W9-BJF-584

LONG LIVE THE KING

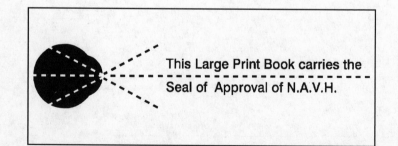

LONG LIVE THE KING

FAY WELDON

THORNDIKE PRESS

A part of Gale, Cengage Learning

GALE
CENGAGE Learning·

Detroit • New York • San Francisco • New Haven, Conn • Waterville, Maine • London

GALE
CENGAGE Learning·

LIBRARY OF CONGRESS CATALOGING-IN-PUBLICATION DATA

Weldon, Fay.
  Long live the king / by Fay Weldon. — Large print edition.
    pages ; cm. — (Thorndike Press large print historical fiction)
    ISBN 978-1-4104-6021-9 (hardcover) — ISBN 1-4104-6021-5 (hardcover)
  1. Large type books. I. Title.
PR6073.E374L66 2013b
823'.914—dc23   2013016099

Published in 2013 by arrangement with St. Martin's Press, LLC

Printed in the United States of America
1 2 3 4 5 6 7 17 16 15 14 13

LONG LIVE THE KING

■ ■ ■ ■

DECEMBER — 1901

■ ■ ■ ■

ADELA ANNOYS HER FATHER

'Will we be going to the Coronation, Father?' asked Adela, in all innocence.

She should not have. He was now in a bad mood. Adela was hungry. She waited for her father to start his breakfast: no one could begin before he did. The last food she'd had was at six the previous evening. Supper had been a bowl of chicken soup (its fourth appearance at the table) and some bread and cheese, from which Ivy the maid had been obliged to scrape away so much mould there was precious little cheese left. The Rectory at Yatbury was an abstemious household, dedicated more to the pleasures of the spirit than the flesh.

'We certainly will not,' her father said. 'I daresay your uncle and his brood will prance around in ermine robes with sealskin spots, but I will not be there to witness it, nor will any member of my household.' He spoke of his elder brother Robert, the eighth

Earl of Dilberne, whom he hated.

'But Father —' said Adela. Better if she had kept quiet. Her mother Elise, a princess of the Gotha-Zwiebrücken-Saxon line, known locally as the Hon. Rev.'s wife, kicked Adela under the table with the heel of a boot, scuffed and worn, but still capable of delivering a painful blow to the shins.

'And I'll have no further mention of this absurd business, Adela, until the whole event is over. The country is still at war and income tax has risen to one shilling in the pound and likely to go up tuppence more. And why? To pay not for the war but for a party. A pointless party for a monarch who is already accepted in law and by the people, in a vulgar display of purloined wealth,' said Edwin. He was the Rector of the small parish of Yatbury, just south-east of the City of Bath in Somerset, and in speaking thus he spoke for many. 'That wealth has been stolen for the most part by piracy; gold, diamonds and minerals wrenched from the native soil of unhappy peoples by virtue of secret treaties, then enforced by arms, intimidation and usurpation.'

The worst of it was that, though he had said grace and been about to crack open his boiled egg, Adela had spoken a moment too soon. Her father laid down his teaspoon the better to pursue his theme. All must now do likewise, since the habit of the house was that its head must be the first to eat.

'I am surprised no one has paraded the heads of Boers on poles outside the House of Lords,' said the Honourable Reverend Edwin, by way of a joke. 'My bloodthirsty brother would love that.' His audience of two laughed politely. But still he did not eat.

Edwin regarded his elder brother Robert, Earl of Dilberne, recently risen to Under Secretary of State for the Colonies, as a man entirely without scruple. Was he not known as a gambling companion to the King, the lecher; and as a friend to Arthur 'Bob's your Uncle' Balfour, nepotist, necromancer and Leader of the House? All politicians were damned and Dilberne was the worst of all politicians, a full-blooded Tory, more concerned with the welfare of his war horses than relieving the miseries of the troops. As near as dammit a Papist, who had permitted his only son to marry a Roman Catholic girl from Chicago, who would no doubt breed like a rabbit and remove Edwin still further from any hope of inheritance. A man married to a wife better fitted to be a pillar of salt out of Sodom and Gomorrah than the social butterfly she was, Isobel, Countess of Dilberne.

'But —' said Adela.

'I have heard too many buts from you, girl,' said Edwin. 'Don't interrupt me.'

'Yes, Father,' said Adela.

She was a pretty if underfed girl of sixteen, with large blue eyes in a pale angelic face, and when her hair was not in tight plaits, as her mother insisted upon, it rippled in thick, clumpy, blonde-red Botticelli waves to her waist. She was doing her best not to answer her father back, but it was difficult, though no doubt good practice for her future life of humility, devotion and obedience. The convent of the Little Sisters of Bethany, where her parents had entered her as a novitiate, she comforted herself, at least kept a good table. On the 21st of May, her seventeenth birthday, she would be off. She couldn't wait.

Adela willed her father to pick up his spoon, and his hand trembled and she thought he would, but he had another thought and put it down again. Adela took a breath of despair and hunger mixed and a button burst off her bodice. Fortunately no one noticed, and she was able to push the button under the edge of her plate. She would ask Ivy to sew it on later. It was a horrid dress anyway, dark brown and no

12

trimmings and too tight around her chest.

Actually Elise had noticed, but said nothing, so as not to draw Edwin's attention to his daughter's bosom. Time passed but brought its embarrassments with it. Ivy the maid suggested from time to time that new dresses should be bought, now that all possible seams had been let out, but new clothes were an extravagance when half the world was in rags. It was Elise's conviction that if Adela ate less she would grow less.

Once it had been a love match — a chance meeting on a cross-Channel steamer in a storm between an Austrian princess and the fourth son of an Earl — but both dedicated to the service of God. The flesh had won over the spirit, the Anglican over the Catholic; they had married impetuously and neither had ever quite forgiven themselves or each other. The proof of their spiritual weakness was the sixteen-year-old Adela. And now she was growing fast, for all her mother could stop it, and worse, turning into a veritable vehicle of concupiscence. It was all her husband, all that any man, could do, and he was the most saintly of men, to keep his eyes away from her changing body. The sooner the girl could be packed off to the Sisters of Bethany the better.

'Better stay home and pray for the salvation of our new monarch's soul,' said the Rector, finding breath, 'than be part of the vulgar display of ostentation and wealth. A double coronation! There is no need for it: she is the man's wife, but he must have her crowned too, Queen Consort — a royal gift much like the bunch of flowers any errant husband brings home to his wife when his conscience is assaulted by his misdeeds.' In January Bertie, Prince of Wales, had ascended to the throne on the death of his mother Queen Victoria. Her reign had lasted sixty-three years: the shock to the country was great, the more so since it now had Bertie, seen by some as a voluptuary, a drunkard and a gambler, by others as a genial if hot-headed fellow, as Edward VII. The new Queen, Alexandra, for forty-three years Princess of Wales, was seen as an angel of docile and loving disposition, though shocked some few by including her husband's mistresses amongst her friends. 'The whited sepulchre which is the Queen Consort's bosom,' Edwin declared with some passion, 'will indubitably glitter with diamonds; but they will be stained by sin and depravity. The King has no shame — he will even flaunt his mistresses in our sacred Abbey, I am told, the whole gallery of them seated together as in any common whorehouse.'

He cracked open his egg but then paused, and failed to remove the shell. Adela had cracked hers likewise but was now obliged to stay the spoon in her hand.

Elise changed the subject and said she hoped Edwin would say as much from the pulpit on Sunday: if he said nothing the Coronation would serve as an excuse for idleness and drunkenness for months to come.

Edwin replied that on Sunday he would have no pulpit, there would be no sermon. That even as he spoke the Church furnishers were at work in St Aidan's refurbishing the interior. In future he would speak not from a mediaeval stone structure but from a plain white table with a white cloth and simple cross: there would be no more incense; there would be no candles, no more mystic Catholic mumbo jumbo. When the pulpit was gone, the furnishers would turn their attention to St Cecilia's gallery, that wormy relic of a false religion, and be rid of it for ever. He glanced briefly at Adela as he spoke, as if in expectation of her protest, and then began to eat his egg, which by now was cold.

'But Father,' said Adela, without thinking, even forgetting that she was hungry, 'please no! The musicians' gallery is so very old and pretty it seems a pity to pull it down. I am sure God won't mind if it stays. Please let it be.'

The Hon. Rev. Edwin Hedleigh slammed the Bible so hard upon the breakfast table that the crockery jumped, and spots of lightly cooked cold egg ended up on the tablecloth, and worse, on the dark red velvety cover of the Bible itself. The Mrs Hon. Rev., dutiful and obedient as ever, leapt from her chair and dabbed ineffectually at the spots with a napkin. Her husband's rages left her shaken and incompetent.

'Old and pretty is hardly the point. I have had enough of your yes buts, Adela. Have you no respect? That confounded gallery is no more than a haunt for all the drunks, rogues and vagabonds of the parish. They shelter there overnight, the better to pursue their filthy habits.'

'Couldn't we just lock the church at night to keep them out?' Adela asked. Her voice quavered, and she despised herself for it, but she persisted. She thought perhaps hunger made her brave. She had no idea what a filthy habit was — no one told her anything — but she had no doubt it was reprehensible. She had so hoped the church furnishers would spare the musicians' gallery. Her father must have written especially to the Bishop of Bath and Wells, asking for a faculty for its removal, and the Bishop had given it. The older things were, Adela reflected, the more unpopular they seemed to be. The gallery, with its delicately carved traceries and oak panel, pale with age, of a dancing St Cecilia the Virgin amongst her musicians — viol, lyre and tambourine — must date back at least five hundred years.

'Let the idolators win? Lock up the house of God? Deny the faithful their solace? For the sake of some wormy oak carving and the relics of a false religion? Are you stupid as well as plain, Adela?' And the Hon. Rev. seized up the Bible and went to his study leaving his breakfast uneaten. He was even taller than his brother Robert, Earl of Dilberne, and as fiery tempered as his brother was genial.

'Now see what you've done,' Elise said to her daughter, more in the hope of appeasing her husband than reproaching the girl, and followed him through to the study.

As for Adela, she ate her egg and toast before anything worse happened, finished her father's, tackled the next two eggs — he always had three eggs and her mother two to her one — swept all available crumbs into a napkin and went out of the Rectory into the frosty morning to feed the robin, who sat waiting on his usual perch on the lowest limb of the oak tree. She was practising thankfulness, and managed to thank Jesus for giving her the parents he had chosen for her, though this morning it took some effort. 'Plain' and 'stupid' had made their mark.

A Letter to the Countess from the Duchess

Tom Fletcher the postman liked his new round very much. It amounted to promotion, though they paid you no more. Here in Belgravia the streets were wide, the houses large and grand, their numbers could be easily read and the letterboxes were under porticos, out of the rain and wind. Far better working here than in the City, where streets had been narrow and twisted, houses and offices crammed together on top of each other, separated by complex networks of alleyways, where horses knocked you off your bike, or splattered the ground in front of your tyres with steaming soft manure, and such numbering as there was, wholly irrational. Also, the letters that came in Belgravia were more interesting than the ones that passed between office and office. One could scarcely begrudge their delivery.

The gold wax seal on this particular

envelope was stamped with two crescent moons and a sun, and had been recognized by the sub-postmistress at Mount Pleasant sorting office as coming from the desk of Consuelo, the Duchess of Marlborough. Consuelo was Mistress of the Queen's Robes, although she was only twenty-four. She had provided her young husband with the two children he required and now had time to spare, and good looks and style aplenty.

The letter was addressed to Isobel, Countess of Dilberne, 17 Belgrave Square, who also moved in the highest of circles, and was something of a fashion icon: perhaps it contained news of what the Queen Consort would wear on her coronation in the New Year? What the dress would look like, the jewels, the possible new crown, were already a source of speculation, even before a definite date was fixed. The women of the nation wondered and chafed at the delay; the men were less concerned. Enough that there was to be a day's holiday and free drinks all round when it happened.

Be that as it may, Vera at the sorting office had tapped her nose when she'd handed over the two crescent moons and the sun and said, 'Keep your ears open, eh, Fletcher, when you call by number seventeen?'

'Don't I always,' Fletcher said, and delivered the letter to the servants' entrance in the basement, instead of the front door, and had a cup of tea with Mrs Welsh the cook while he was at it, and Lily the lady's maid, who looked down her nose at him but whom he rather fancied.

When Reginald the head footman finally brought the letter up to the library, he found Lady Isobel the Countess and her young daughter-in-law, Lady Minnie the Viscountess, packing Christmas gifts for the post. Mrs Neville the housekeeper stood by to fetch brown paper, string and sealing wax as required. Reginald thought the group would look well in a Christmas-card scene, their Ladyships' heads bent together over the task, a good fire burning in the grate and glittering on their diamond brooches, and the deep red vellum of bound books putting a pink glow on their winter-pale complexions. Both were still in half-mourning for the Old Queen — the Earl being a stickler for convention — which meant that some pale lavender and dove grey did not go amiss amongst the black. The two Ladyships looked pretty and cheerful enough, but it was Reginald's experience that for the Hedleigh family such scenes existed only to be quickly shattered

21

by some momentous and unanticipated event.

'Adela Hedleigh, of the Rectory at Yatbury,' remarked Minnie, reading the label written out by Mrs Neville. 'A maiden aunt, perhaps?' She had been a Hedleigh wife for more than a year, and new relatives seemed to keep appearing. No one had taken the trouble to list them for her convenience. Social rules were much more complicated here than they were back home in Chicago. Minnie's father Billy O'Brien gladly welcomed everyone, relative or friend, into his heart and home unless they misbehaved, when he would throw them out, often physically, or even get others to do worse. Her mother Tessa was the same. There was not the layered politeness there was here, no saying things nobody meant, nor was quite expected to believe.

Lady Isobel laughed and said Adela might well end up a maiden aunt, considering her inheritance. At the moment she was an unmarried girl, fifteen or sixteen, and his Lordship's niece, only daughter of Robert's youngest brother Edwin. Edwin had gone into the Church and was reckoned rather strange, indeed, even quite mad and certainly not very nice. He and Robert had had a dreadful quarrel: Edwin had behaved disgracefully. The first son had died in a shocking accident along with his father, which was how Robert, the second son, had come into the title. Yes, there was another brother, Alfred, the third son, who had gone into the army and was now a Brigadier in India, and was mildly preferable to his brother, but not greatly so. 'Neither of them knows how to behave,' said Isobel.

'To know how to behave' was something Minnie, still somewhat awed by the titled company she found herself in, tried very hard to do, and hoped she was succeeding. She longed to know what was in the letter Reginald had brought up, with its great gold wax seal, but knew better than to ask. *'Pas trop de zèle,'* she had heard his Lordship say more than once, *'Surtout, pas trop de zèle.'* Above all, not too much enthusiasm.

'It's not the poor girl's fault that she has the parents she has,' remarked Lady Isobel, 'so I send her a Christmas gift every year. It may well be that one day Adela will seek her family out, though I'm sure one rather dreads the possibility. Edwin is good-looking enough but his wife is very plain and silent, the girl is bound to inherit from her, and Robert cannot abide plain and silent women.'

Minnie felt this was so unfair a judgement

23

that she was driven to speak up.

'But if she is good enough to receive a Christmas gift, perhaps she is good enough to receive an invitation, even for Christmas itself? Families should be together at Christmas time.'

At which her mother-in-law looked at her a little coldly and said, 'Poor little Minnie. You must be missing your mother,' which was another way of saying, since Minnie's mother was so awful and everyone knew it, *shut up and don't presume*. It was the merest flash of disapproval, but Minnie felt her cheeks burning and tears rise to her eyes. And she did, she did, she missed her mother like anything and she longed to be back with the gypsies-oh. The tune kept coming back to her these days, of the song her mother had sung to her when she was a child going to sleep.

Oh what care I for your goosefeather bed,
With the sheets turned down so
    comely-oh,
Oh what care I for your house and your
    land,
I'm off with the raggle-taggle gypsies-oh!

Those weren't the right words: there was a line she'd got wrong, which she couldn't remember, and perhaps it was as well. It was Arthur she wanted, but Arthur was down at Dilberne Court in the country, with his combustion engines and garages, constructing his race circuit in the estate grounds and finding out what it was like to be Managing Director of J.A.C, the Jehu Automobile Company, and designing the Arnold Model 2, while she, Minnie, kept the Countess company. The Countess was charm and courtesy itself and the shopping trips were fun, and Minnie tried to be interested in fashion, but really she was not.

Reginald coughed to draw attention to the letter, still unopened, and Isobel deigned to break the seal and open it.

'It's from Consuelo,' said Isobel. 'The seal is that of the Duchess of Marlborough, do you see?'

'Yes, I do,' said Minnie. Consuelo was a great beauty, came from New York, was a Vanderbilt, and had come to her marriage to the Duke with a railroad fortune. She, Minnie, came from Chicago, was a mere pork-scratchings heiress and her father had endowed less money on his daughter than anyone had hoped, the bottom having suddenly fallen out of the hog market. Railroads, of course, continued to grow from strength to strength. But the whole world knew that when Sunny Marlborough left the church with Consuelo, after their truly grand New York wedding, he had turned to his new wife and told her in the cab that he was in love with someone else, but needed some of the Vanderbilt fortune to save Blenheim Palace from dereliction.

At least when Arthur and she, Minnie, had left St Martin-in-the-Fields after their wedding, Arthur had nibbled her ear and said he loved her, and only her and would for ever: at least she had Arthur's love if not quite enough of his attention. And Arthur was always full of good cheer, whereas the reason the Duke was known as Sunny was not only because he was formerly the Earl of Sunderland, but because he had such a miserable, unsmiling nature. Another English trick amongst the titled — to say the opposite of what was meant and assume everyone around got the joke. Well, one learnt, but one had always to be on one's toes.

OH WHAT CARE I FOR YOUR GOOSEFEATHER BED?

'I'm so very fond of Consuelo,' Isobel was saying now. 'She is so very much like a younger Alexandra, has this very long neck, wears chokers with great style, has a tiny waist, a sweet disposition and, loving good jewellery as she does, is just the right person to be Mistress of the Queen's Robes. How can she not be, Sunny having been appointed Lord High Steward for the occasion; that is to say in overall charge? I do think it is possible to overdo the diamond-choker style, mind you, just a little vulgar and ostentatious. I fear for the Queen. If Consuelo has her way, she'll have the poor dear's front so awash with jewels there'll not be a scrap of flesh showing. I rather wish you could develop a taste for diamonds, Minnie my dear, but you are quite determined never to glitter. Never mind, we love you as you are — and so, apparently, does Consuelo.'

Consuelo, it seemed, had in her letter required Minnie to participate in the Coronation. She was to walk beside Isobel as they processed down the central aisle at the Abbey directly behind the four Duchesses — Marlborough, Portland, Sutherland and Montrose — who were to hold the canopy for Alexandra. The two ladies of Dilberne, both beauties in their own right (*'Oh, Consuelo is such a flatterer,'* said Isobel, with a slight rise of her eyebrows), were to make sure nothing went amiss — crowns could slip, tiaras go awry, jewels might fall, ermine trims tear — and to make things right as circumstances required.

'In other words, Minnie, you and I are to act as lady's maids. Next thing Consuelo will be asking us to carry needle and thread!'

'Little Minnie from Chicago,' was all Minnie said. 'If my friends could see me now!'

'I hope your friends are not so ordinary,' said Isobel, severely, 'as to be impressed.'

Minnie did not explain she had been joking, what was the point? When jokes fell flat better let them lie where they fell. Her father Billy had often told her so. This was not just something else to take for granted. She, little Minnie, the bad girl from Chicago with her unfortunate past, was to walk down the aisle of Westminster Abbey behind the Queen of England and an assortment of duchesses, watched by kings and queens assembled from all over the world, and by the highest statesmen in the land, in all the pomp and circumstance to which humanity could aspire. How could she grumble? She was privileged beyond belief.

Isobel went on reading: 'She tells me the ceremony is to be on June the 26th,' she said, suddenly and sharply, lifting to the light her pale, pretty face, with its high cheekbones and fashionable little mouth so very much in the mode, 'and that Balfour is to make an announcement next week. But I already know that. Why would she think I might not? Robert told me last night. Oh, all these Palace people with their plots and plans and messages from on high!'

Reginald coughed and asked her Ladyship if there was to be a reply, and when she said no, clicked his heels and left the room — no doubt, it occurred to Minnie, to go down immediately to some fly-by-night betting house on Millbank. There he would place a bet on the 26th of June as the day of the Coronation, since bets were open on it, and the exact date currently the nation's preoccupation. Reginald, in Minnie's opinion, was very much a raggle-taggle-gypsy-oh, dark-haired and handsome and not to be trusted, though Isobel seemed to. The trouble with assuming that servants were invisible, springing into life only when needed, was that no one bothered to keep secrets from the lower orders. Anything upstairs knew one minute, downstairs made it their business to know the next.

Her Ladyship went back to the business of wrapping up parcels. Minnie wondered what Adela of the Rectory at Yatbury would be getting. Some kind of dress or cloak, she imagined. She caught a glimpse of what looked like deep red velvet and a flash of very expensive-looking Brussels lace as it was folded into its box. Minnie helped arrange the sleeves neatly and nicely. It was not in Lady Isobel's nature to save money when it came to clothes, even for poor relatives. It would be the most expensive Bond Street could manage. The eventual brown-paper-and-string parcel — the string was green, which did look a little festive and was a little more expensive — still looked rather workaday, so Minnie cheered things up by adding a row of the bright, gummed-paper stickers of garlanded reindeers her mother had sent over in a parcel from Chicago. Isobel winced slightly when she saw them. But then Isobel winced at quite a lot of things.

THE GATHERING STORM

After the robin had eaten the crumbs and
flown off, chirping angrily, as robins will, on
the grounds that the offering had been in
some way wanting, Ivy came out with
Adela's cloak, a grey woollen affair, rather
threadbare but better than nothing, though
hardly what one would expect for the
daughter of the younger brother of an earl.
Not that the Hon. Rev. would have his high
birth spoken of within the village, and it
was wiser not to call him that within his
hearing.

'Take this before you catch your death,'
Ivy said. 'Not that outside is much colder
than in, your ma being so mean with the
coal.'

'There are others much colder than we
are in the world,' said Adela piously. 'You
shouldn't speak so of your employers but
give thanks instead for this beautiful day.'

It was indeed a lovely day; a hard frost

and the tower of St Aidan's next door clear against a bright blue sky. The rising sun was still low enough to make distinct the diamond patterns on the thatched roof of the long tithe barn that backed both church and rectory, and caught the gilded weathercock as it turned slowly in a wind that couldn't make up its mind whether it was westerly or southerly.

'Says you,' said Ivy. She was a girl of great irreverence, big-boned, high-coloured and noisy, nearing thirty and not married. She seemed to Adela clever enough, but had some trouble reading and writing, otherwise no doubt she would have found a better job than maid-of-all-work at the Rectory. She lived in, but sometimes went to stay with her mother in the village, and was allowed to, being what was called a 'treasure' — that is to say competent, reliable, God fearing and honest, though Elise railed against her frequently, as being no better than she should be. 'Perhaps you should be the one thanking God and not crying your eyes out because you can't go and see the Coronation.'

'I am not so, crying,' said Adela. 'It is a wicked waste of money and time which the country can ill afford; nothing but vulgar ostentation. I wouldn't go if you paid me to.'

'Says you,' said Ivy again. 'Me, I'd love to go, see the King and Queen in their robes; I'd stand in the rain for days but they'd never give me the time off. And am I crying? No.'

'If I'm crying,' said Adela, 'it is because my father despises me. I can never please him. He says I'm stupid and plain. Am I?'

It was hard to tell. Her father thought she was clever when she agreed with him, and stupid when she did not. As for looks, the only mirror in the Rectory was above her washbowl stand; a small framed square in front of which she brushed her teeth. It was hard to get an overall view of herself, no matter how she moved the mirror this way and that. Her teeth were white and even, her eyes were blue, her hair a peculiar colour, and even though she brushed and brushed would kind of coagulate into thick reddish-gold clumps, so she was glad when her mother put it into plaits, although Elise tugged dreadfully and could make Adela's eyes water all day. Her eyebrows were quite dark against a good clear skin, except there were often ugly little white pimples round the base of her nose. Ivy told her not to squeeze them; it made them worse. So

33

much, she knew. She could look down and see a bush of rabbit-coloured hair between her legs but did not like to investigate further with her fingers. 'Down there', as her mother called it, was forbidden and dangerous territory. The same with her new bosom. It was beginning to bounce up and down when she ran. Enquiry seemed not so much forbidden as vulgar.

'You look all right to me,' said Ivy.

'Not that stupid and plain matters if you're going to be a Bride of Christ,' said Adela, haughtily. She hated to be seen crying. 'Good is all that matters. And obedient. And chaste, whatever that is.'

'Keeping your legs together,' said Ivy, smirking.

'No really, Ivy, please,' begged Adela, 'tell me what it means!'

'It's as much as my job's worth,' said Ivy. 'But I'll tell you this, your father doesn't think you're plain. That's his problem. But as for Bride of Christ, Miss Adela, I can't see you settling down to be a nun.'

'Not just a nun,' said Adela, 'I would be a proper Sister, and in the end a Mother. I would rise in the ranks. I would not be cloistered. I'd be allowed out to teach. It wouldn't be too bad. They say I have a vocation.'

'They would say that, wouldn't they,' said Ivy. 'They're after your inheritance. That's how convents keep in business.'

'That's a wicked thing to say, Ivy,' said Adela, 'and I don't have any inheritance. Father has nothing, only his pittance as a Rector. His brother Robert took everything.'

'Better be a bride to a man of flesh and blood and lie in a warm, soft bed at night than on a hard, lonely one for the rest of your life,' said Ivy.

'The nuns I met seemed perfectly happy,' said Adela, 'and I don't want another word from you on the subject.'

Her parents had taken Adela to visit the Little Sisters of Bethany in Clerkenwell six months back. She had very much liked what she had seen. Sister Agatha, leader of the postulates, had shown them around. She was dressed in a grey habit with a grey scarf that covered grey hair, was round and gentle and had smiled a good deal. She was also kind and considerate, even noticing with what care Adela carried the ring finger of her left hand. Adela had slammed the finger into the train door at Bath Station as they set off for London and two hours later it still smarted and had swollen up. Sister Agatha inspected the finger and enclosed it between the palms of her hands saying, 'Oh you poor little thing!' at which Adela had started to cry, though it was the last thing she wanted to do. To which her father had said crossly, 'Hardly what Jesus suffered on the cross, Adela,' and Elise had said, 'Don't make such a fuss, Adela, no one wants a cry-baby.'

The finger had given two or three great throbs that had made Adela feel faint, sway, and then had stopped hurting altogether. But Sister Agatha still sat her down and made much of her and bandaged the finger carefully and gently and then asked her if her plaits were very tight.

'Nothing wrong with her plaits,' said Elise, before Adela could say, 'Yes, they are rather.' Which they were. 'I have to do them firmly or her hair's all over the place in two minutes.'

'Hard to think of God,' Sister Agatha had observed, 'when one's hair is pulling and one has a headache,' and somehow managed to ease the hair round Adela's ears so the plaits pulled less tightly.

The next day when Elise put Adela's hair into plaits she didn't pull so hard, and they hardly hurt at all. Her mother insisted on taking off Sister Agatha's bandage, on the grounds that it was ugly, bulky and hardly necessary. Nor was it. The finger, once unbandaged, was no longer a swollen purple sausage with a line of broken skin across the knuckle where it had caught in the door, but its proper shape, smooth and lean like the other fingers and all but healed, just a little pinker than normal.

'What on earth were you making all that fuss about; there's nothing wrong with it at all,' said Elise, but Adela thought it was all very curious and felt quite a spasm of anger against her mother. That and the matter of her plaits. But also anger with her father, for agreeing so easily to her being a Bride of Christ and not stopping her even though that was what she wanted. But she said nothing, and then reproached herself for not loving her father and mother as God said she should.

But she would not mind being a Little Sister of Bethany one bit: not only did they heal your ailments by a simple touch, but the rooms they showed her had been pleasant and warm. The nuns were surprisingly chattery, like a flock of friendly little birds, and there was no great booming voice always coming out of nowhere to startle and discommode everyone. The books on the shelves were more interesting than the ones at home, the food far more sustaining and full of flavour, the praying certainly frequent but no more onerous than at home. They'd said she could join as a postulant when she was seventeen, which would be in six months' time, and she'd said, 'Yes please,' and so all was arranged, and Ivy had no business trying to put her off.

'We'll leave "chaste" be then,' she said. 'But tell me, when my mother says you are no better than you should be, Ivy, what does she mean?'

There was a commotion in the bright sky above them. Crows from the elm trees were mobbing a bird of prey whose presence annoyed them. The garden birds set up their alarm calls in sympathy. The buzzard escaped its oppressors and soared away, all elegance and grace. The garden quietened. A tiny vole landed with a little thud in the grass at Adela's feet. It was soft and warm and apparently unmarked by beak or claw.

'Don't touch it,' said Ivy. 'It's dead. The buzzard dropped it.'

Adela bent down and stroked the little creature's furry back. It opened its eyes and scuttled off into the wintry undergrowth.

'You caught something at that convent,' said Ivy, 'better not caught. I don't forget the way that finger of yours healed when it shouldn't have.'

'It was one of God's smaller creations,'

said Adela, 'and only stunned. Don't change the subject. How can someone be no better than they ought to be?' But Ivy just snorted and went back into the house to put on the cabbage for lunch. It was barely ten in the morning but Elise liked to have the green leaves boiled for three hours or so, the water changed three times during the boiling process to get rid of any poison, then the mush put between two trays and the liquid squeezed out of it, set to dry, kept warm, and the resulting green vegetable cake cut into squares before serving. That way the cabbage was safe to eat.

Ivy wondered if the Palace was taking on extra staff for the Coronation. They might be, but it was not likely it would be the likes of her. She doubted that 'good at cooking cabbage' would be seen as much of a skill. You would have to know someone important, even to be able to scrub a floor the Queen walked upon, in her jewelled slippers, clanking in diamonds and pearls.

THE INVITATIONS ARRIVE

The Lord High Steward's office had reserved seven seats at the coronation ceremony for the Hedleigh family, guests to be chosen at his Lordship's discretion. This was most generous, as Isobel observed to Robert, and more than she had hoped for, the Duchess of Montrose having complained to her over a game of Bridge that she, of a ducal family, had been allocated only four.

'We are fortunate to have friends in high places,' said Robert. The pair were breakfasting alone in the breakfast room, winter sun shone through tall windows, and the new pale-gold brocade curtains flung back more light than seemed reasonable for midwinter. Isobel had gone to Maples furnishing store in the Tottenham Court Road with Minnie, and between them, they had refurnished No. 17 as, Minnie said, 'fit for the new century'. Gone were the heavy mahogany furniture sideboards, the tapestry fire screens, the dismal bronze curtaining and Axminster carpets; everything now was light and bright.

'What friends in particular?' Isobel asked, thinking perhaps Robert meant the King himself, or Arthur Balfour, Leader of the House, or Chamberlain, First Lord of the Colonies, or Sunny Marlborough, now throwing his weight around as Lord High Steward, a post brought into existence only when a coronation hove into royal view — oh, if you reckoned a man by his friends her husband was man indeed and she, Isobel, Countess of Dilberne, was so very proud.

'Oh, it was Consuelo,' said Robert, casually. He happened to be in Sunny's temporary office in Buck House when Consuelo came by with a list of her Majesty's personal guests; they had on examination found three spaces left unfilled so Consuelo had told Robert he could add them to his allocation of four if he wished, and Robert had said, of course, please, yes. How could he not? Hundreds who felt entitled to a place in the Abbey for the great occasion would be turned away. This was good fortune indeed. Now the only question was how Robert was to find homes for three extra gold-embossed invitations.

But Isobel thought, no, that is not the only question. The main one is how does this chit of a girl, with her long elegant neck, with the pretty head perched on top of it — held in place, one could almost think, by the diamond chokers that kept it high — with her tiny waist and her happy smile, manage to turn the heads of so many people, men and women too, that they allowed her to wander freely not only in the Palace of Westminster but Buckingham Palace too, and be the one to hand out these precious, almost sacred pieces of gold-embossed card that meant so much to so few? Dear God, the girl was only twenty-four. Yet she had been married five years, was a mother to two sons, and of all the Duchesses foremost in the land, a foreigner with no breeding, but immense wealth and all the confidence that brought with it. No scandal was yet attached to her name — yet she announced freely to all and sundry that she felt no emotional attachment to her husband, and by implication was therefore free to be wooed and won. That was the question, but Isobel did not put it to her husband. One would not want the possibility put into his mind that he might be the one to win her, not in marriage but quite possibly in bed. The phrase *'Just happened to be there'* was not one any wife was happy to hear. It could so easily mark intent. Nevertheless, it was a bright morning; she had Robert to herself, and would make the most of it.

Minnie and her lady's maid Lily had been packed off to Dilberne Court the previous day. Isobel had been pleased enough with Minnie's company — she learned the habits of the house remarkably quickly for a meat baron's daughter from Chicago — but felt it was important that the girl spend as many nights as possible with Arthur. The young couple had been married for more than a year and still no sign of a baby. If the impossible happened and the quick-witted Minnie turned out to be barren, and if Alfred continued to have only daughters, Edwin would inherit if he survived him. It did not bear thinking about, so Isobel seldom did. It was hard to worry about anything on so bright a morning. Three extra invitations! It was more than she had hoped for. She was wearing her favourite tea-gown, a kind of yellow silk kimono splashed with red flowers, which when she bent forward to study the invitations more closely fell open and revealed more bosom than the servants thought decent. But Robert smiled to see it, and Isobel thought, what a handsome man he is, and how lucky I am that after thirty years of marriage I can still make him smile like that.

'Minnie and I will be processing behind the Queen and Arthur and you behind the King,' she said, 'which uses up our four allocated seats, so we have three over. It would be natural to ask our daughter Rosina, but she will wear strange clothes and like as not alarm other guests by haranguing them about the iniquities of royal ritual in the modern age.'

'But she will be hurt and offended if she knows there is a spare ticket and she is not asked; she is quite capable of behaving if she wishes.'

'But she may very well not wish,' said Isobel, 'and she is quite happy to be hurt and offended. Let it occupy her all next year. Better a real grudge than an invented one. She is quite likely to take her parrot with her to glorify some avian deity, or go without a hat, or let off fireworks. I most strenuously advise against one.'

'I will abide by your judgement, my dear,' said her husband, pacifically. 'But do remember she is your daughter too. I see your father Silas in her. He did what he wanted, said what he wanted, and took no notice of what people thought of him. They are traits better suited to a man than a woman, it is true, but at least she is not *dull*.'

Isobel kept her composure and said that if dullness was a qualification for attendance it might be seemly to invite his brother Edwin and his wife and daughter. Edwin was a Dilberne, and, heaven forbid, in the line of succession to the earldom. She should not have said it, but did so to annoy, and as soon as she had, regretted it.

Robert said, over his dead body, that his brother was a scurrilous rat. And his sister-in-law a pious vengeful little thing, not only dull but plain, and the jubilant crowds who gathered in such number to enjoy the pageantry and fine dresses of the notables who descended from their coaches at the Abbey gates expected to see tall beautiful people not hunchbacks. They would disappoint by coming by hansom cab or even by District line with its fetid smells and grimy walls.

'Then whom shall we ask?' asked Isobel. Better that Robert had disdained Consuelo's offer, but what man would refuse so generous a gift from someone so charming, pretty and young? And why had Consuelo chosen Robert for her favours? He was twice the girl's age, surely, possessed a tenth of her wealth, and held a title a good notch or so below her own. On the other hand Robert was good-looking, sociable and probably, most importantly in the Duchess's eyes, as cheerful as Sunny was not. If she wanted to curry favour with anyone, why did she not set her sights on Arthur Balfour, who was so absurdly clever, kind, unmarried and available? But there were some young wives, the kind really close to their fathers while disliking their mothers, who enjoyed nothing better than to steal other women's husbands, simply because that was what they were. Perhaps Consuleo was such a one? No, Isobel did not like it one bit.

'We could ask the d'Astis,' said Isobel. 'She would give her eye teeth for such an invitation.'

'Too vulgar,' said Robert. 'Too foreign. Lion hunters. All those greenery-yallery people. But we could invite the Baums.' Eric Baum was Robert's financial adviser, thanks to whose backing of Robert's gold and mineral mines Robert was quickly becoming very rich indeed. 'That would at least be useful.'

'So others might observe,' said Isobel. 'Such an odious little man. And what a little social climber she is.'

At which Robert rose to his feet, and said

she must do as she thought fit, these were domestic matters, he must be getting back to the House, old Salisbury was dragging himself to his feet to speak on land reform though heaven knew that after his wife's death the poor old man, once such a fighter, could scarcely speak sense any more. The sooner Arthur Balfour was in place the better.

'Of course,' said Isobel sweetly, 'I shall see to it,' but one way and another she was furious; and once Robert had left the house, she took the three invitations and posted them off along with the Christmas gift to Adela, to the Honourable Reverend Edwin Hedleigh at the Rectory at Yatbury — such a dreary little coal town by all acounts, grown too quickly from its ancient heart, its one claim to fame the mediaeval panel in the musicians' gallery of St Aidan's, the twelfth-century church, showing a playful St Cecilia kicking up her skirts and dancing with her musicians.

Breakfast at
Yatbury Rectory

The letter and parcel arrived at the Rectory as a still grey dawn was breaking over Yatbury. The town's winding wheel had disappeared into mist and fog. Even the weathercock on the squat church tower was barely visible. Tim Peasedown the postman stared with disbelief at the line of dancing reindeers stuck onto the brown-paper-and-string parcel. Such needless expense and frivolity seemed out of place in a hardworking world.

Ivy opened the door to take in letter and parcel. She glanced at the strap of leathery seaweed she kept nailed up above the door. A friend had brought it all the way from Lulworth Cove. When it was dry and limp, it meant the weather would be fine: when it swelled and the buds plumped out, it meant a storm was on the way. Today the buds were well plumped. She did not ask Tim in for a cup of tea. It was not that kind of

48

household. The Mrs Hon. Rev. would have hysterics, and Ivy's boyfriend George wouldn't like it.

The letter was addressed to the Hon. Rev., the parcel for Miss Adela Hedleigh and the sender's address on both was given as Belgrave Square, London. This meant that they would either be returned to sender unopened or thrust into the kitchen stove and burned. She slipped the envelope into the pocket of her apron and was wondering how best to deal with the parcel. She had seen nothing like the row of Christmas reindeers before and did not much care to again: they seemed as if they were bringing the Royal Mail into disrepute, making light of a serious matter. But if she could steam the stickers off they might make a few pence in Bath market, where her mother ran a novelty stall on Saturday mornings, and no one be any the wiser.

Before she could do any such thing the tall, thin figure of the Hon. Rev. himself appeared behind her without warning, up early for his morning constitutional, took the parcel from Ivy's hands, turned it this way and that as if it were something truly loathsome.

'Keep this frippery out of my daughter's way,' he said, 'and ask my wife to put it in the fire at the earliest opportunity.'

Then he strode out into the fog. Ivy watched him through the scullery window and was reminded of some great flapping bird of ill omen. If it wasn't for Adela, she thought, she would simply be off. They were looking for staff at the new hotel in Bath. She cleared the ash and lit the stove; it was the kind that burned anthracite and could perfectly well be kept in overnight, but that was seen as a wicked waste. At Yatbury Rectory cold was good for the soul. As was apparently being always a little bit hungry, a little bit uncomfortable, and washing the dishes in cold water.

'A parcel came for Miss Adela,' Ivy said, when Elise came into the kitchen to make the breakfast porridge. She made it with water and served it with salt. No wonder the lot of them were so thin and solemn. 'It's on the table there. The Reverend said to burn it, but it would only smoke the place out, the way the wind's in the north. It's some kind of fabric, I think.'

Elise turned the parcel over and inspected it carefully. She was wearing a grey dress, which matched the rest of her: hair, hands, face. Ivy thought for a moment there was as much fog inside the kitchen as outside the window but could see it could hardly be the case.

'It will be from her Aunt Isobel,' Elise said. 'She often does this kind of thing at Christmas, such a very vain and frivolous person. The stove is the best place for it. And what are those silly little creatures? What on earth are they meant to be? Like no creature I have ever seen. Is it a very dark morning, or has the time come when I need spectacles? Oh dear, I hope not.'

'It may be both,' said Ivy. 'One day you don't need them, the next you do, my mum says.' This morning Elise was talkative. When her husband left the house and went for a walk, which was seldom, she could become quite friendly.

'I think the little creatures are meant to be Christmas reindeers, walking across the page,' said Ivy, helpfully.

'What have reindeers to do with Christmas?' Elise was puzzled.

'Father Christmas from the North Pole,' said Ivy. 'He brings presents on his sledge.'

'Fairy tales and poppycock!' Elise was indignant. 'At home in Innsbruck when I was a child, St Nicholas came on Christmas Eve and gave you an orange if you were a good child and a lump of coal if you were naughty. Once I was given a piece of coal. I cried a great deal, but they would not tell me what I had done that was bad. I never found out. My husband is not a great believer in presents at Christmas time, and neither am I. Better that Adela does not receive them. Christmas is a happy time, but that is to do with the birth of our Lord, not self-indulgence, overeating and presents brought by reindeer, which harks back to the old pagan ways, and must be rooted out from Christendom.' But Ivy thought that perhaps Elise was trying a little too hard to persuade herself. She was poking the paper with a finger.

'I wonder if it's velvet,' she said. 'My sister-in-law is famous for her gowns.'

'It seems a wicked waste to burn it,' said Ivy, 'whatever it is. Perhaps I should take it down to the Almshouses and give it to the lady superintendent there? On Christmas Eve they distribute gifts for the poor of the parish. Then we'll know it's gone to someone deserving. The Reverend doesn't have to know.'

'Very well,' said Elise and gave Ivy the glimmer of a smile.

Ivy decided she would never marry, not if you ended up married to some man who so crowded your mind you could smile only when he was out of the house.

Later that morning Ivy cut through the churchyard on her apparent way to the Almshouses. She would drop the parcel off at her mother's cottage, reindeers and all. The fog had burned off and the day was suddenly bright and cheerful. The yew trees which stood in rows along the path from the lychgate to the church door were bright with berries — except as ever the one with broad sinewy trunk and gnarled branches, said to date from William the Conqueror, which managed only a few pitiful orange-red berries every year. The weathercock on the steeple glittered in the sun, and was beginning to flash as the wind got up.

As it happened she encountered Adela, and pushed the parcel further into her basket. Better if it was not seen. Adela was in tears, as she so often was. The workmen had been busy the day before, and the remnants of the musicians' gallery, its pale wood splintered and powdery, lay in pieces on the ground, piled ready for the bonfire. Adela was in a state of lamentation, wringing her hands over the wreckage. Was she more like Helen, Ivy wondered, Helen watching the burning towers of Troy, or Dido weeping for Aeneas, or Tennyson's *Lady of Shalott*? Ivy's mother Doreen loved to pin up prints of sad, beautiful ladies on her cottage wall, rescued from her novelties stall, fly-blown and damp-stained though they might be, and Ivy knew and loved them all.

Adela stood and watched, and Ivy too, as a couple of brawny men carried out the old gated pews, almost black with age, to add to the pile for burning. The new open pews, in a lightweight, orangey-coloured wood which Ivy did not recognize, had already been delivered and were stacked against the stone walls. She could hear the uneven sound of axe blade against wood, and looked inside the church door to see a scrawny lad make splintered firewood of the high carved pulpit from which the Hon. Rev. had so often thundered. A few of the older villagers looked on curiously. St Aidan's had a small and dwindling congregation — most had fled to the Methodists at St Bart's, where a friendlier atmosphere ruled and the hymns were more to their taste.

'It's all my fault,' said Adela to Ivy. 'I shouldn't have made Father so angry. Now look. God's punishment!'

'Oh for heaven's sake,' said Ivy, 'God's got bigger things to worry about than you answering your father back.'

Still Adela gulped and wept, and asked if

she could go with Ivy wherever Ivy was going: if she stayed where she was she would die of a broken heart. Ivy said Adela was better fitted for the stage than for a convent, but her heart would break even more if she knew where Ivy was going.

'Where's that?' asked Adela.

'Down to the Almshouses with a Christmas gift for the poor.'

'Let me see it,' said Adela, so Ivy showed it to her. In case the matter of the missing parcel ever arose, which was doubtful, she would have covered her tracks well enough.

'But it's addressed to me,' said Adela, horrified.

'Your father thinks you're too young to receive unsolicited gifts,' said Ivy. 'He told your mother to burn it but I told her it was a wicked waste so she told me I could take it away and give it to the poor.' Ivy crossed her fingers as she spoke, but it was true enough. Her mother surely counted as poor, and enough of the charity gifts that were left at the Almshouses ended up on her novelty stall anyway.

'But it's from Belgrave Square, which means it's from relatives. What harm can there be in it? I don't understand.'

'You know what your father's like about your family. Your uncle's on the wrong side in the House, your aunt's a walking clothes horse, your cousin Arthur married a Papist whore and your cousin Rosina as good as killed her own grandfather. They're all bound for hell. Just let me get it down to the Almshouses and forget about it, there's a good girl.'

'It's very strange,' said Adela, 'that one side of the family should be so very good, like ours, and the other side so very wicked, like theirs. What's a whore?'

'Never you mind,' said Ivy.

'I shall shrivel and die for lack of information,' said Adela sadly. 'The sooner I am a Bride of Christ the better. Well, take my only Christmas present away, Ivy, and give it to the poor. Do you think one feels hungry and cold in heaven?'

'I might drop by Swaley's Farm and see if there's any cream going free,' said Ivy. 'Your ma put out some stale bread for the birds. I could put it aside, and with some cream and a drop of sugar from my mum it'll make a good supper tonight.'

'Thank you, Ivy,' said Adela. She poked the parcel with her finger. 'It feels squishy,' she said. 'Perhaps it's velvet. Please can't I just see what's in it?'

'It's more than my job's worth,' said Ivy, putting the parcel back in her shopping basket, and went on down towards the Alms-houses, missing the first turning to her mother's cottage but taking the second, once out of Adela's sight. This took her past Swaley's Farm, where her boyfriend George worked mornings, milking. He'd already left for Bath, where he was at college, so she stuck the envelope from Belgrave Square in a gap between the plaster wall and one of the milking stalls where no one would notice it, and went and had a cup of tea with her mother.

A Deed Once Done

The enormity of what she had done was slow to dawn on Isobel. She had been feeling over-emotional lately, prone to bouts of crying, behaving quite irrationally, and flushing with embarrassment when there was nothing to be embarrassed about. She knew perfectly well that her worries about Consuelo's closeness to her husband could only be absurd. If anything Consuelo saw him as a father — Robert was so pleasant, wise, fatherly and kind — a Melbourne, perhaps, to the young Victoria. But then again, there had been talk at the time about that; the crowd even chanting 'Mrs Melbourne! Mrs Melbourne!' after her carriage. These things happened. And lately, somewhere in the gossip columns, Isobel had read a rather tendentious comparison between the giddy young Princess Victoria, she of the slender neck, tiny waist and dancing slippers, before age and sorrow clouded body and mind, with Consuelo, princess of today's social scene. Not, perhaps, that the Old Queen had been quite as sorrowful as her later subjects had assumed.

As Queen Alexandra had confided in Consuelo, her new lady-in-waiting, who had passed the gossip on to Robert, who in turn had told Isobel, the King had found out more about his mother's life when he looked into her unsealed coffin than he cared to know. Bertie had found the corpse to be dressed in a white gown with her wedding veil over her face, and seen that in her left hand she clasped a photograph of her Scottish ghillie, John Brown, and only with her right did she entwine her fingers with the plaster cast of the hand of Bertie's long-deceased father, Prince Albert.

'There is some mistake,' the new King accused Dr Reid, her friend and physician, who with the family here at Osborne House had attended the Old Queen's deathbed and recorded her last breath. 'This is neither possible nor reasonable.'

'There is no mistake,' said the good doctor. 'Everything is to her exact specifications. Here, see, on her left, a lock of John Brown's hair — to her right your father's bath-gown.'

'But the left hand is the hand of marriage,'

protested the King.

'I know,' said Dr Reid, bleakly.

'I suppose —' started the King.

'There was always a rumour of a secret marriage,' said Dr Reid. 'But I think not. Sire, do not distress yourself so. All are dead and gone.' As a young man he had attended Prince Albert's death. He was weeping himself.

'Find a bunch of flowers,' said the King. 'Anything. Cover up the photo. The public must not see it. Get the coffin sealed as soon as decently possible. And you are wrong: not all are dead. Get that blasted Indian waiter out of the house at once.'

But the Indian waiter, known as 'the Munshi', declined to leave before the funeral, and Alexandra suggested that it was perhaps wiser to let the Old Queen's favourite stay rather than cast him out: he had letters and documents in his possession it would have been better that he had not. Dr Reid agreed. Abdul Karim had first appeared at the royal dining table resplendent in turban and sash, and gone on to become the Queen's confidant and intimate, to a degree it was impossible to determine. The Munshi, said Dr Reid, was without doubt an imposter, a fraud and a slippery cove who for thirteen years now had been robbing the Queen but whose affection for her seemed genuine enough. He could be allowed to stay for the funeral, as a favourite dog is allowed to follow the coffin of master or mistress. The Old Queen had seen the Munshi only as dotty old ladies often saw their pet dogs or cats, lavishing affection on them, and furious with anyone who dared make an accusation of biting or scratching. The association, Reid swore, had been no more or less than this.

'Dotty old ladies,' said the King bitterly, 'do not sign letters to dogs or cats as from their mothers.'

But he contented himself with demanding that Karim hand over all letters, papers and notes that concerned the Old Queen, and feeding them to the flames of the bonfires in which all mementoes of John Brown's reign were to be burned. The King himself would light the bonfires, with his sisters Louise and Beatrice looking on. The past would be expunged.

'Oh, let the Indian waiter stay,' the King said, in Alexandra's hearing. 'There will be more talk if he does not walk behind his beloved "mother" than if he does.'

Bertie's bitterness, Alexandra remarked to Consuelo, lay in her deceased mother-in-law's apparent preference for a servant than

61

for her own son. Victoria had despised Bertie and let it show: saw only his faults and not his merits: failed to consult him in matters of State: wished that he, Bertie, had died in place of his eldest son Eddy, Duke of Clarence: even blamed him, Bertie, for causing his father's death — Albert had fallen ill on a trip back from Cambridge, where he had been reprimanding Bertie for libertine excesses of one kind and another — and in general made Bertie's life a misery when she could have made him happy. She had done what no mother should do — failed to love her own son. And all the while indulging in her own secret sensual excesses, if the mementoes consigned to the flames at Osborne were to be believed. The letters to Karim signed 'your mother' could only be further evidence of actual insanity, as Bertie had long suspected.

'More,' Robert said to Isobel, 'the Queen is annoying the King very much by telling him that his appetite — once great, not gargantuan, and a worry to herself and his doctors — is in some way connected with his mother's death.'

'The Queen may be right,' said Isobel. She could see it. With every fresh discovery of the Old Queen's love letters to Brown, every fresh curry recipe from Karim unearthed,

Bertie would suffer and come home demanding extra courses for dinner, and he being the Monarch how could anyone forbid him? Alexandra could tell him, his doctors could tell him, that he must eat less and move around more, or he would meet an early death, but death was perhaps what he wanted in his heart. While Alexandra continued to pick away at the odd breast of chicken thinly smeared with mustard sauce, her husband ate with suicidal zeal, puddings and pies and roasts, sauces and gravies and relishes, the better to punish his mother.

'Consuelo says the same,' said Robert, and laughed uproariously. 'You women! The man has the best cooks in the land, why would he not eat? And I daresay he is hungry from making bonfires. I'll grant you that.'

'He is hungry for his mother's love, and now he will never get it,' Isobel said.

'That is what Consuelo infers, but you express it more neatly,' said Robert.

It was meant to be flattery, she could see, and she was duly flattered, although actually it was not original, just something her friend the Countess d'Asti had observed — but why did Consuelo's name keep coming up in casual conversation? Perhaps better that it did than not; at least Robert was not trying to hide anything from her. Still she brooded. She did not enjoy the new pattern of her thoughts; they seemed scarcely to belong to her. They disturbed her sleep. She had begun to wake at four in the morning with a mind full of unreasonable doubts and fears. She had a kind of waking vision of Consuelo's curly black head burrowing into the hollow where Robert's naked shoulder blade met his breastbone. It haunted her.

She had spoken about her state of mind to her friend Freddie, the Countess d'Asti. Freddie came from Austria and was artistic, almost of the *haut bohème,* and knowledgeable about things most well-bred Englishwomen were not. It was Freddie's ambition to go to Vienna and become a patient of the alienist Sigmund Freud but her husband would not hear of it. Bad enough that Freddie was a member of the Theosophical Society, wore flowing Liberty gowns, long strings of large wooden beads, and no longer served meat at her table, since when her reputation as a Society hostess had somewhat dwindled.

'I don't know what's the matter with me these days,' Isobel complained to Freddie. 'Everything upsets me. I lose my temper and snarl where I should smile. I feel that nobody likes me and I certainly don't like them. I am not the woman I used to be.'

'It is the Change,' Freddie said. 'It happens to all of us. You must eat lots of lettuce and it will pass. You will be yourself again and need not bother any more about having babies.'

Which had cheered Isobel quite a lot, but still not enough. She ate a great deal of lettuce and thought it made her feel better. The night after she had sent Reginald to the post with the envelope for Yatbury she had gone to bed unworried and composed. She woke at four in the morning next to Robert. He had returned from the House at midnight, come to her bed and now slept soundly and innocently, showing no sign of wishing to return to his own. She woke as if from a bad dream but there had been no dream, just the feeling that there was something badly wrong. For once, the worries were not about Consuelo. She half slept, half woke. Was it perhaps about the state of the Dower House? She had a vision of her future widowhood clear in her mind; she herself moved out into the Dower House, Minnie reigning over all as the new Countess of Dilberne, and herself, Isobel, demoted to mere Dowager Duchess. The Dowager, figure of fun, was that to be her future? At least Minnie was an amiable girl; aggrieved daughters-in-law, once into their titles, were famous for the revenge they could impose upon their one-time tormentors — roofs left unmended, servants not hired, carriages not available, rats nesting, the cesspit man not summoned, there was no end to it. The one who held the purse strings, as ever, held the power.

But no, it was not that. The Dower House was in no worse a state of repair than it usually was. All over the land dower houses were allowed to go to rack and ruin. Sheer superstition kept them that way; to keep them in good repair was to invite their occupation.

Was it the responsibility of acting as lady's maid to the four Duchesses? Could that be worrying her? Sleep seemed so desirable and yet so impossible. Things could go wrong, it was true: bosoms had been known to fall out of bodices, heels to break; the very greatest in the land were not immune to falling and tripping on their own trains — but she could cope with that. Life was full of mischance, and what she could not deal with, processing up the aisle, Minnie surely could. She was a resourceful girl. No, it was not that.

'My God!' Isobel sat up in bed, eyes wide, as vague thoughts suddenly crystallized into actual memory. Robert stirred; she had spoken aloud; but fortunately, he slipped back into sleep. Three spare tickets to the Coronation, put in an envelope, addressed to Yatbury Rectory, and given to Reginald to take to the post. She had acted on a generous impulse. Or perhaps she had just been angry? At best an extra present for Adela, a girl she had never met or wanted to, but now in all likelihood would. At worst an act of spite against her husband, the man she adored. There had been no covering letter; she had meant to slip the envelope into the parcel, but it had been so perfectly packed and tied up with green string it had seemed a shame to open it up again. She fought for recollection, but found it hard, as if she'd fallen off a horse and forgotten everything on either side of the accident. She remembered Minnie's little reindeer stickers and thinking how hopelessly vulgar they were, but then that she was American and couldn't help it. People from God's own country seemed to have an inbuilt childishness: a liking for the bright and useless. Now Edwin would receive the envelope and like as not assume the tickets came straight from the Palace. He would turn up with his wife and daughter on June 26th and find himself sitting next to the brother he hated, and, eaten up by anger and jealousy, have to watch him process behind his liege lord down the nave of Westminster Abbey. Quite what had caused Robert's falling-out with his brother she did not know, nor had ever wanted to know, but thought it must be to do with his right to his inheritance. Perhaps Consuelo knew; she seemed to know everything else.

She must retrieve the situation. She could not face Robert's wrath when she told him what had happened.

'No,' he would say, not what 'happened' — what you have 'done'.

She would get the tickets back: if she could not, she would say they were lost and set the household to searching: she would write to Consuelo to say she had invited the Baums and Rosina — and then not ask them — and Edwin and family would be stopped at the door and the three seats could just sit empty, as indeed would the family's, until the processing had been done, and the choristers finished with '*I Am Glad*', and the service over, when they would return to listen to Hubert Parry himself playing the organ, waiting for the wedding party to depart. It was only then the lack of occupants would be truly noticed, missing teeth in an otherwise full set of the great, grand and famous — and the post could always be blamed for anything that went wrong.

Oh, for heaven's sake — it was all too complicated: it was Consuelo's fault for not checking the numbers on the Queen's list properly: she, Isobel, Countess of Dilberne, the beautiful one, the competent one, was a peeress of the realm and could not be bothered with such troubles. She, as Countess, was to have a three-inch ermine trim on her train and Minnie, Viscountess, a mere two inches. Their robes would be made of crimson silk velvet, open down the front to show a dress of heavy silver and gold brocade — they must decide on the design — close-fitting, with short fitted sleeves edged with miniver fur. Her arms were still good, thank heaven. Robert would have three rows of dark sealskin spots on the ermine cape that went over his robe, also in crimson silk. Sunny, as a Duke, would have four rows; but the men had no trains to worry about: all the same she would have to check the length of Robert's robe. It had been made for him ten years ago when he came into the title, and he rarely wore it. Elderly peers often tripped over too-long gowns. Better perhaps to get Ede and Ravenscroft to make one up new.

She would not let a matter of invitations spoil her anticipation of the great event. She fell asleep.

In the morning she rang for Reginald and asked him to go down to the post office and see what could be done to retrieve the letter he had taken to the post yesterday. The parcel could go as intended but she needed the letter back.

Reginald, knowing full well the post had gone long ago and that apart from intercepting the letter as it went through the letter-box at Yatbury Rectory there was no way of retrieving it, went through the motions of enquiring at the Post Office. He knew what was in the letter, having steamed it open as was his wont, had marvelled that such valuable contents were being sent by unregistered post, and decided against purloining them. Seats seven, eight, and nine of row four of the west nave of Westminster Abbey on June 26th could mean only one thing, and the risk was far too great.

WHOSE FAULT?

After Ivy had gone off to the Almshouses, Adela sat for a little under the ancient yew and enjoyed her misery. Everything nice was always snatched away from her. Not just a parcel addressed to her — one could understand that, though one didn't like it — a father surely had a right to protect his daughter from malign influences — but all that she had loved about St Aidan's, its very familiarity, the way the sunlight shone through the stained-glass windows at certain hours, at certain times of year, the old pews; the wooden floor, worn down by the feet of worshippers, would soon be gone to be replaced by soulless, practical tiles, easy to wash. All the consoling patterns she knew were to be disturbed. She had loved the elegant flow of St Cecilia's wooden gown: now it lay in wormy shreds on the ground. Even the pulpit was in pieces, and with it her father's dignity. The Rector, at his

71

Bishop's bidding, must now pray at the same level as his congregation, no longer elevated above it as the saints had been above the people. It was too bad, her own superiority as the Rector's daughter was being brought down as his was. No one envied her being her father's daughter, but at least they had respected her.

She had trusted her father to stand up against the Bishop's ecumenical zeal, his strictures that everything must change, everyone be made equal before God — and her father had failed. Why should she pay him the respect she did, since others gave him so little? He was not the man she thought he was. Worse, closer even to home, he had told Ivy to hide the parcel and Ivy had ignored him. He had told her mother to burn it, and her mother had not. And still no one had been struck by lightning, though it was true the day felt heavy, dull, and thundery.

She had somehow imagined that God would be swifter in retribution. 'Swift in retribution' — she liked the phrase. Even God had let her down. She cried a little from self-pity and then pulled herself together and prayed for forgiveness. She must honour her father and mother: these random disloyal thoughts could only be from the devil.

Presently Edwin came out of the Rectory with two young men from Jones and Willis the Church Furnishers, presumably so that all could see how the work of destruction was progressing. Adela thought they were inappropriately dressed, in coats with fur collars and soft felt Homburgs, but it was a new century and no doubt they thought they were arbiters of new thinking. She moved behind a tall gravestone so as not to catch their attention. The taller of the two men was smoking a pipe and tapped it out on the low wall of the lych-gate, next to where the builders were piling the old wood. Adela thought that was sacrilegious; the lych-gate was where coffins could wait under cover for burial, where the preacher could stand to deliver the service during bad weather. But her father made no objection to the liberty the pipe smoker took, and the three of them went back into what they had left of her church, laughing.

The sky was already darkening, though it was nowhere near dusk. Black cumulus clouds were piling up behind the steeple, their paler edges lined with a purpled red. The gilt weathercock swung first this way, then that, unable to make up its mind where the worst danger came from, but flashing a general warning. There'd be a storm in the night. Adela rather hoped so. She loved storms. It crossed her mind that she should check that the embers of the tobacco were properly out as she walked back to the Rectory, but she didn't bother, why should she? It was going to rain, in any case.

Rosina Complains to Minnie

'I think it is outrageous,' said Rosina to Minnie, 'that given three extra tickets for the Coronation, my parents have not seen fit to invite me. Not only does Arthur process, but you do too. Both of you are younger than me, sillier than me, yet you get to dress up in crimson silk and ermine trim and tiara, and I am stuck here in the country, practically walled up like a delinquent nun. You know she haunts the green room down the corridor?'

'I have heard as much,' said Minnie, 'but I don't believe in ghosts.'

'Then you are flying in the face of the spirit of the times,' said Rosina. 'Everyone who's anyone believes in ghosts; the Leader of the House believes in them and holds séances in Carlton House Terrace. They found a planchette board in the Old Queen's room when they were turning out Osborne and burning everything before the public got to know about it. Some say the King got to hear about it and dragged it from the flames and now he has it, and is trying to bring back his mother to tell her she should be ashamed of herself. And even Father had the Psychical Research people down here the other week when you were in London. They didn't find a thing, there was nothing to find, just a rumour that in the year 1701 a servant girl sinned and the lady of the house locked her in the green room without food until she and the baby died of starvation. That's the Hedleighs for you. They care nothing for women. I am the first born, Arthur the second, but I don't even get a seat to sit on at the Coronation.'

'But you keep saying how you disapprove of pomp and circumstance, Rosina.'

'Oh don't be so silly, Minnie. One can hold two different ideas in one's head at the same time. You do it all the time. You love Arthur and you hate Arthur.'

Minnie was too alarmed to speak and Rosina laughed.

'Oh, don't worry about it,' she said. 'All women love and hate their husbands. That's why I'm never going to marry. It's too confusing. That, and having to produce all these little Hedleighs running around, and not a Dilberne amongst them. My children will never get to parade up and down in ermine trim in Westminster Abbey; at least one of yours will. And you're not even English.'

'Rosina,' said Minnie cautiously, 'if you want another title so much you could always marry one.'

'For heaven's sake, Minnie,' said Rosina, 'who would marry me? I think too much. I talk too much, and not the kind of thing anyone wants to hear. Besides, I don't want any old title; I want the one that was denied to me.' She uttered a kind of shuddering sigh. On his perch in the corner of the room, Pappagallo, Rosina's parrot, aroused no doubt by some sense of unusual emotion on his mistress's part, opened a beady eye, squawked, 'Votes for Women!, Votes for Women!', scattered some nut husks around the room for the staff to pick up, closed the eye again and fell silent. Tears began to form on Rosina's cheeks. 'I just want Mama and Papa to ask me to sit beside them when they're doing something special.'

Minnie felt so homesick for her own mother and father it was all she could do not to weep herself. She had found that the English disliked touching one another, but she ventured to put her arms round Rosina to comfort and was not rebuffed. They embraced. Minnie came up to Rosina's shoulder. It was part of Rosina's problem that she was as tall as her father and rather ungainly with it, towering over most men, and, given half a chance, felt always compelled to argue with them rather than to charm, flirt and flatter, as her mother did.

Rosina occupied the west wing of Dilberne Court, the Elizabethan pile that had been the Hedleigh home for so long and seen the family through its many vicissitudes. The house had some forty rooms, accumulated over centuries, most leading into one another — which was annoying but had to be put up with — many staircases and corridors, a few grand halls, a priest hole, a ghost and no central heating. It was more pretty than impressive, with its tall chimneys and added Jacobean attics, but pleasantly situated in five thousand acres of good pastureland, and sheltered by the hills around. It was not at all warm in winter, but the household wrapped up well, though the servants, who were kept busy carrying coals, increasingly longed for their annual migration to Belgrave Square for the Season. In Belgrave Square there was central heating, running hot water and electric light everywhere.

But after the family narrowly escaped

financial ruination as the previous century turned to the new, it had within a couple of years met sudden prosperity, as its current head, Robert, Earl of Dilberne, had transferred his interests to the gold and metal mines of the Transvaal. Now, in both Belgrave Square and Dilberne Court, builders and painters, electricians and plumbers, worked ceaselessly, restoring the place — if not to its one-time glory, at least with a few extra amenities and not in any danger of falling down for another hundred years.

Robert was now obliged to spend a great deal of his time in London — 'running the country', as Isobel put it — and Arthur broadly speaking looked after the estate. Broadly, because much of Arthur's time and attention was now taken up with his new company, the Jehu Automobile Works, devoted to the advancement and manufacture of internal combustion-engine racing cars, which he ran with his new partner, Davey Clacton, in an old mill in the village of Dilberne, one mile from the Court. Luckily, the estate had a competent and honest manager in the form of Tom Shooter, who kept its acres functioning well and in good repair. Arthur's current ambition was to create an automobile racing track, both for testing his and Davey's motors, and to extend the track in time to a proper racing circuit to take in Dilberne and the adjacent village of Samsey. He aimed to have an annual international event underway to start in 1905.

'Pity the poor villagers,' said Lady Isobel. 'The noise, the people!'

'With wheat only twenty-seven shillings a bushel and falling,' said his Lordship, 'they'll live to be grateful.'

'The roar of the engines will be music to their ears,' said Arthur. Steam engines had at least been quiet: the new combustion-engine motors were fast, more manoeuvrable, better suited to hills, but extremely noisy. Racetracks and circuits were the thing of the future, he swore. Road racing was popular, but increasingly dangerous as machines got faster and automobiles more plentiful and likely enough soon to be banned by an interfering government.

'Oh Arthur,' said Minnie, 'I wish we could spend just a little more time together.'

'I love you with all my mind and all my heart,' said Arthur, promising to be home as soon as he possibly could from giving his attention and skills to the split radiator, the problematic flange, the fusing spark plugs — whatever the emergency happened to be. He'd been true to his promise, paying

Minnie so much focused attention her complaints were, for a time, quietened. But it was a bit lonely.

'Well, you married him,' said Rosina. 'I warned you. He's a man.'

It was after an argument with Isobel that Rosina had left her rooms at Belgrave Square and taken up residence in the west wing. The argument had been about Pappagallo, a bird whom, although obviously handsome, the girl kept only to annoy, training it to shriek 'Votes for Women!, Votes for Women!' whenever a man came into the room. It liked to use its beak to scatter birdseed husks around its cage and when let out to fly about the room — which was often — left its droppings everywhere, and in general annoyed the staff. Now a medical friend had warned Isobel of the dangers of psittacosis, a disagreeable and sometimes fatal disease which can be passed from parrots to humans. For Isobel this was the last straw. She told Rosina the parrot had to go. She could not abide it in the house a moment longer. Rosina enquired as to why everyone hated her so, and her mother suggested perhaps it would be as well if Rosina went down to live in Dilberne Court for a while and take the parrot with her. Rosina said yes, rather to everyone's surprise, since she would be away from the lectures and political meetings she loved so much. Perhaps, the family thought, if Rosina was more in the country her revolutionary zeal would be muted. It was unlikely that Rosina could make a good marriage, but she might yet make a respectable one, perhaps to some local landowner.

Rosina was at least someone to talk to, though what she said was often shocking. Arthur talked about engines — and there was a limit to Minnie's interest in chain drives and drum shafts — Isobel talked about fashion and fabrics, and though Minnie liked spending money well enough — as who does not — and had helped greatly in the furnishing and remodernizing of Belgrave Square, was easily bored by talk of the latest styles. You saw, you decided, you spent, and that was that. If you lived in the contemporary world, what appealed to you was contemporary fashion; why worry about it?

And his Lordship seldom put in an appearance, being so busy in London — Rosina would suggest he took more than a passing interest in the young fancy-free Duchess of Marlborough, but Minnie didn't believe a word of it, he being so obviously dedicated to his wife. Robert quite frightened Minnie: she would be struck dumb when he was there at the head of the table. He must think her very stupid. Minnie's father Billy had a different kind of power — amiable until angered but then perfectly capable of strangling an enemy with his bare hands. She was used to that. Her father-in-law was yet more urbane, but would never use his bare hands. He would get someone else to do whatever it was, then alter the law of the land to make sure there were no consequences.

That evening Minnie confided her conversation with Rosina to Arthur when finally he got home for supper, which they had in their rooms by the fire; fresh bread from the kitchens, newly churned butter — properly hung cold beef (Minnie seldom ate pork) with walnut pickle, followed by apple pie (the last of the season's Bramleys) and Cheddar cheese.

'Rosina is really upset about not being invited to the Coronation,' she said to Arthur. 'Can't you do something?'

'It's her own fault,' Arthur said. 'She can't be trusted to behave. I don't blame her; it's just very sad when a girl has brains. She's never going to be happy. And what a man wants above anything else is to have a happy wife. Are you happy, Minnie?' he asked. He liked to be sure.

'Very happy,' she said, and if she crossed her fingers she was sensible enough to be sure he didn't notice.

'That's good,' he said, 'because I am.' Arthur's fingernails were always dirty with engine oil, no matter how hard he scrubbed away at them. She found that rather exciting. Isobel deplored it.

'Anyway,' said Arthur, 'the parents are probably keeping them back for the Baums, or whoever seems suitable nearer the time. There's a good six months to go, after all. A lot can happen in six months. Davey Clacton's talking about adapting Jehu V with a fixed-drive shaft and ring and pinion gear: he reckons we could get her up to sixty-five miles an hour if we did, it's worth trying. A real nuisance, having to stop everything and get into the old ermine and sealskin, just about the time we'll have her ready. All very well for you girls, you love dressing up. That's all that Rosina misses, I'll swear.'

The song kept rising up in Minnie's mind, taking her by surprise. She wished it wouldn't.

Oh what care I for your goosefeather bed,
With the sheets turned down so
   comely-oh,

Oh what care I for your house and your
   land,
I'm off with the raggle-taggle gypsies-oh.

It wasn't even as if their bed was
goosefeather, it was a hard and scratchy
horsehair mattress, which she and Arthur
were quite satisfactorily pummelling the life
out of.

Ivy's Sweetheart

Ivy had gone round to the cottage opposite Swaley's Farm and handed her mother the parcel. It was only sensible and hardly stealing. At least it had not been burned and a parcel destined for Adela was not going to end up anyhow with the poor of the parish, more likely in the wardrobe of some deserving relative of the Lady Superintendent. She was right about the parcel: it contained a truly fancy and expensive piece of clothing, a young girl's nicely made red silk velvet dress, ankle length, with a pink lace collar and crimson satin ribbons, with good seams for letting out, tiny hand-stitching and of very good quality indeed. Her mother reckoned it would fetch at least ten shillings if not more on her Saturday stall. Doreen could get the thatch mended, or at least a start made on it. Ivy wrenched a smile or two out of her mother on the strength of it.

They would have burned the wrapping

paper but Ivy wanted to keep the little reindeers, so they smoothed out the paper and
folded it neatly, and wound the string onto
Doreen's existing roll of odds and ends. It
was green. Neither had seen green string
before. String was meant to be white. But
waste not want not.

As she passed the farm she ran into
George, who as it happened had not finished
up for the day. She took him back round to
the milking parlour and found the tiled floor
and wooden stalls still wet from where he'd
been rinsing down the vacuum tubes which
took the effort out of hand milking, and had
meant another three of his friends were now
without jobs. Fortunately, the tickets had
not got wet, or only a little bit. She showed
them to George who said she should tell no
one what she had done — as if she was
likely to: she'd only left them with George,
who was over six foot tall, so he could
perhaps have a word with Tim Peasedown
the postman, who was barely five foot, to
make sure he denied all knowledge of having delivered either parcel or letter. George
said he would, and would make enquiries.
The tickets might be worth a little: they
might be worth a lot. The seat numbers
could perhaps be altered or removed; he
had friends in the Art Department at col-

lege. It was interesting that someone, somewhere, knew the date of the Coronation. He
pocketed the envelope and nudged Ivy
further into the milking parlour. They would
have to be quick. He had to cycle the eleven
miles into Bath to get to his two o'clock
class with his tutor Mr Edfield on Theories
of Perception. Ivy couldn't be too long
away; the Mrs Hon. Rev. would get suspicious.

George was very clever. Just a few more
exams to pass and he would be qualified to
train as a science teacher. The government
would pay him a guinea a week to do so
and he would be done with farm life and
milking parlours for ever. He was ambitious,
not like the other boys in the village. He
would go far, and then probably not have
time for her, of course, but Ivy would face
that when she came to it.

She crept round behind George and put
her arms round his large frame. They would
only reach so far. She really enjoyed that.
There was no fat, it was all muscle. There
was a difference in scale between the two of
them that she found very satisfactory: he
made her feel tiny, helpless and looked after.
Though when it came to it, she had to
admit, he was more likely to look after
himself than anyone else. He would look at

you intently with his bright wide blue eyes — he needed glasses; a pity, but whoever was perfect — and smile his easy smile and be so innocent and boyish you would end up doing whatever it was he wanted. He was a charmer, with an instant smile and white, even teeth. People trusted him on sight. She was not sure they were right to, but she knew how to look after herself.

He turned her round, grabbed her arms, quick as a flash and steered her round to the hay pile at the end of the parlour where it was comparatively private and had her on her back — she hadn't bothered with knickers — and was into her within — minutes. 'Careful, careful,' she managed to say the other side of her moaning, and he was. He would sometimes ask her to do what the Bible forbade, so he didn't have to withdraw but could carry on, but so far she had resisted. It didn't seem decent and her friend Beryl said it hurt a lot though you got used to it. The last thing she wanted to do was get pregnant, mind you, even though her mother would know what to do if she did, so it was a temptation, just to see what it was like. But she didn't want to end up like Beryl, with a reputation as the village bicycle.

And then he had to be off, but not before

he had given her a lecture on how the vacuum tubes of the milking machines worked, and how and why the cows preferred the tubes to hand milking, facts and theories she perhaps had rather not known. George was like that. You had to stand and listen and be told and agree. But it was worth it.

He was going to be late back that night, he was going to a lecture — but perhaps she'd be able to slip out from the Rectory while everyone was asleep and meet him up at the farm? — his employers were away for the night and they could have a comfortable bed for a change.

'Oh go on, Ivy,' he said. 'Be a brick. I'll sort out the tickets for you. We could get up to a thing or to if we had peace and quiet. You know how I love you.'

Oh yes, yes, yes, love, she thought. Do you believe I'm an idiot?

She said she'd think about it, and asked him what the lecture was and he said he was going to a public séance with some of the fellows from college. They were all interested in theories of life after death. Fame and fortune awaited the one who could prove there was. Most séances were fraudulent — but this particular medium seemed to be genuine. If she was, they'd pay her to call by the college to do a range of controlled experiments. Just as some people had talents — good at art, good at writing — some people, often very simple people, were sensitives, good at communicating with the other side.

'Good at conning gullible folk out of their money, more like,' said Ivy. 'Now there's a way to make a living!'

But she said she'd meet him, sneak out when everyone else was asleep. There was no way she wasn't going to, and he knew it.

AN ALL-CONSUMING FIRE

When the salesman from Jones and Willis, Church Furnishers, carelessly tapped out his pipe on the wall of the lych-gate, a glowing ember flew up in the wind and landed in the splintered wreckage of the musicians' gallery. The wood was dry and powdery. The ember continued to smoulder quietly, stuck under the raised wooden seam of St Cecilia's gown where she'd kicked it up high in her dancing so many centuries ago. The fire started by devouring what was left of St Cecilia and her musicians, and having succeeded in that crept round to the other side of the panel, but its underside was thick with the powder left by a myriad boring beetles, and that blocked oxygen to the flames. For almost twenty minutes it looked as if all would be saved.

It was at this time that Ivy Baines slipped out of the Rectory for a further assignation with the would-be scientist George Topp.

She marvelled at the sudden strength of the wind. There were spots of rain in the gale and thunder in the distance. She counted three seconds between thunderclap and lightning. The storm was three miles off. She'd hoped it would pass at a distance: she didn't want the Rectory roused from sleep to notice her absence. She'd seen no sign of fire, she said later. She passed by Swaley's Farm without noticing a thing.

But a fierce gust from the south-west had sent sparks to wrap flames round the pale, dry, fragile fingers of the charred lute player, and send flaking fragments back down into the pile. Soon the whole bonfire was ablaze, and the lych-gate too.

Whether now it was that the steeplecock was struck by lightning and the roof started to burn, or whether flames leapt from lych-gate to tree and then onto the porch could not later be determined — the thousand-year-old yew with its dark, oily leaves and dry hollow trunk had certainly gone up at some stage, probably early on.

It was a nasty night and few were venturing out. It was not until the flames set off the great expanse of the thatched roof of the tithe barn with what was almost an explosion that Yatbury was roused to danger. The bell tower of St Aidan's itself being out of action, and there being only a single bell at the new Baptist Chapel, there was no possibility of reverse peals, the traditional alarm. The wealthy Methodist St Bart's, its copper spire completed in 1814, an upstart compared to Yatbury's ancient St Aidan's, had twenty-four bells in its belfry, famous for its peals, but was locked at night because of fear of theft of its silver plate by rogues and vagabonds. The telephone exchange was closed. The churchwarden had to cycle all the way to the next village for help.

One way and another it was a full hour before engines from Lacock and Bath arrived. By then most of the able-bodied males of Yatbury were there with hoses, buckets and axes, doing what they could to save church and barn, but to no avail. No one thought to make sure that those in the Rectory had been alerted to danger: it was a surprise to everyone when flames leapt from the barn roof to run down the Rectory walls, devouring dead ivy on the way, to catch the window sills of the ground floor, crack the windows, suck out the heavy velvet curtains, belch them back in again, in flames, and let in a funnel of air to turn the wide central staircase into a furnace and pour heavy smoke into adjacent rooms.

And where was the family? The firemen

checked the master bedroom with its big curtained double bed and, finding it empty, assumed the occupants had escaped: no one had told them there was a child, or indeed a maid. The firemen turned their attention back to the barn: the hoses ran dry: the wind howled. Rain did not fall, but ill-fitting hoses had turned hard ground to sucking mud. Confusion reigned. There seemed to be no one in charge. Putting out flames was one matter: seeking out and imposing their will on the Rev. Hedleigh's life, even to save it, seemed too complex a matter to undertake.

It was fortunate for Adela that Ivy and George came running up to the house when they did: one quick look showed Ivy both that the house was alight and that the family had not escaped to the garden. She hustled George round to the back of the house, and pointed out Adela's window on the first floor, above the back stairs to the kitchen annexe. Flames were flickering round the back door of the annexe and the handle was already hot. George seized it and turned it nevertheless; but the door was locked. He shouldered it open with one powerful thrust and crashed through to the corridor. Flames followed him down the passage; he looked back to find them leaping after him up the stairs like hounds determined to follow their master, come what might. He outran them.

Ivy directed firemen to the two small attic bedrooms where the Hedleigh parents slept, two separate rooms for two hard, narrow beds, and two single horsehair mattresses. The rescuers had to find ladders and manoeuvre them into position in slippery mud and sudden driving rain. It all took time which the Rev. and Elise, alas, did not have.

THE RESCUE OF ADELA

Adela slept: her dreams were troubled, sometimes of fairy princes, sometimes of monsters, often the one melding into the other. She had been reading *The Blue Fairy Book* in bed, and fallen asleep reading, a silly thing to do. She needed to stay awake, in case she heard her mother's foot on the creaking stair, first one from the bottom, which gave Adela time to push the book under the mattress and pretend to be asleep. Not that the book had been specifically forbidden but Ivy had given it to her the Christmas before last, spoils from her own mother's market stall, and one look at the curly blue swirls and slender, waiting maiden of the cover, and Adela had hidden it at once. It would put ideas in her head, it would lead her astray, whatever astray was. She knew the book by heart by now, every illustration, the lineaments of every fabulous dragon, monster, pretty maiden, cruel stepmother and damsel in distress, as delivered in pen and ink by Henry Justice Ford. She was the beautiful miller's daughter, tormented by the hideous goblin, Rumpelstiltskin. Perhaps she was the goose girl, once a princess until her maid betrayed her, waiting for the prophecy to come true: that she would bear the queen's daughter. However one worked that out. Snow White and Rose Red, bear and dragon, came and went in her half-waking dreams, and tonight more than ever. She was hungry. Ivy had forgotten the cream, and the sugar: she, Adela, thank you very much, might as well go hungry as eat dry bread. Come to think of it she would rather be asleep.

She slept, or half slept, luxuriously: she was in love with the shape, the feel of her own bare arm, curved over her head. It was the bare arm of the miller's daughter as Rumpelstiltskin pushed open the door to peer at her with curious eyes, and then the blanket was pushed back. She was uncovered. She was lifted from the bed. She was being abducted. Her nightgown was rucked up: she tried to pull it down, but where were her hands? Hanging down, as was her head, her hair falling free; her body slung over a shoulder, a male shoulder, the prince's shoulder. He hadn't even bothered with the kiss. She could smell burning, she smelled sweat and cows: she could hear crackling, and crashings and hissings; she opened her eyes and stared at white fabric, moving as the body beneath them moved, as she moved. A man's shirt. White linen. That's what a prince wore. Bump, bump, bump; her own body moving as his moved. They were coming down stairs. She turned her head to one side, to save her nose, opened her eyes. Flames. She was being saved from fire; her prince had come, to snatch her from the jaws of death. The house was burning down. Her fault. He had the strongest, broadest shoulders. It was all totally extraordinary yet all totally inevitable. She was coughing: smoke was down her throat. A most remarkable feeling was rising in her: an excitement: a power she could not control both pleasurable and terrible; something you struggled to achieve, it was a bubble: it swelled and swelled, without so much as a by-your-leave, and then it burst, leaving her with the oddest tingling of completion, some need served, some duty done, that all that was meant to be was satisfied, and they were out of the house, and everything was normal again except she was lying on the ground on cold grass with rain spattering onto her face, and a hundred

Rumpelstiltskins staring at her:

Today do I bake, to-morrow I brew
The day after that the queen's child
   comes in;
And oh! I am glad that nobody knew
That the name I am called is
   Rumpelstiltskin!

Where on earth had that come from? The
goose girl had been asked to guess his name,
of course. Someone put a blanket on her
and she thought it would be nice to go to
sleep again, and wake up and deal with
things in the morning.

But Ivy was there looking down at her.

'Who was that man?' asked Adela.

'My boyfriend,' said Ivy. 'Quite the hero. I
hope it doesn't go to his head. He's got
nasty burns on his hands. I'd better go and
look after him. This kind lady here will look
after you.'

And Ivy's face went away.

The kind lady was taking off her own
cloak and putting it under Adela presumably to save her bottom from damp, which
was nice of her. The lady had big teeth and
a big jaw, very many smart clothes and an
air of being in charge.

Adela sat up but the lady pushed her

down again.

'Don't look,' said the smart lady. 'Best not to look.' But Adela had already looked. Firemen were carrying out a single stretcher, and silhouetted against the fiery background was a strange shape, composed of two twisted and charred figures, half sitting, half lying, which reminded Adela of what Ivy sometimes did by way of entertainment: took two matches, put their heads together, lit them, and watched the heads fuse and flare up, the stick bodies seem to rise in the air, embracing and twisting. Elise had caght Ivy doing it and had been very angry, for reasons Adela did not understand.

'Smoke inhalation,' the coroner had declared later. 'They did not suffer.'

'Whole place, up like a torch,' said Ivy's mother Doreen. 'And I'd like to know where you were tonight, my girl, if you weren't in the bed you should have been.'

'Oh thank you, Ma,' said Ivy, sarcastic.

A Journey to Wells

Mrs Henrietta Kennion, the Australian wife of the Bishop of Bath and Wells, had been passing through Yatbury in a carriage on her way home to the Bishop's Palace in Wells, in the company of her nephew Frank, when they noticed smoke and heard a commotion ahead. Although it was so dreadful a night — she had been up most of it attending the sickbed of an old friend — and it was to be Christmas Eve in the morning and a very busy time indeed in the Church Calendar, she had the carriage stopped. She had been horrified to realize that the fire was at St Aidan's, in her husband's diocese, and that the fire, fanned by an unreasonably strong wind, had spread to the Rectory too. She hastened out with Frank into the wet and chaos of the night, and was in time to see, in the reddish, smoky reflected light of flames upon the low clouds overhead, the church steeple with its melting weathercock collapse and fall in upon itself. St Aidan's and its troublesome rectory had been a thorn in her husband's side for some time, but all the same it was a most upsetting sight.

'Magnificent!' cried Frank — who, Henrietta had to remind herself, was a young man who lived for his art — and he ran back to the coach to fetch the satchel where he kept his sketchbook and charcoal. Thus it was that he missed the sight of George carrying the half-conscious Adela out of the Rectory across the threshold to safety, but in time to see her laid upon the ground, and then the firemen, who seemed hopelessly disorganized, bring two distorted bodies out on their single stretcher. It was a horrible sight: the kind you did not forget. It would not be fitting, in the presence of death, to take out charcoal and draw, though he was tempted. He would record it in his mind for future use.

'It's the Reverend Hedleigh,' said Henrietta, aghast, 'and his wife. He's a great trouble to my husband but who could wish an end like this for them?'

'It will have been from the inhalation of smoke,' Frank said firmly. 'They will not have suffered. These are not bodies that struggled to get away,' and Henrietta was relieved to believe the young man. She was fond of Frank: he saw the best in everything, and so the best tended to happen: saw good where others saw evil. She was glad to have him with her, Frank Overshaw, her sister's son aged twenty-nine, born in South Australia. He'd come all the way over to England to study for Holy Orders, and then changed his mind, and now he studied art at the Slade, and wrote poetry for little literary magazines. But he was a thoughtful, supportive and practical person, always prepared to make the best of things and share his good nature with anyone who seemed in need of it.

It was Frank who pointed out that the daughter, her face smeared with soot and mud, her hair wet, whose eyes were open but who seemed to be in shock, might be beneath a blanket but was lying on the ground in a thin nightdress on wet muddy ground. Once she was wrapped in Henrietta's cloak it was Frank who, with the coachman's help, got Adela to the carriage and settled her there under fur rugs.

A large-boned, practical young woman, who seemed to be the maid at the rectory, and was busy with bandages, told Henrietta there were no immediate friends or relatives, the ambulance had been called but would take its time, and the best thing Henrietta could do was take the girl off somewhere safe and warm. Henrietta said this was what she intended to do. It was fortunate that the maid knew the name of the family solicitor — she had taken letters to the post often enough — and was able to write down the firm's name slowly but legibly.

So that was how it came to be that when Adela came to open her eyes, it was to discover herself bumping along in a carriage on the road to Wells, all but naked amongst strangers, her hand held by a woman she did not know but who told her she was the wife of the Bishop of Bath and Wells, whom she knew only as her father's enemy, telling her that her parents were dead.

They asked her what her name was and Adela tried to tell them but, oddly, found she could not. Her lips seemed to be sealed. Adela was a person with a mother and a father; now she was without them she didn't see how she could claim the name. She had seen the entwined and twisted black shapes on a stretcher and if she thought about it knew what she had seen. Everything from now on would be different. It was not necessarily worse. Dawn was breaking. That suggested breakfast. If she ate she might be able to think.

A young man with watery blue eyes and narrow shoulders was sitting across from her, staring at her. He did not look strong enough to fling her over his shoulders. He had a piece of charcoal in his hand and was drawing her. It seemed a great impertinence. He had a silly expression on his face, a kind of devoted intensity which annoyed her.

'I'm so sorry, my dear,' the woman with the big teeth and the large jaw was saying. But she looked kind. She had tears in her eyes. Adela closed hers again.

'I think she's in shock,' she heard the strange woman say. 'Poor little orphaned thing.'

'Death shall have no dominion. The body dies, the soul goes on,' said the young man.

'Oh please, Frank, none of that Theosophy stuff,' said Henrietta. 'Not now. We're all much too tired. And do put away your artistic things. Just leave the poor girl be.'

'But this has to be recorded,' he said. 'She is an angel, dropped from the skies. An angel in great distress, but look at the purity of that chin, the clarity of the cheekbones. How often in life does this kind of thing happen? I feel we are twin souls. I am blessed. It is karma.'

'She could do with feeding up,' said

Henrietta. 'She is much too thin.'

By the time the carriage had reached the moated mediaeval castle that was the Palace of the Bishop of Bath and Wells, Frank Overshaw, unmarried, artist, Theosophist, heir to the hundred-thousand-acre Overshaw Estate in Western Australia, a vast area of scrub and brush, but which included the small town of Overshaw and three working gold mines, announced that he was in love with Adela Hedleigh.

'Oh don't be absurd, Frank,' said the Bishop's wife, whose brother was Governor of South Australia, whose husband had been the Bishop of Adelaide until promoted to Bath and Wells, who knew nothing about her new ward's aristocratic connections, and was never one to be nervous of speaking her mind. 'You have no idea who or what she is. You know nothing about her at all.'

'She is an angel dropped from heaven,' he said, stubbornly. 'She is my destiny.'

Frank tried to take Adela's hand but she shook his off, instinctively, like a cat might shake off an annoying fly.

HIS LORDSHIP FIGHTS BACK

On the morning of Christmas Eve his Lordship called by his family solicitor and financial advisor, Mr Eric Baum, to sign some papers and receive further dividends from the Modder Kloof mine. He was in fine good humour. The news was that the gold seam showed no signs of running out, and the magnesium mines further north, in which Mr Baum too had an interest, continued to produce effectively and efficiently.

Mr Baum pointed out that native labour was becoming more expensive and his Lordship might consider shipping in coolies from China as a cheaper option.

'Rosina wouldn't like that one bit,' said his Lordship and laughed. 'She's a Liberal at heart, the silly girl.'

Mr Baum controlled the urge to raise his eyebrows and snort. He found Rosina a very trying young woman but knew better than to say so. These people fought furiously within families, but bonded instantly at the slightest hint of criticism from without. He let it go, for the moment.

His Lordship announced that he and Isobel were setting off for Sandringham that afternoon to spend a few days over Christmas Week with their Majesties, and Mr Baum nodded, as if this was nothing out of the ordinary. But he was awed and impressed, and marvelled at his own good fortune. He had taken on the Hedleighs and their money problems as a favour to the great financier Ernest Cassel, friend of the new King, and here he was himself within spitting distance of royalty.

'Oh and by the way,' his Lordship then said, 'the date of the Coronation has been decided. It's June 26th. They'll announce it any day now. We have a couple of spare seats in the Abbey. Perhaps you and Mrs Baum would like to take them up? Watch the Dilbernes parading in all their glory? There won't be much sitting around for us, of course. But you're very welcome.'

'I am sure Mrs Baum would be delighted and honoured,' said Mr Baum, as calmly as he could. 'I believe Mr Hubert Parry is composing something for the occasion. She is very fond indeed of Mr Parry.'

To think! Only two years ago he and

Naomi had lived above a shop in the East End. Now this! He was as happy for her as he was for himself. More. Her place in London Society was assured. She had given up so much for him, risked so much, suffered so much, complained so little. Thus love was rewarded.

'Well,' said his Lordship, 'you must be busy, Mr Baum. I'll leave you to it,' and he was off, with a courteous nod of acknowledgement to Rachel the secretary, who once he was gone said, 'Oh Mr Baum, the Coronation!' and all but fainted. Eric Baum had to bring her a glass of water.

He would wait until he got home to tell Naomi. He hoped he would not have to work too late. He would stop by Samuel the jewellers and buy her a Christmas gift. He had bought her a simple gold bracelet for Hanukah but he did not think she would object too much to an extra one set with diamonds, which he had seen at the time but thought too expensive, although in principle Naomi set her face against observing the Christian religious festivals. 'When in Rome do as Rome does,' was Eric's motto. Little by little she would come round to his way of thinking.

But at lunchtime the pattern of the day changed abruptly. The phone rang and it was someone from the Bath and Wells Diocesan Office, with the dreadful news of the calamity that had befallen two of his clients, the Reverend and Mrs Edwin Hedleigh. The caller sounded comparatively young and had a slight Australian accent. Mr Baum found himself oddly unmoved by the news of the deaths. He had met the Reverend and his wife on two occasions and both had been as disagreeable as meetings with Robert were agreeable. He was glad to hear that at least the daughter was safe and well, and said so, but was very conscious of a great deal of hard work ahead. He knew he had Edwin's will in his safe but not Mrs Hedleigh's, which she had intended to send by post. When a married couple died in an accident a matter of who died first might well arise. He asked after the girl — Adela? was that her name? Mr Baum could hardly remember — and was told she was well but shocked and was welcome to stay at the Palace in the Bishop's and Mrs Kennion's care until relatives could be contacted to collect her. Mr Baum said he would be happy to reimburse any expenses incurred, and that he would at once inform the Earl of Dilberne of the unhappy news.

There was a short silence, and then a surprised 'Lord Dilberne is a relative? Lord

Dilberne the politician, the Tory?'

'The Earl of Dilberne is Miss Adela's uncle,' said Mr Baum. 'Edwin is, was, as the younger brother of an earl, properly referred to as the Honourable Edwin Hedleigh, Hedleigh being the family name.'

'Oh I see,' said the caller. 'That's why they all referred to him as the Hon. Rev. I don't think anyone realized it meant anything. They thought he was just a reverend and a real pain in the ass.'

Mr Baum refrained from asking the caller if he was indeed Australian, fairly certain that the answer would be 'yes'. Frank Overshaw had the traits of the colonial, too loud a voice, too open in his emotions, too immediate in his approach to others, forgetful of the restraints of a proper Englishman. Being Jewish himself, Eric Baum did not aspire to Englishness, but was becoming, he found, very sensitive to the lack of it in others.

'Actually,' said Mr Baum, 'if it is of any interest' — it was his experience that titles were of extreme interest to everyone he met, but perhaps in Australia things were different — 'now that the mother has passed away, the daughter will be a Princess in her own right, though relatives on the mother's side will be hard to trace. The line is Aus-

112

trian and somewhat obscure, some kind of Hapsburg dynasty, I believe. Elise, God rest her soul, saw fit not to use the title. The family cut her off when she renounced Roman Catholicism. But all this is of no consequence, of course, in the light of these terrible and tragic events.' He was taken aback by the joyous voice from the other end of the line.

'A Princess!' cried the caller. 'That angel! Of course! She dwells in a palace, how could she not. It is her natural habitat.'

It occurred to Mr Baum that he might be dealing not just with an Australian but also with a madman. He asked for a name, and was given that of Frank Overshaw — a relative by marriage of the Bishop, it seemed, who was helping out in the office, Christmas being such a busy time in the Church Year.

Mr Baum took the number and called Bow Street to ask the police to check reports of a fatal house fire in Somerset. They called back within the hour to confirm the report. All was as Mr Overshaw had described. Telephone numbers and further information were exchanged. He then spoke again to the Bishop's wife, Mrs Kennion, a competent and pleasant woman, and she assured him that the girl was in good hands and had been visited by the Bishop's own doctor.

Mr Baum got Rachel to open up the vaults, looked up Edwin Dilberne's will and groaned. It was as he remembered. Not only was he, Eric Baum, the appointed executor — always a great deal of work for little return — but the deceased, in his Wishes, declared some two years ago, had made a rather extraordinary set of conditions. That he was to be buried in the graveyard at the church where he officiated, St Aidan's, and on no account in the family vault, and that his earthly remains were not to be embalmed. The Wishes were on a separate piece of paper and Mr Baum was tempted to untie the red ribbon which bound the document, detach it and simply throw it into the coal fire which struggled in his grate. It would save everyone so much work. Such wishes were not legally binding. He had remonstrated with Edwin Hedleigh at the time, pointing out that if he was not to be embalmed it would necessitate a very speedy burial, which was not usual in Christian circles, unlike in his own religion, but had been told curtly, that was the point, so he had desisted.

Mr Baum had brought to Edwin's attention that since he was bequeathing all his worldly goods to *The Protestant Review,* his family would be left unprovided for, unless Mrs Hedleigh had means of her own, in which case it would be advisable for him to have at least a copy of her will in his vaults. The Reverend Hedleigh had replied his wife would do as her husband instructed, and forward the will by post in due course. Mr Baum and Rachel witnessed the will, the meeting was abruptly brought to an end; and the Reverend Hedleigh had stalked out into the foggy afternoon, like some tall, stooping bird of ill omen. Mr Baum felt thankful he was not a Christian: there was a movement for reform within the Jewish faith, and that was causing some dissent and bitterness, but nothing like that which still existed between Catholic and Protestant. Not so long ago they had been burning each other to death.

'Glad to see the back of that one,' said Rachel. 'Worse than the fog for standing between a girl and her breath. Is he really the Earl's brother? How can that be? The Earl is so friendly and nice.'

Mr Baum searched further, to be certain, but could find no sign of a will from Mrs Baum, so he called the Bath and Wells Diocesan Office and asked young Mr Overshaw if there was any likelihood of a will being found in the Rectory, and Mr Overshaw said not on your life, the place had been burning like the crackers, it was a miracle the Princess got out alive: the Lord above had leant down and saved his angel.

Mr Baum decided he would not tell his Lordship at once. He would not want the good cheer of the Sandringham Christmas disturbed by such grim news. It could wait until Boxing Day.

ADELA SETTLES IN

Mrs Kennion was a woman of swift decision. It was in her nature to take charge. She had run a home for unmarried mothers back in Adelaide and done it well, by doing, as she was fond of saying, 'what she thought fit when she thought fit'. Within a couple of hours she had the girl homed in the servants' quarters — safe and warm and the rest of the Palace full of Christmastide guests, bathed, fed (cold cuts, potatoes and salad, and a good quantity of semolina and strawberry jam, which the little orphan silently wolfed down), and prayed over — and the child was surely in need of prayer, having been roused from sleep, slung over the shoulder of a strange young man, carried through fire, left to shiver alone in the cold, seen the bodies of her parents carried from her blazing home, sketched in the extremity of her distress by the egregious Frank Overshaw, and now found herself cosy and secure in an unfamiliar bed. Henrietta did not wonder at the girl's silence, and was merely glad that she could eat, and glad that she folded her hands decorously and automatically in prayer.

During the day the doctor was called and declared that the girl was healthy enough, but undernourished and in a state of shock. She roused herself sufficiently to say: 'Please, I am not "the girl". My name is Adela,' before sinking back on her pillows, where she looked most beguiling, her hair washed and halo-like upon white linen, wavy, like a Botticelli angel.

Indeed, young Frank, who kept deserting his office duties through the morning to 'just look in on her to see she's all right', kept murmuring, 'Behold, the angel of the Lord Maitreya!' Mrs Kennion, being herself rather irritable, having managed only a couple of hours' sleep the night before, felt obliged to rebuke him, pointing out that while he was under her husband's roof it would be only polite to keep his Theosophist convictions to himself. Though the Bishop was very much an ecumenical — one of the reasons he had had such a hard time with the Reverend Hedleigh, who was anything but — he would draw the line at the wishy-washy Eastern religions Frank semed to favour. The Theosophical Society, much in vogue at the moment, under the leadership of a Mrs Blavatsky, set out to understand the mysteries of the universe and the bonds between the human and the divine. It seemed to involve vegetarianism and rather a lot of chanting, and Mrs Kennion had no time for it. She had met Mrs Blavatsky and considered the woman a charlatan, with over-large eyes and frizzy hair.

Mrs Kennion dispatched Frank to find out what he could from the solicitor, and he came back with the news that the girl was not only a niece of Lord Dilberne the politician, but a princess to boot. Mrs Kennion cut her nephew off before he could rave further about the wondrous girl — she had never known him in love before: apart from the Theosophy, which presumably he would grow out of in time, he had seeemed perfectly sensible — and hurried off to tell her husband the news.

Bishop Kennion was an impressive, handsome man of fifty-five with the serious face of a senior cleric, quick in thought and slow of speech, and well regarded by his peers. At the moment, since it was the Christmas season, he was extremely busy. He was followed wherever he went by a flock of black-garbed lesser clerics and secretaries in need of instruction. The last thing he wanted was an unclaimed orphan girl on his hands.

The Bishop felt overworked as it was. The thousand-candle services — and extra services meant extra sermons — the Magnificat to be sung at Evensong every day, and today an O Antiphon, always tricky, and the Director of Music complaining that the choirboys were hoarse from too many carol concerts — not to mention the new Archdeacon enraged because his vestments were rose not purple. It was almost too much. This Christmas demands for the services of the exorcist had increased threefold. Why? The Bishop thought it was more to do with the general upset of the population, a real distress of the mind as the concentration camp scandal in South Africa broke, than Satan and his minions tripping hither and thither, but perhaps these things were indeed linked? And now the tragedy of the St Aidan's fire and this pale little waif of an orphan snatched, probably quite illegally, by his wife. The Bishop prayed for forgiveness for his first reaction to the news that Edwin Hedleigh had passed away. It was of relief. The flow of troublesome letters from St Aidan's would stop. It might not even be necessary to rebuild the church. Congregations there had fallen off sharply lately and not even a pleasanter parson was likely to restore them. Once a congregation decamped to the Methodists it was likely to stay there.

'The Earl of Dilberne's niece!' exclaimed the Bishop. 'Hedleigh is — was, God rest his poor tormented soul — Robert Dilberne's brother? And you have kidnapped her?'

'I have kidnapped no one,' said his wife. 'I found one of your young parishioners in trouble and distress and offered her succour.'

'There are temporal powers as well as spiritual ones, Henrietta,' said the Bishop, 'and it is my job to reconcile the two. I admire your impulse to virtue while doubting the wisdom of your judgement. You are too impetuous, my dear. Better have left her for the authorities to deal with: she would be safely in the bosom of her family by now. Christmas is a time for rejoicing, not weeping and wailing.'

'I suppose you think Hedleigh should have timed his death better; waited until, say, Easter Friday.' She should not have said it: he did not smile but looked vaguely pained, which he was good at.

Henrietta wanted to get on. Lady parishioners were to turn up for one of her charity dos — morning tea with scones — at eleven. They would expect strawberry jam but Jenny could lay hands only on apricot and waited for instruction. But the Bishop hated her to 'run about'. *More haste, less speed,* was his favourite saying. So she waited with seeming patience until he had finished on the subject of the Earl of Dilberne.

'As it happens, I know Dilberne rather well. I sit across from him in the House of Lords. He's a High-Church Tory, voted against me on the Charles Gore issue. Come to think of it, the man's near as dammit a Papist. I am sorry if I express myself too forcibly but the Romans have shown themselves more recalcitrant even than the Methodists when it comes to reinforcing unity and collegiality throughout the community of Christ. Dilberne's son and heir, I seem to remember, has married into the Roman Church, daughter of a pork baron from Chicago. There was talk of it in the House. It was felt he was letting the side down. I daresay that was what drove Edwin Hedlegh mad: something certainly did. I have no great symathy with the Catholics: but Hedleigh loathed them. His letters to me on this and allied matters take up three box files. Will you see to it and have them burned, Henrietta?'

'Of course, my dear,' she said. 'One's children may outlive the grave: one's opinions seldom do. They take up too much space.'

He did not seem to hear her; but then he seldom did.

'Dilberne's on the up and up politically. He's one of the Marlborough set — shoots, hunts and fornicates — but Balfour seems to quite like him. I think they even play golf together. Mind you, Dilberne can be charm itself. A born diplomat. I sometimes have a perfectly amiable drink with him in the Commons Bar. Lemonade for me, of course.'

'Of course,' said Henrietta. 'Shoots, hunts and fornicates. I wonder if he is a proper guardian for little Adela?'

'Oh for heaven's sake,' said the Bishop. 'Of course he is. Fellow's an Earl. Just get the poor child out of the house and let me get on with the diocesan Christmas in peace. I am really very busy.'

'Frank says she may be a princess through the mother's line,' said Henrietta. 'A rather obscure foreign line, but she may inherit.'

'Indeed,' said Bishop Kennion, as if it were a matter of no interest. Then he said, 'Where have you put her?'

'There was a nice dry room in the servants' quarters,' said Mrs Kennion. 'We're so very crowded at the moment. Colleagues want to stay on after the candlelight services.'

'Find her one of the moat rooms, my dear,' said the Bishop. 'She'll have to eat with us, I suppose. But there'll be no Your Grace-ing or anything like that. She is to be plain Miss Hedleigh. You must not be so impressed by titles. I hope the girl is decorative?'

'Frank certainly thinks so,' said Mrs Kennion. 'But I really must be getting on.'

'Always so busy,' lamented her husband. 'Some urgent matter to do with jam, perhaps?'

'As a matter of fact, yes,' said Henrietta.

'Just one thing, before you dash off. It seems the Coronation is to be at the end of June, a double ceremony with both the King and his consort crowned. I will be much involved; the tradition is that the Bishop of Bath and Wells, and Durham too, support a female monarch throughout the ceremony, though whether this applies to Alexandra will have to be approved by the Court of Claims. Their records go back a thousand years at least: if only they didn't life would be much simpler. Perhaps you will be in touch with the Liturgical Committee about the detail of the habit, if you're not too taken up with your new charge? I imagine it will be full episcopal regalia. The Church can hardly appear with less splendour than the State. Also be in touch with Ede and Ravenscroft; tell them I will need a new coronation cope; the one used by Henry Law for Victoria was positively humble, to all accounts, threadbare even sixty years ago. Sunbursts of gold thread for such a rare and glorious day in the nation's history would be appropriate, so they need to discuss this with me without delay. Gold embroidery on silver brocade takes time.'

'I will find time to see to it, my dear,' said Henrietta. 'You will look very grand and handsome indeed in sunbursts.' He was a fine figure of a man, she thought, even without his robes. Tall, lean, and nobly featured. She was proud of him. Other prelates easily turned to fat and looked more like Friar Tuck than ascetic grandees.

'Victoria's coronation was a series of mishaps,' he went on. 'My predecessor turned over two pages at once and told the poor little Queen — she was only eighteen, you know — that the ceremony was at an end and she had to be fetched back from the Abbey door. She was mortified, they say.

Things can go so badly wrong if proper attention to detail is overlooked. I can rely on you to see to it, my dear.'

'At once,' said his wife.

Mrs Kennion visited Frank in his office and put these matters into what she saw as his capable hands. If he were more preoccupied with his work, he would be less preoccupied with Adela, and she had no time to act as a chaperone. Jenny the housekeeper had found an untapped source of strawberry jam and by the time the lady parishioners arrived for their morning tea and scones all was prepared and ready.

ADELA IN THE MOAT ROOM

Adela contemplated her future with a mixture of hope and despair. She was a murderess; that was for sure. She had killed her own father and mother if not by intent, then by the sin of omission, almost as bad as any sin of commission. She should have pulled her father's sleeve and pointed out the dangers of the cigar ash, but she had not. His was not the kind of sleeve you easily pulled.

Her last view of her parents was as two black ragged shapes tangled together like dried-up grasshoppers on a single stretcher. Someone had said they had died from smoke inhalation but it looked to Adela more as if a fiery blast had leapt out from hell, blackening and shrivelling, to punish and devour them for some nameless sin. How she wished someone would name it within her hearing. She hoped the undertakers had managed to prise the bodies apart for the burial. She did not think her parents would want to share a single coffin, any more than they had shared a bed in life. It must be wonderful to share a bed. You would never be cold; there would always be someone to talk to. She did not want to think about these things at all, and tried not to. Better remember the song Ivy sung while she worked — she found herself humming it from time to time. It comforted her.

The worms crawl in,
The worms crawl out,
They go in thin and they come out stout.
If you ever laugh
When a hearse goes by
Then you will be the next to die.

Why was it comforting? It shouldn't be: it was vulgar: servant-girl stuff. And where was Ivy? She needed someone to talk to. Mrs Kennion was very friendly, but there were some things you couldn't say to her as you could with Ivy, not that Ivy ever gave much away. The Great Secret, Ivy called it, which girls couldn't know until they were married. It was such a stupid thing not to know: you could study *The Blue Fairy Book* inside out and upside down but it didn't tell you. Or wouldn't, like Ivy.

What did men and women do to make babies? Something terrible, or why did the whole adult world keep it so secret? The bodies of her parents had been found in the one bed. Jenny the housekeeper here at the Palace had told her so. The proof of it was in the memory she tried so hard to forget: the searing glimpse of two burnt bodies entwined on the one stretcher. Had God punished them with fire for the sin of sleeping next to one another, instead of separately? If so, she was spared the sin of responsibility for their deaths. The other memory she could not forget, however confused the event, was being flung over the shoulder of a strong young man as he rescued her from the flames. She could think of nothing nicer than sleeping next to a man. How warm and companionable it must be. Married people did it all the time, it seemed; nuns, never. The Bishop and Mrs Kennion shared a bed, and presumably a bishop would do nothing to risk hell.

She should have been weeping: she was newly orphaned, alone and unprotected in the world, her every possession having gone up in flames. There was a kind of blank page when she thought of her loss, a nothingness where something was accustomed to being, but was that grief? She had managed a few tears because it was expected of her, but they had not flowed easily. People had been so kind and considerate; when she did cry it was from a sudden overflow of gratitude for their kindness. When she thought about her mother all she could think of was that there was no one any more to plait her hair and give her a headache all day. Here no one even tried: they brushed it out for her and let it flow free for a bit before putting it up in a bun. When she thought of her father all she could remember was this tall threatening figure which kept shouting and could never be pleased. Here no one shouted, people whispered in the corridors and scurried here and there about their business but if they saw you, smiled. And she was so comfortable and warm. They seemed to expect her to stay in bed so mostly she did. She slept a lot. They kept bringing her food and urging her to eat up. Fresh bread with great slabs of butter, whole chicken legs and thick slices of ham.

They'd moved her out of a little servant's room into a big one which looked out over the moat, and she could watch the swans. They were such beautiful slender things, trained to ring a bell when they wanted food. But every now and then there'd be a great squawking and splashing of water and flapping of wings when the occasional marauding swarm of ducks flew in from the Cathedral Duck Pond and tried to steal the food. There was a lesson to be learned there somewhere but she was not sure what it was.

Mrs Kennion turned up from time to time to see how she was, sometimes with a strange young man with big watery eyes who looked at her with a stupid expression: but Mrs Kennion would quickly hurry him out, and she was glad. He reminded her of Rumpelstiltskin peering in the door. The old bedroom in Yatbury had been the dream, this was the reality. Jenny the housekeeper had been to the market and bought her new clothes, most of them black, of course, because she was in mourning, but the fabrics were soft, warm, and not at all scratchy.

They told her that her uncle was coming to collect her. She hoped he would not; he was a wicked man, a secret follower of the Scarlet Woman of Rome (whoever she was), licentious and a philanderer (again, whatever) and his wife her Aunt Isobel was little better, a flirtatious Jezebel. Adela had looked her up in the Book of Kings and for once found a reference. She had been thrown out of a window and had her face eaten by dogs, a just punishment apparently for getting mixed up with idols.

Now don't you think?
It's nice to know
The worms are waiting for you below . . .

She was going to hell, how could she not?
There was this terrible other little wormy
thing, waving and rearing its little head
about inside her, like a bean sprouting in
the darkness, reaching for light, crying
thank God, thank God, it is over, I am free.
She had sinned: with every thought she had,
she sinned. Yet heaven was rewarding her,
not punishing her. Sent her to bed in the
goose girl's hovel, woken her up in a palace.
It was Christmas Day. It was assumed she
was so deep in grief she would want to stay
in her room and not celebrate, but she could
hear carols rising from round the Christmas
tree in the Long Hall and longed to be there
and to sing *We Three Kings from Orient Are.*
It would make a change from *The Worms
Crawl In, the Worms Crawl Out.* But they
brought her up a thick meat soup with
crusty rolls in a covered porcelain bowl, a
whole chicken leg, roast potatoes, roast
parsnips and green peas, and a tiny little
plum pudding topped by a sprig of holly
with two red berries in it — it reminded her

of the churchyard at St Aidan's but she quickly put that out of her mind — all served on a heavy silver tray brought up by the butler, accompanied by Mrs Kennion and the Bishop himself. He looked quite kindly, and not at all like the demon her father had described.

After she had eaten every scrap of the meal she turned the soup bowl upside down and found a red Sevres mark, and put it the right way up very carefully indeed. Then she worked out the row of hallmarks on the heavy silver knives and forks; she could make out the lion and a king's head with a crown, probably George III, but would need a magnifying glass to discern the rest. Her father, may he rest in peace, had a little book of porcelain and assayers' marks, which she had sent herself to sleep many a night learning by heart. Gone, all gone, dust and ashes. Never mind: she had enough in her head to be getting on with.

Someone knocked on her door. It was Frank Overshaw, of course, bringing her an offering. It was a shallow silver flower bowl in which three Christmas roses floated, their strange waxy greeny-white petals tinged with pink and slightly tattered about the edges. Adela really did not like them at all, and looked at them a little askance, but

Frank seemed not to notice.

'I shall call you Madelon,' he said.

'Why's that, Frank?'

'Madelon was the shepherd girl who wept on Christmas morning because she had no gift to bring the newborn king. A passing angel turned her tears into Christmas roses. Ah, my Madelon!'

Another knock at the door quickly followed. It was Mrs Kennion come to remove Frank. 'Oh do stop being silly, Frank,' she said, 'leave the poor girl alone,' and whisked him away.

When they had gone Adela looked underneath the bowl, and could make out a harp with a crown on top and so knew it was Irish silver and not very interesting. But she could see the name Madelon might do very well instead of Adela.

THE DILBERNES' CHRISTMAS

Sandringham Estate was very busy, very large, and the house itself really rather new, built of red brick some thirty years ago, and to Isobel's eye had an oddly untidy look, as if a wilful child had been allowed to add bits to some unfortunate architect's plans. It had gables, balconies, bay windows, towers, turrets; the chimneys did not match, a cupola had been added here, a bell tower there. As a palace it lacked the antiquity of Windsor, the scenic grandeur of Balmoral, the scale of Buck House. The outside of the house was so decorated with holly and ivy, festoons and lanterns, it looked more like a Christmas tree than a dwelling, as Robert observed. It was the first Christmas the new royals had been allowed to spend in their own home, and they were apparently making the most of it. They'd always so far had to endure the solemnities of Windsor every Christmas with all its formality, gloom and *memento mori* — and the previous Christmas spent with the Old Queen on her death-bed.

The King had sent a covered brougham to collect Isobel and Robert from the station on Christmas Eve. A sprinkling of snow was falling and the grounds were white, much criss-crossed with the wheels of carts and carriages. The Royal Family had spent the day in an orgy of gift giving, Lily, the lady's maid, who had gone ahead of Isobel, reported. She'd marvelled at the generosity of the gifts the family had delivered in person to all the cottages of the estate, neglecting not the humblest woodcutter, the merest beater — a joint of beef to this family, furniture to another, toys, blankets, pots and pans where they were most needed.

'Everything so gay and festive,' said Lily. 'To and fro they went, the carts piled high: Princes and Princesses walking beside, the King and Queen going ahead, the little grandchildren running along beside, George's four and Louise's three. They love to be with their grandmama. She spoils them rotten. Everyone's happy and laughing.'

Lily declared herself disappointed in the accommodation — she thought the rooms rather small and mean and dusty for a palace. Lily was unpacking Isobel's trunk while Isobel lay on the bed with her feet up and watched. Lily had a real gift for folding and smoothing; little white dextrous hands moving swiftly and carefully, and quite an eye for fashion. One had to put up with an endless stream of chatter; but the chatter was often entertaining enough.

All the clothes were black because the Old Queen had been dead less than a year, and the Court, Robert had pointed out, was still in full mourning. Lily had packed mostly silks — Isobel assumed Sandringham was well heated, though she was already shivering a little and the fireplace was small. Dilberne Court was chilly enough in winter, but had the excuse of being a Jacobean building and prone to draughts, whereas Sandringham was so new — Edward, then Prince of Wales, had had the old house razed to the ground as too small for him and his new bride, and this new version built in its place. But at least, whatever its other shortcomings, as Lily said cheerfully: 'There's no carrying chamber pots about. There are water closets enough.' Though this apparently didn't quite make up for Lily having to share a bed with Princess Maude's lady's maid Mabel.

Maude, now twenty-seven, had been married for five years to Prince Carl of Denmark but kept coming over to stay at Sandringham, leaving her husband behind, and there was no sign yet of a baby. Perhaps there was something wrong.

'In what way "wrong"?' asked Isobel. It was not wise to become over-familiar with the servants, but sometimes one succumbed. One longed to know what went on, and the servants always knew more than anyone else.

'They call her Harry,' said Lily. 'She's ever such a tomboy, though good enough at dressing up and looking grand. All the girls are good at that. None of them are exactly girly, their noses are too long and their mouths too thin. Not made for kissing, if you know what I mean. Louise is the oldest and plainest. They speak of her as Her Royal Shyness. She hates company and likes fishing, which is peculiar. She hasn't managed a son, either, only three girls and when they come to stay, which is not often, her husband the Duke of Fife never visits her bedroom. Toria isn't even married though she's a year older than Maude, and quite sweet and pretty but turns up her nose at her suitors which the Queen is glad of. She can stay and keep her mother company. George and his wife May live in the grounds, so the Queen has him close to her. But only just because May doesn't let him out of her sight, she doesn't want him turning into his father, who would? Just as well, the servants say, that Eddy — he was the oldest son — died ten years ago — he was probably Jack the Ripper —'

'That's enough, Lily,' said Isobel. Gossip could go too far.

They decided on what Isobel should wear for dinner.

'I don't know why you told me to bring only black,' said Lily. 'Mabel showed me the dress the Queen's going to be wearing for the Christmas lunch: it's ever so pretty, in eau-denil figured satin, with a gored skirt that flares at the knee and pagoda sleeves, pouched at the bodice and no high collar, so she can wear her diamonds against the skin. All very much *à la mode.*'

Isobel all but cried out in distress. She would look so foolish in deep mourning if nobody else was.

'Don't distress yourself,' said Lily. 'I brought your purple silk with the sequins and train, and the lace sleeves with puffs. I thought you might need it. Wear it with the white kid gloves to lighten the look. It has a low neckline and it suits you very well. Wear it tomorrow for Christmas lunch. You will not outshine the Queen but look good enough. Eau-de-nil is better kept for the Spring, even if she is the Queen. For tonight you can wear the black silk with the jet bodice. It too has a bloused top, and good jet picks up so many reflections as to almost count as colour.'

Isobel resigned herself to her fate and congratulated herself for having seen promise in Lily when she was a scurvy little thing, a flower girl off the streets of London, and taken her in against all advice.

On the way down to dinner Isobel reproached Robert for having so misled her about what to wear.

'Oh, they're forever arguing about mourning,' he said. 'Alexandra claimed it could end six months after the Old Queen's death; May says it's only respectful to go for the full year. I asked young Frederick Ponsonby and he said safer to go with black. I expect we will find many of the old ways changing now the Old Queen is gone,' he added. 'If it worries you, say a close relative of our own has just died.'

'That would be to invite misfortune,' said Isobel. 'I will say nothing and hold my head high.'

He breathed into her ear and murmured, 'And I may say you look particularly good in black, with your skin so white and your hair so blonde.' Lily had put ammonia and lemon juice in the rinsing water when she washed her Ladyship's hair, to help keep it pale.

Consuelo was rumoured to put sulphate of iron in her hair wash to keep hers dark. Isobel would ask Lily to be more lavish with the ammonia in future. The more difference there was between her and her rival the better. There it was again — the little nagging doubt, the little worm of jealousy which kept sticking up its questing head at the most inappropriate moments. What was the matter with her?

And what was the matter with her that her own easy flow of charming chatter seemed to flow rather haltingly over dinner? She had been seated at the bottom end of the table with Ponsonby, the King's private secretary, on one side and Sir James Reid, the Royal Physician, on the other, as if as a mere Countess she counted for very little. She did not like it: she was accustomed to being a guest of honour.

Robert had been invited because the King wanted him as a shooting companion on the week's shoot: was suddenly she, Isobel Dilberne, to count as nothing?

Robert was seated between the Princess

of Wales — a rather tight-mouthed, stern creature, though at least still in mourning, in high-necked black silk with rather old-fashioned puff sleeves, relieved only by a deep purple brocade chemisette, and a single diamond brooch at the neck — and Princess Louise, a sad-looking girl with a falling-away jaw and too large a nose, also in black, but who seemed in competition with her mother as to how many diamonds and pearls she could get round her neck. Alexandra wore the eau-de nil and glittered more brightly than anyone; the King had the two bottom buttons of his waistcoat undone, not just one, the better to incorporate his increasingly large girth. But this evening, at what the Queen described as a simple family supper, he seemed to swell in good humour as he did in size, and remained benign and talkative. The Queen sat on his left, not at the other end of the table, which was how Isobel would have done things. Those furthest from the throne, as it were, were bound to feel put out. Isobel had a feeling Robert was not enjoying himself any more than she was, but at least he was seated amongst titles, as she was not.

The lively little wire terrier who ran around under their feet was called Caesar. May positively winced as he snapped or leapt up for food, but Maude, the prettiest of the daughters, tiny waisted, seemed to encourage him in his pranks.

'Another meat course with pastry,' muttered the elderly Sir James Reid. 'A *boeuf Wellington* after partridge pie, and that after *ragoût* of mutton. It is beyond belief.'

He was not a great conversationalist, beyond advising Isobel to eat the *choux de bruxelles* or the *aubergines frites,* and leave the *caneton,* and when Isobel declined to do so, warning her at length of the dangers of overeating, which Isobel thought quite unnecessary. Like most of all the other lady guests, Isobel ate sparingly in public, a taste of this and a taste of that, before plates were whisked away. Only Princess Louise, a big, doleful, bosomy girl, ate heartily like her father, not seeming to worry what anyone thought.

And young Ponsonby, who looked quite fun, had eyes only for his beautiful wife Victoria Lily, busily flirting with George, Prince of Wales, heir to the throne — quite uselessly, because everyone knew he was hopelessly emamoured with his own wife, a tendency he most certainly did not inherit from his father. George, an apparently gentle, retiring man, looked baffled but polite, and his wife May looked on with a cold, raised-eyebrowed amusement, while Victoria Lily's gay little laugh rang out around the table. More alarming still, the girl was obviously pregnant, and at a stage where most women would prefer to dine in private. As Robert had pointed out, many things were going to change now the Old Queen was gone. Pregnancy was no longer to be seen as shameful evidence of indelicate behaviour, better hidden.

Isobel felt suddenly rather old. Once it had taken so little effort to charm men. Now she did not even feel like trying. Worse, the dinner was painfully reminding her of what she so seldom liked to recall these days: her own humble origins. Robert had married beneath him: she, illegitimate daughter of a miner and a soubrette — forget that the miner had become a coal magnate and the soubrette become a famous actress — was born to the demimonde and had no business at such a dining table as this. Frederick Ponsonby, whose hereditary business was to know everything — his father Henry having been secretary to the Old Queen — no doubt knew all about her. Ponsonby, like Robert, had been born a second son. Second sons, of course, could become first sons when accident or illness struck: the current Prince of Wales was only thus because his older brother Clarence had died of flu in this very palace. She herself was only Countess because Robert's elder brother had died at sea along with his father. If he had not, she would have stayed only an Hon. Mrs at best. Frederick was only a minor branch of the Ponsonby earldom; he would have to earn his way into titled circles.

'So much advancement in this world happens by chance,' she observed to Frederick Ponsonby, 'and not necessarily because of intrinsic merit.'

But he was trying so hard to hear what his wife was saying he paid no attention to her. She turned to Sir James and said much the same to him, but instead of taking up the point he said, 'Don't worry your little head with matters better suited to an Oxford debating society than to a family dinner,' and added, 'tell me, have you been using ammonia on your hair? You must be careful. It can be most corrosive.' Defeated, Isobel fell silent.

After dinner that evening, the men having had enough brandy and the ladies having seen to their toilettes, all took coffee, more brandy and little almond cakes in the drawing room.

Isobel had eaten frugally, but the company

of the King induced to appetite, and she accepted one of the cakes which the footman offered. It was a mistake: the pastry was powdery and left its traces scattered on the black jet beads of her dress: she had to brush the crumbs away with her hand as unobtrusively as possible. But the tiny crumbs stuck between and under the beads. May noticed, and stared, and looked coldly astonished, and Isobel felt sorry for May's children, and indeed for May's mother-in-law the Queen, who had been the recipient of one or two such looks during the course of the evening. May never said a word out of place, but had the art of making others feel ill at ease, by virtue of their stupidity, frivolity or vulgarity.

Isobel found herself grateful that Arthur had married Minnie, who was incapable of putting on airs, and would be a kind father if only he could think of anything other than motor cars. Thinking of Minnie gave her a pang of acute anxiety — ah yes, the invitations! But she would not think of that now. She, illegitimate daughter of a coal miner, was dining with Royalty *en famille*. She would do her best to enjoy it.

'December is not a good month for our family,' the King was saying. With the move from the dining table his good cheer seemed to have evaporated. 'Forty years ago almost to the day my father Albert the Good died at Windsor, and ten years ago our dear son Eddie in this very house. And it was at Christmas thirty years ago that I nearly met my end of typhoid fever, to the great distress of my good mother. Or so I am told. Though what my mother felt, and what she said that she felt, I now realize, were not necessarily the same thing. One is tempted to bring out the planchette board and ask her a question or two.'

The letters, the diary entries, the busts of John Brown, the statues of Ganesh, the planchette board, recently found, through which the Old Queen apparently tried again and again to raise the spirit of her beloved husband, evidently still preyed on the royal mind.

Hoepner the giant footman approached to fill the King's glass with more brandy, and Isobel saw the Queen nod at the servant almost imperceptibly and the Monarch's glass remained unfilled.

The King, deprived of his brandy, asked for a plate of devils on horseback to be brought in: they came at once as if they had been waiting, not even having to arrive from the kitchen. The King ate heartily. Isobel longed for bed.

Robert brought the conversation away from the dangerous subject of the Old Queen to the Coronation — he had the courtier's natural skill of keeping the conversation on an even keel. Now the King forgot about ghosts and told stories about his mother's coronation in 1837. Victoria had been only eighteen when crowned; the Archbishop of Canterbury had forced the ring upon the wrong finger, causing her pain; the Bishop of Bath and Wells had turned over two pages, bringing the service to an end when it was not over; the crown had been too heavy for her little head to bear; someone had left scraps of food on the altar itself.

'I am the more determined, dear Alix,' he said, 'that my own coronation will go perfectly, be properly rehearsed, every detail attended to. The Empire needs a spectacular ceremony, witness to the grandeur of this nation of mine. It is not for myself that I want pomp and circumstance: that their King should be glorious is no more than the Nation deserves.'

It was quite a speech. Alexandra leant forward and patted the straining stomach.

'Little Tum-Tum,' she said.

The Coronation! All Isobel could think about now were the three invitation cards that should have been sitting safely in her little fruit-wood writing desk, and which Reginald had failed to retrieve, these having gone with the last post and a telephone call confirmed that they had already been delivered, so swift and efficient was the post: and how she must now tell Robert because it would be worse not to, but hardly knew how to set about it.

When, after all had retired, Isobel lay awake in a strange bed, in a bedroom surprisingly small for a royal residence, but with a handsome bathroom adjoining it, containing a most enviable cedarwood water closet, Robert forcibly pulled back the heavy crimson velvet curtains she had closed around the bed, and done so most carefully, fearing they had possibly not been shaken for twenty years or so. He was naked, which was completely out of character, glimmering in gaslight which he had turned down low. He said he had a confession to make, and Isobel's thoughts went at once to Consuelo. Just as Sunny had confessed to Consuelo on their wedding day that he loved another, Robert was now going to tell her, Isobel, that he loved another and that the other was Consuelo. Even as she thought it she knew it was absurd. And of course he did not say any such thing: what he confessed was that he had invited the Baums to the Coronation and he would be obliged if she, Isobel, could see that the tickets were despatched to them.

'It is not that I love their company,' Robert said, 'though I find them pleasant enough, and the little wife to be remarkably intelligent, it is simply an obvious and prudent move, in the light of my new business interests.'

'Of course, my dear,' said Isobel, as smoothly as she could, 'shall I send them all three invitations, or only two?'

'Send them two,' said Robert. 'There is no need to be lavish. How I have mistaken you, my dear. I thought you might send up a great wail of protest, but I am glad that you have not.'

The bed had been turned down by Lily and now he stepped into it naked. Isobel stretched out her arms to him, and did what she imagined many a woman had done to allow herself time to think, encouraged him in the wilder excesses of love. She allowed him to do, for the first time in all her life, what only whores do, and what, it was rumoured, Sunny required Conseulo to do, so by the morning she was exhausted, and a little sore, and no further forward in her thinking at all, other than she could no longer imagine what her objections to the Baums had been. Clouds of dust had indeed risen from the curtains, perfectly visible in the gaslight, so energetic had been his attentions, and indeed her response to them. All she could do was hope that it was not thoughts of Consuelo that had so inspired him to lust, and even thinking, if only briefly, that if such was the case putting up with Consuelo's existence in her life might even be worth it. When Robert went back to his dressing room, his dongle — as he called it: she had no word for it — still so lively he could almost have hung his top hat on it, the wintry light of Christmas Day was already showing through the curtains.

CHRISTMAS AT DILBERNE COURT

In the absence of the parents at Sandringham the young people Arthur, Minnie and Rosina dined alone in the Long Hall at Dilberne Court.

A skeleton staff was left behind in Belgrave Square — the rest decamped on Christmas Eve in three heavily laden carriages, to light fires, dust and generally bring the place back to life. Rosina, when in residence, as she now was — writing about the hardships of the rural poor — always underestimated the number of personal staff she needed.

'I am perfectly happy with a baked potato and an egg for supper, and I can run my own bath and open my own wardrobe, thank you very much.' At the same time it was observable that Miss Rosina — she abhorred 'Your Ladyship' did like freshly baked bread for breakfast and expected clean ironed clothes in the wardrobe, and could fly into a temper if they were not provided, so by the time her personal needs were looked after, cleaning could get neglected. Rooms where she allowed the parrot to fly freely quickly grew musty and required scraping and cleaning without damaging delicate French-polished surfaces. Lady Rosina was not a favourite with the servants. Minnie was less demanding but hot water still had to be fetched for her daily bath and coals carried for her fire. She wore a washable smock for her painting but her studio was up on the attic floor and refreshments had to be brought all the way up from the kitchen.

Master Arthur at least spent most of his days in the workshops and made do with bread and cheese at lunchtime but still liked a good choice of food at breakfast and dinner. It was the staff's experience that the greater part of their work went unnoticed and unappreciated; the family's assumption being that comfort and cleanliness simply happened of its own accord, or through the power of some divine being.

The staff worked late and rose early, and by noon the great dining room was prepared for Christmas dinner at one, the oak beams waxed — an epidemic of death-watch beetle had first to be smoked out — the great chandelier dusted and its many faulty light bulbs replaced — electricity now took the place of candles, not nearly so flattering to the female complexion — and Mrs Neville the housekeeper had worked wonders with the great refectory table. The linen was spotless white, five glasses glittered beside each of the three table settings: the best silver and china had been put out: napkins shaped into white swans: sprigs of holly and ivy, set in cut-crystal bowls, formed a charming centrepiece. Even Rosina allowed herself a gasp of admiration at the sight.

The turkey, a golden, diligently basted giant, reared especially for the festive day on the home farm, and stuffed with veal and pork, was placed early on the sideboard, to rest on its silver hotplate. Three courses of suitable midwinter fare came first — game soup, scalloped oysters and jugged hare — then Mr Neville the butler carved the bird, and Reginald the head footman served roast potatoes and a bean purée from the ornate silver tureens it took strong arms to manage, and ladled plenty of good gravy from the porcelain sauce boats — a wedding gift to the young couple from her Grace, Consuelo, Duchess of Marlborough — followed by mince pies and Christmas pudding lit with plentiful brandy and decorated with holly. In the absence of the Earl and Countess all felt particularly young and free. The servants, knowing that what upstairs failed to eat, they would in time, were cheerful too.

Mr Neville had come up with the best bottles the cellar could provide: from Bordeaux, a Pomerol and a St Émilion; from Burgundy, a Chablis; and for dessert a sweet Sauternes. Also, in honour of Minnie, his Lordship had purchased some rather more dubious wine from outside France, an Inglewood from the Napa Valley, which had not yet had time to gather any cobwebs.

Four hundred years' worth of ancestors looked down from the walls. All were distinguished, most were handsome, few looked exactly likeable. Three of the eldest sons had died unexpectedly in tragic accidents when young.

Rosina had laughed when Minnie asked if it was some kind of curse and said, 'Three in four hundred years isn't many. It happens in all the best families. *Cui bono?* The second sons, of course,' which rather shocked Minnie. The upper classes in this strange, wet, ruined, winter landscape seemed to have ingested a lofty cynicism along with their mothers' milk — but since she supposed that for generations all had been put out to wet-nurses the phrase was misplaced. Perhaps it was the very absence of mother's milk did it? And wasn't it rather tactless of Rosina to bring the subject up at all? Robert had inherited the Earldom on the death of his elder brother. What was she doing here with these people she did not understand? If only they asked her to add her own family portraits, Billy and Tessa O'Brien, with their wide faces, generous features and smiling lips, she would feel better. But she could see it was never likely to happen. It was not individuals who were honoured, just their titles. There was one done by Stanton before he had gone mad and just painted streaks: perhaps she could ask her mother to bring it over when she came. If she ever came. No, she must not think like this. She had made her bed; she must lie on it. It was a pleasant enough bed, with Arthur in it. Love carried you along for so long, then dreams became reality, practicalities began to seem important. She thought she might be pregnant. What then?

She tried not to think about it. The conversation turned to royal rumour.

'Pater's so stuffy about what goes on,' complained Arthur. 'One longs to know. But he shuts up as tight as a clam when it comes to the Palace.'

He talked of how he'd asked his father about the rumour going round the Mews about a letter found in the archives of the House of Lords, written to the Lord Chancellor in the Prince's hand a week before his sudden death of abdominal pains and fever — symptomatic of typhoid, it was true — yet dying so quickly and unexpectedly. Typhoid sufferers usually lingered. In the letter he had asked how one might set about divorcing the Queen of England. Arthur had asked his father if there was any truth in the matter and he had been given short shrift.

'You're a fool to listen to gossip and no child of mine to repeat it,' was all Robert had said, refusing to be drawn.

'And the death of Eddie, Bertie's son: in direct line to the throne,' said Rosina now. 'That was rather strange. The boy may have been half-witted and probably Jack the Ripper, but he was twenty-eight and perfectly healthy. First they said it was influenza: then it was typhoid. Sudden death within the week, like Albert. That must have suited a lot of people.'

'Great-Grandmama as a Borgia Queen!' said Arthur. 'Let's hope the parents get home safe from Sandringham.'

'And poor Bertie got the blame for both deaths,' said Rosina. 'First for his father's

— Albert got the alleged "chill" on his way home from stopping Bertie running off with an actress; and then for his son's — Bertie was off seeing Lady Daisy when Alix was away and he should have been at home keeping Eddie off the streets.'

'Lady Daisy?' asked Minnie faintly. Chicago was as nothing compared to this.

'Daisy Warwick,' said Rosina. 'Bertie's long-term mistress. They're all going to be there at the Coronation in a specially built showcase. His triumphs laid out for everyone to see.'

'That's enough, Rosina,' said Arthur, suddenly. 'He is the King, after all, and Pater's friend.'

After that Arthur and Rosina lost interest in scandal, but began to behave as they would not dare to do in the presence of the Earl and Countess. They became children again. They teased the servants. Rosina declined the soup, summoning Mr Neville and saying animals were her friends and she did not eat her friends; Mr Neville must understand that from now on she was a vegetarian. Arthur chimed in to complain about the absence of boiled beef and carrots from the menu. He could tell from the cutlery, he complained, that there was to be no meat course after the bird, was Cook trying to starve them? What had got into the two of them? They were all desperate, given so much by fate, she decided, but never what they wanted. Arthur had his mother's approval, but never his father's. Rosina had her father's, but never her mother's.

And then hearing herself, to her sorrow, tell Mr Neville that she had joined the Temperance movement and that lips which touched liquor would never touch hers, Minnie had to wonder what the matter was with herself. That she was pregnant? Surely, surely not. Oh, please. She was a slip of a girl, not a woman.

Mr Neville stayed polite, just rather rigid in his body movements; then as the staff ran off to change glasses, add cutlery, squeeze lemons for lemonade, provide turnips, carrots and parsnips to bolster up the bean purée, and set a salted topside to boil, shame set in.

'We are too bad,' said Rosina, 'I know the better way and approve, as Ovid said, yet I follow the worse. *Video meliora proboque, deteriora sequor.* You went to Eton, Arthur, you should know. You are excused, Minnie, because you didn't. We should say sorry because of course we are, but one isn't allowed to say sorry to servants. It is shocking that the most idle amongst us live so well and those that work so hard should exhaust themselves obliging our whims.'

'One can hardly live without servants,' said Arthur. 'And they can hardly live without us. They like a small panic from time to time. One is doing them a favour.'

'You and I could live perfectly well enough without them, Arthur,' said Minnie, 'if we were only back home. The houses are newer and heated and the windows fit, and there are machines to pick up dust and wash the clothes and even the dishes. The few servants we have are black and are happy enough working for us. My father says he'd rather employ them than our own kind, who are so often drunk and dissolute and fall into the machinery, no matter how many guards you put up.'

She didn't add that when whole thumbs or bits of fingers were found in the hamburger mix they were usually white not black. It was the kind of information the Hedleigh family didn't like to hear, even Rosina, who fought so assiduously for truth and justice. Only the lower orders talked of health and horror. Oh, she was learning fast. Too fast.

The servants came, bustled, crashed around a little, rewarmed chafing dishes, and went. Reginald the footman replaced Mr Neville — and Christmas lunch continued with its extra course, except all were now hoist with their own petard, Rosina feeling obliged to eat the parsnips, Arthur the topside, and Minnie to eschew wine in favour of lemonade. None of which any of them particularly wanted. It set them all to giggling again.

'At Eton when it got to this stage,' said Arthur, 'we'd fire butter pats at the ceiling until the beaks stopped us. At Oxford we'd break the places up after a good dinner.'

'Your mothers mistreated you,' said Minnie. If she was pregnant and it was a boy what then? They would make her send him away when he was eight in case he ended up one of those men who never married.

'We are both of us a terrible trial to our parents,' said Rosina. 'They did so want us to be like them, and look at us. I turn out a bluestocking, and you, Arthur' — and she helped herself, as the footman offered none, to a slice of turkey along with her vegetables and a considerable spooning of rich meat gravy, and washed it down with the Pomerol — 'digging up good grazing land, filling the air with noisome fumes which give Mother headaches, frightening the birds, annoying Father's friends, and the King is hardly going to visit a country house where the hoi polloi run motor races round him. We have spoiled their lives. As for you, Minnie, Mother longs for someone to discuss ribbons and fashions with, and all she has is someone who wears a painter's smock, day in, day out, covered with splashes of cobalt blue and chrome yellow.'

'It is the tools of her trade,' said Arthur loyally, 'like the engine oil under my fingernails. We are in a new century. Everything changes. And she had to do something while we wait for the heir.' And he enquired whether Minnie would join him in a slice of boiled beef with carrots; would it not remind her of home, now that Billy O'Brien was moving out of hogs and into cattle and Minnie said yes, though leave out the carrots. Her father could not abide vegetables. She spoke lightly. But it bothered her that he kept worrying away at her father's trade, like a dog with an unsatisfactory bone. His own grandfather had started life as a coal miner, after all.

'I think I may be having a baby,' she said. The staff were listening. She could tell by a kind of sudden stillness in the air. But then they were always listening. 'I don't know,' she said, quickly. 'I shouldn't even have mentioned it.'

Arthur got up and came over and kissed her on the cheek. He looked so pleased she wondered what she had been worrying about.

'Of course you are,' he said. 'How could you not be?'

Rosina stayed quiet and then said, 'Perhaps it's too early to know for sure,' she said. 'If so, you will be in no condition to process at the Coronation, let alone be seen in public. There will be an extra place. Perhaps now Mama will let me have it. If she can't have her daughter-in-law she might just put up with her own daughter.'

'You'd have to sit next to the Baums,' said Arthur, 'who are complete nobodies, just rich. Papa can be so obvious one is almost ashamed.'

There was a crash and a bang. Reginald had dropped the great silver dish which carried the turkey.

George and Ivy's Christmas

George was trying to develop Ivy's psychic powers. Both had time to spare. His hands were still bandaged from the fire, so he could not work: she had no work to do. Farmer Swaley's son Andy, back from agricultural college, had obliged his father by taking over the milking. George, having run in and rescued the Hon. Rev.'s little girl from the flames, was now the local hero. The Bath Technical College was closed for the holidays. Ivy's place of employment was dust and ashes. Her employers were in the mortuary awaiting burial, and no one grieved for them: the village just looked forward to the funeral, though who would provide food for the wake no one knew. It was hoped the Church would: they had been known to put on a good spread if one of their own went. Adela was safe and warm in the grandeur of the Bishop's Palace at Wells. Ivy would go and visit her but thought she might be turned away. She was only the servant after all. But her mother had been told that Ivy could look forward to a substantial contribution from the parish emergency fund towards replacing her bits and pieces.

'Someone up there loves you,' her mother said. 'No mention that you weren't in your own bed when the place went up. You were good to that little girl, I'll say that for you. You can stay with me until you get yourself fixed up.' Everyone was being kind to her, even her own mother.

Doreen had even asked George to share their Christmas meal. They'd had chicken, mashed potatoes and peas and a bottle each of Inde Coope beer, and done themselves proud. Doreen, who always liked a bit of trouser, had entertained George mightily by talking about ghosts; the headless horsemen on the Bath to Wells Road and the legionnaire soldiers she'd once seen marching on the old Roman road up by Dyrham, a spooky place where three Celtic kings had died fifteen hundred years ago. George had been really interested, and asked her if Doreen had second sight, and if so had she, Ivy, inherited it. And Doreen, to Ivy's embarrassment, had talked about how when she was a little girl Ivy had talked about the

165

lady who bent over her bed sometimes when she was trying to go to sleep.

After which she and George had repaired to the barn and nothing would now do but that George was trying to make her shift things by the power of thought.

'Tell you what,' said George now, 'see that button over there?' It was one of the buttons from her skirt which had popped off when she had removed it without undoing it properly, though he seemed to have lost interest in her, only in what he called her kinetic powers. She'd put the button on the table for safe keeping. The table was covered with dust and powdered corn husks and feathers where stray hens had been roosting in the warmth of the milking shed.

'I see it,' she said, sitting up in her scratchy straw bed. 'Why?'

'Make it move an inch to the left,' said George.

'How can I do that?' she asked.

'By focusing your life energy,' he said. 'Using your life soul. That's the kind of language those in the business use, at any rate. I dunno. Just do it.'

Ivy looked at him askance and tried staring at the button for three whole minutes. The time dragged. The button stayed where it was. She thought she saw a little puff of dust go up in the air but that was probably from a draught.

'Told you so,' she said.

'Then what was the puff of dust?' he said. 'Never mind, you looked pretty good doing it,' and leapt upon her, bandaged hands and all. Later he said that he didn't want to be a science teacher, just that he could get the training free, and there were so many suckers out there prepared to part with their money it seemed a pity not to relieve them of it. He was not like any of the other village boys, Ivy could see. But he might well be a sucker himself. Her mother always saw things on the way home from the pub, and Ivy had invented the lady who leant over the bed so she'd be allowed to stay up late. George was so sharp he cut himself.

'If genuine telekenesis fails,' George said, when he finally lay back, temporarily exhausted, 'I suppose one can always fake it.'

'I WOKE,' SAID THE QUEEN, 'I WORRIED.'

A strange whining noise, rising and falling, woke Isobel on Christmas morning. She'd roused Robert, in some alarm. He sat up; listened, said, 'It's the Scotch bagpiper, bringing in Christmas.' And he lay down and fell asleep again.

After that Isobel could not sleep. It was six in the morning: no one would be up. It had been a late night. Most of the guests she supposed would breakfast in their rooms: the grandchildren in their nursery. She wound up her hair without Lily's help, found a black breakfast robe and fur-lined slippers and made her way to where a breakfast room might sensibly be, and where perhaps coffee was being served for early risers.

Maidservants made themselves scarce as she approached, and she was conscious of what a nuisance she must be: grates had to be cleaned, fires lit, carpets swept, Christmas Day or not, and all must appear as if done by magic, not by human sweat and toil. She passed through the great vaulted hall where the Christmas tree stood, a giant Norway spruce, its candles not yet lit, but bright with lanterns, hung with paper chains, and a thousand small ornaments, sweets, toys and bon-bons. Every mantelpiece, every door frame of the hall was hung with holly and ivy: wherever a pine-cone could be placed it had been: beneath the tree gifts for the children were stacked high — Isobel could pick out a drum here, a rocking horse there, a bow and arrow, a bicycle: in corners of the room still further packets and parcels, each with its coloured label, presumably for staff. There was to be a carol concert for family and staff mid morning. Alexandra was known to keep a kind and generous household. All very well, thought Isobel, mindful of the dusty hangings of her bed, the rather tarnished taps in the bathroom, but perhaps better a staff that was in awe of you than one which took your kindness for granted and became slatternly.

When she finally found the breakfast room she was taken aback to see Alexandra already at the table. She turned to flee, conscious of her own informal attire. But Alexandra, slopping over the table in a mauve kimono dotted with yellow flowers, smoking a pink Sobranie cigarette, called her back.

'How nice to see a friendly face so early in the morning! One wakes, one worries, don't you find?'

'Indeed one does,' said Isobel, fervently. A chair was pulled back for her: coffee was poured. It was lukewarm.

'Did the Christmas Piper wake you? I know it's a dreadful noise but it's a Balmoral ritual. The King hates Balmoral but I love it; the place reminds me of Castle Kronborg in Elsinore, stark and bare and Northern. Do tell me, what do you worry about?'

It was a royal command and for a moment Isobel almost told her. 'I worry about whether my husband is fonder of Consuelo Vanderbilt than he ought to be, and I worry about having sent off three invitations to your coronation which were not mine to give —' but fortunately the Queen did not wait for an answer but launched off into her own worries, namely that she might find the weight of the crown too much for her on Coronation Day. It was the kind of detail, she complained, that men overlooked.

'Uneasy is the head that wears a crown,' Isobel said, 'even if it's female.'

170

But Alexandra just looked puzzled and frowned, not understanding the reference, and Isobel felt a flash of sympathy for the King, who so liked the company of clever women he even got on with Rosina, and had asked after her at dinner and when told she was writing a book had said, 'Well done.'

Isobel was not so sure it was well done. Rosina was working on a sociological study of the life and labour of rural workers at the dawn of the new century. They had good reason she said, for discontent.

'But Rosina,' Isobel had said, when asked for her comments, 'our workers don't seem at all discontent. We keep their cottages in good order, we provide firewood in the winter, there is a village school; the doctor calls. What more can they want?' And Robert had not been at all supportive: once you started asking questions, the answers would never be in your favour, and could only result in unrest and agitation.

Robert had been quite right. There had been union activity on the Dilberne estate and an unreasonable wage demand as a result of Rosina's casual 'stirring things up'. Workers who had not known even of the existence of an Agricultural Labourers' Union now not only just knew about it but joined it.

However, in the King's kindly eyes, it seemed a woman who wrote a book, any book, was to be encouraged. Intelligent women were meant to foster intelligence in their sons, though his own daughters, Isobel noticed, were not encouraged to think or argue. Their interests lay in food, clothes and who was related to whom. Alexandra saw no virtue in education. George, heir to the throne, had not even been sent to Eton but been home tutored.

'The fact is,' said Alexandra, fluttering her jewelled hands, 'I do really need to have a new crown.' Even over this early breakfast and still in her mauve kimono she flashed ruby and amethyst rings on her fingers. But then how else should a queen behave? She complained now that neither of the crowns available — one the Adelaide and the other the Modena — was suitable. One was too tall and looked like something out of a music hall and the other too low and not at all splendid.

'And dear Consuelo is bound to wear her new diadem,' said Alexandra. 'Such a pretty arrangement by some fashionable French jeweller: one thousand and ninety-one diamonds. But diamonds can be so heavy — one is frightened her pretty little head would quite snap on that slender neck of hers.' She did not, Alexandra said, want her crown to be outshone at the ceremony, but one must consider the weight. 'And now Consuelo is off to Moscow which is bound to mean more Fabergé. She is a dear good girl but always feels she must have everything that others have, and more.'

She gave Isobel a little meaningful look, or Isobel thought she did. Perhaps the Queen was trying to tell her something; possibly a warning that husbands were included in the Duchess's list? Perhaps the King had looked at her favourably? But surely not: Consuelo was not his type. Bertie liked women with intelligent faces, big noses and strong jaws — until of course the exception came along. Now Alexandra looked at the clock and complained that everyone was very late down for breakfast; there were to be carols round the tree at eleven and it was already nearly eight.

'Half past seven,' said Isobel.

'No, my dear,' said Alexandra, 'the clocks in the house are half an hour fast so Edward can get in more shooting in the daylight. Everyone knows that. It is a very annoying habit but one learns to live with it. I daresay your dear Robert has his annoying little habits too.'

Isobel felt reprimanded. She reflected

173

that breakfasting with royalty was even more
tiring than dining with them. At breakfast,
natural impulses and the remnants of
dreams were too close. The very ceremony
of dinner imposed a more reasonable formality and a degree of forethought. One so
wanted to be liked and approved of by one's
superiors in rank it became impossible just
to speak or act naturally. The greater the
gap the worse it was. She supposed it could
be like that for humbler people in her presence: perhaps when Mrs Baum was with
her equals she did not trip, stumble, and
break things. Mrs Baum — no, that was
another problem for another day. Isobel
pulled herself together, refrained from list-
ing Robert's marital defects, and suggested
that her Majesty have a new crown made, a
shorter, flatter one than the Modena or the
Adelaide, with eight arches which could be
removed to form chokers or necklaces and
perhaps with a St George Cross in front set
with the Koh-i-Noor diamond. That, Isobel
thought but did not say, should put Consuelo in her place.

Alexandra looked at her steadily for a moment or two and Isobel wondered if she had
made yet another mistake. Then the Queen
said, 'My mother-in-law always thought the
Koh-i-Noor brought its owner bad luck. It

174

was large but lustreless and its origins always seen as dubious. It was certainly bad luck that when Garrards ventured to re-cut it in 1852 — I was a child of ten — they managed to reduce its weight from one hundred and sixty-eight carats to one hundred and forty-nine. I understand Prince Albert, for one, was extremely annoyed.'

Isobel felt ignorant. She knew nothing and was worth nothing. But then the Queen smiled suddenly and said, 'However, it is certainly brilliant enough in its present state and the public holds it in high regard, if only because they have heard of it. However, we may possibly think again about Garrards. I wish they'd let me have you, Isobel, as a Lady-in-waiting, but one finds one has very little say in the matter. It has been a political appointment since my dear mother-in-law, at the very beginning of her reign, nearly brought down the Crown because of it. One has to be so careful.'

She patted Isobel's hand and Isobel felt tears rising to her eyes. What was it? Gratitude? Adoration? Surely not. Perhaps she was just tired.

At eleven family and staff gathered round the Christmas tree to join in *O Tannenbaum*. The Duke and Duchess of Wales and the four children came up from York House, the littlest one, Henry, some nine months old, pushed by a nursemaid. Isobel watched the little procession of future kings and queens from the window. All in their turn would marry or be married off to royalty. There was no skipping or larking about; all were serious, quiet and well behaved. Alexandra, greeting them, gathering them into her arms in maternal embrace, was all smiles. Only when May insisted that the children sing *O Tannenbaum* in German did the royal smile fade. Since the eldest boy was in direct succession to the English throne it was not surprising, Isobel thought, that it did.

Relations between the King and the Kaiser were strained, she knew. Wilhelm had publicly blamed his mother, Bertie's favourite sister Victoria, for having insisted on English doctors, not German, at his birth: it was as a result of her misguided faith in her countrymen that the Kaiser's arm was withered. Bad enough that he should so malign his own mother in the past, but when in the previous year she had lain dying in extreme pain Wilhelm had prevented the more merciful English doctors she wanted attending her. It had been a needlessly long and terrible death, for which the King blamed Wilhelm. It was tactless of May, to say the very least, to encourage her children to sing in German, not English.

She said as much to Robert, who said that May was just angry with her in-laws. She was only just back from a nine-month tour of the Colonies with George. May had wanted to stay home with the children — she had a new baby — but the King, the Queen, and Prime Minister Balfour had insisted she accompany her husband. After the Old Queen's death, everyone said, such a tour would serve to reestablish the Crown's continuing power and prestige around the Empire.

'So the children had to stay at Sandringham with the Queen.'

'Naturally. A very sensible arrangement,' said Robert.

'Not if you're May,' said Isobel. 'Not if you know your mother-in-law is going to spoil your children and win their love in your absence. A whole nine months away — leave a newborn, and you'll come back to a child who is nothing to do with you. Poor little Henry! Poor children! Poor May.'

'Poor May indeed,' said Robert. 'She's known as the Dragon. Poor George, more like it. She thinks herself very grand. She despises English royalty, finds them a very paltry, plodding lot, and Danish royalty —

that's Alexandra — even worse. Positively vulgar and brainless. She prides herself on being a Teck of the Württemberg line, a Serene Highness of the original German aristocracy; though God knows her mother was nothing to be proud of. Very fat and impecunious and loud. I think my brother Edwin married someone of the sort, but he keeps the details very quiet.'

'Go as far up as you like,' observed Isobel, 'there will always be someone grander than oneself.'

'Just give up trying,' said Robert, cheerfully. 'Just be glad you have Minnie of Chicago for a daughter-in-law. There can be no competition there.'

Isobel was. She had never herself been a daughter-in-law, Robert's mother, the seventh Countess, having died when he was six, giving birth to her fifth baby, a little girl. He never spoke of her, and so neither did she.

Robert took Isobel's hand while he sang in his deep tuneful voice. There was *O Little Town of Bethlehem* and *O Come All Ye Faithful,* and his Majesty swayed a little as he stood and was brought a chair. Alexandra looked anxious. Then there were little presents for the children. Isobel wondered what Christmas Day at brother Edwin's rectory at Yatbury was like, but it was hard to envisage a place she had never seen. She hoped Adela was pleased with her present. Isobel had chosen it with great care. Something else at the back of her mind; something she had forgotten? Oh dear, ah yes, the missing invitations. She must get the staff to search for them when she got back; but there was lots of time to worry about that. The Coronation was months away, and so much could happen between now and then. And Lordy, as Tessa O'Brien might say, was she tired! Being in royalty's presence was exhausting, as one watched one's Ps and Qs.

ON BOXING DAY

Eric Baum waited until eight-thirty on Boxing Day morning to impart the bad news to his Lordship. It was Saturday, Shabbat, so Naomi made Jane the shiksa maid-of-all-work lift the telephone and dial the call. He wished Naomi would relax; their religion was not so threatened that the slightest infringement would make their whole lives come tumbling down. So much surely was owed to convenience and necessity. Jane was good with the children and he suspected taught them the odd Christian prayer before sleep, while Naomi looked the other way:

Four angels round my bed,
Two at foot and two at head,
Two to guard me while I sleep
And two all night my soul to keep.

It could do no harm, and if Naomi allowed herself this indulgence surely he

180

could be able to switch on a light or make a phone call on a Saturday without being reminded it was the Sabbath? Jane, thank heaven, was amiable enough about what she saw as her employers' eccentricities but then she was given the whole day off on Sunday to make up for it.

He had not yet told Naomi about the invitation to the Coronation. He was waiting for the right moment. She would be beside herself with pleasure: she so deserved acceptance: she was such a clever girl, had given up so much for husband and family. To be seen to sit amongst the peers and peeresses of the realm — Mrs Eric Baum the financier's wife would now be lionized by every Society hostess in the land.

When the girl Jane realized she was calling the royal palace at Sandringham her eyes opened wide and she looked at Eric with an expression he wished he saw more often on Naomi's face — one of awe, almost reverence. She was a pretty girl, he noticed for the first time, with generous lips and long eyelashes, which fell on a creamy pale complexion. The telephone rang in an office at Sandringham and when it was answered, Jane handed the receiver to him with a pretty white hand that trembled ever so slightly.

The minion at Sandringham said that his Lordship was unavailable; he was out shooting with the King. Mr Baum kicked himself. Of course, the clocks were famously set half an hour fast. They would be up and out early, dressed in the strange ritual clothing they used for slaughtering birds. This was what the English upper classes did; they fought and died for their country and they got up early to shoot birds. If they shot each other by mistake they did not complain. They certainly did not, Mr Baum had observed, waste time thinking about their womenfolk. It seemed to be their conviction in their God-given superiority, their belief that God himself was an Englishman, which gave them this immense influence over the peoples of other nations. Disraeli had said their power derived from their desire to talk politics after dinner where others talked about their wives and families.

Mr Ponsonby, the King's private secretary, was called to the phone and Mr Baum said the purpose of the call was not trivial, but to pass tragic news to his Lordship of the death of his brother in the most unfortunate circumstances. Mr Ponsonby was courtesy itself but said the wisest course was to wait until lunchtime when the shooting party was expected to return to the house; he would let his Lordship know without delay and his Lordship would no doubt return the call. Or perhaps Mr Baum would care to speak to Lady Isobel, who to the best of Mr Ponsonby's knowledge had not joined the shooting party.

Mr Baum said that perhaps it would be best if her Ladyship were gently informed by a close relative, and Mr Ponsonby agreed. If Mr Baum's experience of her Ladyship was that she was hard as nails and twice as indestructible, he certainly did nothing to let Mr Ponsonby know it.

His Lordship telephoned Mr Baum at one-fifteen and received the news with apparent calm. But then this was to be expected. If there was weeping and wailing it would be done in private. The relationship between the two brothers had not been good for many years. Mr Baum assured his Lordship that the deaths had been peaceful, the result of breathing in soporific smoke and fumes; that the girl had been rescued by a young local man before the flames could touch her and was safely in the care of the Bishop of Bath and Wells and his wife, Mrs Kennion.

'Ah, Kennion,' said his Lordship. 'Know the man well. Ecumenical ass, voted against us over Gore, but on the whole sound. He'll be responsible. Quite a shock for the child, I imagine, not that I've ever met the girl. What about the mother's side? They need to be told.'

Mr Baum explained the difficulty of finding anyone to tell, the mother having abandoned her faith and her family on marriage, and was of foreign lineage, Gotha-Zwiebrücken-Saxon royalty. The girl was a princess.

'Papists, the lot of them,' said his Lordship. 'Poor as church mice, and everyone you meet a prince or a princess. Well, try *The Times.* Bound to be someone to take her in. So poor old Edwin. Gone. The Hedleigh vault at Dilberne will open up again. He'll be at one with his ancestors and let's hope he finds someone he can get on with. Perhaps you can set about organizing the show, there's a good man? I'm quite busy down here. You should have seen the sky this morning! Couldn't see the sun for flapping wings, at one point. Flying high, too.'

Mr Baum explained that the deceased had specified he was to be buried in his own churchyard and that no family should be present. He left out the bit about no embalming: two days had already gone by: really had he burned the whole document everyone would have been better off. At least this even limited information made an impact, halfway between a choke and a splutter. His Lordship quickly recovered and was as urbane as ever.

'Then my brother must have his own way, Baum. I'll pay, of course. Least I can do. We shared a nursery after all. Very serious little boy. Could never make him smile. Well, too bad.'

Mr Baum asked what should be done about the child, but his Lordship said vaguely to put everything in writing: he'd see to it when he had a moment. Someone called out to him from far away. He was needed. There was a click. He had gone.

Jane, well trained, took the telephone receiver and put it back in its cradle.

'Poor little girl,' she said, 'poor little thing! Orphaned, and at Christmas time.'

She had heard every word that had been said. Well, all had spoken loudly and clearly, as one did, over such long distances.

THE COLLECT FOR THE DAY:

'Almighty God, you have poured upon us the new light of your incarnate Word: Grant that this light, enkindled in our hearts, may shine forth in our lives; through Jesus Christ our Lord, who lives and reigns with you, in the unity of the Holy Spirit, one God, now and for ever, Amen.'

Mrs Kennion fetched Adela down to the kitchens to help knead the dough for the great Epiphany cake. It was called the Three Kings Cake and had a little bean in it which some lucky person would find and be blessed by the finding. It was the kind of thing her father would have hated. Good fortune should come by hard work and not by happenstance. Adela pounded the dough with a will. She felt more at home here in the kitchens where women bustled about, and laughed and gossiped and even burst into song, than she did in the quiet grandeur of the Palace itself. Up there prelates bustled about like black beetles, but no one burst into song out of sheer good humour.

Yesterday she had walked over a stretch of grass to the most beautiful cathedral in the land (they claimed) where she could pray for the souls of her parents under the famous scissor stone of the nave, and listen to the choir practising. The sound brought tears of wonder to her eyes, where tears of grief still refused to come. Once she had thought St Aidan's impressive but compared to the magnificence of Wells, that stocky little church now seemed so small, dull and tame; the musicians' gallery nothing in beauty and complexity compared to the detail of the Cathedral's dozens of carved wooden misericords. And besides, all of her past was ashes.

> The worms crawl in,
> The worms crawl out,
> They go in thin
> And they come out stout.

Forget it. Better sing with the choristers.

> As yet we know Thee but in part;
> But still we trust Thy Word,

That blessèd are the pure in heart,
For they shall see the Lord.

If only she could. There was a cathedral library, where she was told she could come and go freely, where she found rare illuminated manuscripts cheek by jowl with Temperance and Mothers' Union tracts, Samuel Smiles and early editions of John Bunyan. She looked up 'iniquity' in the *Oxford Dictionary* but that it meant wickedness and came from the Latin root, *iniquus*, meaning unfair or uneven, told her very little. They let her take Samuel Smiles' *Self-Help* back to the Palace.

She no longer had to eat in her room, but had been suddenly translated to the Bishop's table, where at dinner time a harpist in a pale green dress and a low neckline played most agreeably. The strange gnawing feeling she had lived with for so long had simply gone. Perhaps it had been hunger. The other guests seemed to be very old: a few had big stomachs and wives with big bosoms, most were thin and desiccated, like dried-out insects. No alcoholic drink was served. She kept quiet and tried to say little, and rubbed her eyes before she went down to the dining hall, with its great table and pewter plates and heavy silver, to make it seem as if she had been crying. 'We must think about your future,' they said, and she smiled and looked vague. She was happy where she was.

Frank Overshaw was the only fly in the ointment — at least he was a youngish person; though he must be nearly thirty, twice her age if she were a year younger — and would keep gaping and gawking and trying to catch her eye. It was embarrassing. He presented himself as a kind of soulful fairy prince, but she had a feeling he might well turn into Rumpelstiltskin on the stroke of midnight. Once he had addressed her as 'Your Grace' and Mrs Kennion had frowned and shook her head at him. She was always shaking her head at him. What was that about? He was a colonial from Australia so she supposed he didn't know how to behave.

Mrs Kennion took Adela to listen to the Bishop preach in his white Epiphany robes and mitre — though not so simple that they were not threaded rather elaborately with gold. How the Hon. Rev. would have hated it. But Adela was enchanted by the procession of choirboys, now in their blue gowns and pretty white ruffs, each carrying their own little candle. If she became a nun she supposed she would never have children. That would be a relief — how such a thing as a baby got out of a body as small as her own she could not imagine. 'In pain and sorrow shalt thou bring forth children,' an angry God had said to Eve after she'd made Adam eat the apple, and no doubt it was true. And if you became a nun presumably you avoided the pain and the sorrow. Though why Eve should take the blame when Adam had actually done the eating Adela could not fathom. It was certainly like the way her father blamed her mother, or Ivy, or Adela herself when he spilt or forgot something ('Now see what you've made me do, leaving a glass where I was bound to knock it over'); or having to go back to the Rectory when he'd forgotten to take his sermon — 'See what you've done! You distracted me when I was busy!'

One of the choirboys tripped over his robe and fell. Adela giggled. She thought of the most miserable things she could to stop herself, as was her custom. She had murdered her own father and mother. She was orphaned, alone and penniless.

The worms crawl in,
The worms crawl out,
They go in thin
And they come out stout . . .

A beam of winter sunlight struck through the red and blue robes of the prophets on the ancient Jesse Window: she thought it was a sign from God and was elated. Had not Jesus come into the world to redeem sinners?

Brightest and best of the sons of the morning, they were singing. *Dawn on our darkness and lend us Thine aid!*

Well, she would show her belief and her gratitude. Like Ruth, in those few short chapters between Judges and Samuel, she would stay true to the faith of her fathers.

BREAKFAST AT
BELGRAVE SQUARE

'If my brother does not wish to be buried in the family vault, so be it,' Robert said. 'I shan't argue. If he wants to be buried in his poxy backyard, likewise. If he bars one from his funeral one is simply relieved one does not have to attend it.'

He'd said that on the afternoon of Boxing Day when Isobel and he were in the restaurant car on the way back to London. The King had insisted that the Dilbernes stood on no ceremony and left for Dilberne Court at once, to be with their family. He even forewent his afternoon's shooting to go with them to the station at King's Lynn and wave them goodbye. 'I know what it is like when a brother dies,' he said. 'My little brother Affie died only a year back. A great naval man but his spirit was broken by family troubles. We called him Affie because he was so affable, but amiability is no protection from death, is it, probably the contrary. I am thankful indeed to be in a happy marriage. It is natural for a parent to die, but when a brother or sister does, it feels like an affront. Part of one goes with them.'

As it happened both were quite relieved to be free of another five days of Sandringham. Robert had been at pains not to outdo the King in the weight of his shooting bag: Bertie was a good shot but Robert was even better. Isobel found long days without male company, and little for the women to do but change their clothes — six times a day was nothing — to be wearisome. She could have gone out with the men, she supposed, but the rattle of gunshot and the sudden flurries of startled wings, not to mention the chill of the winter wind, made her shiver and shake uncontrollably. She marvelled at the difference between men and women: but then the men had been reared in unheated winter classrooms with open windows where hardiness of mind and soul was equated with hardiness of the flesh, and as a girl reared in a bohemian household, where the pleasures of the flesh were welcome rather than abhorred, she had had a softer upbringing.

'For all his Majesty's weight and girth and pomposity,' she said to Robert, once on the train, 'I see why the King is so attractive to women. He understands so much.' But Robert did not pursue the matter. He was disturbed and upset by his brother's death, and it showed itself in anger. They sat side by side in the squishy seats of the first-class compartment while a damp, wet landscape rattled by, and Robert railed against poor dead Edwin. Isobel wondered quite what Edwin had done and said to offend his elder brother; the outrage had evidently been mutual. But if Robert was reluctant to tell her what it was she would abide by that. Her own spirits had been wonderfully restored by the understanding that the invitations to the Coronation would have gone up in flames with the Rectory. Robert need never know. The Baums would have the vacant seats. Their presence was a small price to pay for peace of mind. And perhaps the third seat could now go to Rosina. Rosina let principle over-ride self-interest. It was not so bad a fault, merely an annoying one. And the girl had no husband, no children: if she found a parrot congenial company perhaps it was not surprising. Many women parroted their husbands. Rosina, perhaps more man than woman, as Oscar Wilde had been more woman than man, kept a parrot in lieu of a wife. She, Isobel, must be more charitable. She just did not want the bird in Belgrave Square. It was smelly, musty and little insects hopped in and out amongst its feathers.

'The Hedleigh vault is all the better for Edwin's absence,' Robert was saying now. The Pullman car had been attached at Cambridge, and they ate a late lunch: he had the steak; she had the sole. But he could not leave the matter alone. 'If he does not want to lie with his ancestors, why should his ancestors want to lie with him? But it is a slap in the face. If he does not want us at his funeral, let him find others to pray over him. I will not.'

'But Robert,' said Isobel, ever the maker of peace, 'he won't have expected to die. Given time he might well have changed his mind and made another will. He probably wrote it on a bad day in a bad mood.'

'He should have thought of that,' said Robert, quite unreasonably. 'No one knows when they are going to die. I find it outrageous that he used Mr Baum as his solicitor, having renounced the family in this spectacularly ill-mannered way.'

'Robert,' said Isobel dryly, 'the poor man is dead.'

'What, are you on his side now?' he demanded. Isobel could see it was wiser not to persist, decided to drop the subject, but then like a dog with a bone went back to it.

'But the daughter,' said Isobel. 'Poor little thing! We can't just abandon her.'

'I don't see why not,' said Robert, quite shockingly. 'The father did not want dealings with our side, so let the mother's side look after her.'

'But we know nothing about her,' said Isobel. 'All we know is that Adela carries the Hedleigh name and is your own flesh and blood.'

'She is also her mother's daughter,' said Robert. 'I met the woman once on the unfortunate occasion of her wedding to my brother. She was very plain indeed. From a Catholic family so relatives will be plentiful. I have asked Baum to advertise so no doubt someone will come forward. In the meanwhile she is in the care of the Bishop of Bath and Wells, an arrant ass but without a doubt respectable.'

'Your brother was a very handsome man,' said Isobel, 'just rather unsmiling. Adela may very well take after her father.'

'That is not likely,' said Robert, firmly. 'Looks are inherited from the dam, temperament from the sire. She will have the worst of both worlds.'

'Robert,' said Isobel, 'the girl is not a horse, she is a human being. What is the matter with you?'

Robert relented enough to tell her why, although he had said nothing at the time, he had been so incensed. After Edwin's neglecting to reply to an invitation requesting the pleasure of his company at Arthur's wedding to Miss Minnie O'Brien of Chicago on June 21st 1900, at the church of St Martin-in-the-Fields, Robert had received a letter after the event which he had read, torn, and thrown into the fire. Edwin let it be known that he strenuously objected to the wedding on religious grounds; namely that Minnie was of the Roman Catholic faith.

'But Minnie had taken instruction,' said Isobel. 'She made no objection and was received into the Anglican Church a whole month before the wedding. I hope you wrote to tell him so and put him out of his misery.'

'I did no such thing,' said Robert. 'There is nothing to do with bigots but let them stew in their own juice. Nothing changes their minds: they are deaf to entreaties and blind to new facts.'

Isobel thought there was more to the story than this but held her tongue.

'In the meantime,' Robert said, 'since the Bishop of Bath and Wells has taken her in, unasked and without any reference to me, let the Bishop of Bath and Wells look after her. I believe he has taken the Pledge. *Lips that touch liquor shall never touch mine,* no less. Not that I suppose much touching of lips goes on at the Palace. It is probably just for public show anyway. I seem to remember I once had a drink with Kennion at the Commons Bar and he had a whisky and soda like anyone else. By the way,' he added, 'the girl is a Princess, according to Baum. Of the rather remote foreign kind, a tenuous link with Austrian royalty. But in case you are considering taking her into our own household, which I sincerely hope you are not, it as well that you are aware of her rank, should the link be proved.'

Isobel wondered again at the vehemence of his reaction, and toyed with her crème caramel. She enquired as to exactly what the link was. Robert said she should take the matter up with Baum, it did not concern him greatly. Isobel was enjoying the journey. She found train travel faster and more comfortable than carriage, and its melancholy hooting more attractive than the sound of the road beneath wheels. Robert, like most men, found change difficult, and noticed only the smuts and the rattling and the way steam seeped through the windows.

He stared grimly out of the window at the dank Essex marshes, and brooded about his brother's shortcomings. Isobel was the more grateful that the invitations had been so simply and fortuitously destroyed. She must remember to declare them lost and set the staff to searching. She would write to Consuelo telling her what had happened and asking for replacements. There would be no need to bother Robert with the problem.

She was sorry that Edwin had met his death but it was an ill wind indeed that brought nobody any good. And it was true that the last thing she wanted was a little princess, no matter how plain, sitting at her dinner table, in a place properly occupied by her daughter Rosina, a mere Honourable, and one much in need of a husband, being no beauty, over thirty and politically minded. Isobel herself, being a Countess, was a mere 'my Lady', the girl would be 'Your Grace', possibly even 'Your Serene Highness', and that would be intolerable. And then there would be the business of the girl's coming out, and her eventual presentation at Court, an expensive, time-consuming and tedious business. The dresses were fun, and the new fashions most becoming to young girls — the stiff uphol-stered look the old Queen had favoured was already going out of style — but there was only so much you could do with white, and diamonds were barred to unmarried respectable girls. They were the kind of stones ardent but ignorant lovers bought for mistresses. Isobel's father Silas the coal magnate had bought some superficially superb ones for Isobel's mother, but they'd proved to be riddled with crystal imperfections when she had tried to sell them.

THE FUNERAL

Mr Baum had accepted the Bishop's kind offer of having the Diocese arrange the funeral, since his Lordship was proving dilatory in the matter. Both agreed that it was only sensible to ignore the Reverend Hedleigh's wish to be buried without proper embalming. Coffins could leak, and masks might have to be worn, which could distress relatives. With embalmment, however, and since temperatures were below freezing, the undertaker took the view that with effective embalming the funeral could be left for ten days or more. Burials were considered too grisly a matter for the weaker sex to attend as mourners, let alone organize them, so Frank Overshaw was sent down to do the arrangements with Mrs Kennion to accompany him.

Mrs Kennion had a talent for organization, and it was she who decided St Aidan's churchyard was not in a state to be used —

the ground being more ash, mud and debris than grass, and alcohol having been smelled on the gravedigger's breath. It was Mrs Kennion who organized a search amongst the ashes of the Rectory for a safe, which fortunately was found, blackened but un-damaged, in the debris that was all that was left of the Rectory. The blacksmith was sum-moned to open it and it was found to be empty other than the Last Will and Testa-ment of Elise Hedleigh, Princess of Gotha-Zwiebrücken-Saxony. Mrs Kennion per-suaded the evangelical Vicar of St Bart's to agree to have the burial there. 'I've had most of poor Hedleigh's congregation here for some time anyway,' he said. 'I might as well have him too. Not an easy man.'

Henrietta had consulted her husband as to the propriety of such a move and the Bishop allowed it. He was something of an evangelical at heart, a keen ecumenicist, and perhaps thought it would do Hedleigh's soul good if his body rested amongst Low Churchers. He had a word with the coroner who allowed the burial to precede the inquest, in the lack of suspicious circum-stances.

There was a sizeable turnout for the funeral — tragedy always drew a crowd — the newspaper headlines had been bold and stark, and ghouls loved to gather. Such local church dignitaries as could be spared from their duties were there and even a handful of their wives, breaking tradition to attend. Adela was there — Mr Kennion had said she was far too young to attend, but Adela had tackled the Bishop himself to get his assent, and won it. Her powers of persuasion were impressive; perhaps it was because she so seldom smiled that when she did it was hard to resist: the sweet, soft voice, always polite but slightly implacable, was persuasive in argument. She was a Hedleigh after all, Mrs Kennion thought, and one should not forget it. They got their own way.

But heaven knew what went on in the girl's head. Mrs Kennion had written, on Adela's insistence, to the Little Sisters of Bethany who said, yes, they had heard of the girl's bereavement in the newspapers and there was certainly a place for Adela as a postulant when she turned seventeen in May. Some convents took girls at fifteen but it was an Anglican working order and they preferred girls to enter the religious life only when they were sure of their vocation. The father had signed the necessary papers about her upkeep and so forth, but in the circumstances, they would wait to hear from her guardians. The sense and competence of the Little Sisters quite impressed Mrs Kennion.

There had, so far, been no message from his Lordship, which rather surprised Mrs Kennion. There was to be no rushing to the child's rescue, it seemed, princess or not. Perhaps when the mother's will was read it would be a different matter. In the meanwhile Adela was a devout child, with her head very much screwed on the right way, and was quite definite in her desire to be a Bride of Christ. There were worse fates. It was a teaching order; she would be free of worldly concerns and be of use in the world. The girl seemed reluctant to be handed over to her uncle's care and from what the Bishop said Dilberne was hardly a suitable guardian for a child with a serious and religious temperament.

Mrs Kennion had to admit that after a short stretch of good food and rest at the Palace Adela was filling out nicely, had learned to hold her head high and had lost the slightly cowed stance she had shown when she first came to the Palace. It would not even occur to anyone now to put her in the servants' quarters. However, it was a big step in a young girl's life to enter a convent, and though it was perfectly possible for a postulant to leave the order before becoming a novitiate, and after that a nun, few did so. Lord Robert would no doubt show up sooner or later and would decide.

A rare ray of sunshine struck through the stained-glass windows of St Bart's and caught a wisp of fair hair which had strayed from Adela's bonnet and turned it to a streak of gold in the gloom of the church. Adela turned her face up to the sun. It was the face of an angel, pure and intent. Mrs Kennion saw Frank gazing at Adela in adoration. His interest seemed more spiritual than physical, which was just as well. Mrs Kennion felt rather sorry for Frank. He so obviously worshipped Adela and had made the mistake of letting her know it: as a result she thought the less of him for it. Men had no idea how to captivate a woman: in Mrs Kennion's experience it was done by showing no interest in her at all until she began to wonder why.

Ivy, the maid-of-all-work at the Rectory, was sitting a couple of pews back from Mrs Kennion and the funeral party. She was a bouncy, cheerful-looking girl but to Mrs Kennion's eyes rather too forward. It would have been more correct for the maid to sit nearer the back in deference to her betters, but then what servant these days knew how to behave? And why should they? Were we not all equal under God's eyes?

The boyfriend, George, the one who had rescued Adela from the flames, sat next to Ivy. Their bodies touched. One must be grateful, of course, that he had saved Adela from the flames, but Mrs Kennion did not like the look of him at all. He bore himself brashly, and was well built, even good-looking, but she thought he seemed untrustworthy, someone who pretended to be honest but was not — what they called at home a chancer. He smiled too widely with too-white teeth: Mrs Kennion was sure that his spectacles were of plain and not magnifying glass. That was what crooks did in Australia, to appear more earnest than they were. She did not see why they should be any different in this country.

Mr Baum came late, meeting the funeral party at the graveside. He was a man very much from the city, tall, thin, like some kind of predatory eagle, who thought very well of himself, and treated them all, Mrs Kennion thought, like country bumpkins. Which she supposed, after all, they were. But his shiny elegant pointed brown shoes and yellow waistcoat were hardly suitable for a country funeral, and when he left as soon as was decent after the final sods had been flung on the coffin, instead of waiting for the tea and ginger cakes in the vestry, which Mrs Kennion had taken it upon herself to provide, all were relieved. Now they could relax. Mrs Kennion had to run after him, a galleon in full sail, to hand him Elise's will and other papers. She had not read them: she was honourable, a bishop's wife.

Minnie's Alarm

While the Princess sat in the church and contemplated the coffins of her parents and reflected on mortality, Minnie sat in Rosina's room and sucked boiled sweets to settle her digestion. Rosina was being very kind and had sent Reginald down to the sweet shop in the village to bring back half a pound each of pear drops, ginger balls and lemon slices. Mrs Neville had decanted them from their paper bag into an elegant silver bowl before bringing them up to Rosina's room, and smiled with special meaning at Minnie, and said, 'I hope they help, your Ladyship. The ginger works best.'

There was no privacy, there never would be, ever again. That morning Arthur had gone down to his workshops as usual, but actually singing, seeing Minnie's morning nausea as proof of what all had been waiting for. Minnie could no longer dismiss her early-morning queasiness as too much wine the night before or too hot blankets or too vigorous lovemaking — she was pregnant. She would have to tell Isobel who would tell his Lordship who would shake Arthur's hand vigorously and congratulate him and say something like, 'And about time too.' She would write to her parents in Chicago and her mother would offer to come over to be by her side and Minnie didn't want that. She certainly wanted Tessa to be by her side but she did not think she could bear Isobel's impeccable politeness and raised eyebrows as Tessa spoke her mind on how the baby's nursery should be a warm sunny room next to his parents', not the cold attic quarters on the third floor which had served the Viscount and his brothers and sisters well enough, not to mention their forebears for the last four hundred years. It would be endless. She must tell her mother not to come.

Rosina agreed.

'Just give in,' she said. 'You'll never win. Put up with it, see it through. You will give birth to a future earl, not a baby. They will give it to a nanny and nursemaids to look after and bring it down for you to look at twice a day and send him off to boarding school when he's seven, in case he grows up to be like Oscar Wilde. He will be very polite to you but he will love his nanny more.'

'Never win!' squawked the parrot. 'Never win!' and with a flurry of his beak joyfully scattered nut husks from his food tray far and wide, and then laughed uproariously.

Minnie laughed too; she couldn't help it. She saw why Rosina kept the bird. It was good company. Mrs Neville was right. The ginger had helped. She felt quite normal.

'But why are you so sure it will be a boy?' she asked.

'If it isn't they won't notice,' she said. 'Just put it to one side and wait for the son to come along. At least you've proved you're not barren, that's the main thing. If you only have girls the title will go to my Uncle Alfred in Bombay, if he outlives Arthur. Then if he dies without sons it would have been Edwin, he was next, only now he's gone.'

'Edwin's gone?' asked Minnie. 'I wrapped up a parcel for Adela only the other day. No one said anything about her father being "gone".'

'He only went the day before Christmas Eve,' said Rosina, 'and I only heard the other day. There was this horrible fire and they both went; and the church, and the house. They didn't suffer; they died in their sleep from smoke inhalation. Don't look so shocked.'

'Shocked!' squawked the parrot. 'Shocked! Any old iron, any old iron!'

Rosina got up and threw a shawl over the parrot's cage. And while Minnie gaped and blinked Rosina explained there was a family feud, her uncle did not want to be buried in the family vault so his wishes would be respected and at least it meant no one had to go into mourning, or to go to the funeral, which she believed was today. It was very sad but no one liked him very much.

'They had family feuds in the old country,' said Minnie. 'But not in Chicago. No one has time for them.'

'Just like your mother, Minnie,' said Rosina. 'Everything in God's Own Country is better than your own. Remember this is your country now.'

'At home there's a lot of noise when people die,' said Minnie. 'Weeping and wailing and embracing, and everyone gets drunk and the wake goes on for days. Here's just so silent and the waters close over. I don't know if I can bear it.'

'I don't see that you have much choice,' said Rosina. 'You can't get divorced unless Arthur does something truly terrible, which he won't; if you run away they'll keep the baby and never mention your name again.

And if I were you I'd change to water-colours: the smell of oil paints and turpentine will upset Mother. I'm surprised she hasn't mentioned it already.'

'What about Adela?' asked Minnie. Rosina had the knack of finding one's weakest point and going for it. Minnie the hopeful artist. The best thing to do was not react. 'The poor little thing! Homeless and orphaned. Is no one going to take her in?'

Rosina pondered.

'It's a matter of breeding,' Rosina said. 'I wouldn't think so. Father's so into horses. Only daughter of a fourth son, and one who's not quite in his right mind at that? A religious obsessive, must have been quite mad not to want to be buried in the family vault? Her mother, Austrian minor royalty? — No, they'll find someone on the mother's side and hope the girl will vanish back into impoverished obscurity. She's landed on her feet anyway. The Bishop of Bath and Wells has taken her in. There's some talk of her becoming a nun and that would suit everyone.'

'A nun!' said Minnie, in horror.

'I'd be a nun,' said Rosina. 'Only I don't suppose they'd let you keep a parrot. At least they wouldn't keep pestering you to get married to some man you don't really

212

like, or snubbing you because you don't look or feel the way you're supposed to. I don't want children anyway, any more than you do.'

'But I'm very happy to have a baby,' said Minnie. And she realized it was true. She wanted to give birth to a little boy like Arthur, with bouncy brown hair and crinkly eyes and a lovely smile to look up at her with trust and love. She would worry about him being sent off to a boarding school when the time came. She wouldn't worry too much if he turned out to be a girl. She didn't like feeling ill, but she'd put up with it. She was disappointed about missing the Coronation, that was all. She would miss walking down the aisle of Westminster Abbey behind four Duchesses, in a fitted brocade dress with a long train and a two-inch ermine trim — though the day would come when she'd take over as Countess from Isobel, and be entitled to three inches. She was beginning to feel like one of them, and it was good. She crunched the rest of the ginger sweets.

A CLASH OF ADMIRERS

Adela was relieved to see that Ivy, as she had hoped, was amongst the mourners. It was because she so much wanted to see Ivy, and cry on her shoulder, and saw no other way of doing so, that she had gone to such lengths to be allowed to attend.

'Oh please, please let me go,' she'd begged Mrs Kennion. 'And then I can settle down to the fact that they're —' To say 'dead' seemed unaccountably rude to her parents, so it came out rather lamely as 'passed over'.

'It isn't seemly,' said Mrs Kennion. 'It's a very modern fashion for women to go to funerals, and in any case you're too young. Ask the Bishop, if you want, but he's bound to say no.'

It had taken some courage to argue with the Bishop: you never knew with men; they could so easily erupt with rage, bang the table and shout, but she had his wife's permission and had spoken cheerfully and softly and smiled, and it had worked. It was how, it seemed, Mrs Kennion dealt with the Bishop. Her mother, faced by her father, had seldom smiled, but just lapsed into more passive dolefulness, which gave him more liberty to behave as badly as he felt inclined.

Adela walked slowly up the aisle behind the two coffins, one large and one small, and tried to not to think of what was in them, and the practical business of getting two melted-together bodies properly separated, and how she should be crying but was not, but rather tried to pretend she was walking up the aisle as a Bride of Christ, and the funeral march was really the wedding march. St Bart's had a fine organ, better and bigger than the one at St Aidan's, as her father had often complained. But now there were no coffins, just Jesus with his gentle smile and crown of thorns waiting for her by the altar. Alas, the vision would keep changing and the crown of thorns and robe dissolve in favour of a faceless young man in a cotton shirt about to throw her over his shoulder and run off with her, against a background of flames, noise and general chaos. She was damned, confounded, hopeless. Three quarters of the way up the aisle, just before she was meant to take her place in the front row, she caught sight of Ivy, and felt such a surge of pleasure and relief it was all she could do to continue the mournful pacing, and not run off to embrace her.

Then she saw that the figure next to Ivy was the tall, broad, fair-haired young man of the smoke and flames. He, like Ivy, was smiling at her. His teeth were very white, perfect. All of him seemed perfect, more dream than reality. Except he was wearing spectacles. She walked on.

Be still, my soul; your best, your heavenly
   friend
Through thorny ways leads to a joyful
   end . . .

All sang, or rather piped and squeaked, the final hymn. It was not at all a full-throated congregation. Adela could pick out Ivy's voice — she was a strong, enthusiastic hymn singer, so much so that the Rev. Edwin would rebuke her for drawing attention to herself — and from next to her a strong male voice, powerful and confident. Frank Overshaw was sitting just behind her; his was a tentative, apologetic kind of voice, annoying and over-reverent; as if the old masters in Tibet to whom he kept alluding had somehow denatured him.

After the final hymn Adela pushed her way through the crowd to find Ivy, they embraced, and George joined them. He was taller and broader and younger than most around. 'My fiancé,' said Ivy.

Adela tried to reconcile this information with the George who was waiting for her at the altar and failed and found tears were pouring down her cheeks. Now she was really weeping, great sobs and gasps she could not help. As they left the church people murmured and sympathized. 'Poor little thing!' 'All in one night, father, mother, home, everything!' and someone — 'She's far too young to be here,' and then she was laughing so hard she could hardly breathe at all.

'Hysteria,' said Ivy, coolly. 'George, she needs a slap.' Before Adela knew it there was a sharp sting across the cheek, first one side and then the other, more startling than painful, and she could breathe again, and she was staring up at George, who was staring down at her. She could not read the expression on his face.

'I didn't mean so hard, George,' protested Ivy, and then George himself was whirled round and there was Frank Overshaw, squaring up to him with fists clenched; and one of the fists hit George's jaw, but it lacked power, and George merely staggered and recovered his balance. Now Frank was on the ground clutching the bottom of his stomach and gasping, moaning and writhing in the mud; George was laughing.

Someone else dragged Adela off to the graveside to watch the coffins being lowered into the open grave. She composed herself enough to throw the first handful of soil, as was expected. First the big one, then the little. It was raining and the mud made her hands dirty. But at least she had behaved properly, and cried for everyone to see. And she did miss them. They were what she was accustomed to.

The worms crawl in,
The worms crawl out,
They go in thin
And they come out stout . . .

Well, perhaps. She remembered a time when Ivy had left the joint in the oven overnight and they had had to eat up the charred remnants the next dinner time. There was not much nourishment in it, you were just left with a dusty mouth black around the edges and the faint flavour of what might have been. The worms would come out pretty much as thin as they had gone in.

Mrs Kennion behaved very strangely on the way home in the carriage, sitting stiffly and seeming not at all friendly.

'I told the Bishop you were too young to come,' was all she said to Adela, snappily, 'but he wouldn't listen. And as for you, Frank —' and that was all. Frank sat pale and winced at every bump, of which there were very many. The road from Yatbury to Wells was rough. Still, the funeral was over and Adela could lean back beneath a rug and dream of St George and go to sleep. In her dreams, he did not wear spectacles.

■ ■ ■ ■

JANUARY — 1902

■ ■ ■ ■

THE SEARCH FOR LOST INVITATION CARDS

'By the way,' said his Lordship to Isobel, 'you did send off those invitations to the Baums?'

'Oh goodness me,' said Isobel. 'I forgot all about them. I'll do it this very morning. But there's lots of time.' She had forgotten all about the Baum invitations, what with one thing and another. She would have to declare them lost and set about a general search in the household, which of course would fail to find them, and then declare them missing. It was a perfectly ridiculous thing to have to do, but she could see no other way out.

'The days pass by quicker than one likes,' said Robert. 'This Coronation takes up a deuced amount of time. The King wants a new open landau built, at great expense to the public purse, but what if it rains all day? We can use the Coronation coach his mother used as an alternative, a gold spec-

223

tacular, but it's deuced uncomfortable. William IV said it was like being abroad in rough seas. And what about everyone else? Do we need alternatives for all the landaus, or shall the footmen just carry umbrellas and put up with looking ridiculous? At least Sunny is back from Moscow and he's a stickler for detail. Consuelo is being a great help: she has a female eye for what things looks like which we men tend to overlook.'

'I'm sure she'll be a great help,' said Isobel. 'Did she have a good time in Moscow?'

'I didn't ask,' said Robert, 'but she was wearing a diamond choker I hadn't seen before, so I expect she did.'

'What, isn't that a little, well, ostentatious? Diamonds to the office?' asked Isobel.

'Oh dear me, no,' said Robert, 'she seldom visits Sunny in his office. She meets with the Queen at Marlborough House should they both be in London. No, I saw her snipping a tape at some slum clearance ceremony for the London County Council. If it is Consuelo's duty to glitter, she glitters. She is a very remarkable woman.'

'I daresay,' said Isobel, perhaps a little shortly.

'But so are you,' said Robert, rather hastily, 'in your own way.'

They were breakfasting in Belgrave

Square. Isobel was wearing a pale yellow tea-gown in silk shantung, made by Fortuny, vastly expensive, being embroidered round the neck with a host of tiny silvery shells gathered in the South Seas. The gown was barely corseted, and, showing the natural flow of her body as it did, was not quite suitable for breakfast. But others maintained it suited her very well and Robert appreciated it. Not, Isobel hoped, that Robert had ever seen Consuelo in a tea-gown. Isobel had a delicacy of beauty which Consuelo could not aspire to. Isobel was a delicate English rose, Consuelo had the strong features of a woman with Cuban blood. She had detected in herself of late a tendency to buy clothes on the grounds that they would not suit Consuelo, rather than that they suited her. What was the matter with her? There was something standing between her and common sense: something like a black cloud of fog, which drifted in and out of her brain. In the meantime it was a very pretty tea-gown. She was being very careful not to drop food on it.

Most of the staff were still down at Dilberne Court but Isobel found she quite enjoyed this state of affairs. The sense of not being overlooked, not being endlessly talked about downstairs, every movement noticed, watched and dissected, was quite liberating. It was like being a child again, in the house in Old Conduit Street where she grew up amongst artists, writers, theatre people, the happy, clever, illegitimate daughter of an actress mother, but frequently visited by her father Silas Batey, the coal magnate from the North. She was wealthy now, and grand, the scandal of her birth long forgotten, almost even by herself, but perhaps she was no happier now. It might be that to have had an unhappy childhood was good fortune; life was likely to get better. To be a happy child was to want to re-create that childhood all your life. She had been to see John Gay's *The Beggar's Opera* at the Surrey Theatre when she was fifteen and watched her mother play Polly Pea-chum.

'Oh Polly, you might have toyed and
    kissed,
Been wooed at length and never won.'
'But he so pleased me and he so teased
    me,
What I did, you must have done.'

That was the night she realized that Silas Batey the occasional visitor was her father, that Polly, the bad girl, had done it with

226

Silas, otherwise she, Isobel, would not exist. The tune kept running through her head, oddly comforting. Robert, the second son of an earl, had come along and pleased and teased and then, surprisingly for one of his class and kind, had married her. And she'd had Arthur, who had pleased and teased Minnie, who, like Polly, had been pleased and teased before, by an artist called Stanton. Well, it was a small sin: when it came to it Isobel was pleased the girl had some life in her.

But she, Isobel, would have to see about the missing invitations. There could be no forgetting them, and letting what happened just happen. Too late now simply to confess all to Robert. He was well aware of her early resistance to the Baums' inclusion in their family life — bad enough to have him as a lawyer and financial adviser; though he had certainly done well enough in that latter capacity. Even so she certainly did not want the pair sitting next to the Dilberne party listening to Parry's anthem, in full view of every lord and lady in the land. It gave them quite unholy status. But Robert wanted it for reasons of his own and so he would see to it that it happened. He would not forget. Like the King, Robert might appear cheerful but he was always watchful. He had begat a son who took after him. If Arthur appeared lightweight, it was the better to mask a steely determination. Robert applied his to politics, Arthur to his engines, but it was the same kind of energy. How else had he won Minnie, how else persuaded his poor mother, and indeed his father, that it was reasonable to turn acres and acres of Dilberne's green and pleasant land into a race track for noisy, smelly, oily engines to career around?

But she must telephone Mrs Neville and ask her to search for an envelope missing from her writing case: she would say it was unlikely but possible it had got amongst Miss Minnie's things when she travelled down to the country. She picked up the receiver. The call would have to go through Mrs Flower, who ran the telephone exchange at the back of the village store, and no doubt listened in. Then she remembered that she had asked Reginald to post the letter, and worse than that, asked him to retrieve it. He would remember posting the letter, and say so — she could of course offer him money to stay quiet — but that way absurdity lay. Better keep things simple; an unsuccessful search of Belgrave Square would have to do. Then — yes, a stroke of genius — she would suggest to Robert that she have an apologetic lunch with Consuelo to ask for a replacement of the missing invitations. And the lunch would cure her, Isobel, of the madness of her suspicions.

Or if it did not, well, at least she would know where she stood. She hoped she had not been naïve in believing the invitations had gone up in flames. It certainly seemed unlikely that anyone would follow them up. She thought about the red velvet dress that had gone to the niece in the same post. Poor little girl! She had wished her well then and still did. Why had she found herself so absurdly sensitive about having a 'Your Grace' at her table? Because she was just back from Sandringham and was humiliated by being a mere Your Ladyship amongst so many Your Royal Highnesses, and that only by marriage? Probably. It was absurd. But Robert had certainly not wanted the girl included in the family, and had made it very clear. Adela would have to manage on her own.

ADELA MANAGES

It was in the middle of January that Adela found herself waking in the big four-poster double bed in a pool of blood. Not a big pool, but enough to terrify her. It was coming from 'down there': her stomach was aching in great clenching pains: she was wounded; God was punishing her for burning the Rectory down, for failing to grieve for her parents. She was bleeding to death, and deserved to.

'Ivy, Ivy,' she called in her head but there was no Ivy. 'Mama!' she called aloud but of course that was useless. There was no Mama. So she rang the bell and a maid came. Adela asked for Mrs Kennion and presently she came bustling in, threw back the bedclothes, looked and laughed, saying it was perfectly normal; it happened to women every four weeks; it meant she was a woman now, not a girl, and must behave like one. The body was getting rid of all the rubbish it accumulated every time it didn't make the baby God was waiting for her to have.

'Every month?' asked Adela, aghast. 'How long for, every month?'

'A week,' said Mrs Kennion. 'But less if you're lucky. Once you're married you'll be glad to see it, it means you're not having a baby.'

'But I'm going to be a nun,' said Adela. 'I'm not going to get married. Does it still come?'

'Of course.'

'That isn't fair. Does it have a name?'

'It's called the curse,' said Mrs Kennion. 'God's curse on womankind for tempting Adam. Although personally, Adela, I have always thought Adam should have known better than to accept the apple in the first place. Cheer up; it's not the end of the world. It's more like the beginning.'

Enough girls in trouble had passed through the House of Mercy Mrs Kennion ran back in Adelaide to convince her that of the twin evils of ignorance and promiscuity, ignorance was the lesser. The menarche had been a shock to the girl, unprepared as she was. But then few gently brought up girls ever were prepared, and rightly so: too much information about the facts of life could only encourage sexual activity in the curious and energetic young, leading to disgrace, ruination and some poor little baby with no place in the world. A shock at the menarche was a small price to pay. She herself was a mother of sons, not daughters, and felt quite privileged to have witnessed Adela's transition from childhood to womanhood. It happened only once and it was important that a girl be amongst friends when it did. She was happy to have been there to help.

Jenny the housekeeper came to change the sheets and clean Adela up. Mrs Kennion left to get back to her busy life, no doubt to see about the sunbursts on the Bishop's coronation robes, which had been central to the conversation at the dinner table for the last few days.

'This is how we do it,' said Jenny, producing the oldest, thinnest sheet she could find in the linen press. She cut the hem with scissors in strategic places, ripped the sheet with her hands into some twelve oblongs, and made a neat pad of fabric out of each one. She used three stretches of hem, one long, to go round her waist, and two short, to fall down back and front, to contrive a belt, and handed her two sturdy safety pins with which the pads were to be attached.

This was the business of womanhood.

'They are called rags,' Jenny said. 'Always keep them in a private drawer, wash them unobserved, dry them in secret, re-use them or you won't have a sheet left in the house. Never let a man know they exist. Don't hang them on the line for the neighbours to see. It is a great shame to be seen with a stain on your skirts, so always check before you leave your room. Don't complain to anyone about the pains, not if there's a man about who can overhear. It's a woman's secret. It goes on until you're fifty. I'm sorry you don't have a mother to tell you this. Poor wee waif.'

'But how do I know when it's going to happen?' asked Adela.

'You have a few days' notice,' said Jenny. 'When you find yourself quarrelling with everyone and you can't sew a straight seam, and you hate the man you ought to love, why then you know it's on its way.' It seemed a kind of incantation, worse than the wound and the blood, the real curse.

Such dreadful pains in her middle overcame Adela that she took to her bed for the day, and huddled up with a stone hot-water bottle, telling the maid who brought her lunch (haricot soup and broiled steak) that she had a headache. She wanted to tell Ivy

what had happened but where was Ivy?
Adela wept. She was alone in the world.
Where were her aunts and uncles, where
were her grandparents? She wanted the
Countess who had sent her a Christmas
parcel to come and snatch her away. She
might be wicked, might deserve the fate of
Lot's wife and be turned into a pillar of salt,
but at least she was kind: the little row of
reindeers kept coming to her mind as
comfort. Presently the pains abated. She
consoled herself with the idea that she was
to be a nun, and from now on she would
have sisters and mothers aplenty. Since the
female condition was what it turned out to
be, it was as well to live one's life out in a
convent. No wonder nuns chose to wear
black skirts and keep themselves to themselves. Anything else was hypocrisy. Love
was hypocrisy: purity was hypocrisy: women
were kept away from altars for good reason,
and only men were allowed near. The world
belonged to man, and always would. Women
were too near the animal, too much of the
body, not enough of the soul. Real women
were not the romantic ethereal creatures
that Burne-Jones painted or *The Blue Fairy
Book* described. Women were Creatures of
the Bloody Rags, and that was that. Her
parents were right. She was unclean. But

only three months to go and she would be with the Little Sisters of Bethany, away from this life of indolence and luxury, this palace posing as a bishop's home. She did not want to go to hell.

By now the soup was cold and the steak was not the kind that melted in the mouth, though the onions and carrots were good: she ate up and mopped up the gravy with bread and felt almost happy again.

■ ■ ■ ■

FEBRUARY — 1902

■ ■ ■ ■

A New Career for George

Ivy's kindness to Adela over the years had not gone unnoticed in Yatbury. Her absence from her proper bed on the night of the fire was somehow overlooked and she was awarded £200 from the parish funds to rehouse herself and replace her belongings. This may have had something to do with a fondness for Ivy's mother Doreen on the part of the Parish Council clerk. He visited Doreen weekly, being a widowed man. Ivy's return to her maternal home after the fire was proving a little awkward.

Ivy's gentleman friend George, Adela's rescuer, lost no time in using Ivy's funds to set up in business in Bath. He had finished with his exams and was looking for employment as a science teacher, while spending some useful hours working as a lab assistant at the college. He thought he could profitably use such spare time as he had trying his hand at the afterlife business. Ivy agreed to come in with him: she had been out of a job since the fire. It seemed something of a laugh. People were gullible, but seemed comforted by the idea that the dead lived on and could be contacted. It was no great crime to make money out of them. George, along with his tutors and a handful of students in the new Department of Paranormal Studies, had come to the conclusion that a few genuine and talented mediums did occur amongst the many fakes, just as a few great artists would always turn up amongst the many who daubed away. And as some artists specialized in miniatures, some in still lifes, some in landscapes or portraits, so some of those with a special talent for the paranormal would find themselves specializing in telepathy, or teleportation, or had the gift of prophecy or communication with those passed over.

'I don't understand a word of it,' Ivy said.

'You don't have to,' said George. 'Just stand back, trust me, and wait for the money to roll in.'

She did trust him. Since the funeral, since he'd become a local hero, since he'd struck Adela's young man to the ground — a lolloping colonial with glasses — he seemed to have grown in energy and determination.

'We'll take lodgings in Bath,' he said. 'You

can't go on moving out whenever your mother's fancy man chooses to come round.'

'It's not all that often,' Ivy said, 'and I don't mind. My mum does everything for me.'

'I mind for you,' he said. 'It isn't decent. Next thing he'll be turning his eyes on you and you'll have to say yes or he'll take your mum's name off the parish poor list. I'm warning you. You don't know men like I do.'

'But living in sin with you wouldn't be decent either,' she protested.

'Just say the word,' he said, 'and we'll be married. I'm mad for you, Ivy. You know that. It's bad for my health. I'm beginning to get headaches. It's all your fault.'

She believed him. She'd led him on; she couldn't deny it, 'Never lead a man on,' her mother had said. 'Once you've led them on they can't stop without getting ill. It all builds up inside and they get headaches and sometimes die.'

He took her to Woolworths in Milsom Street and she waited outside while he bought her a threepenny brass wedding ring. Then he took her to the gardens down by the river, knelt on one knee, took her hand, slipped the ring on her finger, and said she was now his wedded wife.

'Oh do get up, George,' she said. 'You're making a fool of me.' At which he looked quite hurt, so it occurred to her that he might really love her. They took lodgings together in a boarding house in Bath, Ivy wearing a brass wedding ring from Woolworths and calling herself Mrs Topp. She could have wished for a more elegant name, but if you took a man, you took his name with you. They spent many an enviable and noisy night cavorting about in the creaky bed, neglectful of the other guests. The coiled wire springs of the bed, worn through by rust, had a tendency to snap under pressure and poke through the horsehair mattress and cause nasty scratches, but otherwise the second-floor front of the Journey's End Guest House in Station Street served their purposes well enough. Ivy quickly overcame her distaste for illegal sex: you got used to it soon enough and it did not end you up with a bun in the oven.

They went all the way to Paulton on the bus to visit Purnells the printers to discuss using colour lithography for the leaflets and flyers Ivy was to distribute in Bath, but the sour-faced man behind the counter took one look at George's sketches for *Princess Ida of Bucharest, the World-Famous Clairvoyant and Spiritualist,* and shook his head.

'I won't have none of Witch of Endor stuff on my premises,' he said. 'Gives me the creeps. What will my men think of me?'

'Why,' said George, 'they'll think of the good they're doing the widows of the parish, bringing them news of those who have passed over, and work for free!' But the printer was not moved. He did, however, suggest that old man Pitman in the Caledonian Road might treat them more kindly, being into heaven and hell and angels and that kind of thing.

'Princess Ida is an angel sent down from heaven to help us poor mortals,' George said.

'She looks pretty much like flesh and blood to me,' said the printer, looking Ivy up and down, in a way that was hardly respectable. 'Wouldn't you do better, young man, with someone more, shall we say, ethereal?'

On the way back to Bath George nuzzled into Ivy's ear and murmured he was glad she was flesh and blood, and his hand strayed where it should not, but the conductor began to look uneasy so thankfully George sat up straight and looked respectable.

After that they went to visit Pitman & Co. just down the road from George's college

— George told her on the way he'd given up being a science teacher: these days there were easier paths to fame and fortune for an enterprising fellow. The owlish young man who served them at the printing works behind the shop told them that old man Isaac Pitman had died a couple of years back, that he was his great-nephew Ronald, and was now running the business. George showed him his sketches for the leaflets —

Princess Ida of Bucharest,
the World-Famous
Clairvoyant and Spiritualist.
Levitation and Spirit Mysteries.
Watch While the Dead Return from the
Other Side.
Hear What Your Loved Ones Have to
Say to You.

— and Ronald became quite excited, his round glasses shivering and glittering in the electric light.

Ronald turned out to be not only sympathetic to ideas of the afterlife — old man Pitman had had direct experience of the Celestial Kingdom — but was himself a fan of the great medium Charles Foster, having had the good fortune to attend one of his Salem Seer séances, and witnessed him in conversation with the poet Virgil.

'You've come to the right man,' Ronald said. 'It is so important for the people to understand that emanations from the other side are not a matter for fear but for reassurance' — and offered to do colour printing at cost price and access to the secret block of the Cherub Angel of Wisdom kneeling at the feet of the Maker, which old man Pitman had engraved just before his death.

'I knew the right person would come along,' said Ronald, 'and here you are. Only trust in the Lord.'

'Luck's on my side,' said George later, studying the card Ronald had given him, on the back of which was now written an address in the Royal Crescent, that of a wealthy devotee of the afterlife. Ivy could see that it was true. George was lucky in the way most people she knew were unlucky. She still didn't quite trust him but life with him was a hundred times better than life without. She would stick with him. She liked the way men looked at her nowadays. George said it was because she was 'aware' and transmitting life-force energies, and she believed him.

He changed his plans. He would put off the public séances until he was more secure in what he was doing: the big money was in these, no doubt, but they would start small in the darkened drawing rooms of the Royal Crescent. They would refine their skills on a gathering of the hostesses' wealthy friends, who paid good money to sit round in a circle holding hands — and learn to concentrate on what went down best — voices from the other side, spirit guides, the planchette board, mysterious knockings, or simpler tricks of telekenesis, hypnotism, the sudden chilly wind, the extra finger of the rubber glove and so on. Ivy would be the medium: with her extra powers of attraction she would have no trouble: he would teach her how to go into trances and come out of them convincingly. George would manage the technical side of things.

'But no one sensible will believe me,' she said.

'People who want to believe, believe,' he said. 'And that's that.'

'It doesn't seem right,' Ivy murmured once or twice, 'cheating those poor people,' as she practised rolling her eyes and connecting with the infinite.

'We are not cheating them,' said George crossly, 'we are providing them with a service.'

A few nights more and George had persuaded her that her qualms were foolish and naïve. It was better not to find fault, in any case. He did have a tendency to lash out, or go to the pub and sulk. 'I wish you looked a little more mystic, Ivy,' he'd complain. 'More underfed, like the Hon. Rev.'s little girl, not such a strapping country wench, more in tune with the other side, like an angel. Then we'd really make money.'

He was trying to work out how levitation could be achieved in a drawing-room setting. 'Some kind of pulley contraption,' he supposed, 'a board on which a girl's lying under a black blanket. The board gradually rises, the blanket goes, the audience is too transfixed to see a prostrate girl in white rise in the air to notice anything else. The accordion has started playing and the audience is hearing that, not wheels creaking.'

'But there are only two of us doing it, George,' Ivy pointed out. 'It's too complicated.'

'You are such a wet blanket,' he said.

But later that night he sat up in bed and said, 'Of course. You're right. We need a third person. Adela! I knew it would come to me.'

'You're out of your mind,' said Ivy, alarmed.

'Why?' he asked. 'You were always good

to her, she owes you a lot. She owes her very life to me. Time for her to do something for us. We can be her family.'

'No, I'm sorry,' said Ivy. 'You don't understand. She's just not our sort. You'd have to kidnap her first.'

'Then that's what we'll do, he said, and hurled himself upon Ivy, seizing her breasts as if they were handles, pounding the flesh as if it was rising dough, then on top of her, his great thing in her mouth, driving down like a piston, almost suffocating her so she tried to push him away, angering him so he pounded her this way and that as he seemed to feel she deserved, out of the softness here, pound, pound, into the tightness there, pound, pound, without ceremony. Someone from the outside world pounded on the ceiling with a broom. George just pushed her head further into the pillow so she couldn't make a sound and continued with yet more ferocity, as a man whips up the horses when asked to go more slowly. By the time he finished she was half-conscious, swirly in her head. She quite liked the rough stuff, but could see it could go too far.

After that he was sweet and kind, and told her he loved her and she believed him, and they started planning how to get hold of

Adela. They agreed it might take time. Jenny the housekeeper up at the Bishop's Palace had heard from Ivy's mother Doreen that the girl's family wanted nothing to do with her, and that in any case she was going to enter a convent as a nun in May.

'So we'll be rescuing her,' said Ivy, 'not kidnapping her?'

'See it like that,' said George.

The landlady, blushing, asked them to leave, they were disturbing the other guests, but George was charming and complained about the rusty springs of the bed breaking and they ended up staying in a better room on the first-floor back and with a new bed, without even paying any more. You had to admire him. It was the downstairs tenant who went.

A Prime Minister in Waiting

His Lordship called in to see Arthur Balfour at the House of Commons, and found him at his desk, his handsome head bowed over his papers, and his great blue melancholy eyes tired.

He seemed pleased to see Robert, rose to his feet and extended his hand, urbane and charming as ever, but seeming more puzzled than usual by the demands of the material world.

'Ah, Dilberne,' he said, 'a friendly face at last. The least judgemental of my colleagues.'

'I'm not in the Education Office,' said Robert. 'You are quite safe.'

He and Balfour had met on occasion in the past over a whisky at the Royal St George golf course, admired each other's drives and agreed to be in favour of the new Haskell golf ball, the bouncing bounder of the tees, which so alarmed the more staid members of the golfing fraternity. Nowadays poor Balfour had little time for golf; he was determined to get the nation's children educated while his own party and clerics of every hue stood in his way.

'I'm not even PM,' he said. 'But poor old Uncle Salisbury's grown so old everyone behaves as if I am. He can still make a fine speech but that's all. Everyone hates me. Simple yeas or noes are beyond me.'

'I beg to differ,' said Robert. 'I've watched you choosing your irons, and you never hesitate.'

'Oh, golf. I can manage rain and wind well enough, but people? No. They are far more unpredictable. Every light remark I make is scrutinized, every decision criticized. I am more accustomed, frankly, to the adoration I received when I played the philosopher and affected indifference and languor. And now this Coronation — the King insists on pomp and ceremony and I daresay he's right, but the cost escalates, and I am required to defend him with facts and figures, which I loathe. It is all most unsatisfactory.'

'You still seem to have the critical adoration of any number of women,' observed Robert cheerfully. 'Be content with that.'

'Oh that,' said Balfour, dismissively. 'That

is easy enough. So long as one inclines one's head to a lady at dinner and appears to be paying careful attention to any kind of nonsense they fall in love at once. Then they go away and persuade their husbands to vote for one. But you know this very well. I have seen you inclining your head quite often in the direction of the delectable Duchess.'

'Consuelo, can you mean?' asked Robert, not without alarm. Had it really been so noticeable?

'Oh don't reproach yourself, dear fellow,' said Balfour, who Robert had long ago decided had the gift of reading minds. 'Half the chaps in London feel the same and half the women are in a frenzy of jealousy. But no one doubts her virtue, while wondering how on earth she managed to marry such a *little* man. She can, after all, afford her own diamonds.'

'Dukes are thin on the ground,' said Robert. 'Earls are two a penny, alas,' and lured him off to the House of Commons bar for a tot of whisky: two good-looking men with fine moustaches, neither as young as they used to be, but with their political futures before them.

Balfour expressed surprise that Robert was still in town and not off on his estates 'killing things' and Robert said he had had more than his fill at Sandringham and now had his wife with him in Belgrave Square: she was, as he was, taken up by matters to do with the Coronation, and it was best to be in London. 'A storm of trivia,' said Robert. 'Of ermine trims and silver slippers, but my wife makes short work of it.'

'Alas,' said Balfour, 'I have no wife.'

Twenty-five years since Arthur had lost the love of his life, his cousin May Lyttleton, to typhoid fever. He had stayed unmarried, and many, including Isobel, wondered why. 'It is not in the nature of men,' she had said, 'at least normal men, to love anyone for more than a year who is out of reach and out of sight. And to be dead, like poor May, is to be both.'

To which Robert had replied sternly that Balfour was the most normal of men. He did not hunt or shoot like other men but at least played golf and was frequently seen in the company of attractive women, although admittedly often other men's wives, and he did not want further conversation on that subject. Nor was there.

'We must see it as a relief,' said Balfour now, 'that the New King is so unlike the Old Queen in his happiness to show his face in public, and it is true that his dependence upon public affection rather than military might may well save the country money in the long run, but in the short term it is damned expensive on the public purse!' And he asked for an account of Robert's Christmas at Sandringham.

'I cannot pretend not to be interested,' he said. 'But I will not ask you to be indiscreet.'

'It was most agreeable and most relaxed,' said Robert.

'Ah yes, banging away at birds,' said Balfour. 'One is sorry for the women, who have nothing to do to but change their clothes ten times a day, while dead birds fall all around. I wish our royals would learn to play golf. You're a horseman, I believe.'

Robert agreed that he was, but added that a good shoot on a bright winter's day was hard to beat.

'Always tactful, Dilberne,' said Balfour. 'Now tell me. Was there any talk of the Shah of Persia?'

'I am not a Foreign Office man,' protested Robert. 'I know horses and I know gold mines: ask me about wars and colonies and trade by all means, but please, not diplomacy. But yes, the King has set his face against asking the Shah to a State dinner: yes, the King feels the Foreign Minister should not have offered the Shah the Order of the Garter, when it was in the King's gift, not the government's. He has made this obvious enough to you himself, I know. The King is sensitive at the moment and anxious not to be overlooked.'

'He is so like a child,' said Balfour. 'Yet so very large in person one forgets. But I daresay his heart is in the right place.'

Robert protested that indeed it was. The King had declared that he was going to present at least part of Osborne House to the nation, for the benefit of wounded soldiers.

'Rather for his own benefit, I suspect,' said Balfour, 'to better expunge all memory of the abominable Brown and the even more abominable Munshi, which have so blighted the King's memory of his mother.'

Robert murmured that the King's upset was understandable. The Queen had replaced his father as husband with Brown the ghillie, and himself as son with the Munshi, an Indian waiter. The insult could not be greater.

'I fear the public sees something a little less innocent than that,' said Balfour. 'You know rumours keep circulating that she had an actual marriage to Brown? Though I daresay the nation will be happy enough to accept Osborne, by way of apology.'

'It was Queen Alix's doing,' said Robert, soothingly. 'She has a soft heart and cares for the welfare of wounded soldiers. We shouldn't look for sinister motives when none exists.'

'Oh Dilberne,' said Balfour, 'you are such a diplomat and such a liar. You would do well at the Foreign Office.'

When Salisbury either retired formally or died there would be a new government and a new Cabinet. Robert could see this conversation, which had at first seemed so casual, was serving as an interview. Perhaps Balfour saw him as rather similar to himself, a Tory by family and tradition but a Liberal at heart? But he was no Liberal.

'No,' said Robert firmly. 'I would not. I too prefer to be liked than disliked.'

'Treasury?' asked Baldwin. 'To all accounts you wheel and deal most successfully.'

'My advisers do,' said Robert. 'I am an innocent.'

He remembered the tickets Consuelo had given him. Isobel had been foolish enough to lose them, throwing them out with other papers, but had been going to ask Consuelo over some ladies' lunch to replace them. The Coronation was months ahead but Robert must confirm it had been done. On such small details preferment depended. Isobel had already shown she was quite capable of forgetting to send what she was not enthusiastic about sending — it must not happen again. It was a pity she dismissed the Baums as social climbers: both seemed pleasant enough to him, and even engaging.

Balfour did not probe further and then startled Robert by asking if Robert and his wife would care to join him in a séance, which he and a few scientist friends were organizing at his house in Carlton House Terrace.

'Do not worry,' said Balfour. 'We have a group of well-established cynics from the Psychical Research Society to overlook what goes on, and the medium herself is well recommended. We will put politics to one side and concentrate on philosophy. Whether or not we live on after death is as least as interesting as the fate of the Liberals. Or do you see it as so many do, as humbug?'

'I haven't given the matter much thought,' said Robert. 'But we would be delighted to come along. Though I fear Isobel is rather sceptical on these matters.'

'It is hard to stay sceptical if you have witnessed these things with your own eyes,' said Balfour.

The answer, thought Robert, might well be to take care not to witness them by not holding séances and tapping tables. But then the whole world seemed to be at it, a fashion first set by the Old Queen as she tried to bring poor Albert back from the grave, and with her own death had found new energy. Even the King entertained himself and his guests with a planchette board. Now every kitchen maid, every drunken ploughman staggering home from the pub had seen a ghost. Balfour was known to seek the spirit of his lost May from amongst the shades, and it was seen as a harmless folly, product of a profound and lasting grief — but to be widely known for it would do his reputation as a rational and competent leader of men no good at all. On the other hand, outright dismissal of his ideas would hardly be politic.

For his own part he could see that Heaven was 'to be with God', and that to throw a few sinners into a boiling pit was the only way justice could ever be achieved in a cosmos so clearly short of it. He could see that the finality of death was hard to comprehend, but beyond that he would not go. His own brother Edwin was scarcely cold in his grave, and his death was certainly hard to believe, let alone grieve for. But he saw no signs that the 'spirits' lingered on; he was not so credulous.

'I am open to conviction,' said Robert, crossing his fingers like a schoolboy.

A greyish-brown fog was beginning to seep up the Thames, clouding the windows so that passing boats outside became vaguely visible passing shapes, rather than definite and detailed reminders of industry and success. His Lordship shivered, recalling the time in this very place that Isobel had nearly left him, having discovered a passing act of indiscretion on his part. But he hoped he had learnt his lesson. Consuelo was very fond of Balfour, but, Robert hoped, in a daughterly way. She saw something spiritual in him. Well, Robert was fond of Consuelo too, and he hoped in a fatherly way, though if she looked for anything spiritual in him she looked in vain.

But Arthur was telling him about his old tutor, mentor and friend, the classical scholar Frederick Myers, with whom he had set up the Society for Psychical Research. Myers, Balfour assured him, was already communicating with him from the other side. He had passed over some six months back, but now, through reliable mediums, specialists in automatic writing, selected in advance from all over the world, was already beginning to send messages from the other side, using classical references of which only the one passed over could be aware. Robert cut him short, saying he must be off to see Isobel. When Balfour got onto this particular hobby-horse, really it was a lot of tosh.

■ ■ ■ ■

MARCH — 1902

■ ■ ■ ■

WHO IS FAIREST OF US ALL?

As Adela's mind and mood swung like the St Aidan's weathercock, first one way then the other, her body was changing too. There was a waist where none had been before and budding bumps on her chest. A kind of cheerful determination was building up inside her. It couldn't only be because she was warm and well fed, and the first crocuses of the year were showing, it was because her mother was gone and so her body as well as her soul was free. She was still looking forward to the Little Sisters of Bethany but perhaps not as much as she had been. Her mother had described the sin of vanity as looking at yourself in mirrors: *Mirror, mirror, on the wall, Who is the fairest of us all?*

The answer was to have as few mirrors in the house as possible. In the Rectory there'd been just a square of one next to everyone's ewer and basin for looking in when you washed your teeth. Adela had sometimes wondered if she would see Rumplestiltskin's teeth and not her own if she looked, so she'd try and get them clean by rubbing with bicarbonate and finger alone, but it could be messy.

Adela, in her new naughtiness, could see her mother might well rather not look at herself for fear of what she would see, but what was true of the mother was not necessarily true of her daughter. She would find out: there was a large mirror over the fireplace in her room, mottled glass with an ornate gilt frame. If she climbed up on a chair and tilted the mirror towards her she could see the full length of her black-clothed self any time she liked.

First she bolted the door to make sure no one could come in. Ever since the strange episode at the funeral — when she had disgraced herself with hysterics, Ivy's young man had cured her with a slap, and Frank had intervened and there had been a scuffle — Frank was always popping in and out, like some jack-in-the-box. It was not right. She was not a child any more, she was a grown woman. He should stop it. She needed a chaperone. She wanted to slap Frank to wipe the serious, soulful look off his face; the smile when his lips smiled but his eyes didn't.

She climbed on the chair and by wedging a copy of *Self-Help* from the Palace library beneath the frame she found she could see very well.

At first she looked tentatively and shyly, then boldly and longer. Yes, she was right. She looked like Ruth the Moabite in the illustration in one of the children's books at Sunday school. The corn was a strange orange shade but the image had been memorable. Ruth the Moabite, the beautiful widow, stranger in a strange land, weeping amongst the alien corn. To be orphaned was probably sadder and even more dramatic than being widowed. Yes, she was Ruth herself, bereaved, beautiful, tragic, brave.

But what if she took off all her clothes? She felt her mother's shock, her father's horror. She flinched before the shouting. 'Are you stupid as well as plain?'

Have you ever thought, as the hearse
   goes by,
The worms are waiting for you and I . . .
   ?

She positioned herself in front of the mirror so she could see the length of her body:

she let her hair fall free from its tight bun. She took her clothes off, piece by piece, and dropped them on the floor. She did not look until they were all off.

She had nothing to compare it to, never having before seen a picture of a naked human body, male or female, let alone a real one. What she saw now was good: its planes and curves pleasing. Her breasts were bigger and more rounded than she had thought, not little peaky things at all. She was so pale, almost to the point of transparency. She was rather splodgy and freckled too, but that was the mottle of the old mirror. Her head was too big but that was the way the mirror was tilted. She liked the way her hair rippled almost to her waist. She like the way the bush of darker hair, where her legs joined, seemed to centre the whole.

She was no longer Ruth the Moabite; she was Burne-Jones's Princess Sabra, thanking St George for rescuing her from the dragon. She'd seen the painting of the Princess Sabra in a catalogue left behind by mistake by the Church furnishers; she had admired the richness of the flowing fabric, marvelled at how an artist could make the flesh come to life. Her father had found her looking and removed the book. It was sacrilegious; the Church gone mad, fallen into eroticism and heresy. He had shouted. A bit of plaster had fallen from the ceiling. She, Adela, knew what it was to be rescued. Her own St George had flung her over his shoulder and rescued her from the flames.

Or perhaps she was Millais's Portia? Ivy's mother had a water-stained print on her kitchen wall. Beauty, strength and judgement, all at once: what one must aim for. She was shivering. Enough of all this. She must cover herself up. She removed Samuel Smiles and the mirror fell back into place with a puff of dust. She climbed down from the chair.

She quickly dressed again. White underskirts, black petticoats, high-buttoned black moiré dress, long black sleeves, little black laced boots. She scraped the golden hair back in the bun. But everything had changed. She was all these women. She was Ruth, sick for home, she was Sabra, the rescued, she was Portia the wise, but most of all she was Eve, who had succumbed and eaten the apple. She had an intimation of the pleasures of the flesh, and how they were at odds with the aspirations of the soul. You had to choose. She had chosen a life of devotion to God and to others, but perhaps she was wrong?

She was sitting on her chair, bent over the

better to lace the row of buttons on her last shoe, when the door pushed open and there was Frank. She had thought she had locked the door, but now could see that the mediaeval lock was more theatre than actuality. You slammed the great bolt across, but there was no socket. The real lock was a tiny hook and eyelet, which she had failed to see.

Had he been watching her, like Rumpelstiltskin? It was silly to see him like a wicked dwarf; he was so obviously not, with his upright carriage, clear skin and the wide candid eyes. He had been training to be a missionary in Australia, bringing the word of God to a place of savages, typhoons, crocodiles, kangaroos and houses on stilts where termites gnawed. He was brave and good, Mrs Kennion said. Now he was bringing her a glass of cordial. He did not meet her eye.

'Mrs Kennion asked me to bring you this, Miss Adela,' he said, in his soft light voice. 'It's a lime cordial they make locally and it has health-giving properties.'

'Thank you very much, Frank,' she said, and he went away.

It was perfectly possible that he had come up to her room in all innocence, as was his wont, found the door ajar, seen it as an invitation, like Rumpelstiltskin peered at her naked form, and only when she was down from her chair and properly dressed again had let his presence be known. It was possible, but not probable. At least the incident would not be spoken of, any more than had the scuffle at the funeral. But Adela was left with a strange feeling of excitement and repulsion mixed; of more to come. She could see it was probably to do with 'the curse' she now had to endure and that Jenny and Mrs Kennion had described as the rubbish left behind when you didn't have babies. The two were interlinked. If only there were someone to explain it to her, but there was not. The medical books were no help. They described the mechanics of the female menstrual cycle, but not how it made you feel. What it made her feel was naughty, defiant, and jumping up and down and making faces at other people.

The worms crawl in,
The worms crawl out,
They go in thin
And they come out stout . . .

Don't think about it.

A Trip to Bath

'I hope you are not having second thoughts,' said George to Ivy. They were walking hand in hand up the road to the Registry Office, there to give the fifteen days' notice required before registering a marriage.

'Well, I am,' said Ivy. 'I don't want to think I've been married for the sake of £200 worth of parish relief money.'

'Think yourself lucky,' said George amiably. 'You're a bad girl. Everyone in Bath knows. Who else is going to marry you?'

'All kinds of men who want my two hundred quid,' said Ivy. 'I'm not daft.'

'Your mother wants it for her roof,' said George. 'I know. I like your mother. Get her to put up with one more winter and we'll not only re-thatch but put in running water too. It's a promise. The money will come pouring in.'

'Says you,' said Ivy. 'And this business of kidnapping Adela. It's daft. Even though she's willing she's still under age. It's bound to be against some law or other.'

'So it's worry keeps you awake at night,' said George. 'Funny. I could have sworn it was me,' and he bumped against her as they walked so she got a fit of the giggles, forgot her qualms, and signed the necessary papers.

'If you go to the bad I can't testify against you once we're married,' she observed. 'Is that why?'

'I'm marrying you because I love you,' he said. 'You are so suspicious. It makes your eyes go squinny: it doesn't suit you. Careful I don't fall out of love with you.'

'You be careful I don't change my mind before the fifteen days are up,' she murmured.

They went to the Post Office where he started a savings account and she transferred £200 from her account to his. She was already spending three and sixpence a night on the boarding house and fares had mounted to a good two shillings. Nothing was cheap. They took the bus to Wells and strolled round the Cathedral and then crossed to the Bishop's Palace where they knew Adela was imprisoned. They pretended to be ordinary sightseers and watched the swans being fed. Ivy swore she

271

saw Adela looking out of one of the windows at the swans, but George said she was being fanciful. It was just too easy and she could see that it was.

'But it's the kind of thing she'd love to do,' said Ivy, regretfully. 'It's all so poetic.'

'You saw it because you wanted to see it,' he said. 'It's the kind of thing we learn at lectures. You just be guided by me, Ivy. I'm your husband.'

'Not yet you aren't,' she said. But he jostled her from the back and she could see that she was as good as.

They were pleased to see that all kinds of people — clerics, servants, delivery boys — wandered up and down the drawbridge and though there was a porter's lodge saw that for the moment at least it was unmanned. If Ivy put on a maid's bonnet and George a coachman's cap it would be easy enough for them to get in and out. But they needed to know exactly where in the palace Adela was. The longer they spent wandering corridors the greater the danger of being challenged and detected.

They could see they'd have to think about it, and took the bus back to Bath — another fourpence — where they had a cup of tea and bought some good crispy cod and chips wrapped in the *Bath Advertiser* to take back to their room — another eight pence for the two of them. It was strange that he now had nearly all the money but she was expected to pay. She said as much.

'I wish you didn't keep getting that squinny look in your eye,' said George. 'I'll fall out of love with you. We don't want that. It would spoil everything.'

It would too. She tried not to look squinny even if she still felt it. She handed over the eight pence.

The next day George's eye fell on an advertisement — which he could just make out despite the grease — in the discarded newspaper wrapping from their fish-and-chips. It was, he said, 'meant to be', which was not the kind of thing he'd usually say but he seemed excited: it was for a public séance to be held that night in a school hall behind Pierrepoint Street.

George said going to it was necessary research. He already knew what went on but she also needed to — after all she, not he, would be the one on the platform. It was worth the investment of two shillings and sixpence a head. She said he should pay: it was a capital expense, not sundries. He sighed.

'Squinny again,' he said. She didn't want him to fall out of love with her, and paid up, and remembering how once Adela had practised forgiveness, she tried practising trust. It gave her such a nice warm feeling she quite fell into the habit of feeling it.

The world-famous Mrs Tate was appearing with her spirit guide Hui Neng. George said she was probably a fake and these false mediums brought serious research into disrepute, and Ivy said but they themselves were going to be fakes and George said that was beside the point. Ivy shrugged and let it go.

The hall was full: there was standing room only: the room was steamy with damp coats, noisy with coughs and colds, and made foggy with smoke from oil lamps and cigars. Most in the audience were elderly women of the down-at-heel widow variety, but there was a fair sprinkling of the better dressed, and quite a number of student types. Everyone wanted to know about life after death. There was someone there from George's college.

Mrs Tate made her entrance. She looked, rather disappointingly, like the farmer's wife from Devon she was, in a not very crisp white blouse and a rather dusty navy skirt, not at all smart. She stood alone on a stage, empty other than two chairs and a plain table covered with a cloth which hung halfway to the floor. She talked in a high, refined voice for some ten minutes about the peace and presence of the Lord and the happiness of the other side, where the dead were finally at peace and restored to the wholeness of their youth. The audience liked and trusted her. She stopped talking mid flow, and her eyes began to roll upwards. She grunted and then as Ivy and George watched she turned into an elderly Chinaman. What kind of trick could turn smooth apple cheeks into dusty, wrinkled hollows, narrow European eyes into slits, change female into male, a mane of hair into a pigtail and a circular embroidered cap, an ordinary plain blouse and skirt into a flowered silk robe? To which George said, 'A change of lighting, of course.'

The audience sighed in wonder and satisfaction. The spirit guide Hui Neng had taken over Sylphia Tate's body. No one now must disturb the union or when he left for the other side he might take her with him.

'This is for real,' said Ivy.

'She took off a wig and screwed up her face, that's all,' said George.

'It's so hot and smelly in here, George,' pleaded Ivy. 'Can we go?'

But George's hand was on her arm, and forceful. She stayed where she was.

'That tablecloth reaches the floor,' said George. 'They've painted the lower half black so it matches the back wall.'

When Hui Neng spoke it was with a strange accent and a high reedy voice that might well have come from the other side of the grave. He, or she, looked upwards into the fog of cigarette smoke and oil fumes that rose from the crowd. The audience looked upwards too.

'Are you there? Yes, I hear you now, Fan Yip. I see, a message from Henry for Mary.' There was a sharp rap from the ceiling. 'Sorry, Fan Yip. Not Henry, Harry.' There was a sharp cry from the audience.

'Harry, is it you, my darling?' and a sob of pain. The audience gasped. So did Ivy.

'Oh, for heaven's sake, Ivy,' said George. 'There are four hundred people in this crowd. How can there not be a passed-over Harry?'

'Oh do hush!' said Ivy. 'People can hear you!'

Hui Neng/Mrs Tate and Mary had a conversation in which Mary asked Harry if his leg was still giving him trouble, and Fan Yip quoted Harry as saying he was young and strong again and Mary would be joining him soon in paradise, and when she asked how soon, said before next Christmas.

Mary gave a little shriek. Hui Neng said time on the other side was different, being eternal, and quickly went on — to a little boy coming through from the other side, he had a caliper and big eyes, was there a mother present looking for a son with a caliper and big eyes, and found a father if not a mother. Was there a pet mouse? The father said not a mouse but a pet dog, and Hui Neng said the voice was indistinct, the wind of heaven was blowing strong today from the other side, and the lampshades above the table began to swing, so moving shadows crossed to and fro across the audience.

But now Sylphia Tate was moaning and twitching and a kind of white mist was coming from her mouth and ears, and forming in front of her into a shape, no, two shapes.

'Ectoplasm,' said George. 'Gossamer and a draught. Look beneath the table.' It was hard to see because of the dimmed lights and the fog of smoke and oil fumes. There was a disturbance in the audience. Someone had fainted.

'They pay someone to do that,' said George.

But Ivy's heart was beginning to pound. On stage two shapes were beginning to form, a man and a woman. One was the tall

277

craggy impression of Edwin Hedleigh, the other was that of little Mrs Hedleigh, both misty and dissolving and reshaping as clouds do, and cartoon versions at that; but them, nevertheless, her employers come back to take her with them to where they had gone, for the sin of going with George and letting them burn to death. She wanted to move, to flee, but she was paralysed. Others were also making for the doors.

Someone was screaming. The reedy voice turned into a croak. 'Fire! Fire!' and flames seemed to leap from Mrs Tate's mouth.

'Camphor,' said George. 'Take two parts of aquavite to one each of quicksilver and liquid styrax and set a match. Flames appear but do not burn. A simple trick. Our Professor showed us in the lab. For a moment even I was convinced. It's the fumes in here. Shall we go?'

'Stand back, stand back,' Hui Neng was saying to the ceiling, as if to unseen spirits crowding in. 'So many of you! Such a busy time.'

On the stage Hui Neng himself seemed alarmed. His voice squeaked like chalk on slate.

'Death comes unannounced. The Avenging Angel. Death comes by flame and smoke. No, no.' Now his voice was guttural again: a voice from hell. Mrs Tate was back, jerking and fitting away, leaning back stiffly.

George and Ivy made for the door.

'But that was them,' wept Ivy. 'The Hon. Rev. and his missus.'

'Don't be stupid,' said George. 'The Rectory fire made quite a stir. They study the local papers when they arrive at a town, and pull something like this. One tall man, one short woman, easy. She's pretty good, Mrs Sylphia Tate, I'll say that for her. Two and six a head and they're making a fortune. If there was someone like Adela on the platform we could charge three shillings — and they'd line up.'

'Rather her than me,' said Ivy, pulling herself together. 'But I can't say I like it. Too spooky.'

'Then we'll make the voices come from heaven not hell, and charge three and six. You're married to a genius, Ivy.'

'Not quite yet,' she said.

The Illusionist's Shop was still open, up the poor end of Milsom Street, and they went in together and bought some castanets, a guitar, some black paint, some gossamer and a rubber hand with a stout clip on the wrist and rubber fingers, and when George said it was for private work the shopkeeper came forward with a novelty number from

America, a little miniature fan run by a battery. The whole lot came to fifteen pounds, eight and thruppence and George said it was cheap at the price, and Ivy paid up happily. But it did all seem somehow grubby as a collection of purchases, especially the rubber hand.

George slipped next door to the chemist, where he bought a bottle of chloroform and some gauze pads but Ivy didn't know that.

Minnie's Condition

Mrs Flower at the post office telephoned through to the station master at Brighton to tell him that the 10.00 train needed to make a detour and stop at Dilberne Halt. The fifth Earl of Dilberne had sold the land to the Brighton Railway Company in 1835 on condition that the train stopped at the Halt whenever so required by any occupier of Dilberne Court. Reginald drove Lady Minnie and Lady Rosina to Dilberne Halt, where they caught the 10.25 train to London at 10.30. They were on their way to see Lady Isobel. Minnie had news, good and bad, for her mother-in-law: Rosina wanted to get in some shopping and go to a debating club the following evening when Mr Gilbert Chesterton was rumoured to appear, and William Butler Yeats, over from Ireland. It seemed that Rosina was in correspondence with Seebohm Rowntree and he was coming down to London to attend

— it was to be an argument between the rationalists and the idealists — but Minnie was not to let her mother know.

'He is a happily married man,' Rosina was at pains to tell Minnie, 'it is a meeting of minds, that is all.'

'In that case,' said Minnie, 'perhaps I could go with you?'

'It is in Bedford Park,' said Rosina, 'one of the new garden suburbs, and the houses are all pebble-dashed with peculiar chimneys: it's very writery — and I don't think it will suit you at all. You have to get there by steam train and you are in a certain condition and I'm sure once Mama knows she will not let you go anywhere at all.'

'Then I will go first and tell her afterwards,' said Minnie. She had heard of Bedford Park; there was a school of art and Pissarro had lived there and T. M. Rooke still did, the famous artist who knew Ruskin and had worked with Burne-Jones. 'We will spend two nights away.'

'Papa and Mama are there with only a couple of servants,' objected Rosina. 'It is a great deal of trouble for them.'

'Oh for heaven's sake, Rosina,' said Minnie. 'I promise not to overhear whatever you say to this Seebohm of yours, and not tell a word to anyone if I do.'

'We will be talking about rural poverty, that is all,' said Rosina, then added, 'more's the pity,' and smiled. She had a pretty smile, and when she used it, thought Minnie, looked ten years younger.

Minnie asked what the name of the club was and Rosina replied the I.D.K. debating society.

'What's I.D.K.?' asked Minnie.

'The I Don't Know debating club. When anyone asks you for the password you say I.D.K. and they let you in.'

'Then nothing in the world will stop me going,' said Minnie.

Mrs Neville had packed a lunch hamper, but they decided they would far rather eat in the Pullman restaurant car, so they found an empty third-class carriage and decanted the packed lunch — hard-boiled eggs and ham; butter, cheese and rolls; and apple pasties and ginger cookies especially for Minnie — onto the bench and left it there for the next lucky passenger, and made their way to the restaurant car. No one would know. They felt very delinquent and very happy. Now Minnie was resigned to her condition, she had stopped feeling sick. She put it down to crystallized ginger.

The good news that Minnie planned to give her mother-in-law was that a baby was on its way: the bad news, from the doctor, was that it was likely to arrive in the last week of June and that it would be unwise for Minnie to attend the Coronation.

His Lordship Passes By

His Lordship knocked on the Lord High Steward's door. Accommodation for his Grace the Duke of Marlborough had now been made in the Offices of the Lord Great Chamberlain in Buck House, the Marquess of Ancaster being even less busy than usual. It was a rather splendid room overlooking the Gallery: nicely if rather eccentrically furnished as a drawing room, with white lace curtains, plump crimson chairs and sofas, some darkish landscapes of rocks and storm clouds, heavily framed ornate mirrors and a couple of potted palm trees, but the whole dominated by a great mahogany desk, as if everything that had not fitted in the rest of the house had ended up here because there was nowhere else for it to go. A small light voice told him to come in, and he found Consuelo seated behind the desk, rather briskly sorting papers, her plentiful black hair piled on top of the little head, fixed by a couple of Spanish-looking combs, and her frail body and slender neck dwarfed by the size of the desk.

'Oh Consuelo,' Robert said, 'I hoped to see you, but I thought Sunny would be here.'

'Sunny is off lunching with William Waldorf Astor, who is immensely rich and immensely powerful and even more miserable than Sunny, but we need him on our side because of his magazines, so at this very minute I daresay Sunny will be chomping through roast beef and Yorkshire pudding at the Carlton Club. Poor Monsieur Escoffier, he creates these wonderful dishes, but has to cook for all these people who will only ever eat what they were given at Eton. He may have better luck with William, of course, who is American, and so will favour hamburgers, but at least spent some of his childhood in Italy, and of course the King, who never went to school at all, is always partial to something new. They say the King learnt his love of sauces when he was the Prince of Wales and he and Lily Langtry used to frequent the Savoy, where Escoffier worked until they fired him and César Ritz for stealing fine wines. You did not know that? It had to be hush-hush because chefs know only too much about where the bodies are hidden. So Robert, no Sunny today, you will have to put up with me.'

She seemed very nervous, thought Robert. Chattering on, as if to fill an awkward space, to give time to a lover hidden in the bedroom cupboard to slip away. Or indeed, as a woman chatters on when waiting for the lover to make the first move, holding him with her eyes.

'The King assured poor Sunny that Lord High Steward is a purely honorific title but of course it is not. It turns out to be his duty to see to everything that other people are likely to forget. The Earl Marshal is too old to remember a thing, likewise the Archbishop of Canterbury. There will be four hundred peers and peeresses in the Abbey and four thousand ordinary people. So many what ifs. Like what will happen if it rains? Where will everyone's umbrellas go? If someone runs out of the crowd waving a gun? If the red carpets have been eaten by moths when they are taken out of storage? If Astor's *Pall Mall Gazette* digs up some real scandal about the Old Queen? Luckily I am very good at what ifs. Do come in, Robert, and sit down. And it might be wise to shoot the lock on the door, so no one walks in on us. Then pour yourself a drink. No, don't ring for the servant, they will only talk if they find us alone together.

Pour it yourself. A man alone in a room with a woman always causes talk, even though I am known to be above suspicion. Indeed, it is because I am above suspicion, and no breath of scandal ever touches me, that others long to blow me away on winds of disgrace. One must always be on one's guard. But no one ever comes in here. We are quite safe.'

Robert could see he had a choice, either to go, which might seem rather rude — the little light charming voice, with its faint American overtones, seemed in no hurry to fall silent — or to shoot the lock on the door and pour himself a drink.

He did the latter.

'Robert, I would like some whisky too,' so he poured her one — but was not whisky a man's drink? — and added a little water and she came out from behind the desk and looked up at him, and then sank down in one the armchairs. Her dress was very proper, high-necked and long-sleeved, a dark red which seemed to match the chair: its sides rose up on either side to frame her. She looked up at him, and her eyelashes were very dark against the clear pale skin of her cheeks. There was a glittery belt around her tiny waist. She seemed breakable, and very young. She sipped her drink not as a man drinks from a glass, straightforwardly, but with the hand curled round it, as if it were something precious but forbidden to be savoured in secret. Their secret.

'You and Arthur,' she said, 'two men to depend upon! I so love Arthur. He is one of my truest friends. Such a fine disembodied spirit. Pure, logical, like listening to Bach. Those blue eyes, that immense distinction; transcendent, spiritual. But disembodied, Robert. That's the trouble. Disembodied.'

Quite suddenly she sounded immensely sad, and started to sing in her little light voice, but as if she were singing to herself. The voice hardly escaped from the confines of the tall wings of the chair. He had to crane to listen.

I leaned my back against an oak
Thinking it were a trusty tree,
But first he bended and then he broke,
Thus did my love prove false to me . . .

'Oh Consuelo,' said Robert, before he could stop himself, 'what happened?'
She sang:

Oh love is handsome and love is kind,
Bright as a jewel when first it's new,
But love grows old and waxes cold

And fades away like the morning dew.

'That's what happened,' she said. 'Love fades away like morning dew. The thing about you, Robert, is that you're not disembodied. Bright as a jewel! Do you like my hair combs? Lalique; enamel and sapphires. A real find.'

'True, I am not disembodied, very much not so. I am a married man and twice your age. And yes, I like the combs very much. And the belt. Are those sapphires too?'

'Ah yes but very rare, they're pink; shaped like acanthus flowers linking the gold medallions. Fabergé. Sunny gave them to me last time we were in Moscow. They were far too expensive but of course only a tenth of what he spent tiling acres of roof at Blenheim, at my father's expense. I could have bought them myself but it's nice to be given things.' She asked for more whisky. It seemed the least he could give her; he poured her more, a little more than seemed reasonable, and for himself too.

He should not have mentioned the belt. It drew attention to the gold medallions round the waist and the waist was so little. Robert pulled himself together. He was not quite sure what was happening, but he did his best to be businesslike, and remember the purpose of his errand. 'Consuelo, I came to ask you a favour. You very kindly gave me three spare invitations to the Coronation, to sit amongst the peers.' He stayed standing. His instinct was to kneel in supplication in front of her.

'That is so,' she said, 'Arthur Balfour asked me to. Arthur Balfour pares away every nonsense, every folly, to get to the heart of things. But so disembodied.'

'My foolish wife has mislaid them,' said Robert. 'Is it possible for you to give me replacements? I have offered them to the Baums and they are expecting them.'

'Ah yes, the Baums. So very sensible of you. Arthur told me to put them by. How tall are you, Robert?' she asked.

'I am not sure,' he said, 'perhaps six foot and one inch. But the invitations —'

'Arthur Balfour is six foot and two inches, Sunny is five foot and six inches. Why do you call your wife foolish? I think she is a very clever and charming woman with great style and of all the countesses I like her the most.'

'I called her foolish by way of apology for her having mislaid the invitations. In that sense yes, she is foolish. In no other.'

Consuelo stood up and smiled at him. He supposed she was some five foot seven inches, with her straight back and fine neck, and the little waist.

'How many inches do you think my waist is?'

'Really, Consuelo, I have no idea, and I don't think this is a very fitting conversation for us to be having.'

'Why ever not? It is only about feet and inches. See if your hands will meet around my waist.'

If he put his hands around her waist he would embrace her; there was no way he could not. His hands would meet around her waist, he was sure of that. It was smaller than Isobel's: his hands, big and clumsy as they were, would not quite meet around his wife's middle. But did Consuelo want him to kiss her? He could not be sure. He felt like a blundering ass, out of his depth. Women had thrown themselves at him before, and mostly he had repulsed them. Occasionally, not.

'It is very tempting, Consuelo, and I am very honoured, but I think I had better not.'

'Oh dear,' she said, 'I do hope you were not thinking — really I am only interested in measurements. I think you had better go now, Robert.'

She went over to the door and slid back the bolt, seemingly offended.

'The invitations —'

'Your wife has already been in touch with me about them. I am meeting her for lunch at the University Women's Club and I will give them to her then.'

She held the door open for him to go. But as he went she said, 'Do call again and see me, Robert. Sunny is so often away at lunchtimes. And you are so, well, embodied!'

He hastened away, hopelessly confused.

■ ■ ■ ■

APRIL — 1902

■ ■ ■ ■

FRANK'S WOOING OF ADELA

It came to Adela that when she had watched the swans on the moat fight off the ducks, the ducks were like the nuns, with their white wimpled heads and dark bodies, and the swans like princes and princesses. The ducks were vulgar and in the right — why should they not have what others more fortunate had? — the swans elegant and beautiful and in the wrong, given everything and sharing nothing. More and more, she found, she was on the swans' side, and she shocked herself. Perhaps Satan was creeping into her soul: it was possible, she supposed, to be very, very bad and not know it. Why was there no one to talk to about these things? If she tried people looked at her as if she was a little odd. She had no friends. Jenny the housekeeper's daughter Agatha was about Adela's age but curtsied and shrank away from her as if she had the plague. Perhaps people thought misfortune was catching, and if you touched an orphan you would lose your own parents? She missed Ivy. Ivy was only a servant but cheered her up. Ivy was unfinished business: someone with whom she could talk about the past, so at least she had a past; as it was she had somehow sprung fully formed into the world on Christmas Eve, 1901. And Ivy had not even seen fit to come and visit her, too caught up with her new boyfriend. What was it men did to women that made them look so happy and want to brush up against one another all the time? The answer was something very simple, but finding out was like trying to reinvent the universe.

Adela gave up thinking and went back to her book and the story of the Little Mermaid — she had just discovered Hans Christian Andersen — and it made her cry, which was why she had given up reading and gone to watch the swans at war with the ducks. The Little Mermaid loved her prince so much she gave up her tail for legs and whenever she put foot to ground it was like treading on knives. But the love and the sacrifice did her no good at all. What was Mr Andersen trying to say? The prince would always get the princess? The swans stuck to the swans? It was too bad.

When there was a knock at the door and

it was Frank, she was relieved. He was bringing her lime juice, his now customary mid-afternoon offering. His slight nervous tic, which Mrs Kennion attributed to his being, as she put it, 'highly strung', seemed today rather worse than usual. But he smiled affectionately. His pebbly eyes were kind and his smile patient.

'Lime cordial, Miss Adela.'

'That is very kind of you,' she said, 'but you know, Frank, I am becoming quite grown-up, and if you need to talk perhaps we should do so not in my bedroom, but in the library?'

'You don't know how much of a child you still are,' he said. Adela was suddenly put in mind of how the snake charmed Eve into eating the apple. She wondered if the sin lay more in Eve eating the apple in the first place or in tempting Adam? Couldn't Adam take the blame for his own sin? Her father had been rather like that with her mother. If he forgot his prayer book when he left for church, the fault lay not in his own forgetfulness, but in some other random fact: Elise had not been quick enough bringing his socks, or Ivy had not sewed on a button and so put the prayer book out of his mind, or she, Adela, had made him angry with her stupidity. But what was Frank saying, in his ironed-out, flat voice?

'But you will grow up soon enough and I am happy to wait for you.' Perhaps Frank was a serpent, slithering over grass? Twitch, twitch, went the muscle at the side of his mouth, reaching for his ear. Poor man. Mrs Kennion said he had been lured away from true belief by false gods, though apparently you could not exactly call the Buddha a god, merely a great preacher, so it was excusable. Mrs Kennion thought the world of Frank, and said Theosophy was only a stage he was passing through.

'But very well, we'll go and talk in the library,' Frank agreed and carried her drink as they walked together down the long stone corridor towards the library. She tried not to brush against him, but his arm always seemed to be in the way of hers. Their hands had touched once, reaching for the pepper pot at the Bishop's table, and then his skin had felt cold and hard; like marble she had thought then. Now she saw it differently; it was like snakeskin, rough if you stroked it one way, smooth and slippery if you stroked it another. She was probably just stroking the wrong way.

When you got used to the splendours of the Palace dining table the conversation was so polite and dull — about the correct readings and the great Cranmer and how the creation of the Local Education Authorities would affect Church schools — she almost missed her father's rantings. There was nothing to do but eat. Once she'd seen Frank changing place cards so as to sit next to her, and she was pleased, because he was only twice her age and not three or four times, as everyone else seemed to be. But then he only wanted to talk about the Oneness, Inner Peace and meditation, which sounded to her pretty much like staring into space and falling asleep, which she'd been doing a lot since her parents died anyway. He was being just as boring as anyone else. On the other hand what was wrong with people being boring? It was meant to be enough for them to be good, and Frank was certainly good, with his patient smile and kindly bearing, as if nobody else had reached his spiritual plane, or ever would. He didn't drink wine or touch meat. He thought she, Adela, was an angel, which was flattering, but also meant that he somehow owned her or thought he did.

'You're quite the little bookworm,' he said to her, as they turned into the sepulchral gloom of the library. 'I admire the way you make the most of your time.'

'My choice of book is quite limited, I'm

sorry to say,' she said. 'There's a review in *The Times* — they pile up here in the library — about a book by this woman called Elinor Glyn called *The Visits of Elizabeth,* which I would so love to read.'

'O dear me, no!' said Frank, seemingly alarmed. 'That's not the kind of book it will do you any good to read. It's salacious and better not written.'

'I can only tell that by reading it,' she said.

'It's not the kind of thing a man wants his wife and the mother of his children to read.'

'Yes, but I'm not your wife or the mother of your children,' said Adela. One of the advantages of being worshipped by a man, it seemed, was that you could be rude to him and he did not notice. Or perhaps it was that they didn't listen to a word you said, being so full of admiration at the way you said it. 'I want to know what men think they have a right to know and women have to be protected from.'

'Knowledge comes in its own time,' he said. It was the kind of thing he did say, along with 'All is illusion', which always seemed to her a not very cheerful thing to have to listen to.

'I expect you are right,' she said, to which he replied, 'I know I am right.'

Adela sat down at one of the reading

302

tables and he sat beside her and not, as she would have expected, opposite her. He took her hand. Her instinct was to snatch it back but she let it lie there. Snakeskin, she reminded herself. Stroke it the right way. He was quite pink in the face and his high wing collar cut into his neck. It looked very uncomfortable.

'Your glasses are all misty,' she said. 'Shall I clean them for you?'

He took them off and handed them to her. He looked much better without them; his eyes lost their pebbly look. She used some of the soft silk of her sleeve to rub them with.

'You are so sweet,' he said. 'Little Adela.'

He told her he had asked the Bishop's permission to speak to her and had received it, and Mrs Kennion's too. In a month or two, he said, Adela was going to join the cloistered life and it was a noble ambition. But she was without parental or family guidance and she was very young.

'Do try and be precise, Frank,' said Adela. She wondered where she found the temerity to speak to him in the way she did. For some reason he made her cross. He was sneaky, like a snake. 'It's not cloistered. Little Sisters of Bethany is a teaching order. I will be out in the world all the time.'

'But you will still be able to be a Bride of Christ,' he said. 'To renounce the flesh is a very big decision for a young girl to make. You are a little young to make it, or to understand what you are doing.'

'If I could read *The Visits of Elizabeth,*' she said, 'I might understand it a little more. And I don't have a great deal of choice in the matter. I have to go somewhere. I can't remain a charge on the Bishop's goodwill for ever. My family show no sign of wishing to claim me. What do you suggest?'

'Marry me,' he said. She snatched her hand away.

'No, hear me out.' His glasses were misting up again. She did not want to go through life cleaning them up.

'I have finished my time here,' he said. 'Too right I have. In May I'm sailing for Western Australia. We are a Dominion now: we can rule ourselves. A new bonzer land to build, a land of the future. Europe's old, finished. Landscapes to paint, wider and larger and grander than you can believe. Edge of the old black stump, I'll give you that, but shapes and colours to entrance your mind. And opportunities. My uncle's died: I have the land, I have the power, I have the wealth. I'll go in for oats. Low-acidity soil, great market potential. Breed horses too, perhaps. We have the best in the world. The home country spent one hundred thousand pounds on nags during the war, and as long as there's people there'll be wars. But most of all I'll have you. I'm bringing back the real prize from the old world, the most beautiful woman ever born, that's you, Adela, I knew from the moment I set eyes on you in that carriage. The Divine Essence put you in my way, sent smoke and flames to guide me, showed you to me in that mirror; they had chosen you as mine. They have a plan for us.'

He wanted to start an industrial school for the abos in Murchison, teach them proper painting, get them trained in art as well as mining; they loved caves but had to learn to gaze at the stars. 'People say they're not human, from another planet, but they're just like us, just haven't yet caught up with us, that's all. You'll come to love them, as I do.'

There was no stopping him. He was like her father, only he was unblinking, and staring into her eyes; his face was too near to hers. She thought he did not brush his teeth enough. His breath was not very nice, only it would be impolite to turn her head away. He said there was leprosy, only no one admitted it, he meant to start a colony.

'Leprosy?' she asked, alarmed. 'Isn't that when your fingers and toes fall off?'

He said he'd keep her well away from it, he worshipped her, every bit of her, even her little toes, when they were married he would sleep with them in his mouth. She thought she had misheard him, unless this was the great secret of married life. She could imagine Rumpelstiltskin behaving like that, creeping up on you and grabbing your feet. But hadn't Frank said 'when' not 'if' they were married? He hadn't yet given her a chance to say no. He was overwhelming her with words, as her father had done, only instead of saying she was stupid and plain he seemed to think she had secret powers and was beautiful.

'I need you, Adela. You are *sattvika:* pure, so beautiful, from another, higher world. You are mine to save, mine to protect. My karma.'

Now he was saying he'd heard Henry S. Alcott speak in Melbourne when he was a boy: he'd had a vision, the wisdom of the Buddha must combine with the good oil of the Christians: all must stand under one umbrella of faith: universal brotherhood, the transmigration of souls made more sense than heaven, where all one did was stand about and sing. Where was the striving, the self-improvement in that? Adela could do the same work as the Little Sisters of Bethany in a new land where it never rained, only a hundred times more usefully. She could make a difference.

'You must be the bride of a flesh-and-blood man, Adela, not a statue on a cross.' Hadn't Ivy said something like that once? 'Christ, down the plughole, a splendid girl like you?' It burst out of him. Then, reverting to the calmer language of the Palace, 'Choose life itself, my darling, and not a dull safe shadow of it. I am here to teach and lead you. Choose life with me.'

It was quite a speech. He had prepared it but passion came breaking through, so he sounded quite mad. He was trembling. Adela leant forward and took off his glasses: so misty she thought he could barely see out of them, cleaned them and returned them. His hands were plump and white, and twice the size of her own.

'Aren't there crocodiles?' she asked. She was half joking, bathos after so much fine speaking, but he did not understand jokes.

'There are a few,' he said. 'A few salt-water bastards around the mouth of the Ashburton river but that's further north.'

Then he said, 'How about it, my splendid bush girl, how about it?' and she laughed and saw she could do the laughing for both of them, just by listening to him.

Adela tried to think, but he had exhausted her with words. She longed to travel, to see the kangaroos and the koala bears for herself. The convent had seemed agreeable enough when she had been half starved in Yatbury: inevitable for her when she discovered the curse of womanhood; now she was not so sure. The nuns were such a dowdy lot, ducks not swans. Frank might be peculiar but Australia would be an adventure. There were lots of black swans near where he lived up a river he called a creek. Perhaps she could train them to come when a bell was rung.

'But I don't love you,' she said. Was this an obstacle?

'Not to worry,' he said. 'A wife comes to love her husband if she's young enough. I'm a decent man, Adela. I'll love you as a husband should. My bloody oath! We have a house waiting for us, the white ants have been at it but we'll soon get rid of the bastards. You'll have to train the servants, but the native women aren't too bad as nursemaids. A bit of white blood in them and they're fine.'

Adela had a vision of a lot of little children with pudgy hands and thick glasses running round her feet, and big white ants trying to eat her toes. She longed to get back to the story of the Little Mermaid, but Frank was squashing her fingers, breathing into her eyes. There was dandruff on his coat collar. There was no stopping him.

'We could build a little white temple down in the township, bring Theosophy to the natives. The Dreamtime and Nirvana are pretty much the same. Have you heard of Annie Besant?'

She shook her head.

'I'll teach you.'

His finger moved up and down on her wrist. There was a horrible fascination in it. If he talked for long enough she would do whatever he said, just to stop him.

'The thing to do with the natives is never let them taste alcohol. Their metabolism won't stand it. Their marital goings-on can seem strange when you're fresh from the homeland, but you'll soon get used to it. The thing we have to do is to set them an example of married love.' He squeezed her small hand more. 'Princess!' he said. 'Princess! My Eostre!'

'Who?' she asked.

'The Saxon Goddess of the Spring. In hermetic lore the Queen of Creation. All bursting forth in abundance.'

'Oh,' she said.

'What a hot little paw you have,' he remarked.

'Because you're holding my hand so tightly,' she said. He loosened it a little. She felt grateful.

'I shouldn't have looked in the mirror,' he said, 'but I did. I can't say I'm sorry because I'm not, my bloody oath! But we'll hit it off, I'm sure enough of that. We'll make a fine pair, the two of us. I'm not bad looking either, I can say that for myself. Your birthday is on the 21st of May.'

'How do you know that?'

'I looked it up in the parish records,' he said, as if it was the most obvious thing in the world. She supposed it was. He knew everything about her. When he saw her naked in the mirror ownership of her had passed to him. 'It's better for us to wait until you're seventeen, otherwise there's probably the matter of permission from a guardian, and your uncle Dilberne doesn't seem too good at acknowledging that's what he is.'

Adela felt a pang of self-pity. Unwanted, rejected, orphaned, not good enough. At least Frank wanted her, and seemed to want her badly. She must find out more about Eostre.

'So that's settled. The *Cuzco* sails from

Tilbury for Sydney on Monday the 25th of May. Stops off at Fremantle with the mail, and drops us off too. All fixed. We'll be married on Friday 22nd of May in the Cathedral. The Bishop has space at one o'clock. He himself will give you away, the Canon will do the service. Everyone wishes you well! It's all arranged, my darling. You'll find your future husband quite a man for detail! We will have a shipboard honeymoon. Good seas that time of year till we get to the Cape, we'll be fine. You'll have to wear a black dress for the ceremony, of course, because of your parents, but it's perfectly proper to have a white veil. I consulted Mrs Kennion on the point. I so long to see my little girl in a white veil!'

'But I don't want to miss the Coronation,' she said. It was all she could think of to say. Perhaps she could run away before the time came. But where? How? She'd had a vague feeling that she could run away with Frank if needs must, but now it was Frank she must run away from. If she could.

'You will be *my* Queen Consort,' he said. 'Isn't that enough for you?'

'I want a wedding present from you,' she said. '*The Visits of Elizabeth* by Elinor Glyn.'

He was silent for a moment. He looked at her with eyes that were dewy and gleaming and happy. He bent his head and pressed his lips to hers and then forced a little edge of tongue in between her lips. It was totally disgusting. She tried not to show it.

'Beaut!' he said, satisfied. 'Dinkum! *The Visits of Elizabeth* shall be our own. We'll give it a read and then go to it hammer and tongs and pray for forgiveness later. You'll know what it's all about by then. Too right.'

'But what is it all about?' she entreated. 'Tell me!'

'Not yet, not yet. It's a surprise,' he said, 'a great big, big, wonderful surprise, my darling!'

She rose to her feet, smoothed down her black dress and went back to her room, while he gazed after her with infinite joy. What fate offered you on a plate, she thought, it was rude to your Maker to reject. For many years she had let others make decisions on what she ate, wore, thought, felt, said — now she could decide for herself. She might have decided on something completely awful but it was her decision to make. And she longed to see a kangaroo. All the same when she went to bed she cried and cried, she was not sure why, but at least orphans were meant to cry and she finally had. But Mrs Kennion too had let her down, handing her to Frank on

a plate. Everyone just wanted to be rid of
her.

IVY AND FRANK AT DOREEN'S

Ivy had left a note at the market stall for her mother to pick up when she took over on Saturday, and on the Monday she and George called by at Doreen's cottage. The thatch needed money spending on it, and her precious prints — Goliath and the Lady of Shallot and Helen of Troy and some sweet little kittens and even sweeter rosy children in a Pears soap advertisement — were all looking rather the worse for wear, what with the damp and water actually coming through the kitchen ceiling. Ivy felt bad about that. She had given most of the parish money to George when it should have gone to her mother.

Doreen said as much. George said,

'But what about your fancy man on the Parish Council, Doreen? Fine figure of a woman like you. He should make an honest woman of you; he's the one to mend your roof.'

'No one knows about that,' she said. 'What have you been saying, our Ivy?'

'Everyone knows,' said George, 'or will soon.'

After that Doreen behaved. She liked George, with his jolly smile and dancing eyes, and his appreciation of a woman's worth. If it wasn't for Ivy she'd be after him herself.

She'd seen Jenny at the market on Saturday, she said, they'd even had a cup of tea together. She'd brought the subject round to Adela. Jenny said the girl spent most of her time looking at the swans on the moat. Yes, she'd been given the best room in the Palace, first floor just to the left of the portcullis.

'It was her,' said Ivy. 'I told you it was her I saw in the window!'

'All in the mind,' said George, shutting her up. He couldn't bear to be wrong, even in retrospect. 'Let your mother get on!'

It seemed the lock on the door was faulty; had quite rusted away with age. Everything in the Palace was beginning to show its age. The door seemed locked but the floor wasn't level so its tendency was to stand ajar. Jenny had been at the market buying yet more clothes for Adela. Everything in black, of course, but Jenny had drawn the

315

line at crape, so scratchy, she went for a good bombazine, although it was twice the price. Crape was far too dismal for someone so young. Adela was bursting out of everything. She was in one of those growing spurts girls sometimes go through. Mind you, she'd just come on for the first time. Poor little thing, she had been quite shocked. Her daughter Agnes had done the same, but she'd warned Agnes what was going to happen to her, she didn't care what people said. Ignorance might be bliss but it was still a shock to a growing girl. Adela had quite a bosom now. A few months and she'd turned from a miserable little waif into a real beauty. She was reading her way through the library, Jenny said, not that she'd find much to interest her there. It seemed a real waste to shut her up in a convent for the rest of her life. Jenny didn't understand the way her family had just abandoned her. The wrong side of some family feud, it seemed, on the father's side; something religious on the mother's. There was a rumour that she was an actual Princess, which Agnes believed, but was probably a lot of stuff and nonsense, only they had put her in the best bedroom and she was allowed to dine at the Bishop's table. She knew which knife and spoon to pick up which was more than a lot of the old codgers knew these days. She had a really good appetite, and if a footman passed a dish before her eyes she could be relied upon to eat some, even spinach. She had a beau already, Mrs Kennion's nephew Frank, who had come into a fortune and was off to Australia and had been alone in the library with her for at least half an hour without a chaperone, but it wouldn't come to anything: a girl like Adela wouldn't look twice at someone like Frank Overshaw. He might be rich but he had pebble glasses and was very plain. His socks were smelly and the laundry girls would only go near them with tongs.

'Jenny certainly talked a lot,' said Ivy.

'People confide in me,' said Doreen. 'I have that kind of face.'

'I think we know all we need to know,' said George. He seemed very happy. He handed over a wodge of fivers to Doreen and said, 'That's for the roof, Doreen. Just don't let Fancyman get away with it. He's a churchwarden at St Bart's. I saw the way he looked at you at the funeral. Lock the back door against him until he comes to heel. He will.'

There was something about a roll of banknotes when a man takes them from a bulging wallet and peels them off one by one and hands them over, even though you'd handed him the notes in the first place. It made him seem generous and you feel grateful. Ivy felt quite jealous. But it was probably only about forty pounds in all, enough for her mother to get the roof ridge done, at any rate, and the kitchen roof mended and even a paraffin stove to dry the place out and rescue the prints, but the whole roof would be more like eighty pounds.

'Ooh, you're such a one, George!' said Doreen. 'If only all of my gentlemen were as generous as you!'

Ivy asked her mother if she still had the red velvet dress she'd taken from the Rectory the day before it burned down and Doreen said yes she had. Ivy asked her to take it out and Ivy shook it out, and all admired it. It was a quality dress.

George said they didn't want to miss the bus to Yatbury, they should get back to Bath as soon as they could. He wanted to make a move tomorrow.

'More haste, less speed,' said Ivy and asked her mother for a pair of scissors and a needle and matching thread. George asked what on earth was she up to.

'If a girl's been wearing black for the past few months,' said Ivy, 'she'll be glad to see a

318

bit of colour, and there are a few seams I'm going to let out.'

'I follow your reasoning,' said George. 'I'll say this for you. You're not slow. We'll show her a new world, a new life. We'll be doing her a favour. She was light as a feather when I took her through the flames. A child. A different kettle of fish now, to all accounts.'

'Don't get any ideas,' warned Ivy.

'Aren't I married to you, Ivy, queen of my heart?'

'Not yet you aren't, George. *Georgie Porgie pudding and pie, kissed the girls and made them cry.* Go down to the cowshed and get the envelope I left hidden in the cow stall while I do this.'

'Why?' asked George. 'Nothing we can do about those: they'd bar the Abbey door to the likes of us. They're just fancy tickets. Unless you can sell them in the market, Mother?'

'Can't do any harm,' said Doreen. 'Someone might want to frame them, hang them on the wall. Curiosities.'

'I think Adela ought to have them,' said Ivy. 'They're rightfully hers.'

'Yes, but she's rightfully ours,' said George.

'Supposing it's true and she is a princess, then the Abbey's where she ought to be. In

319

Westminster Abbey on the 26th June with her own kind.'

'Not if she's foreign, she's not,' said George. 'Supposing we don't hurry up and she sails off to Australia or goes into a nunnery, and we lose her?'

Ivy sewed more quickly, while her mother put on the kettle to steam the fabric and bring up the pile where it had been mistreated. All agreed Adela would look a picture in it on a platform, with its trailing ribbons and fine pink lace. George went off to fetch the invitations. They left the envelope with Doreen for safe keeping and caught the bus back to Bath.

A LATE BREAKFAST

'For heaven's sake,' said his Lordship. 'First it's sign papers so she can go into a convent, now it's notification that she means to get married. Can't the girl make up her mind?'

'Robert,' said Isobel, reproachfully, 'you are the girl's uncle. We need at least to take an interest.'

'You've changed your tune,' said Robert. 'But you are looking particularly pretty this morning.' So she was: Spring sun was shining in the tall windows of Belgrave Square, and catching the dust motes in the air. His wife's fair hair was caught up and falling in tendrils from the top of her head. She was wearing a yellow silk tea-gown with a splodge of bright red flowers all over it, and her eyes wide and trusting. She was being very nice to him, these days, summoning him out of his dressing room when he thought he least deserved it, being a little drunk or noisy, and welcoming him into her bed just the same. He'd hardly given the matter of Consuelo a thought, what with one thing and another. He was busy. Had he been more certain of his reception, or younger, or had more time on his hands, or had a less satisfactory wife, he might well have pursued the matter of Consuelo, or at least slipped by Sunny's office in Buck House one lunchtime just to see what would happen next, but he had not. So far.

There was the problem of the two hundred cavalry horses left in Natal. A decision was needed: a sea voyage was hard on them: these great big sturdy, round-hipped, magnificent chargers, who could carry nineteen stone on their backs, and had breeding and pluck enough at the end of a long day to charge a retreating enemy and cut him to pieces, suffered dreadfully from seasickness and exhaustion. Up to four percent could be lost on the voyage. Were they to be shipped home, and replaced by the little Cape horses, plentiful and cheap, the skinny little lean-shanked ill-fed things the Boers got about on, or sent off to India where the cavalry was short of them, or mercifully left where they were by a grateful nation? But two hundred horses at £20 a head, less £160 was £3,840, multiplied by however much a change of policy would lead to —

and now this troublesome niece he had never met or wanted to who couldn't make up her mind whether to marry or go into a nunnery — what did he keep Baum for, what was his wife for, but to look after this kind of thing?

Two letters had come in the same post. A shortage of servants was all very well, and offered privacy, but he'd had to pick them up himself from the hall floor and bring them to the breakfast table — it simply didn't occur to Isobel to do it — and use an ordinary and rather buttery knife to open them. He could hardly appear in the House with a smeary coat, and would have to change, and where was his valet?

One letter was from Mrs Kennion in Wells asking for his approval to the marriage of Adela to a relative of her own, one Frank Overshaw, a young man of twenty-nine, of good character, well able to provide for a wife, being the owner of a large estate in Western Australia, and indubitably fond of Adela. The feeling between them seemed to be reciprocal. The Kennions had apparently become very attached to Adela, and felt confident that it was a good and sensible match and the girl was mature enough to know her own mind. It was as well, as they were sure his Lordship would agree, that if she was in the least unsure of her vocation marriage was a preferable choice for a girl of seventeen than to enter a convent. If his Lordship would take the opportunity to visit the girl and her fiancé they would be most pleased to receive him: they were sure Adela would welcome the chance to become acquainted with her most distinguished family.

His Lordship, snorting, had read the letter aloud to his wife.

'I daresay she would,' he said. 'But I'm afraid her father put paid to that. She must get on with her own life. She will be seventeen, and can surely choose for herself.'

His brother Edwin kept rising from his grave, demanding his attention. Perhaps he should have gone to his funeral, laid him to rest, but if you were banned from that funeral in a spirit of enmity, the estrangement could only remain permanent. Isobel seemed not to understand.

'But Robert,' Isobel said, 'she is so very young. Her parents have so recently passed away. She may be making a dreadful mistake. You can always run away from a convent — well, it has been known — but you cannot run away from a marriage. And Australia is so far!'

Robert said nothing. He opened the letter

from Baum. Again, the knife was buttery, what was he meant to do? Open it with his teeth? Baum said there seemed to be no relatives on the mother's side wealthy enough, and certainly not young enough, to take the girl on; the facts of her right to the title of Princess were established and there was also talk of an inheritance which might have come into play on her mother's death, property in Vienna now beginning to fetch in a good income as rural land became city land. Robert thought he would call by Baum's office when — when! — he had a moment to suggest that perhaps the lawyer didn't hurry his investigations until Adela was safely married and passed into her husband's legal care.

At least if the girl wasn't a postulant a convent wouldn't get its hands on her inheritance: better that it should come the husband's way. He pushed the letter to one side, as if casually, and Isobel did not enquire as to its contents.

'She is after all a Dilberne,' Isobel was saying. 'The Bishop's wife will probably see tea and sandwiches as a fitting wedding feast, and think any old dress will do for the bride. It simply will not.'

'The Bishop took her in, let the Bishop be responsible,' he said. 'Kennion is an ass but

I daresay one can accept his advice on the girl when it comes to matters of matrimony. It seems to boil down to whether Kennion or I am the busiest, and I would claim that distinction. Mind you, he is arguing with the Court of Complaints about supporting the Queen at the Coronation, which is Bath and Wells's prerogative. Consuelo reports Alexandra as saying she is healthy enough, and since Kennion needs to lead the King in his responses, let him worry more about learning his lines properly. She doesn't need supporting, she says, unlike her mother-in-law Victoria at that bodge of a coronation, weighed down by the weight of her own crown — let the Bishop of Bath and Wells concentrate on poor old Temple of Canterbury, who is eighty at least, and support him when he stumbles, as he is bound to. And more, she wishes the Bishop to concentrate on singing the litany briskly; the litany being the most tedious part of the ceremony for everyone. Previous bishops of Bath and Wells, Alexandra points out, have made terrible mistakes in coronations. Everyone's getting very nervous,' Robert said, 'with only eight weeks or so to go.'

At least he was laughing. But why Consuelo again? If her, Isobel's, suspicions were unfounded, why did Robert feel the constant need to mention her? The sun seemed to go in: the dust motes to stop dancing.

Things had been going so well: such a pleasant visit from Minnie and Rosina. She was more than happy that Minnie was with child, and happy that Rosina's temper seemed so much improved, so that she almost seemed an ordinarily loving daughter — why did her own peace of mind have to be so threatened by this chit of a girl, this lively little Duchess half her age? Half her age — perhaps this was the crux of the matter? The black fog was closing in again.

'I wish you knew more about horses, my dear,' Robert was saying.

'Horses?' Isobel enquired, mystified. She found the beasts that so preoccupied her husband rather repellent, unruly and unpredictable creatures, and had always been relieved that neither of her children took an interest in them. Arthur preferred his engines, Rosina her books, Minnie looked good on horseback, but was beginning to show and must put it off for the time being. It struck her as outrageous that Robert seemed more preoccupied with the fate of the English cavalry horses stranded in South Africa than with his own family.

'Forget horses, my dear,' she said. 'The people will look very oddly at you if you let your own orphaned niece marry in haste and with no proper ceremony. It will do you no good in the public estimation.'

He looked at her rather coldly, she thought, but at least said, 'Do what you want about it, pay the Bishop a call, inspect this gift horse of a husband in his mouth to see the state of his teeth, just do me the favour of not bringing the girl home.'

'Her name is Adela,' said Isobel, 'and her blood runs in your veins.'

Love nests, she decided, could be uncomfortable after a while: if there were dust motes in the air it was because there was too much dust about: she would ask Minnie and Rosina to come up to Belgrave Square and keep her company, and bring servants with them. Now Minnie was pregnant it was probably safest to keep her away from Arthur's bed — she had no doubt he was an ardent lover — and she would have Rosina to keep her company, and really she did not mind the parrot too much; the creature could be really quite amusing. Rosina could bring it with her if she insisted.

Robert left the breakfast table and went up to his room to try and find a new collar and for lack of a valet scattered garments far and wide. Some days one felt younger than others. Today was one of those days when Spring was in the air and young lads and lasses went a-courting, but he was not a young lad, he was a peer of the realm and had responsibilities. But affairs of State still mattered, and perhaps he would call by Sunny's rooms at lunchtime and if Consuelo was there she might talk to him about horses. Her father was a horse breeder, after all, though she probably knew more about thoroughbreds than the war horses which now preoccupied him, be they cavalry, gun, artillery or humble mules.

On the way out he called out to Isobel to check that she had put the invitations to the Baums in the post. She came out of the breakfast room to say she had yet to have lunch with Consuelo to get replacements, but was doing so in a couple of days; there was lots of time. Also she needed to discuss with Consuelo who was to process with whom on the 26th in Minnie's absence. She would arrange a visit to the Bishop's Palace to see Adela after that. He must remember that she too was busy.

THE ABDUCTION OF ADELA

Now they knew where her room was, Adela's rescue was simple enough. Ivy wore a black servant's dress and George wore a flat cap and a handyman's leather apron and looked like someone on his way to fix the pipes. The porter's lodge on the drawbridge was unmanned. No one challenged them. A few prelates wandered the corridors with prayer books and papers; a few servants bustled around with trays of food but seemed to take strangers in their stride. When guests came to stay they brought their servants with them. Adela's room was easy enough to find, and she was inside it when they pushed the door open. It was almost too easy. George said later it was as if God had been watching over them.

Adela lay on the great bed reading; her fair hair startling against the red velvet of the bed cover and her black dress. George, remembering the child he had carried through the flames, was shaken by the difference in her.

'My,' said Ivy, 'you have grown up.'

Adela, startled, put down her book and hurled herself towards Ivy, almost knocking her down. 'Oh Ivy, Ivy,' Adela cried. 'Why have you been so long? Have you come to take me away? Where are we going?'

George saw to the door, jamming the lock with the end of the window pole while Ivy helped Adela off with her black dress and put on the red one, made her take down her hair and wrapped her in a pale-blue serge coat. George tried not to look. Ivy said she was coming with her and her new husband George, they had a plan, they were to live in Bath. George was the one who had saved her from the fire and did Adela recognize him? Adela blushed almost the colour of her dress and said yes, she did.

'Saved you once,' George said, 'I'll save you again,' and Ivy wondered quite what she had let the girl in for, but it was done now. What would be, would be.

Adela wanted to leave a note but George stopped her. Ivy wanted her to take her few belongings but Adela refused, saying that would be stealing. Nothing was hers, everything was borrowed. The three of them walked out boldly, Adela with her head held high, her hair loose, her clothing bright, looking like someone no one had ever seen before but would want to see again, and still no one challenged them.

George said she had a fine future on the stage, she was a born actress and Adela blushed again. On the way home on the bus she went on about how she didn't want to be married and go to Australia, but it had suddenly seemed better than being a nun, and how then it seemed too late to stop it, and she felt like a rabbit being hypnotized by a snake. Ivy felt better about it all. It was only a few weeks until Adela's birthday and no one would then be able to say she had been coerced into running away, but had gone of her own free will.

The landlady had kicked up a fuss and said she wasn't having an extra, a girl who for all anyone knew was no better than she should be, in a room for two, and George forked out for an extra room, without too much argument. They had fish and chips in the front-floor back.

'Ivy,' Adela said, 'I'm so much older now. Please tell. What does "no better than she ought to be" mean? Is that me now?'

'Not yet,' said George, 'not yet. We'll get too good a price for you as you are.'

Adela looked puzzled.

He was joking, of course, about something Adela didn't understand but Ivy did. Later that night Ivy found the bottle of chloroform and the gauze pads in the pocket of the coat George had worn on the bus, and worried. But he'd never have dared to have used it, surely. It might have ended up in the law courts and a really heavy sentence. They tried to be really quiet that night, because of Adela in the next room.

NEW HORIZONS

A drop of cerulean blue dripped from the end of Minnie's brush, and she bent down to mop it up with her turpentine-soaked rag. Mr Neville the butler, who had come all the way up to the East Wing attic with Minnie's mid-morning beef tea, intervened.

'Let me call a servant to do that, Miss Minnie,' said Mr Neville. Minnie ignored him and only succeeded in leaving a nasty smear of blue on the polished floor. He raised his eyebrows slightly as he went away. Rosina, who had settled in the studio to watch Minnie paint, which Minnie rather wished she wouldn't, said, 'Now you've annoyed Mr Neville. You really need to give the servants work to do, Minnie, otherwise they get nervous in case they lose their jobs. They're worried enough that the parents have so few looking after them in Belgrave Square. Supposing we learned to live without them? Then what would they do for employment? And are you sure the smell of oil paint isn't bad for an unborn baby?'

'Quite sure,' said Minnie.

'Is that a fur waistcoat you're wearing? I know it's draughty up here, but I hope not. An animal has had to die to keep you warm. I don't approve of the infliction of pain on any sentient being, man or beast. George Bernard Shaw is of the same opinion. Is it mink?'

'It is beaver, Rosina,' said Minnie, 'and my mother gave it to me to keep me warm.'

'You should be content with wool,' said Rosina. 'That at least is only theft, not murder. The sheep goes on living.'

Minnie tried to ignore her and went on painting. It was a landscape: the long and majestic avenue of oaks which lined the quarter-mile drive from the gate to the front steps of Dilberne Court. It was what she could see from her window.

'But Minnie,' said Rosina, 'trees aren't blue in the first place, but green, and the oaks are still not in leaf so why are you painting in blue leaves that aren't even there? Do you know better than Nature?'

'Rosina,' said Minnie, 'I am an artist, not a copyist. Try and understand. I paint a mixture of what I see with my eyes and the truth of what I see in my head.'

'But we are in a new century, Minnie. I think a photograph will always be more truthful than a painting, and certainly take less time to produce. Could you not be a photographer? It would be less messy.'

Minnie put down her paintbrush and asked if Rosina was setting out to annoy, and Rosina stopped pouting and laughed and said yes, she supposed she was, it was a habit of which she was trying to cure herself, and apologized. She had toiled all the way up to the attic to tell Minnie that they had both been summoned to attend the Countess in Belgrave Square that very day, without so much as a by-your-leave. She, Rosina, was to abandon her book just as she was getting to the index, and Minnie was to abandon Arthur's bed not to mention her easel, and neither had any choice in the matter, any more than Minnie had a choice as to what colour the nursery was to be painted, or which local wet-nurse was to be engaged. Moreover they were to go by carriage, not train, because Minnie would not want to expose herself to the public gaze.

'The public is welcome to gaze on me as much as they want,' Minnie said. 'I am having a baby, and proud of it. Why should I pretend I'm not?'

'Because this is England and not Chicago. It's embarrassing for everyone. A public and shameless declaration of what you have been up to in bed.'

She had married into a family of aliens who pretended no one had sex, a race who never acknowledged weakness, physical or emotional, who did not weep or get drunk at funerals, or run to the side of orphaned family members, or countenance pain if they fell off a horse and broke an arm, but just remounted and got on again. They demanded servitude and got it. Insisted on inequality and were not defied. She was going to give birth to another one. Well, they ran a mighty empire. It could be worse.

Arthur was in Coventry for the week, discussing the possibility of a motorized landau to follow the coaches at the Coronation. Daimler were to provide a twenty-two-horsepower four-cylinder vehicle, which could reach forty-five miles an hour if it had to, which on this occasion it certainly wouldn't, could be armour plated if assassination was feared, and was fairly impressive. Arthur, whose very presence carried an implicit promise of increased Royal patronage, was trying to persuade Daimlers to incorporate the Arnold Jehu's new electric ignition system into their future designs.

Daimler, he was able to argue, was regrettably German in its roots; English input would do much to help the firm's credibility in the British market. It was working. He was turning into a business man as well as an engineer. Minnie, who was developing quite an interest in the way the automobile trade worked — it was not so different from selling hogs, after all, and at least machines did not squeal when slaughtered — had suggested to Arthur this particular route to Daimler's essentially Prussian heart, and it had worked. She would be happy enough to spend the week in London. She looked forward to another meeting of the I.D.K. and another lively argument between the rationalists and the idealists.

Rosina cheered up. In London, Minnie reminded her, she would be able to pay the £3 membership and work in the peace of the London Library, with access to far more books than she could find in the Boots Booklovers' Library in Brighton. And even run into her literary hero George Bernard Shaw writing some play that went on for ever about the meaning of everything.

'You mean,' said Rosina, 'that I might find some vegetarian husband there. I am thirty-three years old. I was born to be an old maid. Too late.'

'Thirty-three's nothing at all. George Eliot married when she was sixty. She was a writer.'

Rosina laughed. 'That is no comfort, Minnie. She was a scandalous woman and a freak and plain as a pikestaff, and the man she married killed himself almost at once. You know even our little cousin Adela, not yet seventeen, her parents scarcely cold in the grave, is engaged to be married to a rich colonial farmer twice her age? They are to be married any minute and leave at once for Australia.'

'I thought she was going to be a nun,' said Minnie. 'But perhaps she decided any man was better than no man at all. I certainly would have. This is the first I've heard of it. I suppose the news came through the shipping clerk to some hotel concierge to the servants in Belgrave Square through Mrs Flowers at the local telephone exchange, and by-passed the family altogether.'

'Reginald told me,' said Rosina. 'Mother didn't even bother to mention it. More evidence of my failure in the marriage market, I suppose. Reginald also told me she's actually a princess of the Gotha-Zwiebrücken-Saxony line.'

'But that's rather useful,' said Minnie. 'She could replace me as Isobel's partner walking up the aisle in the Abbey on the 26th. If she hasn't already been whisked off to be the only princess in Australia. She might have to stay by Royal Command. She may not be of the direct Dilberne line, being daughter of a fourth son, but any connection on the Gotha side might count. Imagine if she was allowed six inches of ermine trim, twice as wide as a countess's!'

'Ah, Minnie,' cried Rosina, 'you really have become one of us. I am quite cheered up and Mama says I can take my parrot. She must be in a good mood.'

ISOBEL AND CONSUELO
SEEK COMMON CAUSE

Isobel and Consuelo, Duchess of Marlborough took tea in the University Club for Ladies near Hanover Square. They were not members by right, neither having a university degree, but Consuelo's name opened doors anywhere. They chose the Club because home was never free from servants' gossip, the maître d'hôtel of any fashionable meeting place was likely to be in the pay of gossip columnists, but here they would be spared tittle-tattle, and two ladies lunching alone together would not draw attention, and cause comment. It was dowdy but they could put up with that. The food was a rather different matter. They ordered a cream tea but when eventually it came the scones were heavy and solid and Consuelo claimed she could taste gelatine in the unnaturally stiff whipped cream and the sour tang of boric acid in the raspberry jam. It was tea-time, not lunch, because Consuelo said most of her lunchtimes were taken up.

'These blue-stockings always pay more attention to their minds than their appetites,' observed Consuelo, and not in the normal, well-modulated, low-pitched voice of the English aristocracy, but for once, in her irritation, allowing its original rasping, American twang to show through. It must have been years, thought Isobel, since the daughter of Vanderbilt the railway king had let food pass her lips that had not been created by the finest cooks in the world. No doubt it was a shock. Isobel herself, though with a father wealthy enough, had been reared in rather hardier circumstances, and had eaten pie and mash from a street stall often enough, waiting for her mother to emerge from the theatre after the show.

Consuelo sent the food back and asked for thin brown bread and butter, which arrived so thin and delicate it was almost like lace, and Consuelo savoured it, seeming to cheer up at once. She handed over an envelope with three Royal invitations in it, saying dear Robert had asked her to bring them with her. They were replacements, she emphasized. They did not want empty seats on the day, but nor did they want peers fighting over places, a spectacle to be gloated over by the watching hoi polloi. Isobel said she had given enough dinner parties and organized enough charity events to realize the importance of forward planning. The row seated seven: the Dilberne party was only four, absent until they returned to their seats for the Parry anthem. Robert had told her the seats were going to the Baums, which was what Balfour had suggested, Baum being a director of the new Anglo-Palestine Bank and Baum's wife being, as was Balfour himself, a great admirer of Handel's oratorios — this latter was news to Isobel: perhaps she had dismissed Naomi Baum too easily? There was one further seat to be allocated. To whom did Isobel suggest it should go?

'My daughter,' said Isobel, magnanimously. 'Rosina.'

'But of course, Rosina. Isn't she the clever one?'

'That is so,' said Isobel. Word got round. No wonder the girl had not married.

'She will not be entitled to a coronet, of course,' said Consuelo, 'but do remind her to wear a nice hat, though not one that is so tall as to block the view. A nice straw will do very well with a bird of paradise wing round the rim and perhaps a diamond hat pin. Though Garrard have the prettiest ones in emerald and crystal at half the price. Do you think I should ask for some more bread and butter? It reminds me of my nursery. My mother was always off building houses, but she found me nice nursemaids.'

She ordered more bread and butter, and it came so quickly Isobel thought they had been recognized.

As soon as she was face to face with Consuelo, Isobel remembered how much she liked her. Fears and suspicions fled away. It was absurd to suppose this pretty, cheerful, brave girl took any undue interest in his Lordship, let alone that he returned it. She was half his age, and she was safely married: as was he, and if she occasionally felt the need for advice, who else to turn to but someone like Robert? Just as now, finding herself in trying domestic circumstances, she turned to Isobel for matters to do with the Queen's coronation jewels. It was perfectly normal for Robert to bring her into the conversation whenever he could — half the men in London claimed to be infatuated with her. Sir James Barrie himself said he would cross London just to get a glimpse of her getting into a cab. Only her own husband managed to look bored and gloomy whenever Consuelo approached. Yet Robert reported that she shared an office in Buck House with Sunny, and was apparently effective and efficient, a go-between twixt the Queen — she was Mistress of the Robes, an astonishing post for one so young — and the Lord High Steward, which by tradition was the Duke of Marlborough's duty whenever a coronation hove into view — thrice a century being the national average.

On the way to the Club, the black cloud had descended and Isobel had wondered whether there was not to be some dramatic confession scene when the mistress declares her love to the wife, but that was just something for penny dreadfuls and not real life, and certainly Consuelo would not choose the University Club to do it, where the scones were heavy and the jam tasted of boric acid.

Sitting opposite each other at a window table for two, they could have been taken as mother and daughter, two good-looking, fashionable women, the older accepting of life, the younger anything but inconspicuous, no matter where she went or how she tried. The slim figure, the straight back, the long neck, emphasized whenever time of day allowed by a jewelled choker — little chin and mouth and a clear high brow, a tiny, rosy mouth and huge, smudgy black eyes in an elfin face — could there be Red Indian blood? — and then the pearls — even today it seemed she could not be parted from them — two short strings over the collar of the green pleated taffeta of her high-necked dress, a third swinging free and almost down to her waist. The Palace was out of mourning, Queen Alexandra appeared in pale pastel flower prints, and anyone who was anyone could breathe a sigh of relief, and be in colour again.

'I wanted your opinion on the Koh-i-Noor,' said Consuelo now, leaning confidentially towards Isobel across the table, as well she might, the subject of the conversation being what it was. 'The Queen has set her mind on it for the crown but to me the stone looks dull. It had not been well cut. We don't want her to be a laughing stock. Potentates from all over the world will be present: the last thing we want is for the Queen of England to be outshone. And I worry about the King Edward Sapphire for the Monarch's crown, though that is Sunny's business, not mine. It's so spectacular it looks as if it came out of a joke shop.'

'Consuelo,' said Isobel, 'why ask me? You know more about diamonds and sapphires than anyone else I know.'

'I know about pearls,' said Consuelo, 'and they're easy. Though they say they'll soon be able to culture them artificially, and then they'll be two a penny, and no one will be able to tell the difference, so we'll have to give up wearing them. But diamonds are a different matter. And the Koh-i-Noor! Its reputation so exceeds its worth. The Old Queen was convinced it was unlucky.'

'Only for Kings,' said Isobel, 'not for Queens.'

'But the real problem is the Queen's penchant for any old jewellery. So long as it sparkles she'll put it on. She'll come across an emerald brooch, stick it on any old where but next to a pink sapphire, bury both beneath some crude crystal necklace and a string of pearls, and add a diamond choker high enough to strangle her. I love jewels, and so does Sunny, but at least I know where to stop. She's fond of you, Isobel, she was so happy with you at Christmas, will you please talk to her and teach her a little taste?'

'I'm afraid it may be rather late in her life to learn,' said Isobel, 'but I will do what I can should occasion arise.'

She took the opportunity of explaining to Consuelo that Minnie was expecting and would be in no condition to walk in the Coronation, indeed to attend at all. Her condition would be too obvious. The baby was expected in the first week of July.

Consuelo flushed with joy: she seemed delighted. Isobel was accustomed to the outrage that usually struck the very rich when their plans were thwarted but no. Consuelo's pleasure was instant and sincere.

'But that is wonderful, Isobel. Little Minnie! An Earl to follow in Robert's footsteps: I hope he grows up to be as wise and wonderful as his grandfather, who is second only to Mr Balfour in greatness. I am sure he will be, proud and strong. Minnie is so sensible. She is like me, American and practical. She will get the necessities over with, she will produce the heir and the spare and then be free to get on with her own life, as I do. It is perfectly possible to be as happy in this country as at home: one must just learn the rules and follow them scrupulously. And the men here — quite extraordinary, they mumble and look reluctant and aloof, but then they pounce, oh how they pounce! American men are all talk and precious little action. But tell Minnie she must be terribly, terribly discreet. Not a breath of scandal, not now or for posterity. Oh Isobel, I am afraid I have shocked you!'

Isobel was indeed aghast, conscious of other tables listening in; but what exactly had Consuleo said? Not a child for Minnie, not a grandchild for her, but a grandchild for Robert. Robert the wise and wonderful. The men who mumble but pounce. The black fog was stirring around Isobel, clutching her ageing womb, narrowing her eyes and her thoughts. She made an effort: opened them, cleared them.

'I am not in the least shocked,' Isobel said, as if nothing untoward had happened. 'But of course we mustn't forget the baby may be a girl.'

'I have the two darling little boys,' said Consuelo, 'for which thank God, one brave and bold like my father, the other like Sunny. If they had been girls I would have had to go on and on until two sons were achieved. Of course Robert's grandchild will be a boy. Your husband is to be Prime Minister, Isobel, after Arthur Balfour the disembodied has drifted off into space. Robert is so firmly bodied. But why did he not tell me about the new child, why did he leave it to you to tell me? I don't understand: men are so strange, but I suppose Robert is so, well, English. I had such a good long talk with him the other day at lunch. We talked about war horses and cavalry and how my father, who is a great horseman, believes tracked motor tractors will soon replace the war horse. Are you interested in horses, Isobel?'

'No,' said Isobel.

'Ah no, of course, Robert said you were not.'

Isobel felt a sudden stab of anger. Consuelo was quite deliberately taunting her. She was in effect saying to Isobel, 'I can have him if I want him.' Isobel had met her sort before. The kind who loved their fathers and despised their mothers, and now liked older men, the ones with wives to upset and marriages to break up, who, having failed to replace their mothers in their fathers' affections, couldn't see a happy marriage without wanting to destroy it. Realizing what she was dealing with, Isobel's head cleared wondrously. Consuelo had declared war, but had also revealed herself. She would toy with Robert like a cat with a mouse but not pounce. She would not risk indiscretion, she had said, and Robert was too naïve to be discreet. Isobel was safe enough.

Her Grace continued to complain about her Majesty. 'And now she wants to borrow my seventeen-strand pearl necklace for the occasion. Her very best is a mere fifteen. Is one even allowed to say no to monarchy? I fear not.' She asked if Isobel would like to see the treasures she, Consuelo, had brought back from Moscow. The jewellers there were so skilful and imaginative. She was taking her new treasures to the bank. 'I ordered one of the Fabergé eggs they talk about; they usually only go to Royalty but the dear little man made an exception for me. Sunny can be very nice when he is in a good mood — the trouble is he so often isn't. He's a little man, of course, and can hardly help it. All little men are Napoleons, and must have their own way, however strange that way may be. But in Moscow Sunny behaved like an angel. Look. Let me show them to you. The bank must wait just a minute.'

Consuelo produced a little blue velvet reticule which she emptied onto the white tablecloth.

Isobel felt the tables were ridiculously small. The ruby earrings practically fell into the butter dish, and the pin of the fragile amethyst and garnet brooch pierced the bread. A diamond necklace followed. All glittered tremendously. There was a muffled gasp from the next table. Isobel felt it sounded very like disapproval, but what could you expect in a place like this?

Consuelo let the diamonds trickle through her fingers.

'Sunny in Moscow is one thing,' she said. 'Sunny in New York is quite another. We were married in New York, you know. I was eighteen. I stood at the altar and looked up at him shyly in love and trust, but he didn't look at me, he was looking over me, past me into space and I knew he was longing to be marrying someone else. There were three of us in the marriage. No matter. I am a good wife. And there are always jewels, aren't there, to comfort one. Hard and cold, but at least for ever, as love is meant to be. Alexandra loves them too but goes too far. Every necklace, bracelet, brooch masks a disappointment.' Her dark eyes glittered. Isobel thought for a dreadful moment she was going to cry. The tops of her little shell-like ears flushed pink. But she just laughed her delightful little laugh, and threaded the jewels back, one by one, into her bag. The blue-stocking ladies, their entertainment over, went back to their rubbery scones and puffed-up cream.

The two ladies parted apparently on the best of terms. Isobel felt quite benign, poor flailing Consuelo could be forgiven; she was hardly to be taken seriously, the more so because she wanted to be. She was like some child's tinselly cut-out toy and if Robert was entranced, it was hardly surprising and would come to nothing. She felt immensely generous and forgave Robert too though for what she could not be sure. But as they were leaving the Club Consuelo said, 'I am so happy for Minnie: just so very trying that she now can't follow behind the canopy. I can't think of anyone else pretty and smart enough to accompany you, Isobel. Perhaps I'll just scrap the idea and have nobody, and you can join in with the other countesses. I'll think about it. I'll let you know.'

The bitch. Isobel went back home, at least with the invitations, and resolved to get them into the post to the Baums that very day, and to hand the remaining card to Rosina. What had she been thinking of, trying to disown her own daughter? The black fog again, now happily dispersed. Tomorrow she planned to go all the way to Wells to meet with Adela and discuss the wedding, acknowledge her too as one of the family, and see what could be done to help.

There was uproar in Belgrave Square as the cab dropped her off. Three large covered brakes were parked outside No. 17, apparently too wide for the mews entrance, so that a mass of indoor servants and their possessions were being disgorged into the street. All could have been managed more easily in four broughams. Reginald's fault. She would have upbraided him but needed to ask him to drop the invitations for the

Baums into the post before she forgot. What an intolerable fuss, she thought, about seating for three at a King's Coronation.

Mrs Baum Waits

It was a beautiful Spring and Mrs Baum's garden in Golders Green, two years in the making, was showing the benefits of the attention lavished upon it. The daffodils had made a wonderful display and the gardeners were tying back their green spikes to make way for a dozen budding shrubs. Jonathan Reuben and Barbara Ruth were enrolled at the prestigious City of London School on the Embankment, though the promised Hampstead Tube line had still not materialized. It was a day school, so heaven knew how she would get them there, but she would manage. It was unfortunate that Jane, who although a *shiksa* girl had been so good as a nursemaid and general help about the house, and whom she had come to treat almost as a friend, had given in her notice so suddenly and for no apparent reason. It would be hard to replace her. But the building plots on the road were being quickly taken up and quite a little community, like the Baums fleeing from London's East End, was growing up fast around them. A little row of shops including a Kosher butcher was now within walking distance. She could not be the scientist she had hoped to be, but perhaps her daughter would.

Eric had bought her a very splendid Bösendorfer grand piano and she had set up a little choral society in her front room, and a Saturday *shul* for the children. Eric had given in to her demands to call the children by their middle names, respectively Ruth and Reuben. He was, thank God, now in no danger of apostasy but proud of his religion, being now so well established in society, and indeed a director of the Anglo-Palestine Bank. There was little point now in assimilation. And had not Lord Robert asked them to sit with his family in the Abbey at the Coronation? It was a great honour.

She thought perhaps she had contributed to his acceptance into high society. A year or so back she had been invited by Lady Isobel to a charity dinner at which the Prince of Wales had engaged her in conversation, since when many doors had opened. She had encountered Mr Arthur Balfour, a friend of Lord Robert's, at the inauguration of the Royal London Voice Choir and talked at length with him about Ebenezer Prout's sterling work re-orchestrating Handel's *Messiah*. It had been a most exhilarating conversation — though Eric had looked blank and not known what was going on. Well, let him get on with the money — what he was good at, she would get on with culture. Mr Balfour, everyone said, was going to be the next Prime Minister and would do much to promote the arts. She sincerely hoped so. Not since Disraeli had the country been governed by anyone remotely cultured. Now she waited for the invitations to come dropping through the letterbox. His Lordship's business interests were so intertwined with Eric's she had no doubt they would.

Naomi had started a small local branch of the Zionist Federation in her front room. They met monthly: it was for women and many came, their husbands for once not objecting to their absence, such was the cause. The ladies would read and discuss Theodor Herzl's work and someone had embroidered 'If you will it, it is no fairy tale' on a banner and pinned it up above Naomi's splendid Adam fireplace. All present looked forward to the creation of a new and perfect society, a land of peace and plenty, where ethics would prevail over greed, where Jews of all nations could live without fear or persecution. The most determinedly religious stayed away: furious in their belief that Zion must wait until the second coming. But these were a gentle lot. Tonight they were going to discuss the dreadful plight of Jews in Roumania, and someone was bringing forward the idea of Uganda instead of Palestine as the new homeland. Naomi did not think it would be well received: Israel was not a geographical but an historical and spiritual concept. Nevertheless she would let the idea go forward. All discussion was good.

Naomi was in her bedroom dressing for the occasion, and thinking she needed fewer guests or a bigger drawing room — the orthodox ladies seemed to wear more voluminous skirts — than the ones who turned up for choir practice. She would wear something pretty but modest and perhaps, to liven things up, the pretty diamond and gold bracelet Eric had bought her last December. She had almost refused it at the time: still perhaps a little over-sensitive when it came to observing proper ritual. One should not succumb to the lure of a pagan festival like Christmas, she had told herself: she had already had a more than satisfactory Hanukah gift in the form of a very similar bracelet in twenty-three-carat gold, only without the diamonds, but it was so pretty she had over-ruled her scruples, and fastening the clasp now, was glad that she had done so. Eric, back from work, came bounding up the stairs to her room, and she could stretch out her pretty wrist for him to admire, and kiss.

'Two things,' he said. 'Both good news! One, I have bought us a building site in The Bishops Avenue, the new road that joins the Heath to Finchley. The Church is selling off plots large enough for palaces, and that's what we shall build!'

But apparently it was not good news. Naomi snatched back her wrist before he could kiss it. In the silence Eric could hear Jane moving about downstairs in the drawing room, setting up for this evening's meeting, wavy hair flowing free. When she was working overtime she refused to wear a cap. Naomi, as ever, wore a black wig: he had never insisted on it, let alone pointed out the inconsistencies of her rituals: it was her doing. Eric hoped it was not his doing that Jane had handed in her notice — she was so pleasant to watch moving around that he could not help doing so — and a chaste kiss or two could hardly have come amiss: she was almost one of the family — but perhaps it was just as well she was going, for whatever reason. It could be hard not to covet one's handmaid, and perhaps even excusable, thinking of Hagar and Abraham, but he loved Naomi dearly. It was just she seemed to find enthusiasm so difficult. The Bishops Avenue was a huge step up.

'But Eric,' she was saying, 'we have only just got settled here. And anyway, why should we want to live on ground, as you boast, named after Christian bishops? We are Jews. And the daffodils have been so lovely: the lawn is finally grass not mud: I have made friends: I have a good butcher. What about my choir — what about my Ladies for Zion — they don't want to have to traipse across all London — I'll lose everything I've taken the trouble to build up. We will stay where we are.'

He felt his temper rising. He did so much for just a kind word from her, and so seldom received it.

'For heaven's sake, Naomi,' he said coldly: he could be unkind if she could — 'The Bishops Avenue is only around the corner, and "here" is going to be next to impossible when the Crematorium goes up practically next door; you have campaigned against it often enough. I will not have my children

360

growing up in the shadow of its chimney, for the sake of some daffodils and the Ladies for Zion. We are a good Jewish family: we live where I say we live. I work hard for what we have: I give you everything, everything — today I hurried home with these — at least pretend to be grateful!'

'These' were two invitations to the Coronation in a blank envelope sealed with a crescent moon and two suns. Reginald had dropped it off by hand — Eric Baum suspected because her Ladyship could not bear to write out a North London postal address. Well, a Bishops Avenue address would be harder to despise. They were very large plots and very expensive; the Church evidently preferred to sell to its own. Others had bought for less. He had run for the bus to get the invitations home to her quickly; two causes for exultation. Now this. She did not even open the envelope but looked at it with distaste and dropped it to the ground.

'A good Jewish family?' she enquired, her voice hard and raw, so different from when she spoke to the children. 'So you say. But one in which the husband does not care to observe the laws of purity?'

It seldom happened, but it had. The ritual bath took a long time coming. He was a vigorous man.

'You deny Mitzvah,' he could not help retorting. 'You deny me unreasonably. You are rebellious. I could divorce you.'

'Oh divorce me,' she said, 'please do. Why has Jane handed in her notice, I ask myself?'

'Any stick to beat me with,' he said, lamely. She had been like this when her mother died. He could not endure it.

'I do everything for you,' he said again, and it was true. She was why he lived and worked and breathed. 'I give you everything.' He was beside himself.

She did not look down and concede as a good wife would, but moved the safety clasp of the bracelet and at the same time flicked her wrist so the bracelet flew off and into the heart of the fire.

'So much for your everything!' she said. He bent down, picked up the envelope, straightened, took his time to tear envelope and contents in half — thick, stiff and not easy — and flung them into the fire after the bracelet.

'There goes your Coronation,' he said.

Panic and Confusion

'But this is absurd,' Rosina said to her mother. 'Why can't we go by railway like anyone else?'

'Because to get to Wells you have to change trains twice and you know what these small lines are like,' said her mother.

'Or by automobile? Please, Mama!'

'Nasty oily things,' said Isobel. 'Always breaking down.'

Rosina thought her mother was behaving very erratically. One moment she felt herself to be the object of what almost amounted to dislike: the next of an admiration that was almost too uncritical. Isobel would flush as if embarrassed when there was nothing whatsoever to be embarrassed about, or seem to grow hot when the wind was cold and throw off as much clothing as she decently could. Now she had got it into her head that she needed to turn up at the Bishop's Palace in a coach and four: it was, she said, a question of status. Two women could not just turn up on foot walking from the station.

'We can, you know, Mama,' said Rosina. 'Or we can hire a brougham at the station and arrive in perfectly good style.'

Rosina thought perhaps it was the coming Coronation that had so disturbed her mother, shaken her confidence, taken her back to a childhood in which she was less than no one, just a clever, bright, pretty child out of the *haut bohème,* conceived the wrong side of the blanket, who had married well, and slipped into a high society which so quickly forgot her origins she had almost done so herself. But now, a notch or two higher up, finding herself in the company of royals and duchesses, she showed the unease of the lowly born. Rosina, though she griped and struggled against her lack of formal title, had no such problem.

She said as much to Minnie and recited the flea nursery rhyme:

Big fleas have little fleas
Upon their backs to bite 'em,
And little fleas have lesser fleas,
And so, *ad infinitum.*

Minnie said it was like the Jonathan Swift

piece about vermin only teasing and pinching their foes superior by an inch, and Rosina was grateful that God had sent her a sister-in-law who at least understood what she was talking about.

The practicalities of getting the old disused coach out of the Dilberne Court stables and the organization and time now required to effect a coach journey of a hundred miles or so, were such that her Ladyship agreed to a train journey. Rosina was greatly relieved. Minnie wanted to go too but the Countess would not hear of it: it was Minnie's duty to see to the welfare of her child, not amuse herself. Reginald, in the absence of an available man, was to accompany the party, and Lily as lady's maid. Isobel would have taken more staff but an earlier phone call to the Bishop's Palace made it clear that accommodation for servants was limited. The young man who ran the Bishop's office, approached the day before, had spoken with a colonial accent, and was polite enough — if not quite, Isobel thought, 'one of us', but seemed slightly taken aback, when they announced their forthcoming arrival. Perhaps, Isobel wondered, this was the prospective groom? She felt instantly suspicious of his motives, but knew herself well enough not to give in to the doubts and fears that these days so easily grabbed hold of her thoughts, like an attacker seizing her throat. But if you just waited they would melt away.

It came to her on the journey that Reginald and Lily were rather too fond of each other and it would have been wiser for her not to have chosen this particular pair for the journey. But she felt safe with these two — they were willing and spirited, not dozy or easily cowed as were so many of the staff. The servant classes increasingly lacked initiative, accustomed as they were to being looked after.

They travelled without reservations, and at Paddington discovered panic and confusion. There had been some stoppage on the line which meant that their train was to run without first-class carriages, was overcrowded, and the station-master nowhere to be seen. Reginald found them seats in second class, but Lily, if she was not to stand, would be obliged to share their carriage. Reginald found a seat in third class, Rosina wanted to go home and wait until the trains were running normally but Isobel over-ruled her. She wanted to arrive when she said she would arrive. Rosina sulked and said very little.

'I really don't understand the need for all

this haste,' she said at Slough. 'I hope she's grateful. All this for a cousin we tried to ignore.'

'Adela's very young,' said Isobel. 'We don't want her making a mistake that will spoil her life.'

'When she was going to be a nun she was even younger. That brought none of us running,' observed Rosina.

Isobel patted her daughter's arm pacifically. Once you realized that what Rosina said was not in any way malicious, but she just spoke the truth when others did not, it was possible to be fond of her. The girl was too clever for her own good, and especially for any man she might encounter, and that was a misfortune. But most families had old maids in them. It was bound to happen; there were not enough men to go round.

As they left Reading Rosina said, 'But then of course we realized Adela was a Princess, although from the wrong side of the family, and now nothing will do but that we go running to her side, to all our great inconvenience.'

'She is very minor royalty, darling,' said Isobel, and entertained her daughter with tales of tea at the University Club for Ladies with the Duchess, though Rosina seemed more interested in whether her mother had

had a sighting of Beatrice Webb, a social reformer and a rather plain woman.

The first-class dining carriage was still attached, and Isobel and Rosina had a not very good lunch of a steak and kidney pie overloaded with kidneys which might have been none too fresh. But they shared a very good half-bottle of a Bordeaux. Lily went with Reginald to stand at the bar and when she joined her employers in their compartment again she was smelling of beer and giggling.

At Pewsey Rosina said, 'I wonder why our cousin is marrying in such haste? Can she have got herself into trouble? In which case it might be wiser not to visit her and not to know.'

'For heaven's sake,' said Isobel. 'She is a clergyman's daughter and a Dilberne.'

'Exactly,' said Rosina and Lily forgot herself and giggled.

At Newbury Rosina talked only about the Speenhamland system which originated in the town, and was something to do with the fixing of the wages of agricultural labourers about which Isobel knew little and cared less. Apparently it featured largely in the book which Rosina was writing at the instigation of one Seebohm Rowntree, another social reformer. A strange name but

Rosina seemed very caught up with him, although he was married. She had met him at some dining club.

As they ran into Westbury, Rosina said, 'Perhaps there's an inheritance involved and he's marrying her for her money. He may be a rogue and a villain.'

'That's why we are in a hurry,' said Isobel.

'To save her virtue?' asked Rosina. 'I hardly think so. If it's gone it's gone.'

Lily had fallen asleep otherwise no doubt she would have giggled again.

They changed trains at Witham Friary and settled back into more comfortable and cleaner seats. Lily sat with them. It was easier.

'I know!' said Rosina. 'I've solved it. We're in a hurry because now Minnie's out of the picture you need someone pretty and smart to process with at the Coronation, or Consuelo will relegate you to the any-old countesses. You want the wedding deferred and the sailing postponed so you can walk beside a princess. Let's just hope Papa is wrong and she's pretty and smart but don't hold your breath.'

For a moment she thought her mother would hit her, but Isobel just said,

'Rosina, you're so smart you'll cut

369

yourself.'

At the Bishop's Palace all was alarm and consternation. Adela had disappeared. She had not come down to dinner the previous evening, but Frank had already disclosed his proposal of marriage and Adela's acceptance of it in a manner perhaps more colonial than English and it was assumed she was too bashful to appear in public. It was only the next day that the maid bringing her breakfast found her bed still made and no Adela. The Palace had been searched at once, and then the grounds, and after that the Cathedral itself, in case she was lost in prayer. Frank was noisy and disconsolate, and ran around searching where others had already searched. He was not totally unattractive, Isobel thought, and too earnest to be a villain. Isobel was reminded of the confusion earlier that day at Paddington Station. People ran to and fro as if movement itself could solve a problem. Prelates prayed noisily and scuttled about in groups, Adam's apples waggling (Rosina's phrase) over high clerical collars.

Mrs Kennion greeted her guests with scant courtesy and a quite uncalled-for 'and about time too'.

The Bishop said, 'A pity Dilberne never bothered to turn up in the first place. She'd be safely in a convent by now.' Reginald and Lily disappeared into the bowels of the Palace. A weeping parlourmaid, Beth, lead Isobel and Rosina to a room which they were expected to share, and did not seem to want to unpack their bags for them but rather to talk. Dr Winnington-Ingram, the Bishop of London, Beth said, was convening a conference on the evils of incense and the problems of confession and absolution. He had no wife and his socks were smelly. Three senior policemen had been summoned from Bath. All three held different views on Adela's disappearance: the first wanted the moat and ponds drained at once, the second held the view that the girl had run off with a lover — as girls were wont to do — and the third seemed to think that Frank had done it, taking the fact that he was to leave the country for Australia as all the evidence that was needed. They had at least managed to agree to a poster of the missing girl going up in police stations around the country, with a £10 reward for finding her. Beth had a poor opinion of all three of them; her own view was that Adela had run off to her convent to get away from Mr Overshaw's philosophizing: they had better look for her there.

'Tell me,' said Isobel, who was lying on

the bed still with her cloak on and her shoes off. 'What does Adela look like?'

'She's lovely,' said Beth, after a moment's pause. 'Too lovely ever to be dead. God saved her for a reason.' Then she said she must be off to see to the Bishop's socks, which had to be washed and dried overnight. He had no spares. 'In my experience bachelors never think,' she said.

Isobel could see no point in continuing the visit. She saw Dr Kennion briefly. He said he had cancelled the evening's dinner but would be pleased to see the Countess and her daughter at breakfast. All joined her Ladyship in anxiety for the girl's safety. She had been with them at the Palace for only a few months but all had come to love her very much in spite of her not being family.

Isobel was exhausted and went to bed, where the mattress was hard and the pillow was as unforgiving as a Scottish parson — which, come to think of it, Bishop Kennion was — but sent Rosina off to find out what she could about Frank Overshaw and his motives. Rosina returned to say she had found him weeping in the library, very much upset, and spilling tears onto a clutch of rather good sketches of Adela which he himself had drawn. She had better go back to the library to save them from ruin. In her opinion Frank was a good artist, far better even than Minnie. At least you could tell what his paintings were meant to be.

By one o'clock in the morning Rosina had not returned to her room, and with a sudden chill Isobel realized that if one girl could disappear in a well-peopled palace, so could another one. She got off the bed — she had given up any thought of sleep — walked darkened corridors until she found the library, and listened at the door. There was the sound of two voices, and both sounded reasonable and animated; they were talking about the oneness, the wholeness. She risked the creak and pushed it open. They were talking over one another.

'The wise do not grieve,' Frank was saying. 'My bloody oath!' And then something like: 'The thing to hold on to is that the spiritual essence of a body does not perish but merely changes its form following the death of the physical body,' and Rosina was saying something like: 'As Socrates said to Crito, "Be of good cheer. Before they can bury me they have to find me, the real me, and how will they ever do that?" '

Isobel left them to it. She went back to bed and this time slept soundly. Rosina was in the other bed when she awoke and Isobel asked no questions.

Breakfast was a gruelling experience. Frank did not appear. Rosina did, but was no help, as though she were in a trance which precluded speech. Isobel did what she could to be bright, positive and responsible, conscious that in Robert's absence she must speak for the family.

The Bishop was not in a good mood, glowering at the head of the table, the handsome head bowed over porridge, which he took Scottish style, with salt but no sugar or cream. Henrietta Kennion was behaving rather like a fluffy hen, pleasant and chirpy, as if trying to neutralize the Bishop's apparent ill temper. She was looking dreadful, her hair standing on end, her jacket buttoned up awry, but Isobel imagined that it often was.

He rose to his feet as Isobel came into the room.

'Ah Lady Isobel,' he said. 'It is so kind of you to spare us a moment from your busy schedule. I wrote to your father Silas once, concerning a charity for the daughters of coal miners, but he was too busy to reply.'

Isobel said nothing, but smiled sweetly. Silas had hated the Church and all its works.

'Busy-ness seems to run in your family,' the Bishop observed, but did not elaborate.

The Bishop seemed to know a great deal about a great many things. He would have known Edwin, and perhaps been told that Robert was only a second son who had married Isobel before he inherited, and that she, Isobel, was Silas's bastard daughter by an unknown actress. 'Your husband is no doubt busy helping Mr Balfour with an education bill that is to destroy the moral fibre of the nation.' Explanation enough, Isobel thought with relief, for the Bishop's ill temper.

'I do not think the moral fibre of the nation will be destroyed by raising the school-leaving age from ten to twelve,' Mrs Kennion spoke up, rather bravely, Isobel thought, since the Bishop was obviously in no mood for disagreement. 'And surely the Bill strengthens the position of the Church.'

'Do not talk about things you do not understand,' said the Bishop. 'The Bill is a socialist plot to stir up the Wesleyans and put education into the hands of the County Councils.'

Isobel glanced over to Rosina, fearing that the word socialist might bring her back to contentious life, but it did not, for which Isobel was thankful. Rosina continued to stare into space, and had not touched her food. She was sadly lacking in social graces: one did what one could with one's children, but blood would out. Rosina was remarkably like her grandfather Silas, who, as Robert would have it, 'followed his own dree'.

But she should be paying attention to the Bishop. 'We are doing all we can to find the girl, naturally,' he said, 'but I find myself most reluctant to drain the moat at this juncture. To do so would disturb the swans — a great attraction to our many visitors. We will have the moat dragged, of course, though the likelihood of finding a body is minimal. It is possible she will just walk in through the door, having put us all to a great deal of trouble and expense, though the police warn us that with every hour that passes it is the more unlikely. You did not know her well, I gather, Lady Isobel? You cannot advise us as to her temperament?'

'I have never met her,' said Isobel.

'Extraordinary,' said the Bishop under his breath. 'And she apparently so close a relative.'

He suggested that perhaps his Lordship would see fit to raise the present reward for information which the police had suggested, and the Bishopric had put up out of its own funds, money which could otherwise be used for the poor of the diocese.

Isobel assured the Bishop that her husband would of course increase the reward

— ten pounds did seem rather a small amount for the recovery of a daughter of a deceased local cleric — to perhaps fifty pounds or so. The Bishop said yes, it would be more appropriate and no doubt Dilberne with his gold mines and imported Chinese labourers had money enough to spread around.

Mrs Kennion said if the reward went unclaimed she could give it to her own charity, Mercy for Women, in Adelaide, where it was much needed.

'If only,' Henrietta said, eyes to heaven, 'money alone could solve the world's problems.' 'Or that it would save a man's soul,' added the Bishop. 'Strange, I must say,' he went on, 'that the girl ran off having just received a proposal of marriage. My wife encouraged it, though I had my doubts about its wisdom. The other possibility, of course, is that my wife's nephew may have slaughtered her, sacrificed her to one of the strange gods to whom he adheres. Do not look so agitated, my dear, I am only joking. But we must, alas, face the possibility that the girl has not met with some accident but deliberately done away with herself, so recently bereaved and no family coming forward to claim her or comfort her until too late.' He took marmalade for his toast.

'But you are not eating, Lady Isobel? Perhaps conscience bothers you? Your imagination? You see Adela lying there, in some lonely ditch, frozen, or dashed beneath the iron wheels of a railway train? Pray take some kippers: they are very plump and good. The hens are not laying, or I would suggest eggs. Good for the delicate digestion. And your daughter has eaten nothing at all, I see.'

'Oh, Kennion,' said Henrietta, 'you are in one of your moods. Take no notice of him, Lady Isobel. He is in a fuss about his flowerburst cape, which he must wear for the Coronation. It has come back with quite the wrong stitching, gold where there should be silver and silver where there should be gold. You know how these husbands can be in the morning. I am sorry you have had to witness it. And we are all in a tizzy about poor dear Adela. I had been so looking forward to the wedding. And now Frank must sail away to distant lands without the company of a bride.'

'Frank this, Frank that, Frank the other,' said the Bishop. 'And may I remind you, my dear, that the Coronation is not such a small thing as you seem to think.' It occurred to Isobel that the Bishop had had a monumental scene with his wife that very morning, and she, Isobel, had been unfortunate enough to get in the way. 'The role of Bath and Wells is central to the anointing of the monarch,' he went on. 'It is a pity that you have trouble acknowledging the significance of sacrament, but I suppose one must remember you are a colonial.' He rose to his feet, a tall, majestic figure. 'I have important matters to attend to. As I say, it is a great pity the child has gone astray, but the matter is in the hands of the proper authorities. If I may be frank, Lady Isobel, my own belief is that being the child of a spiteful father, as I always found the Reverend Hedleigh to be, she has done away with herself simply to spite her benefactors.'

And he stalked out. Isobel caught the train back to Paddington as soon after breakfast as she politely could, dragging a reluctant daughter behind her. Rosina seemed not to have taken in a word of what went on over breakfast. Nor was she forthcoming as to what had gone on between her and Frank. It was a boring journey back home. But the unpleasantness of the breakfast seemed a proper punishment for sins of omission, if not commission.

■ ■ ■ ■

MAY — 1902

■ ■ ■ ■

Earning a Living

Adela was a fast learner and a good worker, George had to hand it to her. She was also in love with him; he could tell that from the way she would drop her eyes whenever he caught hers, and would stumble over words when replying to anything he said. He only had to make a move and she would look up at him with worshipping eyes and do whatever he wanted, and he could not deny he was sometimes tempted, and the thought of her asleep in the next room certainly fired him up. But he didn't want to upset Ivy, and anyway he didn't go after children. Whatever the law said sixteen was still young. A slum girl grew up early; Adela's kind took a long time ripening. When she reached her seventeenth birthday he might feel differently. The fact of her virginity was a kind of asset he hoped he would not have to realize but if the worst came to the worst always could, to further capitalize the business.

At first there were police posters up everywhere advertising a £50 reward for information leading to the return of Adela Hedleigh to her family.

'I could do with fifty quid myself,' said Doreen, 'to finish off my thatch. All I have to do is drop a hint to Jenny. I bet Adela looks good in that dress. They all think she's dead but I know better.'

George had to hand over £50 to keep her quiet. There was no mention of any 'princess' on the poster so all assumed that particular fantasy had come to nothing. Lots of little girls dreamed they were princesses who had been switched at birth. The sketch on the poster didn't look anything like Adela for a start — done by the Australian fiancé, apparently: there was a lucky escape! — and by the time Ivy had hennaed Adela's hair, and darkened her eyebrows she looked just like the Carlotta St Cross she'd chosen as her new name for her new life. She still went on asking what was meant by 'no better than she should be', and both George and Ivy refrained from answering, 'Someone who looks like you, dear.' But it did make them laugh. Quite a lot of laughing went on. They were a team, and a jolly one, all with their new lives.

Miss Reynolds the landlady was now on their side — she gave them a proper English breakfast with eggs, bacon and black pudding, and in addition, for their health, she said, an orange each; they had bread and cheese for lunch and fish, chips and mushy peas wrapped in newspaper from Seafoods restaurant most evenings for supper.

They saw it as their business to train Carlotta up. She seemed a natural, and loved an audience. She longed to do platform work. They'd taken her to a couple of small private séances up in the Royal Crescent — four shillings a head — one featuring as the medium Miss Maia of Tottenham, a real dab hand at tipping tables. Jehovah himself had turned up to that one, accompanied by peals of thunder and a floating trumpet.

Miss Reynolds lent them a spare room to practise in and even served as an audience as the nimble Carlotta crept about the room dressed in black and her face smeared with Nuggett boot polish and learnt how to stay invisible and tip tables by lying on the floor by pushing away supports rather than having to lift from above. It was her idea to play The Last Rose of Summer on a real trumpet, painted black, placed behind the silver one, as it rose in the air on invisible strings.

'The best ideas are the simplest,' she said, and George could go along with that. She was better than Ivy at going into trances, turning her eyes heavenwards and rolling them before passing out, managing the while to look ethereal and even beautiful, where Ivy managed just to look mad. Ivy could get a clear note on the trumpet. Carlotta struggled rather. Lights tucked under Carlotta's fading red hair gave her the appearance of having a halo; tucked under Ivy's, Ivy looked gaunt and more spectral than the shades she was meant to attract.

'You be the medium,' Ivy herself suggested to Carlotta, 'I'll do the crawling about on the floor. Honestly, I'd rather. I don't have the heart for audiences.'

So Carlotta became not Princess Ida of Bucharest, but Princess Ida of the Cherub Angels of Wisdom, and Isaac Pitman's great-nephew added an extra line to the leaflets: *Words of Advice and Comfort Straight from Heaven to You.*

They took tickets to another séance, where the medium presented herself as Mrs Ada Pennington: strange childish voices issued from her mouth and spectral figures floated from her nostrils. Or at any rate they formed when they were a foot or two beyond her nose.

They puzzled for a time as to how this was done: Carlotta said she thought it could be done with a fan blowing a very fine white gauze which would wrap itself round a wire frame, but then, after the apparitions had been sent back to hell from which they came (*Samuel 1, verse 28*), brushing against her hair while they fled, she found her hair was sticky with ectoplasm, and changed her mind and said it could possibly be a spun-sugar frame, not wire, and boiling water had been used to collapse the figures, but some had stuck to the floating gauze. Next day she boldly went back to the house, told them they were guilty of fraud, demanded her three two-and-sixes back and got it. George marvelled. She seemed afraid of nothing.

A platform event with an audience of a hundred and fifty with famous medium Rosa from Paris cost only two shillings a ticket. The medium's customary familiar, a tabby cat, lay sleeping on the table when Rosa made her entrance. She was very fat and had a moustache. She brought with her a Bible, a bowl, a lily and a bell and placed these on the table next to the cat, to ward off any evil spirit.

'Best to be on the safe side,' said Madame Rosa. 'One is very vulnerable to possession by demons when in a trance.'

She went into the expected trance and slumped back into her chair, not so deep as not to be able to receive greetings from the other side, introduced by Rosa's spirit guide the Indian chief Hiawatha, who spoke much like anyone from rural Somerset, and summoned up an Uncle Eric, recently passed over, who spoke of how life and health was restored on the other side, when suddenly Rosa's snores were replaced by demonic guttural groanings, and the cat leapt into the air spitting and yowling and ran off. The audience gasped at the time, and though a few left complaining it was no demon, just a cheap trick, someone had jabbed the cat with a pin, it was remarkable how many remained to watch Rosa wrestle with her demon.

'Money for old rope,' said George to Ivy, 'I told you so.'

Carlotta watched carefully and took notes. Some things became apparent. If you first talked about evil spirits people believed in them. If you shivered and said you felt a cold wind, others felt it too. If you made an audience concentrate on moving a bell on the table they thought they saw it move and didn't notice when another hand moved the lily. If you hoped for a sign from a passed-over loved one, the more you paid the more likely you were to receive such a sign.

George described it as 'the power of suggestion'. Carlotta said it was more like 'the power of wishful thinking'. Ivy said she was almost out of money and the sooner they started making money, not spending it, the better. Her mother's roof was leaking again.

By the time George's poster about Princess Ida of the Cherub Angels of Wisdom brought in a booking for a session above Jolly's, a smart draper's shop in Milsom Street, they had their act worked out. Mrs Henry, who had booked the session at short notice, ran a costumier business and called George in for an interview. She had invited a dozen of her best customers to the entertainment and tea and cakes afterwards; her regular medium had fallen ill. Could Princess Ida oblige? George looked at the wording of the invitation card and was pained. What he offered was not an entertainment, but a profound experience, a meeting of the two worlds, the corporeal and the spiritual. If she would change the wording on her invitation, he would be happy. The dead were not to be mocked, any more than were the living. Mrs Henry — having seen the two letters of recommendation that George produced, one on good thick paper and signed in an educated hand by a Mrs Kennion from Wells and another, more workaday, on thin, lined, but headed paper, from a dairy farmer in Yatbury, both attesting to Princess Ida's great and rare talent in communicating with loved ones — agreed to do so.

George got a good notion of the room, was able to check to what degree the drapes kept out the light, the whereabouts of furniture and fittings, and so forth. Doreen, having been assured that money was shortly on its way to mend her roof, helped out with information as to Mrs Henry's friends, family, and customers.

All worked out very well. Princess Ida rolled her eyes convincingly, and John the Baptist materialized in front of her, half naked, to the shock and pleasure of the company. He was very well muscled and oiled. A glowing ball circled above Carlotta's head (it dangled from the end of a fishing rod held by Ivy, who had a strong arm and a steady hand) and was black from head to toe. St John the Baptist spoke, saying that he was a burning and a shining light returned from the other side for those who were willing for a season to delight in his light, and then he faded out. As did the glowing ball over the Princess's head.

Princess Ida uttered a few phrases, which she had learnt from Frank, about the hidden mysteries of the universe, and how all must learn to love one another and be at peace, and forgive any who had offended them that day, and then answered questions from the audience as to what they were to do to be saved. Her words fell easily into patterns she remembered from her father's sermons. The accordion suddenly played the tune of *The worms crawl in, the worms crawl out* — apparently of its own accord; a few people laughed, and the atmosphere was broken. There was a break for tea and cakes, during which George put his clothes back on and his glasses and returned to the parlour as Princess Ida's manager. Ivy washed her face and hands and took off her black clothes and put them in a bag to be reclaimed after the show, and came into the parlour as a guest who had been delayed waiting for a bus.

'George,' Carlotta asked, getting in as much seed cake as she could manage and still look ladylike. 'Whatever made you play the accordion? The worms crawling song? It made people laugh.'

'But I didn't,' he said, surprised. 'I tried to set it up for "The Last Rose of Summer" as in the Daniel Home book but I gave up. It was too complicated.' He had found the Daniel Home exposé of fraudulent mediums in the College library and now used it as his Bible. 'I didn't hear any accordion, anyway. Perhaps it was Ivy?'

But Ivy denied it. She'd never played the accordion and never wanted to.

George said in that case Carlotta had set it off herself. It was her powers acting up.

'I don't have powers,' she said, but she felt chilled. It was the last thing she had expected. She had done enough experiments while George tried to test her psychic powers: lifting things by willing them to lift, breaking cups by sending hate waves at them, reviving wilting plants by loving them, guessing what objects other people were thinking of. She had managed to revive a plant but that was probably because she'd felt sorry for it and watered it while no one was looking. She had come very low in paranormally gifted charts and she was glad of it.

But George, for one, could see that what happened next was very strange. Mrs Henry seemed right as rain as she poured tea and served cakes. Most of the company was at the window, watching a rather spectacular thunderstorm raging over the hills of Bath. Few saw her drop the teapot and fall into a kind of fit, go into spasms, roll about on the floor and in a few merciful seconds lose consciousness. Those who did see busied themselves with the spilt tea, the broken pot, or else looked politely the other way. George, standing near, thought for a dreadful moment that Mrs Henry had expired. He took her pulse but could have sworn that there was none. But Carlotta knelt by her side and whispered something in her ear, and Mrs Henry's colour returned and after a few minutes she sat up, stood up and drank more tea — someone brought in a new pot and fresh cakes — and nibbled her almond slice as if nothing had happened. The whole episode could only have taken three minutes.

Carlotta, hungry as ever, chose the pink meringues, eating at least three: otherwise seemingly unmoved. Ivy, at the other end of the room, dodging admirers while pocketing the string which linked the drawer of the painted French armoire to the fishing rod, had not even noticed Mrs Henry's collapse.

After the break the guests settled down in

a circle round the big table and held hands. George and Carlotta joined them. Ivy kept the rubber hand under her skirt. Candles spluttered briefly, only for a chilly wind out of nowhere to blow them out. The thunder had not cleared away; the atmosphere was heavy. George, respectable in his suit, deciphered what the planchette board had to say. A child spirit declared himself as Harold, an eight-year-old who had died from drowning six years back, but now happy in paradise. Mrs Henry wept and said her eight-year-old nephew had died in a boating accident and never been found. Princess Ida gave a little speech about how science had proved the continuation of life after death and the existence of the universal over-soul, and how she would be giving away sacramental ribbons from the table in the hall after the session.

The guests went away convinced; none asked for their money back. People even left money for the free ribbons (stock from Doreen's stall she'd had trouble moving) in the Cherub Angel of Wisdom's collecting box. Mrs Henry required forty percent of the takings but George easily beat her down to twenty-five percent. She did not argue. She seemed slightly dazed. Perhaps she knew it was a small price to pay for her life.

George said as much to Carlotta but she didn't seem to know what he was talking about.

'What did you say to her?' George asked Carlotta a week or so later. He had been shaken by the incident, but it seemed prudent to say nothing. Things were going very well as they were; bookings were pouring in, they had a stage show to prepare and the healing business was something he knew little about.

Carlotta looked blank and said she couldn't remember; something like, 'You poor thing,' because that was what she felt. It must have been horrible for poor Mrs Henry to have lost her little nephew the way she did. The pointer on the planchette board had moved by itself, she said: she couldn't stop it. George let the matter lie. Young girls often had psychic powers which faded when they got older.

Ivy let out a few more seams on the red velvet dress; soon it would be too tight. Carlotta's hennaed hair had faded with frequent washing to a reddish gold, and if she stopped penciling her eyebrows she looked more like an angel and less like a whore.

'What's a whore?' asked Carlotta and Ivy laughed and refused to tell her. Carlotta would again be Princess Ida for the next show — a hall which took three hundred and fifty people — and if she came over as some pure creature hovering between the two worlds, so much the better. She would hardly be recognized now. No one had come forward for the reward, the wanted posters had fallen off the walls, and a girl's body had been found in the Kennet and Avon canal. She was forgotten.

George went all the way to Southampton Buildings in London to talk to the examiner at the Patent Office about the possibility of patenting his new device, the Distant Accordion, and was told new laws made it practical, though still expensive. George's other idea of patenting the whole show they had devised under the business name Life after Death Ltd., or L.A.D., as a kind of blueprint which could then be leased out nationwide, was seen as impractical.

A MEETING OF
THE I.D.K. CLUB

Minnie thought Rosina was acting strangely. Some days she glowed and blushed and seemed twenty, other days she looked cross and pale and rather old and anxious. Minnie would have thought she was in love, but how, when? Rosina and she were back at Dilberne Court; Rosina back in her room with Pappagallo finishing her index; Minnie herself back in her studio, though mostly sitting rather than standing because her centre of balance had changed and using watercolours because the smell of oil paint made her dizzy. Arthur was being most attentive, and came back from the workshops every lunchtime to make sure, as he put it, 'her gears were in good order', and was so gentle in bed it could be rather aggravating. She was not about to rust through.

Isobel had called Nanny Brown out of retirement to look after the new baby. Minnie worried that perhaps, having seen both Rosina and Arthur through their growing years, Nanny Brown might be rather old and tired, and the kind to believe a good dose of laudanum was the way to keep a baby tranquil, but Isobel laughed away her fears. Experience was important, and Nanny Brown could be relied upon to choose nursemaids — three would be needed — that were not slovenly or unkind. And when Nanny Brown turned up she seemed such an amiable old duck, and Arthur so pleased to see her, that Minnie gave up worrying. She was in Rome: she would do as Romans did.

Minnie called by Rosina's room one morning to hear the parrot squawking not 'Votes for women', but clucking and chirping, 'I love you, I love you,' as Rosina, greatly embarrassed, tried to throw its cloth over its cage. The parrot, seemingly angered, jeered a few more defiant 'I love you's' loud and clear before lapsing into silence. Rosina refused to elaborate, but asked Minnie to come with her to another meeting of the I.D.K., this one at Carlton Gardens, which Arthur Balfour would be hosting.

'I can't possibly,' said Minnie. 'Your mother would never allow it.'

'She needn't know,' said Rosina. 'We will do it within a couple of days. She is so taken up with ermine trim and getting the Queen's diamond fringe girdle to fit round the royal waist she will not notice. We will tell everyone we are going to Brighton for a day's outing, because you need the sea air. You are eight weeks or so away from your date, so it is perfectly safe. We will manage to miss the last train home and be obliged to stay with my good friend Louisa Martindale in Brighton — I will warn her — but actually we will be in the Savoy. If I can't listen to some intelligent conversation I will go mad.'

'You have already,' said Minnie. 'Who is it? Seebohm Rowntree?'

'Good heavens no,' said Rosina. 'That is a meeting of minds, not bodies.'

'Then who?'

'I am not going to tell you,' said Rosina. 'I care for him but I do not know what he thinks of me. He writes to me from time to time but so strangely it is hard to tell. He has a beautiful mind.'

'I am glad to hear that,' said Minnie. 'Is he a rationalist or an idealist?'

'An idealist,' said Rosina, indignantly.

'Then it must be true love,' said Minnie, sadly.

She thought she had better go with Rosina if only to serve as her chaperone. Her sister-in-law had invited her anonymous beau to the meeting and he had agreed to come. It was hardly proper. And she, Minnie, also longed to get out of the house.

Carlton Gardens was sufficiently grand to please anyone, with its pillars and wide Nash windows, and the guests, some fifty of them, sufficiently intelligent and talkative. Minnie, who had become quite accustomed to the peace and slowness of the countryside, felt almost alarmed by the noise of argument, and fervent opinions defended to the end by noisy and passionate advocates. Over drinks before dinner Rosina pointed out people she knew and claimed were famous, a number of Fabians — little-by-little-socialists — H. G. Wells and George Bernard Shaw from the rationalist camp, and from the idealist camp the Chesterton brothers, though both seemed to be arguing bitterly, and writers from the *Saturday Review.*

A strange thin man who claimed to be its editor came up to Minnie and congratulated her on her condition and told her he had rewritten the Lord's Prayer to its great advantage and when she politely asked him in what way said he had changed the words 'for thine is the Kingdom, the Power and the Glory', to 'the Kingdom, the Power and the Beauty'. Minnie agreed it was an improvement and he went on to complain about the weakness of his digestion and how when he had been obliged to stomach-pump the contents of his lunch that day he had found whole peas, to his horror completely untouched, in the contents. Minnie, rather taken aback, was suggesting he tried chewing his peas so they arrived in a more manageable state, but did not get very far: a rather dandyish writer by the name of Edgar Jepson with a lean intelligent face and a good moustache quickly dragged him away, saying Harris was a genius and a fine editor, but not a fit companion for a young lady. Minnie thought this was probably true. For the most part the guests were male but Rosina pointed out Beatrice Webb, who looked fierce and intimidating, the notorious Violet Hunt and her very plain lover Ford Madox Ford and the children's author Edith Nesbit, who seemed quite friendly and normal and even rather pretty, though batting her eyelashes at GBS who was so busy talking he did not seem to notice.

An etiolated man of venerable mien silenced everyone by proclaiming, 'Ha! A thought.' All waited and he announced that war had a glorious effect on the noble qualities of man.

Clearly no one agreed. Jepson broke an

embarrassed silence with his full-blooded dismissal, saying loudly, 'Ha! Call that a thought?' and the noisy rhetoric of the evening resumed. Jepson had a quite frightening book published that very day, it seemed, called *The Garden at 19,* all about the Great God Pan surfacing in a London suburb and putting paid to respectability. He belonged to the Golden Dawn literary movement, had friends like the abominable Frank Harris and the peculiar poet Walter de la Mare, and as such had no respect at all from the fashionable rationalists.

At nine a simple dinner was served at individual round tables, and a comparative and welcome peace fell as watercress soup, followed by roast beef and Yorkshire pudding was served with plentiful gravy. GBS, a vegetarian, was handed instead three hard-boiled eggs. They were a hungry lot, Minnie observed, tending to eat as if this might well be their last meal. But thinking back to Stanton, the artist lover of her early years, this constant gnawing hunger in the presence of free food seemed to be symptomatic of so many writers and artists. There was a vacant seat next to a disconsolate Rosina. The place card remained, for one Frank Overshaw.

'I suppose that's him,' Minnie said to Rosina. 'The one who isn't here. Frank Over-shaw, one of the jilting kind. Eat up your apple pie and Cheddar and forget him.'

'I can't,' Rosina said. 'We have an affinity. We are joined in the oneness, together in the Dreamtime. There is so much for us to do together. The strength of it frightens him, that's all.'

At this point Arthur Balfour stood up at the top table and greeted his guests, saying that no philosophy in the present age could be other than provisional, and how remark-able it was that mankind, who unlike the birds and the bees could apprehend reality, so delighted in the exercise of reason, for which cause this evening all of opposing views were gathered together — and so on and so forth. All trooped down to a lower lecture hall, where the panel arranged themselves. Frederick Bligh Bond, an archi-tect, sat with the idealists and said as evidence of the continuation of life after death the Society for Psychical Research was to hold a short, live, twenty-minute séance in which Princess Ida, the talented and well-known international medium from Roumania, was to raise a spirit from the dead, and convince the unconvincable. The announcement was met with whistles and catcalls from the rationalist ranks and cheers and claps from the idealists. The lights dimmed. There was a small commotion from the back of the hall; someone was arriving late. Rosina and Minnie both turned to see who it was and saw Rosina's father, Minnie's father-in-law, the Earl of Dilberne, in the company of a tall slim young woman with a swan-like neck, black thick curly hair and a rosebud mouth. She was shrouded in a black velvet cloak and obviously wanted to be unnoticed but there was no unnoticing her. It was Consuelo, Duchess of Marlborough. If by nothing else you could recognize her by the glitter of diamonds at her throat where the edges of her cloak failed to hide them.

Minnie and Rosina looked at one another, and without a word, and simultaneously, found a side door and slipped out of it. Their leaving was not noticed. Arthur Balfour would have to do without their polite goodbyes. It was too bad. What have I done, Minnie thought, what have I done? Worse, what has *he* done? Her own father-in-law?

The enormous marbled baths of the Savoy, the giant showerheads, the good paintings in the corridors — one or two of them originals, but which? — the lights twinkling on the Thames, a few early coronation wreaths swinging gently from the lamp posts, the serene face of Big Ben as seen from her balcony window, did much to calm her. But what Minnie wanted was just to be home in Chicago with her mother.

NEXT YEAR IN JERUSALEM

'What have I done?' asked Naomi Baum, weeping.

Her husband had burned his hands snatching the bracelet from the fire. The gold had not lost its shape or the diamonds dimmed, but Eric's right hand was raw and blistered. Jane had run into the garden and fetched some comfrey leaves, great green tough prickly things which the gardener should have got rid of but hadn't. These she folded between muslin and then soaked and mashed the poultice in vinegar and water, with a splash or two of slippery elm, and now handed to Naomi to wrap round her husband's hand. She had moved so swiftly and competently. Mr Baum wept too, from pain and misery mixed.

'No, what have *I* done?' asked Mr Baum, of the universe. 'Your invitations! What have we both done?'

The doorbell rang. The first of the Ladies

for Zion had arrived. Naomi asked Jane to go down and let them in, explain their hostess had a sudden migraine and could not be there to welcome them in, but suggested they hold the meeting without her, making sure that someone remembered to take the minutes. Jane asked if it would be all right if she stayed for the meeting, and Naomi said, of course, yes.

'Poor Mr Baum,' said Jane, as she went. She seemed to be crying too, and Naomi wondered how she could ever manage without her, while Mr Baum realized that whatever he had done to upset Jane he should be careful not to do it again: if Naomi loved him there would be no temptation. Perhaps the girl would withdraw her notice: perhaps everything would be good again.

'It's my fault,' said Mr Baum, 'please don't let us be like this.' And they sat on the bed together and rocked and wept gently in each other's arms. 'I don't understand,' he said. 'I give you everything.'

'I know,' she said, 'but it's not what I want.'

He asked what it was she did want and she said she didn't know, but she would live wherever he wanted and never refuse him again. Soon they were laughing as much as crying at their own sudden attack of silliness. Eric said he would tell his Lordship the invitations had been lost, and would have them replaced.

'Won't that be awkward?' she asked, and he said yes, it would be but he would do it happily.

She said no; she was going to a rehearsal of the Handel Society in the Queen's Hall, and would explain the situation to Mr Balfour himself; no doubt replacement invitations would be forthcoming. Eric acknowledged it would be a relief if she did that. His relationship with Lady Isobel was not easy and she, not his Lordship, was in charge of the family's social arrangements.

'It's easier to know what you don't want than what you do,' Naomi said. 'What I don't want is living my life as a special case: I so hate not quite belonging, people feeling sorry for me. I love my religion and being what I am, but I simply do not like being one of the dispossessed, the wretched ones.'

The next day Eric stayed at home to nurse his hand and did not go into the office. Late in the morning they walked up to The Bishops Avenue to look at the building site he had bought, Naomi chose the one she preferred, though both looked pretty much the same, desolate and dusty, and the land

408

around arid. She said the land, like all of Hampstead Heath, was not fit for much; it could manage a few roses and a lawn but not much else. It was the scree from an old glacier, stones and rubble built up in its path in the Ice Age. When it got to Hendon the glacier stopped and all the rubbish came tumbling down. Eric marvelled at how much she knew. She reminded him that yes, before the children she used to go to lectures at the Royal Geographical Society, and so did he: he had been a mining man before he was a financial genius. Then she did something strange. She knelt down in the dust and scooped up some soil and let it trickle through her fingers.

'I know what I want,' she said. 'I want to go home. Next year in Jerusalem, all that.'

'You don't know what it's like,' he said. 'A dusty, dangerous land.'

'I don't care,' she said. 'It's my land, it's where I belong, where my children belong. It's not enough for me to make The Bishops Avenue bloom again, though that would be hard enough. I want to build a new land, of peace and plenty and justice, where all are equal and all are free.'

'Yes,' he said, 'and taxes will be high. You are such a socialist! You will be very uncomfortable: so will the children.'

'They will grow up to be real people,' she said. 'Tall and handsome and strong.'

'If they grow up,' he said. 'That's the problem. They are safe here.'

'That's not enough,' she said. 'Being safe. I want you to sell these plots of land. They are in the wrong place. I want you to buy one on Mount Zion.'

He thought for a little.

'No, not Mount Zion. Inside the old city walls is safer and better. More expensive, mind you. I don't think I could bear communal living.'

'Very well,' she said, 'Inside the city walls.'

'No more diamonds,' he said, 'no more maidservants, just basic next year in Jerusalem. It will be hard work. You will have to take off your wig.'

'I'd take it off now,' she said. 'Except I'd look such a sight.'

They walked back hand in hand. Jane remarked upon how happy they looked and they told her their plans. She asked if she could come too? She had given in her notice because she was so bored, everything was so dull, the local boys so weedy and pimply. If she could have time off to go to classes, could she take her notice back? She loved Reuben and Ruth, but she wanted to make the desert bloom, too, the way the Ladies for Zion had been saying. She wanted to be included in the family. They loved each other; she'd seen that. The way Naomi had bandaged Eric's hand. In her house everyone shouted at each other. Perhaps she could convert?

They hardly knew what to say, other than, 'It's not simple.'

A STRUGGLE WITH BELIEF

Frederick Bligh Bond of the Society for Psychical Research was right; the séance offered was a most interesting and fascinating demonstration of the continuation of life and death. It was of course humbug, and fairly obviously fraudulent. His Lordship did not understand why Arthur Balfour, a perfectly intelligent man, went on wasting his time and intelligence on charlatans. It was one thing to engage in a dinner debate about the decline of religion and the rise of superstition — whether, as Shakespeare said, 'the instruments of darkness tell us truths' was always good for a debate — but to ask your friends to sit through twenty minutes of a woman in a darkened room having fits and talking to spirits was quite another.

But Consuelo seemed excited by the prospect — she was interested in the esoteric arts, as so many of the very wealthy were. They looked for alternatives to the hell they feared they deserved. The likes of Balfour, on the other hand, comparatively impoverished, while perfectly sure that he deserved heaven, perhaps hoped to control death in the same way as he controlled life. The death of friends and family simply offended him.

His Lordship hoped that the others, a bibulous crowd, would turn up soon; their cabs seemed to have been delayed. Being seen alone with Consuelo was not altogether wise, and yet she so often managed it. Perhaps she had little men running after her, peering into windows, overhearing her conversations, recording her every move? Did she want to persuade Sunny to divorce her, and was providing him with evidence against her, to spare him the trouble of finding it himself? He would not put it past her. The others turned up, to his relief, including Sunny himself, and all moved into the row reserved for them, and the show began.

Princess Ida turned out not to be not some puddingy housewife but an extremely pretty young girl with a refined face and an educated tongue — very different from the ordinary run of lady mediums, who tended to look as if the spirits coursing through from the other side had drained them of looks, style, and intelligence. There was a kind of slackness and coarseness of personality which kept company with those who dealt too closely with the occult. But Princess Ida, who wore a childish dress — too tight, in faded red velvet — and had an ethereal air. When they adjourned for drinks he heard Gilbert Chesterton's brother Cecil compare her to a Botticelli angel but Edgar Jepson, the gathering being of its nature refractory, retorted: 'More like one of Alphonse Mucha's Moët et Chandon White Star Line advertisements.'

At least Princess Ida didn't foam or twitch when she went into a trance, just drifted off into a kind of angelic, blissful state in which you could believe that her real home was heaven, whose comings and goings it was her task to report. When she spoke in tongues they were melodic rather than guttural. Raps both startled and amused, and seemed to have a sense of humour, tapping out the sound of *The Death March* or *Lillibulero* at wholly inappropriate moments, accompanied by an accordion that played by itself. Only when a lost and wandering soul that was transmitted through the planchette identified itself as being that of May Lyttleton, and talked of searching high and low for her engagement ring, credibility lessened. It just seemed too obvious. Every-one knew how Arthur Balfour had pined all his life for May, and had thrown their engagement ring into the coffin with her body. 'May' faded back into wherever she had come from and the session came to an end. Then something happened that shook even his cynical Lordship.

A sparrow had flown in through the open window into the hall and had been flying about happily above the audience's head — there must have been a good eighty people present — and chirruping away, before deciding it wanted to leave but, finding no way out, flew into a panic and hurled itself between one wall and another before dash-ing head first with a thump and a cracking of glass against the tall window behind Princess Ida's table — George had just opened the curtains to let in the light and demonstrate the absence of any fraudulent appliances. The bird fell instantly to the ground: it was obvious it was dead. Princess Ida got up from her chair, cradled the little limp creature in her hands and stroked its feathers for a little. Then she said quite loud and clear, and slightly crossly, 'Do wake up!' Whereupon the sparrow did just that, open-ing its eyes, struggling to its feet, and within moments opening its wings and flying off unerringly through the window by which it had come in. Heads turned to watch it as it went. It seemed so cheerful, so normal.

Silence fell.

'It was stunned,' said a voice from the audience, 'that was all.' The voice came from the rationalist camp. The audience had divided itself roughly into two, the idealists on the left, the rationalists on the right, choosing the propinquity of the like-minded, as, his Lordship had noticed, people will usually do if left to their own devices.

'No,' said another. 'It cracked that great window. That bird could not ordinarily have survived.' That came from the don't-knows.

'It had a heart attack?' said someone else irrelevantly.

'It's a miracle,' piped up Consuelo, from the front row where the grandees sat — so it carried more weight than perhaps it should have. 'First it was dead: then it was alive. We watched a miracle.'

'It was a trick,' grumbled the rationalists. 'Imbeciles!' His Lordship, agreeing, decided that chicanery could indeed be the only answer.

The grandees left the I Don't Knowers to their noisy debate, and gathered round Balfour in his antechamber. He seemed not to be much concerned with the incident of the bird. May had come back from the other side and spoken to him. He was distressed, happy and overwhelmed all at the same time. He seemed to feel the need to explain. 'We were indeed engaged,' he was saying. 'It was her voice, the dearest girl, I would know it anywhere. I had the ring, ready to give her, before the illness overcame her. I put it in the coffin. It was the least I could do.'

'I know the story, Arthur,' said Consuelo, with surprising acerbity. 'But knowing you, I don't suppose you got round to actually asking the poor girl. Ever the bachelor!'

Balfour ignored her. The Society for Psychical Researchers were agreeing that Princess Ida had a well-developed mediumistic talent, and that they would ask her to participate in their next controlled experiment. She was indeed very pretty.

His Lordship slipped away and took a cab back to Belgrave Square and Isobel. Whatever game Consuelo was playing it was dangerous. He would steer well clear of her in future. One had to be very careful of pretty faces. Look at the S.P.R.: faced with an obvious piece of trickery (though how it had been achieved, he had no idea) a pretty face reduced them all to idiocy.

A Night at the Savoy

Rosina was in the lobby of the hotel, engaging with the reservation clerk, suggesting that perhaps the reason she had been given an inferior room was because she was a woman, when Frank Overshaw, flustered and distraught, came in through the swing doors of the lobby.

Seeing Rosina at the desk, he crossed over to her saying, 'Oh, your Ladyship, Rosina, I am so pleased to have found you! I thought we'd missed each other!'

To which Rosina replied crossly, to the reservation clerk as much as anyone, 'I am Lady nobody, I am reserved under the name of Miss Rosina Hedleigh,' and gestured Frank to wait on one of the armchairs under the great central chandelier. The clerk seemed to believe Frank, since instead of arguing, as he had been inclined — there was nothing wrong with the room, other than that the maid had neglected to turn down the sheet and pull the curtains to on her late-night round — saw fit to upgrade her to one of the superior rooms: one argued with Misses, but not with Ladies.

By the time the room was sorted out Frank had quite recovered his composure. He took her to the bar, and though the bartender looked surprised he consented to serve them Manhattans. Rosina watched while the bartender had a surreptitious word with the concierge who had a word with the desk, who looked over to where they sat and nodded a discreet approval. She was not a lady of the night.

'I missed the train,' he said. 'I was wrangling with the Bishop. Mrs Kennion had become hysterical. I regret nothing except causing trouble to my Aunt, who has been so good to me.'

'I thought you had changed your mind. I sat there at the dinner table next to an empty seat and told myself he is just another deceiver, a man who likes to lead women on with false hopes only to dash them at the last moment. They delight in it. There are men like that.'

'Not Australians,' he said. 'They don't have the bloody time.'

'Hush, Frank,' she said. 'That's a word for the Australian bush, not the Savoy.'

'Then the sooner we have you out there the better,' he said, 'so you can say it too. My bloody oath!'

He said the purser of the *Cuzco* was happy with the change of name on the tickets but would be pleased to have a glance at the marriage lines, if only to keep the owners happy. Serious efforts were being made to keep undesirables out of Australia. 'I told him I was marrying a Lady of the Realm and he soon shut up.'

The problem, and why he had missed the train, was that the Bishop refused to give Rosina away, a girl he hardly knew, or permit the Canon to marry them. The Bishop found it outrageous. A man could not simply replace one girl with another in order to suit a shipping company's timetable.

'I can see it is unusual,' said Rosina, 'but it is certainly practical.'

'And there is the question of the banns,' said Frank. 'I had forgotten about those.'

'Then we will get married in a Registry Office, not a church,' she said. But he balked at this: he wanted to be married to a girl in a white veil.

Both said they loved each other, agreed they were made for each other and had probably met in another life. Then they had another Manhattan; and then another Manhattan. He said he'd had a wonderful dream in which poor Adela appeared in the guise of Eostre the Saxon Goddess of Spring, with flowing robes and flowers in her hair. She gave him and Rosina her blessing and wished them well. Adela's fate had been to die in the fire: a mistake had been made, now corrected. Rosina had been the one intended for Frank Overshaw. Karma had been served: all should be happy.

Rosina thought perhaps the dream was a little self-serving, but belief was so much easier than doubt. She had finished the index: the book was at the publishers: she wanted very much to go to Australia and look after the aboriginals, and teach them mining. Her own family had a mining background. There was a new study called ethnography: she had been to a few lectures: it was all about the origins of different cultures: she would do some studies.

She could see that Western Australia was the back of beyond, and probably very uncomfortable. But Frank was a decent man, and she did not see that Theosophy was any stranger than anything else anyone believed in. The acquaintance was certainly very short; but they had got on very well in the Bishop's Palace: embraced sufficiently in the library to understand it would be pleasant to embrace more, gone on to exchange increasingly fond and intimate letters — he had enclosed some sketches of her, which had not been at all lacking in imagination — and she had been so upset when he had not turned up at the I.D.K. dinner she could almost say truthfully she loved him.

She would miss the Coronation but she could put up with that. She would miss Minnie but Minnie would soon be having a baby. Her brother Arthur cared only for engines, her mother cared only for clothes, her father only for politics and, if tonight was anything to go by, girls young enough to be his daughter.

She did not want to stand by to see Isobel's distress when her father's secret came out, as secrets always did. She only hoped the scandal would not be public. It was the kind that could rock nations, if the girl in question was who Rosina thought it was. She would rather go to Australia.

She assumed her parents would give her some kind of allowance. Frank said he had more than enough wealth for both of them, but it was always advisable for a woman to have at least some money of her own.

They had another Manhattan and worked

out ways of smuggling Frank up to her bedroom. The best way, they decided, was for her to say goodnight and go publicly to her bedroom and for Frank to take another room in the hotel and join her later. No one would be fooled but the proprieties would be observed. Frank did not quibble about the unnecessary cost. She was glad of that. One would not want to be stuck out in the Australian desert, or anywhere, with a mean man. She would have to face her parents' wrath, but she would worry about that to-morrow.

The next morning Minnie was taking breakfast in her room; her condition was now most obvious no matter how full her skirts, and while the intellectuals of the I.D.K. delighted in their advanced thinking, guests at the Savoy were of a more conventional mould. She was surprised when there was a knock at the door and was taken aback when Rosina came in, accompanied by a youngish man she did not know. Rosina introduced him as Frank Overshaw of Western Australia, her betrothed; they were to be married by special licence and sail for Freemantle within the week. Their tickets were booked. No, her parents did not know: she would be going round to Belgrave

Square with Frank that morning to tell them.

Minnie remembered what living with Stanton had been like, in that other world, long ago and far away, when the unexpected and rather alarming was a day-to-day occurrence. She recovered from her annoyance that Rosina had misled her so and wished her and Frank every good fortune. She declined to go with the happy pair to Belgrave Square. She would make her own way back to Dilberne Court to be with Arthur. She was feeling perfectly well, thank you very much. She thought Frank Overshaw a little strange and not someone she would have married but every girl to her own taste.

She rang for room service and ordered breakfast for her guests. There would be some talk but really in the circumstances what did it matter? Frank Overshaw asked for Bircher-Muesli, a concoction of raw oats, nuts and raisins moistened by cream and lemon juice. Minnie tasted it and found it quite delicious.

CARLOTTA TURNS SEVENTEEN

After the gig in Milsom Street bookings for Princess Ida had been steady: there had been enquiries from as far away as London. Carlotta continued to do the platform work, George to plan and manage lighting and props, and Ivy took the money, kept the books, and helped out George. They developed a few extras: psychokenesis, in which Princess Ida lifted a chair in the air by the power of thought and moved it towards her before sitting in it; another one in which a panama hat materialized out of darkness to land on someone's head. That always got a laugh. Levitation would need another person. They did small private sessions and larger public ones, which proved to be less profitable after you paid for the hire of the hall and overheads. George's only problem was deciding which way forward to take the show. Raising the spirits of the dead was their mainstay, but this didn't bring in a class audience, just the poor and the gullible who had very little to spend. They expected ectoplasm, too, which was messy stuff and hard to control, and which both Carlotta and Ivy hated. The show, he reckoned, had to be positioned somewhere between a music-hall act, an uplifting demonstration of the power of the human mind when released from doubt, and spooky voices from the grave.

They'd moved to London when they had built up a good enough network of connections. Mrs Henry had good contacts in fashionable circles there. George observed that Princess Ida's looks and cultivated voice opened many doors that would otherwise be closed. They'd rented rooms in a boarding house on the fifth floor of a big house in Earls Court: the advantages being that it was cheap and their comings and goings would not be noticed, or the strange equipment they carried about: the disadvantage was the stairs. Ivy did most of the housework and cooking and complained that Carlotta didn't like getting her hands dirty.

'Well, she is a lady,' George had rather rashly replied and Ivy had gone off into a huff which had lasted days. It was remarkable how a sour face affected takings.

George could see something had to be done. Jealousy was rearing its ugly head. He was fond of Ivy, and had resigned himself to Carlotta being out of his league; yet wondered quite why. He would look at her on a platform, the way she moved, spoke, inclined her head, with a kind of reverence that ill became him, a young entrepreneur of the new century.

Carlotta moved about the house with a childlike confidence, laughing and chattering, which made him feel fatherly. But he was not her father. He could not do without Ivy: he did not want to do without Ivy. She was of the flesh rather than of the spirit, he doubted that Carlotta would ever consent to what Ivy consented to, and nor probably would he want her to. The rational thing would be to live in a *ménage à trios:* if men proposed this, women sometimes consented. Half a man, they thought, was better than no man at all. Ivy could probably learn to settle into it; Carlotta was so off into her own head she might not even notice. One way or another he imagined she knew all about the birds and bees by now. How could she not? He and Ivy made enough noise.

In fact he was confused; he thought perhaps he was in love. The tune of *Come into the garden, Maud* kept coming into his head. Granted, he had worked the accordion to play the first few phrases but it kept surfacing in his head:

Come into the garden, Maud,
For the black bat, night, has flown.
Come into the garden, Maud,
I am here at the gate alone . . .

The lover, waiting, while the scents of the night drifted around. Beautiful. He wanted to call her Adela. She had never been a Carlotta, this girl he had rescued from the flames, her arms so trustingly, childishly, round him. May the 21st was going to be her birthday. She seemed to have forgotten. She had put her past behind her so admirably. She looked ahead into the future, straight as a die, clear-eyed. Perhaps he should encourage her to go into the healing business but then she wouldn't want him any more. He wanted her to need him. She looked blank when he mentioned the Mrs Henry business, and just said it must have been some kind of fit. And of the other night's bird incident, all she said was she had stroked the creature, it had recovered and then flew out.

What was odd about that?

'What was odd,' said Ivy sourly, 'was that a bird dashed itself to pieces in the first place, possessed by a demon, like as not. Things are getting too spooky.'

Carlotta had been all set to do a child's voice when the young woman who'd died of typhoid fever had come through and taken over. George said he'd intervened to seize the moment; having done so much research he didn't want to waste it. But he knew in his heart it wasn't true. The voice had been echoing all around. It was kind of a phenomenon that did happen. They'd talked about it at college as 'a non-conscious intelligence': an energy that happened when a lot of people were concentrating on the same thing.

A week or so after this conversation, when Ivy's mother in Yatbury fell ill, Ivy had to go and sort things out. This meant she had to leave George alone with Carlotta and she was none too pleased, but there was little she could do about it, except to warn George to leave Carlotta alone. Once done, of course, she regretted it: tell a man what to do and he will do the opposite. One show had to be cancelled and another simplified so that George and Carlotta could manage.

So it was that George was able to take Carlotta to the Prospect of Whitby to

429

celebrate the birthday she had forgotten all about. They travelled by pleasure boat to Wapping. It was a truly beautiful evening. George surprised Adela — he would call her that name from now on, he said — by quoting Tennyson, though she suspected much of it came from *Come into the garden, Maud.*

He held her hand, and she wished he wouldn't. She had hero-worshipped George for a time, but it was hard to adore someone who lived so close to you: they were just people, with noses to blow and tempers to lose. He was like a brother and brothers and sisters didn't hold hands that way, she knew enough now to know that. It was still a bit vague, but a girl she'd met in a queue had explained what men did to women to have babies. It seemed they did it even when they didn't want babies. It was rather revolting but judging from George and Ivy it was enjoyable, once you had realized it wasn't someone's death throes. 'No better than you ought to be' meant you did it when you weren't married. George was moving his knuckle up and down in her palm, and talking about the evening star, Venus. She wanted to laugh, it was so unlike him.

She would rather he didn't call her Adela; that was another world she had once lived in, full of flames and fire and palaces and complete unreality. But he seemed bent upon it. She wished Ivy had been able to come; it spoiled things not to have her around. She never knew what to say to men, they struck her dumb.

The Prospect of Whitby was an enormous public house with lots of rooms and little stairways leading to nowhere in particular, and she wondered why he had taken her to this place of all places. When George had called her Adela again she'd had a vivid memory of the dining hall at the Bishop's Palace, with the harpist and the gold candle-sticks — Babylonian, her father had called it. Now George led her into a bar that was full of men and women in a state of more or less undress and intoxication sharing cigarettes; it seemed a very odd place to have come to. Here he plied her with glasses of gin and tonic. She had rather too many, which she supposed was his plan. She did not like the smell of the cigarettes: he smoked but she certainly did not.

He said it was her birthday, she was seventeen and it was time for them to know each other better. He knew a place where they could go. He slipped his arm under her jacket and squeezed her breast. He said he loved her.

'That's a strange way of showing it,' she said. 'It hurts.'

He said she had cast a spell over him. He wanted only to serve her. Adela! Adela! He beseeched her. She could see this was so much nonsense. She remembered Frank Overshaw wanting to take her off by ocean liner to teach the aboriginals of Western Australia mining. This one only aspired to a river boat and Wapping. She thought she was worth more. She could tell the difference between a fairy prince and Rumpelstiltskin. She slapped his hand very hard and told him to stop. He did so at once and took her to a place where they served rather good steak and kidney pie and beer, and there was no nonsense from him any more. She was relieved. He was her brother again.

■ ■ ■ ■

JUNE — 1902

■ ■ ■ ■

THE CORONATION LOOMS

Arthur Balfour was surprised when Mrs
Baum called to visit him at Carlton Gardens
on the morning of the 2nd of June. As it
happened he was at home. It was a momentous day. First thing that morning he had
authorized Broderick at the War Office to
release the news of the official ending of the
South African war. The King had been
informed. The Bishop of Stepney would announce it at his evening service at Westminster Abbey. Prayers would be said and bells
rung. The nation could proceed to the
Coronation in good cheer. A great trial was
over. Not only that, the nation's wealth
would be greatly increased by the emptied
coffers of the now annexed Boer territories.
There would be a lot less carping about the
cost of the Coronation.

Balfour had intended to take the rest of
the morning off by playing a round of golf
at Henry Tubbs's golf course in Hendon,

but the weather was so bad it hardly seemed worthwhile. It was a disappointment; the course was only nine holes and the members were eccentric, insisting on wearing a uniform — scarlet with brass buttons — but old Tubbs was an amiable enthusiast and always good for a golf conversation. There were precious few places near central London where a man could play, and he needed his mind clearing. His uncle, Robert Salisbury, would most likely be stepping down next month: as his successor he must make final decisions as to his new Cabinet, not be taken by surprise. Ritchie, tough but loyal, should probably replace Hicks Beech as Chancellor. Financial matters grew more complex, loomed larger in the nation's understanding of itself than it should, but there it was. On the home front a letter from Mary Elcho which would need thinking about before replying. And of course, May's voice still echoing in his ears; that had disturbed him greatly. It was one thing to search, another to find.

And then of all things there was Naomi Baum tapping at his front door. Well, he would let her in, he would see her. It would stop him brooding, as he'd hoped a round of golf would do. He knew Naomi and liked her, a spirited young woman who sang beautifully and was wife to Mr Baum, who had saved so many of his landed colleagues from financial disaster, and who was a leading light of the Handel Society. It was good to talk to someone from the ordinary world. He made her sit down and talk. There had been some trouble with their invitations to the Coronation, it seemed. Theirs had come, at his instigation, to the Dilbernes via Consuelo. He remembered having delegated the task to her. These invitations were like gold dust. How had it ended up at prime ministerial level, with this damp woman — the rain had not stopped all day; jubilant crowds would be having a hard time of it — on his doorstep?

'I could say I lost them,' she said. 'I could say they blew away in the wind, I could say the dog ate them, but I think I will tell you the truth. There was a domestic tiff. I threw a diamond bracelet in the fire and in retaliation my husband threw the invitations.'

'What, the highly responsible Mr Baum?'

'I drove him to it,' she said. 'In penance I have come to see you.'

That made him laugh.

'And now you want them back again?'

'Of course.' He called his secretary and asked him to sort it out, and when Mrs Baum rose to go he asked her to stay. He asked if she was going to hear Clara Butt singing Elgar's *Land of Hope and Glory,* and when she said she had her ticket booked, asked her to bring back news of it; he would not be able to find the time to go. They chatted about this, and that, and why Handel was so dear to the English heart. In the course of the conversation she said she and her husband were to buy land in Palestine.

'I hope that doesn't mean your husband's talents will be lost to us,' said Balfour. 'It would be too bad if he ends up growing vegetables in a desert.'

'I don't see it quite like that,' she said, 'and nor should you.' She was bold and serious. She didn't prattle on, as so many women did. But then she belonged to a bold and serious race. Quite extraordinary how through their nomadic life the Jews had clung, century after century, to their rituals, their religious beliefs, always in the face of hostility. Now the new wave of pogroms, this time in Roumania. They deserved a better deal.

'It may be desert,' she said, 'but it too would benefit from a little Handel, a choir, a string quartet. We will build concert halls and theatres, as well as grow vegetables. There is nothing wrong with vegetables.'

Another starry-eyed idealist, he thought,

but the idea caught his fancy. The new land
a handful of international Jewry demanded
seen in a different light — not just an armed
encampment, but one ruled by a concert
hall, with Bach and Handel drowning out
the sound of warfare. Unlikely, but the most
surprising things could happen. He was not
surprised she had tiffs with Baum, or he
with her, but she had the great gift of enthusiasm.

He laughed politely, changed the subject,
and asked how Baum was getting on with
the Dilberne household. He thought he'd
caught a glimpse of the daughter at the
I.D.K. debate but she must have left early.
He gathered there had been some trouble?
Naomi was pleasantly indiscreet. Balfour
had the feeling she did not like Lady Isobel
very much. Apparently it was true: the
daughter had run off practically overnight
with an Australian, after a marriage by licence.

'Isobel wanted Bishop Kennion to officiate, but he refused. He said the groom was
a Theosophist and worshipped strange gods
and graven images: a Bishop only married
Christians.'

'Reasonable enough for a Bishop, I
daresay,' said Balfour. 'Though many today
manage to add Theosophical leanings to

their Christian faith.'

'The Bishop could have chosen a dozen other reasons,' said Naomi. 'The Dilberne girl was so desperate to get away from home she threw herself at the Australian, who just a month back had been engaged to poor Adela, the one who disappeared and was found drowned. Lady Isobel had been too busy with her charities to visit her. The shipping company wouldn't refund Adela's ticket so he married Rosina rather than waste the fare. Well, that's what they're saying. It's going to be a disaster.'

'I hope there was a little more romance than that,' said Balfour and Naomi softened and said yes, she hoped so too. She only had it all from Eric, and the matter of Adela's inheritance was driving Eric mad.

'Anyway,' she said, 'the young couple sailed away on the good ship *Cuzco* with no bands playing or flags waving, in disgrace because they'd spent the night together in the Savoy. Eric got the bill.'

'At least they have a daughter off their hands.'

'But she left with nothing but a husband, a Gladstone bag and her parrot. Her father refuses to give her an allowance. It would never happen in a Jewish family. And now with her daughter missing Isobel has to

parade at the Coronation with the Countesses, not behind the Duchesses. Poor thing.
She won't like that. I try not to be nasty
about her but I can't help it. She did send
us tickets for the Coronation, I know,
though that will have been his Lordship's
doing, not hers. I'm talking too much, I
know, I'm nervous.'

She fell silent, embarrassed. Balfour asked
her if she was looking forward to the Parry
anthem and she said she was, very much.
And up to a point to the Elgar rendering of
the National Anthem.

'You doubt that either will rise to the
heights of Purcell or Handel?'

'I hope you don't think me unpatriotic,'
she said, 'but no.'

He agreed that earlier composers wrote
for the glory of God more than monarchs,
but it was perhaps understandable if in such
a year as this modern composers devoted
themselves to national pride. She conceded
a point, and asked after the health of the
King.

Balfour was surprised: so far as he knew
the King was perfectly healthy, dedicated as
ever to duty, caught up with the detail of
the Coronation, even down to the designs
licensed on ceramic commemoration mugs,
and the decoration on lamp posts along the

Mall. Potentates and dignitaries from abroad had already been sighted bowling along through London in their carriages, only occasionally colliding with automobiles that were slow getting out of the way. Commonwealth and Empire troops with wonderful headgear had been seen on parade. London boroughs had promised tenants a day off work and free beer for everyone; street parties were being organized. Twenty-four days to go and expectation was building nicely. If the weather was bad now it would be better by the end of the month.

'The King has taken to a milk diet in place of his evening meal,' he said. 'So much I've heard. But I imagine it's due to vanity rather than ill health. His waist is forty-eight inches and bigger than his chest, as happens to many a man of his age. I daresay that like a bride he wishes to be at his best on this day of days. Ceremonial sashes must fit, ermine capes hang gracefully. The Queen is the same. She eats like a bird.'

Naomi said she had heard a rumour that the King had lumbago; she knew it to be a very painful ailment and she hoped it didn't mean he'd have to hobble up the aisle to receive his crown. Balfour laughed.

'Though his Majesty has to crawl up the aisle he will get there, while pretending it doesn't hurt one whit. He will die rather than let his people down.'

He asked Naomi what her religion had to say about death.

'Very little,' she said, surprised. 'I suppose we think how we conduct our lives is more important.'

'No belief in an afterlife, in the continuation of life after death?'

'No,' she said. 'Why?' He found himself confiding in her; told her about the séance and how May's voice had come to him out of the past, so much like her yet not her.

'A voice of your own creation,' she observed. 'You want to hear her; it does not mean you did.' He liked her. So many people said what he wanted to hear — friends, colleagues, lovers — all wanting praise, acknowledgement or preferment.

'But I heard her. It was not an illusion. A shadow of her living self, but still her. The dead do lack the clarity of the living. Sometimes I think they are just shadows of the real thing, an echo imprinted on the past. If one could only be sure. It is very annoying to have to live with such uncertainty. No one can prove that God exists, but neither can they prove that he does not.'

Mrs Baum said that so far as she was concerned, dead was dead. Balfour laughed.

'It would certainly be something of a relief to think so when it comes to political enemies. One does not want them to live for ever; one reserves reincarnation for friends and family, I find.' It was wise to appear light-hearted about these things.

But he came to the decision that he would invite Princess Ida to a further séance and see what came up. He had resolved to keep away from the paranormal: hearing May's voice had been most disturbing, and there had been some talk of a demon-possessed bird which had hurled itself into a wall and killed itself. A sense of debilitation and oppression could descend when one trespassed into the next world. But another foray seemed appropriate. May's voice had sounded less as if it came from heaven as from some vast echoey waiting room where the dead waited to be housed in their new lives. Hers had not been an easy death: the wait would be long before mental equilibrium was restored; it fitted with the theory. Just one more time. The S.P.R. thought very well of Princess Ida; she had been very *sympathique,* as well as pretty.

The secretary came back with news that the matter of the invitations had been solved: the replacements would be with the Baums in the next post. His Grace the Duke of Marlborough wished to speak to Mr Balfour when he had a moment. Mrs Baum rose to go. Mr Balfour said he had enjoyed the conversation, which was true. He privately thought it was rather a waste to lose such an excellent couple to Palestine, but he rather liked the idea of European-style tiffs and Handel on Mount Zion. Let neurosis and exultation be exported. The rain had still not stopped.

LADY ISOBEL WAITS

The storm over Rosina's abduction — as Robert saw it — by a colonial mountebank and fortune hunter, who had a poste restante address and lived amongst primitive savages in a land populated by convicts, redback spiders and kangaroos, for some reason put paid to Isobel's black fog. There had been such a scurry of activity — perhaps that's what she lacked? Things fell back into proportion. She soothed Robert as best she could. He was angry with himself, the Bishop of Bath and Wells, Frank Overshaw, herself, and Rosina in that order.

She too was annoyed with Rosina, not least because she had lured Minnie out on an excursion on false pretences when she should have had her feet up, and then abandoned her in London to make her own way home. Though why Minnie had not just made her way to Belgrave Square Isobel could not imagine. But at least she had come to no harm and was now waiting her time out in peace and comfort. The baby was kicking well and was carried high, so it was sure to be a boy. Nanny Brown was installed and waiting. Minnie had been so passionate about requiring no wet-nursing that Isobel had given in; the baby would feed the modern way, with condensed milk. Isobel had to agree it had done Minnie well enough.

That of course was not the worst of Rosina's sins; marrying without her father's consent, and though Minnie had said nothing about what happened at the Savoy, no doubt breaking the rules of decency and common sense by giving herself to a man before marriage. And she herself was at fault for not supervising Rosina more closely when they spent the night at the Bishop's Palace. Men without families too often got what they wanted and then moved on. But Rosina had been lucky. More, Frank Overshaw's 'family' turned out to be some connection, however loose, with an ex-governor of Adelaide, which was better than nothing but not enough to placate Robert.

'But Robert,' she had said, 'would you rather the girl ended up an old maid than married a commoner?'

'I'd rather she stayed unmarried than she

447

married the fool of a man she has,' was all he'd say. 'Theosophy! Bunkum! The Great Oneness, all that. Did you hear him? And I thought Rosina was a clever girl!'

'A clever girl agrees with her husband,' said Isobel primly, thus fuelling Robert's outrage further. She found herself oddly thrilled by her daughter's leap into the unknown. She looked forward to the first letters home. When Robert threatened to give Rosina no allowance she said she would pay it herself out of the miserable scraps of her own inheritance, and he capitulated. She put that down to his bad conscience.

Robert felt bad about his initial rejection of Adela, his own brother's daughter. He felt bad about his inability to mourn Edwin.

He felt extremely bad about the girl's disappearance and apparent *felo de se*. The coroner had thought so — the same coroner who had passed judgement on the parents' death now passed judgement on the unhappy child — the verdict was suicide when the balance of her mind was disturbed. At least she could be buried in sanctified ground, next to her parents. At least Robert had consented to go to that funeral and very upsetting for everyone it had been.

He felt bad about putting himself so much in the wrong in the Bishop's eyes, and saw fit to speak ill of him as a result: after first all but kidnapping the girl the Bishop had failed to protect her and look after her, and once she was gone, had made little effort to find her.

He felt bad about Frank Overshaw because he, Robert, had failed to find Rosina a better husband. Because he had not loved his daughter better. Or so it seemed to Isobel. His instinct was to blame others for his own failings. He was, after all, a man. He blamed Isobel for not having saved him from himself. He blamed her because he had a brief almost-flirtation with Consuelo, Duchess of Marlborough and then had thought better of it.

The night before Rosina had ignited the fire of his rage, he had told Isobel about his evening at the I.D.K. dinner, the séance, the company, the debate. The prettiness of Princess Ida. The folly of Mr Balfour who had allowed, even encouraged, the debate, pretending an interest in science but actually serving his own ends, assuring, he hoped, a victory for idealists; but how Mr Shaw and Mr Wells had routed Mr Chesterton and Mr Belloc. How the séance had been a disgrace of its kind, exposing Mr Balfour to public ridicule, when the voice of his former lady friend, long dead, had spoken and a bird had been brought back to life. How Consuelo had disappointed him, crying out, 'It's a miracle,' when it was obvious to all intelligent people that they were witnessing a fraud.

Isobel assumed that the reason for this outburst of information was to tell her that whatever it was it was over. He was disappointed in Consuelo.

Later that night when she was safely in his arms he told her why he had turned against Edwin. It was because Edwin had turned against him. It was not just Edwin's refusal to come to Minnie and Arthur's wedding; that could be put down to general disagreeableness, a difficult wife and bigotry. These were cardinal not mortal sins. But Edwin had also written to say that he had proof in the form of a letter from his father to his mother accusing her of adultery over a long period; asserting that neither Robert or Alfred were his sons, but Albert, the eldest, and Edwin, the fourth, were. That therefore he, Edwin, was by rights the earl.

'I did not believe him,' said Robert. 'The man is mad who impugns his own mother. My father never wrote any such letter. It was not in his nature. I burned my brother's letter and heard no more from him. Which was just as well, or I would have killed him.'

This off his chest, he fell soundly asleep, and Isobel, who had never met her mother-in-law, was left wondering if this could possibly be true, and thinking that if such a letter ever had existed, with any luck it would have gone up in flames, together with the invitations she had so rashly sent out, hoping to bring the family together.

A Queen Is Dressed

The new King and Queen were moving out of Marlborough House and into Buckingham Palace, but by degrees. Their daughter-in-law, the new Princess of Wales, back with her children after her nine-month tour of the Empire and anxious to settle into her new official residence, found the move going rather slowly. But with the date of the Coronation looming, Alexandra at last moved her extensive wardrobe to Buck House. It was here that Consuelo and Isobel found themselves inspecting the clothes set out by the staff for the great day. Alexandra was on her way back from Windsor, where the King had decided to stay, at a distance from domestic turmoil, busying himself with changing the staff's livery from blue to brown with the help, or as he felt, hindrance, of Horace Farquhar, Master of the Household.

The King would not, Alexandra complained on her arrival, could not, leave well alone. Nor would he come with her to London for the rehearsal at Westminster Abbey which she felt was so necessary. It was all very well for him, of course: he would have the Bishop of Bath and Wells by his side, instructing him, telling him where to go and what to say and when, and she, the Queen, would have no one. She would have to remember the prayers and the moves herself. The Bishop would assist her up the steps — she being a woman it was assumed she needed supporting — but then he would desert her for the King. If anyone needed supporting, Alexandra observed, it was Archbishop Temple, who was at least eighty and liable to expire any minute.

The Queen sent Isobel and Consuelo to the Robing Room while she retired to bed and took some lemon tea. She was not usually given to complaint, Isobel thought, let alone being critical of the King. But perhaps she was just tired.

'Troubled is the head that wears a crown,' said Consuelo, once they were in the Robing Room. The Queen's new crown stood on a plinth in pride of place, looking, both thought, rather cheap and ridiculous, as if borrowed from Mr Maskelyne.

'It's a disaster,' Consuelo said bluntly. 'It's

ugly. It's squat and has too many arches.'

'I think the idea was that afterwards you could turn the arches into diamond necklaces.'

'Most strivings for economy are misguided,' said Consuelo. Isobel was obliged to agree. Even the central Koh-i-Noor diamond had not been improved. It had been re-cut and seemed smaller and duller even than before.

The coronation dress sat on its dressmaker's dummy, Alexandra's shape and size, adorned with its jewels, bisected with its imperial purple sash, and was another matter.

'Magnificent,' said Isobel.

'Magnificent does not add up to style,' said Consuelo.

But for once it did, thought Isobel. The dress was made of a kind of liquid gold fabric, designed and cut in India, Isobel knew, at the instigation of Lady Curzon who as Vicereine of India knew where to go and what to buy. If ever there was a woman who understood luxury, Consuelo conceded, it was Lady Curzon, née Mary Leiter. The dress had then been finished in Paris and tinkered with in London. It had a low square neckline, and a lacy ruff sprinkled with diamonds, amounting to jewelled epaulettes: an almost Queen Elizabethan effect and very clever. Down the centre of the skirt was a panel hung with Queen Victoria's famous set of diamond-bow brooches, from each of which pendants fell; probably sapphire, Isobel thought, but certainly very pretty. A diamond-fringed girdle outlined a narrow waist. But it was hard to see the bosom of the dress for the jewels. The Dagmar necklace — notoriously one hundred and seventeen pearls and two thousand diamonds linked by gold medallions — had suspended from it, reaching to below the bosom, the large, ancient, elaborate, enamelled Dagmar Cross. It had been given to Alexandra by Frederick VII when she married the Prince of Wales, now her husband the King of England, certainly a great possession. But also round her neck she wore her favourite nine-string row of pearls, finishing up with Victoria's diamond coronation necklace, worn as a choker. And creeping up from her waist all was then covered with brooches which had taken her fancy, including a large diamond-pin cockade with turquoise which would look better on a hat, and somewhere lurking there a glimpse of a really nice blue sapphire, but much was covered by the rather erratic fall of the nine-string pearls, crowded by the silver, gold and pearl droplets of the Dagmar necklace.

'It may be too much,' said Isobel.

'One can never have too many diamonds,' said Consuelo, who seemed to have decided enthusiasm was the better part of valour. 'Every time Bertie took a new mistress he would buy Alix diamonds or sapphires. With Alice Keppel it is turquoise. Now Alix is the Queen she wears them all with pride. They were her consolations; they are her victory now. I know about consolations. I buy my own, mind you.'

'Then I am pleased I own only a modicum,' said Isobel.

'You are very lucky in your husband, Isobel,' observed Consuelo. 'A good man in a naughty world.' She put her little hand on Isobel's arm: she wanted understanding. 'I do so want Sunny to divorce me and set me free.'

Ah, thought Isobel, so that was all that was about.

'But he will not,' said Consuelo. 'I give him every cause, or pretend to, but it is not really in my nature to be bad, and he knows it.' Isobel thought she was almost crying.

Consuelo couldn't say any more, and Isobel was rather glad of it. The Queen had come into the room, wearing little more than a silk wrap. She looked good in it, flattered by its simplicity, a fine figure of a woman, nearing sixty but handsome still, a slight limp and a tendency to stoop because of her height, but when she remembered to hold her head high, upright, brave and resolute.

'I am quite restored,' she said, 'and ready for practice. This is not just a gown to try on, I realize, but something I must learn to walk in and move in. Do you like the crown?'

'We love it,' chorused the Duchess of Marlborough and the Countess of Dilberne.

'I mean really,' Alexandra said, and when they hesitated, added, 'I know. It was a mistake. But it is too late now. And the King loves it so that is that. I will just have to carry it off.'

It took Consuelo, Isobel and two lady's maids three hours simply to transfer to the living, talking, moving Queen what was on the still and silent dressmaker's dummy. The jewels were almost all pinned or hung by now. Isobel murmured that without the pin cockade the other jewels would come into their own. Alexandra looked doubtful. But Consuelo, recovered from her fit of conscience, was mischievous.

'That would be such a shame,' she said. 'Jewels are there to be worn, especially if they are of personal significance.'

'Quite so,' said Alexandra, satisfied. 'I do so love the cockade. It is one of my favourites. My husband gave it to me. It's a miniature Fabergé fan. Diamond, gold and turquoise.'

Isobel thought she caught the lady's maids exchanging glances and smirking. Turquoise gladdened Mrs Keppel's heart, everyone knew. It was said that there was to be a special enclosure in the Abbey for the King's favourites, past and present, but not everyone believed it. The cockade pin was added.

The jewels were all on now, and Isobel had to agree, whatever the outfit was, it was magnificent.

The Best-Laid Plans
of Mice and Men

It was such a lovely June day, thought Minnie, she would walk down and see Arthur. The baby had fallen quiet, and stopped its barrage of kicking, while giving her the occasional nudge just to show it was all right. The day was not too hot, not too cold, a gentle wind, the smell of honeysuckle in the air, and of new-cut grass where the gardeners had been scything. She would take the short cut to the workshops so no one would see her. Nanny Brown hated to let Minnie out of her sight, saying the baby would be here any day, but her physician Dr Hodson gave it another two weeks. She was very attached to her baby now, though she couldn't quite see how it would ever get out. She'd said to Dr Hodson that she presumed it was the same way as it got in, from between her legs, but that had made him look rather shocked. But then many things made him look rather shocked. She persisted and said it needed a very small hole to get in but such a large one to get out, how did it happen? Dr Hodson was vague and said that Nature knew what it was doing, more or less letting her know that it wasn't hers to enquire, but his to inform. She was a healthy young woman, that's all he would say, she should call for him when the pains were two minutes apart; he would come straight away from Brighton. He had a reliable car — a brand-new Arnold Jehu with automatic ignition, he told her with pride — and before she knew it she would be sitting up in bed with a new baby in her arms receiving visitors. She'd got a look at his obstetrics bag once and it was terrifying. Strange metal instruments to claw, drag and crush and God knew what, and little bottles marked 'poison'. Minnie told Dr Hodson that a midwife not a physician had attended her birth in Chicago, and he said that was barbaric: here the medical profession was doing what it could to keep midwives out: they were a dirty, slovenly, drunken lot who killed more babies than they ever saved.

Isobel wasn't around to ask questions of: she was too caught up in the Coronation, only days away. Minnie still felt disappointed that she would miss this event of

460

events, though the very idea of parading in a hot ermine-lined gown and wearing a tiara seemed oddly trying. The aim of all life was surely to sit down and be comfortable, though no doubt that was her body speaking; it was so very vocal, these days.

Rosina was no longer there to answer questions. Rosina was gone; Pappagallo was gone. Rosina would have looked up some medical books and given her some facts. She hoped Rosina would be all right. It was dreadful when people sailed away out of your life like that. Her mother had sailed away out of her life, or perhaps she had sailed away out of her mother's?

There was no point in asking Nanny Brown anything: Nanny Brown seemed to think everyone she encountered was a child who had to be reminded that 'those who asked no questions wouldn't be told no lies'.

Arthur said he knew everything about the inside of engines but he would rather know as little as possible about women's insides. Men had engines, women had babies. He would say anything for a smart phrase.

But such a lovely June. A blackbird singing a fresh melody on a branch, trying it out for size, clucking and chucking, and then trying it again. She walked slowly and happily down to the workshops. She could see them from a distance, smell the occasional waft of engine oil, hear the generalized clinking and clanging workshop noise, the occasional roar of an engine being tested for size, or vibration, or speed, or whatever his engines happened to be currently aspiring to. She was glad Arthur was the man he was: that he had something to strive for: he didn't have a great deal of time for her but then he wouldn't have any time or attention for anyone else. His father had a wandering eye; she could only hope Arthur had not inherited it. She had told no one, not even Arthur, that she'd seen his Lordship out with Consuelo Vanderbilt; such things were better not reported. Isobel would be devastated. And perhaps in any case Minnie had been mistaken. Though it was rather hard not to recognize her tall, impressive father-in-law, let alone the infinitely glamorous Duchess.

She couldn't be bothered walking any more, she felt sleepy. The imperative was to sleep, not walk. She took off her cloak, it was getting hot anyway, and put it on a grassy bank for a rug and lay down on it. She would have trouble getting up again she was so top-heavy, but she would worry about that later. She watched a lark soaring into the sky. She fell asleep. When she woke her skirt was drenched. She was ashamed of herself. She must have wet her knickers as if she was a little girl. She hauled herself to her feet. She would get to the workshops and with any luck nobody would notice. These were men who loved engines: they didn't notice much else. She felt a rather sharp slow pain as she walked up the ramp to the workshop where Arthur was usually to be found. The pain was rather like cramp, only a strange place to have it. Cramp usually came three times and then let you alone if you waited for it to do its worst and then it released you.

Arthur was running an engine and standing over it with a stop-watch in one hand. He looked at her with pleasure. She was glad of that. She was unexpected. Supposing his first reaction had been irritation? She couldn't have borne that.

'I think I am having the baby,' she said. 'If only they told me more I would know more.'

He took a rug from over the back of his office chair and she lay down on the oily floor. Her skirts were wet. Perhaps it would be better to get back to the house, only she couldn't work out how to do it. Another of the cramps came and she asked him to time it. He did. Then he timed the next pain. He said there was a minute between them.

She said, 'Dr Hodson said every two minutes, then to call him. But it's still only one.'

'We'll wait then, until it calms down to two. I suppose it's like an engine cooling down.'

'I expect so,' she said. 'Do you mind if I stay here? I don't want to get in your way.'

'I'm always delighted to see you,' he said.

He was relieved, though it seemed rather strange, lying down on the floor the way she was. There was another rather bad pain and a strange blocked feeling between her legs.

'I don't think this baby should wait any longer,' she said. 'Get someone to go and fetch Dr Hodson. Near the clock tower in Brighton, that's where his surgery is.' Someone roared off to Brighton. It was seventeen miles. She heard Arthur ask if anyone knew anything about babies, but nobody did. They were all quite young, apprentice mechanics.

It wasn't exactly pain, anyway, just an extraordinary feeling that Nature knew best and there was nothing she could do about it. She was caught up, whirled up, in something amazing. She was lying down; legs bent, everything exposed. Arthur with his sleeves rolled up and something coming out of her, with a couple of pushes which she couldn't have stopped even if she wanted to, which she didn't. She looked down and saw that Arthur held a baby in his hands, its head covered with sticky stuff. It needed to be washed. The baby opened its mouth and made a noise, and then there was a kind of answer from inside her, another final surge and then there was something squishy and messy like liver lying on the rug. That would have to be washed too. Arthur looked very surprised.

'That was quick,' he said. 'I thought it took days.' The baby let out another cry. It sounded angry.

'It's a boy,' he said, 'unless girls look like that too when they're born.'

She had a look.

'I wouldn't think so,' she said. 'But no one tells me anything.'

'What do we do now?' he said. He seemed to be crying. Sniffing away, at any rate. She felt quite energetic, as if there was a lot to be done.

She looked.

'I expect you have to cut the cord thing in the middle,' she volunteered. 'People don't go dragging something like that round with them all their lives.'

He studied the baby, the cord, and the lump of liver.

'Navels,' he said. 'I see. How we all begin. Well, well. I see.' He tied two knots in the cord with string and snipped the ends with some moderately clean wire cutters. He boiled up the tea kettle and poured the boiling water over the cutters before using them to cut the cord between the two knots. 'I learnt the importance of boiling water in the Cadet Corps at Eton. In time of war and tumult.'

The baby was looking round and searching for something to put in its mouth. Her breasts seemed obvious so she pulled one out of various layers of clothing and put it in the baby's mouth. It nuzzled around a bit and then began to suck.

'You are clever,' he said, admiringly.

'You're not bad yourself,' she said.

Nanny Brown came bustling in, in a state of fine panic, looked, saw, tore off a piece of extra skirt and wrapped it round the baby without dislodging its mouth. Someone had sensibly gone to fetch her.

'You are clever,' she said to Minnie, and to Arthur, 'You are a one, Master Arthur.'

Dr Hodson arrived an hour or so later, up at the house.

'A lightning birth,' he said, 'I've heard of it but never seen one.'

'You did not see much of this one,' Minnie

pointed out.

But he smiled at her in a quite friendly manner and said, 'I told you, you could leave it to Nature.'

She smiled back. But then she would have smiled at anyone. She was in a state of adoration. It was different from anything she had known before. She and Arthur shared it.

They were safe.

They decided not to tell Isobel at once but to wait until the Coronation was over. It was only a few days away, after all.

A Room Set Aside

Isobel was waiting on the Queen in Buckingham Palace. It was Sunday: the Coronation was to be on the Thursday. She had been summoned by telegram, and was at Buck House within the hour, although her plans for the day — lunch with Freddie d'Asti, a final dress fitting — had to be set aside. She had thought Alexandra was safely in Windsor with the King, to arrive in London only on the Tuesday, to have rehearsals in the afternoon and all the next day. They would need them. The rituals were elaborate.

Isobel walked through from Belgrave Square and found the sight most stirring. The cavalry were out, helmets glinting, hooves drumming: the decorations up — great wreaths and loops of flowers, the flags already down the length of the Mall, symbols of national pride and confidence. The streets were crowded, people already gathering days in advance: visitors from abroad everywhere, their strong, open colonial faces obvious, so different, alas, from the pinched, tired faces of her countrymen. But how they smiled; how everyone smiled. The future beckoned and it was good. Isobel was much moved.

But Alexandra was not smiling. Isobel found the Queen pacing the drawing room, smoking pink Sobranie after pink Sobranie, nervous as a girl before her wedding, and full of complaints.

She had wanted an extra rehearsal at the Abbey on the Monday, she said, but the Earl Marshal had failed to arrange one: if she was to kneel at St Stephen's altar for the anointing she needed to see how her bad knee would react, how her skirt would behave, and would the ruff be disturbed when she took the sceptre in her right hand and the ivory rod with the dove in her left. In other words, thought Isobel, she was nervous.

'The Dean said he was trying to fit me in — no one has tried "to fit me in" since I was a girl: it is outrageous, am I not the Queen? This coronation has gone to everyone's heads! He said it was difficult. The stands and floral decorations were still being put in. But I am hardly going to stand in their way, one small woman. The choirs and orchestras were rehearsing round the clock, he said, as if that was our fault.'

It was true, Isobel knew, that the music their Majesties had chosen was not easy, but according to Robert, according to Balfour, most admirable; everyone of contemporary note — from Elgar and Parry to Sullivan, Saint-Saëns, and a host of others — was to be represented.

'And then he said his choristers were more accustomed to Handel, Mozart and the polyphonic composers than this modern stuff. This modern stuff! He would not have dared say this in front of the King.'

'How is the King?' asked Isobel, hoping to divert her.

'He is still not well,' said the Queen, as if it was by-the-by. 'In fact he is in constant pain and it makes him very bad-tempered. But I am not easily defeated. If I cannot get into the church, the church will come to me. I have sent for Kennion, who is the Bishop of Bath and Wells and is to officiate on the day because Canterbury is so old everyone thinks he will die mid ceremony. I have had to take poor Kennion away from his Sunday services, but it is his traditional duty to support me. He can hardly refuse.'

Isobel had no inclination to encounter

Bishop Kennion — how the past did keep catching up with one, she reflected; her last conversations with him and his wife had hardly been pleasant, and over the matter of Rosina and Frank Overshaw — although mostly conducted by her husband, and through the post — almost rancorous. She had hoped never to have seen him again. Yet here he was, and at the door. She thought it best to make herself scarce, and went to inspect the Royal dressing rooms and admire the crowns. As it happened she passed Kennion in the Quadrangle, striding along with flunkeys on either side running to keep up. The palace flunkeys were on the whole little short squat men, she had noticed, Cockneys out of a family tradition of royal service. His face was thunderous — he clearly had better things to do — and he did not recognize Isobel — why would he? Isobel was just another annoying person to have passed briefly through his portals — and she kept herself unobtrusive until he had passed.

The Queen was in a better mood after Kennion had gone, and drew Isobel into conversation about Rosina — how word gets round, thought Isobel — and her elopement. 'Not exactly elopement,' said Isobel, 'just rather sudden.'

Over lunch the Queen said her own second daughter, 'Toria, was thirty-five and still unmarried, being such a thoughtful, serious girl. But at least she could keep her mother company into her old age, which was what one hoped for in at least one daughter, did one not? She seemed to feel rather sorry for Isobel for having ended up with so few children to spread around, and then being so careless of the one she had. Eloped! And to Australia, where there were no crowned heads, just Governors General and endless deserts. And then all of a sudden she began to cry. Her eyes welled up and her mouth went down. She sniffed and gulped and felt for Isobel's hand.

'It isn't fair,' she said. 'I do so much for him, feel so much for him. I've been so worried for him for so long, and he doesn't care for me one bit. He only likes his clever women, one of the stands he's had put up in the Abbey is for them. The loose box, people call it. Trophies of the stud. That's why the Dean was so difficult, he's upset too. It's disrespectful. The Abbey is dedicated to God, not fleshly lusts. Yesterday was the last straw. He was so horrible at Windsor I walked out. I've never done that before. Called a carriage and came here and I haven't slept a wink.'

She was, Isobel realized, talking about the King. The staff stood by, no doubt listening, but to Alexandra they were invisible.

'And he didn't even come after me!' the Queen wailed.

It seemed that the King had been complaining for some time of vague pains. He was off his food, and languid, which he put down to not having enough meat. He would not slow down; if he wasn't receiving guests, he was dining out. He'd been playing host at Windsor to members of the King's African Rifles and a troupe of Maori warriors. He wanted to see everything, welcome everybody. He was excited and flushed and every now and then he would double up with pain. He hated doctors. Boats were lining up at Tilbury and Southampton carrying visitors vital to the national interest. The Great Park had been opened up for the tented quarters of Canadian and Australian troops. He felt he had to inspect them. He would not disappoint his people. He'd stopped visiting Mrs Keppel, but he would not stop eating. Yesterday morning she'd put her hand on his forehead and it was hot. To be feverish in the evening was nothing; to be feverish in the morning was not a good sign.

'But didn't you call the doctors?'

'He said I mustn't. If I did he would tell them to go to hell. He said in his experience wherever doctors gathered, someone died. I went against his wishes, I called Sir Francis Laking. Of the three I inherited from my mother-in-law he's the only one I can stand. Broadbent looked after Albert on his deathbed and didn't save him and is very plain and very corpulent, worse than Bertie. Reid's loyal but knows far too much about everyone's private affairs, especially the late Queen's, rest her soul. So I was left with Sir Francis: though he is rather short. For some reason the taller the doctor the more one trusts them. Don't you think, Lady Isobel?' She had stopped crying, but spoke wildly.

'It is certainly the case,' said Isobel, agreeing with royalty as she had found one was only too wont to do, though she had never given the matter much thought. Her own family kept remarkably healthy. She thought about Minnie and the coming baby, and had a sudden pang of anxiety. Perhaps she should be attending to her instead of to this weeping Queen? But Minnie was of robust stock and hated a fuss.

'I knew it was bad when Sir Francis turned up unannounced,' Alexandra was going on, 'and Bertie was quite nice to him and even lay down and let himself be examined. Sir Francis didn't seem worried and said it was probably just a rather stubborn chill to the stomach, and the best thing for the King to do was rest, even going to bed before dinner. The King lost his temper and told him he was a fool of a doctor, there was no way he could rest, he had far too much to do, and only dinner kept him going. Then I suggested perhaps he shouldn't go to rehearsals at the Abbey but preserve his strength for the Coronation itself. I could go on my own.'

'It might be a very sensible idea,' said Isobel. But the Queen was in tears again, the latest Sobranie sodden and limp in a feeble hand.

'And then Bertie turned on me. He roared and shouted and said I was a fool and an idiot and drove him mad, and I should go and look after my jewels and parade up and down as I thought fit and leave him alone for once. So that's exactly what I did. He has no business behaving like that to me. I love him. I care for him. I worry for him. And this is how he repays me.'

'The King is not well and in pain,' said Isobel. 'He will be very sorry for what he has said as soon as he is himself again. You will forgive one another soon enough. Don't distress yourself so!' So much she seemed to have said to innumerable wives in the past. Royal wives were apparently no different.

Alexandra seemed comforted and sniffed a little and the tears stopped flowing.

'Sir Francis said he would move into rooms at Windsor to keep an eye on the King in my absence,' she said. 'Let him face the royal rages for a change.'

'But he really wasn't worried about the King's health?' asked Isobel. In Alexandra's place she would have been — extremely.

'Oh no,' said Alexandra. 'A chill to the stomach. What a fuss!' And they went down to the dressing rooms to have a last look at the crown and the way the jewels were placed on the mannequin. Alexandra looked again and then asked Isobel to wait on her again the next day; she was such a comfort.

And that was the end of all serenity for by noon next morning who was at Buck House door but a rather agitated Sir Francis Laking and two colleagues, introduced as Dr Thomas Barlow, who seemed a nice enough man and had a good beard, and Dr Frederick Treves, appointed surgeon general to the King. Alexandra said this was the first she'd heard of it; why, was there some question of surgery? She seemed not to care for Treves: a very military and rather bombastic man, the kind who seemed uninterested in anything women had to say, but was at least tall.

Sir Francis did not beat about the bush. He said he had come to ask permission to set up a small operating theatre in Buck House. Equipment would be brought up through the day from St George's at Hyde Park Corner. The King was coming up that day by special train from Windsor. He was suffering from perityphlitis. A surgical operation must be performed at once to treat an inflamed and infected right iliac fossa, the source of which lay in the vermiform process of the caeca. It must be found and removed. Peritonitis had set in and they would operate at once, praying that they were not too late.

The Queen looked from face to face. Isobel could only admire her composure.

'Is it dangerous?' Alexandra asked.

'Frankly, Ma'am, yes. It is at the very edge of today's surgical expertise. We must be prepared for all eventualities. But we do know that if we do nothing the King must die.'

The Queen stood, swayed a little, shook off Isobel's arm and then recovered her composure. She has six children, thought Isobel, she is accustomed to sudden bad news. More, she is a queen. When others panic, she must not.

'Well, Sir Francis, you do surprise me. Does the King know?'

'We have told him, Ma'am, but he will not listen. He will not have the Coronation cancelled.'

'Of course not,' she said. 'He will not disappoint his subjects. We will see what he says when he arrives.'

'Ma'am, he has no choice.'

'Could you not have told him earlier? He will have very little time to recover before he must be at Westminster Abbey. The Coronation service is long and tiring.'

There was a short silence. The doctors did not say what was clear to Isobel; that the King had little chance of life, let alone getting to the Abbey. He would die un-anointed.

'It is hard to diagnose. We have had our suspicions. We hoped against hope,' said Laking.

'How very unwise of you, Sir Francis.' She was at her most regal.

'Ma'am, by the Grace of God the King will survive the operation.' Treves spoke for the first time. 'But it is still a grave assault against the body. He will be in his bed for some time.'

'Days, weeks?'

'Months, Ma'am.'

'And are you an expert in these matters, Dr Treves? I must remind you that the King is a strong and healthy man.'

'It is my subject, your Majesty,' said Treves, with great patience. 'Which is why I have been brought in. I have performed more than one thousand vermiform removals in this country and in South Africa. We are talking about a pouch-like structure where the small and large intestine join. It is unnecessary to our survival as human beings — a vestigial trace of our evolution, it is believed, a mere appendix to it — but nonetheless fatal if infected and not removed. The pouch is sensitive to disturbance and may burst during the operation. That is our problem.'

'Fatal?'

'My own little daughter Hetty died under the knife in just such an operation. The knife was mine.'

'That is hardly reassuring, Dr Treves. I am surprised you tell me.'

'It is the truth, Ma'am.'

'And you, Dr Barlow?'

'I attended your mother-in-law on her death-bed. I know the family history well. It can be helpful in such cases.'

'How very cheerful!' she said. And then, 'What does vermiform mean?'

'The shape of a worm,' said Dr Barlow, thus tested.

'How very unpleasant!' the Queen said. She made a decision, and dismissed them. 'Very well, you must do as you see fit. You may have your room. The staff will find you anything you need. I shall wait for the King and see what he has to say. It is his body, after all. But to cancel a coronation at two days' notice is unthinkable.'

She waited until they were gone and then said, 'Stay with me, Isobel. The family must be called. Our son George will be too distressed to be of much use: 'Toria will look to heaven for help; May will tell me it is all my fault. How quickly life can change. I remember how it was when our son Albert died. One hopes, and then hope dies and nothing is ever the same again.'

In the evening they played backgammon as if nothing was amiss. But the Queen's limp, which that morning had been negligible, became quite noticeable. Isobel stayed the night in a palace filled with dread. The lady's maid who brought her night robes enquired, she noticed, not whether the King would live, but whether the Coronation would be cancelled.

The next morning Isobel looked in at the make-shift operating theatre. It was a large, pleasant room looking over the grounds at the back of the house. Nurses in their voluminous skirts and little white ribboned caps were scrubbing down the walls and furniture. Lord Lister himself was there, to make sure the required state of antisepsis was achieved. He was full of misgivings, saying to Laking it was better to let the King die in peace than subject him to so much pain and stress. He had known too many patients die on the table during the procedure for comfort.

'But not many kings,' was Treves's response. 'Courage, man, courage!'

At which Lister smiled grimly and required the surprised nurses to remove their skirts and work in their petticoats to reduce the risk of infection. If he had his way they would chop off their hair as well and burn it.

And then the King returned, in what Alexandra referred to as one of his 'difficult moods'.

It was something of an understatement, Isobel thought. When he was not doubled up in pain, or claiming death was better than disgrace, he ranted at his doctors. He was suffering the most terrible torment man had ever known, or monarch endured. The choice the quacks presented him with was nothing short of satanic. He would rather die than cancel his Coronation.

'Then he will die,' mouthed Treves to Isobel.

The King raged on: the doctors were fools and charlatans. He would declare his abdication now and perhaps they would leave him alone. He threw Laking out of the room, telling him to take himself and his accursed profession with him. He told Lister he was a fool, and a germ did less damage than a surgeon ever did. The Queen was listening in silence, the doctors in mixed outrage and terror. Then she spoke.

'You would be in a much better temper, dear, if you simply had it done. You may not be able to stand it any more but neither can I.'

The King seemed to return to his senses and looked at his wife as if for further instruction.

'You will simply go to sleep, my dear, and you will either wake up, or you will not.'

He thought about this for a moment and then said: 'That is not necessarily the case. A man could go to hell.'

'Not on my account,' she said. He regarded her with great affection.

'Then the Coronation is postponed,' he said. 'You may announce it.'

He turned to his doctors, apologized, and after that behaved like a lamb, doing what he was told, lying quiet while they administered chloroform.

Isobel took a walk while the doctors worked. News had got out that the King was seriously ill, likely to die under the knife. The streets were deserted, sorrow had struck, no one smiled any more. Here was a King loved by his people, and if for his faults, not in spite of them, so it was. But how quickly joy could turn to fear. Fear spread. The worst could happen. If the King could go, everyone could go. All were vulnerable. She thought of Minnie for some reason, and prayed for her safe delivery. She prayed for the royal family, for her own; for all bishops, priests and deacons, just to be on the safe side. She included Bishop Kennion. When she returned the operation was over.

THE KING IS DEAD — LONG LIVE THE KING!

It had seemed that the King was dying. The operation had gone successfully. The offending pouch was out, and had not burst in the process, though when the forceps laid it on the receiving tray, it had exploded with an alarming energy, producing an intolerable stench. Many had all but run for the doors. But the King himself seemed to be drifting away. Those who were accustomed to death-beds knew the signs: the pallor, the sense of fading away, the arrested breathing. No breath at all, seemingly, for an unconscionable time and then a deep, slow, sad breath, more like a sigh. People had seen it too many times not to recognize it. Dr Barlow slipped from the room and used the telephone. If they had lost the King they should at least make the most of the death-bed scene. It was advantageous to have heads of state present when a monarch died. Disraeli had been present when Prince Albert passed on. Barlow tried Lord Salisbury, who was too indisposed to come to the telephone but sent a message saying he should be in touch with Balfour at Carlton Gardens. Dr Barlow did so. Balfour walked down the Prince of York Steps into the Mall and was inside Buck House within fifteen minutes. Barlow waited for him.

When Arthur Balfour arrived he came in the company of a young woman he introduced as Princess Ida, currently involved in experiments for the S.P.R. — the Society for Psychical Research. She had, he claimed, powers as a healer. She should be allowed into the King's room.

'It can do no harm, man, it might do some good.'

Barlow hesitated. He feared coming up against Treves's aggressive scepticism, or Laking's supercilious raising of eyebrows, but he was an older man than either of them, nearing seventy, and had known many strange things happen. He would like to end up a baronet. The Queen's Indian waiter had assured him such was his 'karma', but the Queen was dead, and the Indian servant was dead, and the promise had not yet come true. Besides, it was hardly prudent to quarrel with Prime Ministers, though this one was not like any other he had known. And

Princess Ida was a sweet, gentle girl, and titled. He let her into the death scene. No one noticed. The laboured breathing had almost stopped. The family wept. Barlow had been with the family long enough to read what was going on. The Prince of Wales, waiting for the mantle of power to descend, looked frightened. His wife May was weeping, yet conscious of relief to come: now at last her children would be out of Alexandra's clutches; she could give them the proper disciplined upbringing they needed.

The King breathed his last, or seemed to. The Dowager Queen stood, raised her arms to heaven, and wailed. Princess Ida slipped into her empty chair, and watched the still, calm face for a moment. All passion spent.

'You poor man,' she said, and stroked his cheek with her long pale finger, weeping a little. She was thinking of her father.

'What the devil —' said Treves —

'This is too bad!' said Laking —

Alexandra moved to slap the girl's hand away —

Princess Ida looked surprised, a little aggrieved and entirely innocent, and drew back her hand, reproachfully.

The King's eyes shot open. He stared into space for a second and then sat bolt upright.

He winced, as the stitches in his belly stretched. He looked round the room.

'George,' enquired the King, and then thundered, 'George!'

George stepped forward. The lamentation in the room took its time to subside. It was hard to make sense of what had happened. The doctors blinked. But Alexandra now stroked the King's living cheek and her tears were of simple joy. She did not care what had happened, Isobel knew. Alexandra loved the King. It was enough that the King lived.

'George,' said the King, loud and clear, 'your time has not yet come. I have work to do.'

He closed his eyes and fell asleep, a deep, healthy, pink-cheeked slumber.

'A miracle!' cried Barlow.

'A successful operation,' said Treves.

'The King has survived,' said Sir Francis. 'It is for you to inform the nation, Mr Balfour.'

HAPPY EVER AFTER: A POSTSCRIPT

Later Isobel was to write to her husband in London from Dilberne Court: *'I don't know what happened and none of us ever will. But I think perhaps the King encountered the spirit of his mother in the borderland between life and death. I think she apologized, as well she might. In any case he has been much happier since he came back to us. He eats only moderately, has lost inches from his girth, looks much better and is busy reforming the navy. His recovery had been so quick one would almost think the whole thing was in his mind if it were not for the horrible smell of the ruptured pouch, which was all too real. The Coronation will be in August. The ceremony will be shorter and simpler. So many grandees had to go home after the cancellation, there are fewer to impress, I daresay. But the flags and the bunting can come out again. And now Minnie is back to her proper shape, she can process with me behind the Duchesses.*

She will see her Coronation. And so will Adela. She can sit between me and the Baums. She slips so easily into Rosina's place.'

As Isobel stood next to the young Princess Ida at the King's death-bed which was not a death-bed, she had become aware of what the girl was wearing. It was a rather faded red velvet dress with a pink lace collar and scarlet ribbons. It seemed familiar. She could remember buying it. The hems had been let out once or twice: you could tell: an inch or so of darker fabric either side of the seams. The girl had hair which reminded her of Arthur's hair. She held her head the same way Arthur did. She looked at the world with the same cheerful innocence which was not innocence as did Arthur. They were cousins. Isobel turned and said: 'You are not Princess Ida at all, you are Adela.'

'Yes, I am,' said Adela.

'I'm your Aunt Isobel,' said the Countess of Dilberne, embracing her. 'Time to come home.'

So Adela came.

The employees of Thorndike Press hope you have enjoyed this Large Print book. All our Thorndike, Wheeler, and Kennebec Large Print titles are designed for easy reading, and all our books are made to last. Other Thorndike Press Large Print books are available at your library, through selected bookstores, or directly from us.

For information about titles, please call:
(800) 223-1244

or visit our Web site at:
http://gale.cengage.com/thorndike

To share your comments, please write:
Publisher
Thorndike Press
10 Water St., Suite 310
Waterville, ME 04901